Gillyflower Kid

Gillyflower Kid

A Novel

by
Christine Brückner

Translated from the German by
Ruth Hein

FROMM INTERNATIONAL PUBLISHING CORPORATION
NEW YORK, NEW YORK

Originally published in 1975 as *Jauche und Levkojen*
Copyright © 1975, Ullstein Verlag GmbH, Frankfurt and Berlin

Translation Copyright © 1982 by Fromm International Publishing
Corporation New York, N. Y.

Printed in the United States of America

First U. S. Edition

Library of Congress Cataloging in Publication Data

Brückner, Christine 1921–
Gillyflower kid.

Translation of: Jauche und Levkojen.
I. Title.
PT2603.R7753J313   1982   833′.914   82-13531
ISBN 0-88064-006-5

W*afting*
through my open window
is the mingled smell,
constant here and elsewhere,
of manure and gillyflowers,
the former predominating,
offering a universal image.
Life is not simply
a bed of gillyflowers.

—Theodor Fontane
to his wife, July 18, 1887

1

A few minutes earlier, a child had been born on Poenichen. The baby's eyes were tightly shut, as if to ward off the bright light of morning, and not even gentle taps on its bottom could produce a cry. But the infant squirmed, breathed, was alive. The midwife had taken the baby's measurements–42 centimeters long; using the kitchen scales, she had determined the birth weight– 2,450 grams. These, together with the date and time of day–August 8, 1918, 7:30 A.M.–she had entered on the official certificate. Now the baby, diapered and attired in blue jacket and cap, slept nestled among the em- broidered blue pillows of the Quindt family cradle.

The baby's mother, Vera von Quindt, née von Jadow, confined for once in her life and never again, had insisted on an agreement according to which her child–not even conceived at the time the agreement was reached–be born in the Charité Hospital in Berlin, where a young doctor, one leg amputated below the knee, was on duty in the obstetrics division. Though one of her staunchest admirers, he was unsuitable as a husband–not a member of the aristocracy and without any imminent prospects of establishing a private practice in one of the better residential sections of Berlin. For obvious reasons, his name was not mentioned when the agreement was worked out.

The memory of a winter of turnips and even further reductions in food rations had made the young Berlin woman take a second look at the Pomeranian manorial estate. She was twenty-four years old, dark-haired, pretty but without a fortune, and her dancing partners had lost their lives at the Somme and the Marne–"row upon row," as Vera's mother was wont to say. In light of her situation, and hedging her bet with a number of conditions, Vera von Jadow accepted the proposal of twenty-year-old Second Lieutenant Achim von Quindt, sole heir to Poenichen.

Though, as behooved their family's rank, the wedding took place at the Hotel Adlon, concessions were made to the war. The bride's father was not in attendance because, as military postal director, he was unable to obtain leave. There were no ushers; the bridesmaids followed the bridal pair two by two, wearing their Red Cross uniforms. The bride wore hers as well, and the groom was in field gray. The wedding was in field gray.

The groom's parents had come to Berlin for five days. Baron von Quindt, not yet quite fifty, became known as Old Quindt from the day of his son's marriage. He wore the uniform of his regiment, in which he still cut a good though somewhat stocky figure, with the rank of captain of cavalry.

When his son and heir joined the army in 1915, Old Quindt saw to it that the young man was assigned to the regiment in which Quindts had served from time immemorial–heavy armored cavalry. Immediately thereafter he put in for his own discharge, which was granted all the more readily as during the battles in Masuria he had contracted the rheumatism that was to plague him for the rest of his days.

In his after-dinner speech, delivered immediately following the clear mock-turtle soup, Old Quindt noted, among other matters, "The Quindts have become an endangered species; they cannot furnish the fatherland

2

with more than one soldier." His son, Achim, Quindt went on, was the last war loan he would subscribe for; the first two had been in gold marks, and those had been hard enough to raise. For his part, he had been engaged on the Eastern front. At this point he reminded his listeners of the Battle of Tannenberg, in which he had participated, and he toasted Field Marshal von Hindenburg–an accolade he never omitted from any of his speeches–adding that his son would now be engaged on the Western front, which was at a far remove from Poenichen. His wife cast him a glance signifying, That's enough, Quindt.

"I do whatever you tell me, Sophie Charlotte, and even what you don't tell me. I'm about finished anyway. My dearest new daughter-in-law, you are from Berlin, and Berliners have their own way of thinking about the Pomeranian landed gentry, which is why I want to take this opportunity to tell you and the other Berliners what Bismarck once said: 'A genuine member of the landed gentry is just about the finest thing Prussia'–whether he meant Brandenburg or Pomerania may be an open question–'has produced.' "

While waiting for the applause to die down, Quindt took an envelope from his pocket, removed a letter, and spread it out. "This day, Achim, makes you the possessor of a letter from Bismarck. You are familiar with its contents, as is your mother. All too familiar, she might say if she were not such a lady. I will read it to all of you. 'My dear Quindt'–the addressee is my father–'In our nation it is not always easy to be a patriot. One man thinks of Pomerania, and that makes it easier. Another thinks of Prussia. Still another thinks of the entire German Reich. And each considers himself a patriot. On Poenichen, patriotism weighs less heavily. The man who works the land loves the land he works, and that suffices for him.' You, my dear daughter-in-law, will have to get used to the idea that on Poenichen we work the land. To return to the letter: 'My wife begs yours for the recipe for the Poenichen game pâté. Ever yours.' Signed with Bismarck's *Bk*. I shall keep the letter safe for you until you return."

Once more he turned to his daughter-in-law. "You are marrying a very young man. But anyone old enough to risk his life in war for his country–I deliberately do not say 'for Kaiser and country'–is old enough to beget life."

His wife tried to prevent him from growing even more specific, but he waved her away. "I know what I am saying, and everyone at this table knows what I mean." He raised his glass and toasted the bride.

Then he turned his gaze on his wife. "The Quindts by marriage were never the worst. They freely chose to become what their husbands could not but choose to be–Quindts on Poenichen. To the ladies! My grandfather was conceived during the Napoleonic Wars and fell in the Battle of Vionville as part of the Third Prussian Corps. My father conceived me during the War of Eighteen Sixty-six . . ."

If the bride had had any doubts about her assigned task in life, by the end of this after-dinner speech she understood perfectly.

After four days of marriage, spent in the hotel, young Quindt rejoined his regiment at the Western front, and the older Quindts took his wife back to Poenichen with them. First the express train from Berlin by way of Stettin to Stargard, then the local, and finally Riepe, the coachman on Poenichen, who met the party at the train station in the closed carriage–known as "the Plaid" after the interior upholstery.

The young bride brought nothing more than a series of hampers and grips. For the moment her trousseau– furniture, linens, china, and silver for the projected town house in Berlin–remained in Berlin. For the moment she would be living in two of the guest rooms in the manor, the so-called Green Rooms. For the moment— that meant: until the young baron returned, until the war was over.

By the time the horses turned into the leafless avenue of linden trees, dusk was already falling. When the manor house appeared at the end of the avenue, Vera exclaime, "But it looks classical. You mean one of you Quindts visited Greece?"

Old Quindt confirmed her guess. "Yes, but he didn't stay long enough. Pomeranian classicism."

And where was Poenichen located?

If you wish to take the trouble, turn to the map of Germany in your atlas. Depending on the year it was published, the area of Pomerania will be surprinted in red or black with the legend "At present Polish Zone of Occupation" or "Under Polish administration." The names of the cities and towns may be given only in German, or in German followed in parentheses by the Polish names, or only in Polish. The discrepancy should not be interpreted as a political issue. Though at the moment of our story it is already evident that the First World War can be ended at best by an honorable armistice, Pomerania is not yet lost!

Look for Dramburg, a county seat (Polish: Drawsko), situated on the river Drage, its inhabitants numbering less than ten thousand. Roughly thirty kilometers southwest of Dramburg lies Arnswalde (Polish: Chos- zczno), hardly larger than Dramburg, also a county seat; then, to the southeast at about the same distance, the German Krone (Polish: Walcz), no longer in Pomerania but already in West Prussia, part of the former Kingdom of Poland, a county seat as well.

By drawing three straight lines to connect these three towns, you come up with what will pass for a right-angled triangle. If you determine the geometric center of this municipal triangle, you will run across Poenichen. Poenichen estate and Poenichen village, 187 souls, 22 of them currently away at war. Two lakes, named Poenichen Lake and Blue Pond by an unimaginative ancestor, to the south of Poenichen heath. An area of ten thousand acres or more. Called "Pomeranian Saltshaker" by some, "Pomeranian Wetlands" by others, both apt; in the possession of the Quindt family for close to three hundred years.

As was always the case with furlough babies, the birth of this child could be predicted almost to the day. From the first everyone unashamedly stared at the young baroness's stomach as soon as she stepped out of the house. When she wanted to go riding, Riepe said, "Would the Baroness please be very careful and only take an easy gait?" At which she threw him one of her bright, angry glances and put the spurs to her horse. In midmorning Anna Riepe fixed her a large cup of bouillon. "That'll be good for the Baroness in her condition!" For each serving of soup one pigeon gave its life. The dovecote emptied measurably.

Spring came, then the beginning of summer. In the sheepfold the newborn lambs bleated; the geese led their goslings along the village green; in the farmyard the sows rolled in the sun next to the steaming compost heap while the piglets clung in double rows to their mothers' teats, making smacking noises; in the paddock the foals stood at the mare's udder; and on the round flower bed outside the manor house the bitch Dinah lay suckling her five puppies.

In her condition, Vera felt like a dam. She spent most of the day in a rocking chair she had had moved onto the verandah. In the shade of the potted palms she leafed through the illustrated magazines her mother regularly sent her from Berlin. Her girl friends' letters spoke of serving at the railroad stations, of looking after

6

the troops, of infirmary trains. Now and again a postcard brought greetings from the front, addressed, not to her personally, but to the Quindts on Poenichen. Terse messages, brief questions.

Compared to her monotonous life in Pomerania, the goings-on in Berlin seemed to her eventful and seductive. Holding the cup of pigeon broth, she forgot the turnip dinners; the warm, tiled stove at her back erased memories of poorly heated rooms in the Berlin apartment; attended by Riepe and his wife as well as by the chambermaid, she took no account of the rigors of serving in the Red Cross. Like most women, she was inclined to miss what she did not have rather than to enjoy what she had. She dreamed of dust-free bridle paths in the Grunewald, flanked by young officers.

Launching herself with the heel of her tiny boot, she rocked without intermission until Old Quindt finally said, "Take it easy, the boy will get seasick—unless he's already decided to join the navy!"

Women were necessary, and he was not remiss in matters of courtesy; children were equally necessary. But he cared little for either women or children—or, unlike his wife, for animals. For years he had cherished the idea of turning Poenichen into a forest preserve. He was partial to trees. "Trees are never in the wrong," he said now and then. For the time being, however, the forests were being cut down because of the increased consumption of wood occasioned by the war. There could be no thought, now, of reforesting—the labor was not available—but it was Quindt's intention to turn the cut areas into "peace forests"—not wood factories with quick-growing inferior conifers, but mixed forests with good brushwood. German forests!

Quindt's nationalism and patriotism were most clearly expressed when he dwelt on the forests, on the land. At such times Quindt, generally a level-headed man never too far from irony, tended to grow solemn.

7

Addressing the Prussian regional diet as a delegate, he had allegedly declared, "We Germans, and especially we Prussians, must learn at long last that even a grainfield can be a field of honor. To that end we must spend our lives working, rather than losing our lives." Understandably, this statement, uttered in 1914 shortly after the outbreak of war, brought him applause only from the wrong side, from the Social Democrats. Since he appeared in uniform, however, he was spared a reprimand from the leadership. Nevertheless, he calculated the consequences and begged permission to resign his seat.

After the war the statement was cited with greater frequency, and one journalist characterized it as a "Quindt-essence." It would have been easy to compile a compendium of such Quindt-essences, but surely no one was interested. His "fields of honor" would soon make Quindt seem a desirable candidate once more, though only for the regional diet to begin with. We shall return to this subject. Back now to the verandah, where his daughter-in-law was rocking vigorously.

From the outset there was no doubt that this child, awaited on Poenichen not only by its mother and grandparents, would be a boy. Following a mysterious law of nature, each war produces a greater number of boys than of girls. Besides, it was a saying in Pomerania, "The younger the father, the more likely a boy."

After the great spring offensives of 1918 the Charité Hospital was filled to overflowing with wounded soldiers. Vera's mother wrote that conditions in Berlin were worsening steadily. "Ca-ta-stroph-ic," one could almost hear her voice. It was practically dangerous to go out into the streets. She urgently advised her daughter against undertaking the arduous train trip to Berlin in her condition.

Vera therefore made arrangements for the child to be born in the largest hospital Stettin could offer. Every

8

detail had to be discussed all over again. Riepe would drive her to Stargard in the Plaid, and Old Quindt himself would travel with her to assure her of male protection should the riots have spread to Stettin by then.

Dr. Wittkow, physician to all on Poenichen, who had been treated as one of the family for twenty years, paid a weekly call on the expectant mother. He was allowed to take her pulse and was given a look at her tongue, but that was all. In answer to his question whether the baby was moving, Vera said, "You're not going to help it into the world anyhow, so what do you care whether it's moving?"

Courtesy was not among the symptoms of her condition, as everyone soon realized. But she was forgiven— wasn't she carrying the Quindt heir?

Beginning in mid-July, Frau Schmaltz, the local midwife, was seen in the manor house with increasing frequency; at first, it is true, only belowstairs, where she held exhaustive discussions with Anna Riepe concerning the young baroness's physical build and fitness for childbearing. "They don't have no different ways of birthing children in Stettin than they do on Poenichen," she said, gulping down a last sip of elderberry juice fortified by Anna Riepe with a shot of home-distilled spirits.

When the labor pains began five days before the estimated time, everyone was certain: only a boy could be in such a hurry to make his way into the world. There could be no question now of either the Charité or Stettin, not even of the Dramburg hospital. Riepe hitched up the horses to fetch Dr. Wittkow on the double, and his wife sent Dorchen, one of the housemaids, to the village to call the midwife, just in case.

Meanwhile the older Baroness sat restlessly at her daughter-in-law's bedside and tried in vain to recall the only birth at which she had ever been present—her own son's. Old Quindt, marching up and down the hall out-

9

side the Green Rooms, perforce also remembered the birth of his son, a recollection he usually made a point of avoiding. Belowstairs Anna Riepe ordered the stove fired up and the water kettles filled and heated. At that moment Dorchen appeared with Frau Schmaltz, who was breathing heavily and eager to get to work. The Baroness ceded her seat at the bedside of the laboring woman, taking up a new position at her husband's side in the hallway.

Morning dawned, not gray but red, promising another hot summer day. After an hour the sun could be seen rising behind the stand of locust trees. In the farmyard the engines were starting up; it was threshing season.

Riepe, returning alone, was the harbinger of Dr. Wittkow's impending arrival; the good doctor was confident that since this was a first birth, there would be a considerable wait. So it came about that Schmaltz the midwife undertook the delivery—just as she did for every other baby born in Poenichen.

"The little baron has arrived!" Within minutes the word was out in the barns, in the cottages, and on the threshing floor.

The joy in the male heir, however, lasted no longer than two hours, when Dr. Wittkow's one-horse shay drove up. Frau Schmaltz's head appeared at the upstairs window. She was waving the certificate triumphantly; once more she had succeeded in stealing an infant away from the doctor. She made a distinction between his babies and hers, and she maintained that distinction until the infants had been confirmed and even after they married.

Dr. Wittkow took the new mother's pulse, was shown her tongue, and said, "Fine, fine. Now get some sleep, Baroness. You've won the first battle on Poenichen. A brief skirmish, my compliments." He was fond of

10

using military terminology; it made up for not serving at the front.

The doctor turned his attention to the sleeping infant. He examined the baby's tightly swaddled navel, and his trained eye observed that the child was of the female gender. The midwife reddened to the roots of her gray hair. "A baby is a baby," she finally said, but it was clear that she would never forgive the physician his discovery. Subsequently Dr. Wittkow entered "Female" on the certificate, went into the hall, and announced, "The boy's a girl."

Shortly before ten o'clock Old Quindt ordered the flags flown, and Riepe went to get them from the kennels. "And I want to extend my congratulations, Baron, sir, even if it turned out to be only a girl. The young baron's still young, and once the war is over, there can be plenty more babies."

"Could be, Riepe, and then again, maybe not. But it could be. Although the Quindts—sometimes I think their time is past, just as the Empire's time is past. And what's to become of Prussia if the Allies succeed in their breakthrough? There won't be any stopping them then, and on Poenichen we'll see a thing or two. . . . Any news of your Willem?"

"No news, Baron, sir. Not for two months."

"If one's son is a second lieutenant, and if that son's father-in-law is with the Military Postal Service, one manages to get more frequent news. None of that is how things should be, Riepe. These differences, I mean. A son is a son, that's all."

"But between the young baron and my Willem— there's a world of difference there."

"Really? You really think so? You talk like a conservative."

"And sometimes the Baron sounds just like a socialist."

"Well, that's all right; everyone takes the road he must, and in the end that's the Christian way. But the Reds have no Christian purpose, and neither do the Black Shirts. The two of us, we manage to get along. Both of us are fifty years old, both have spent all our lives on Poenichen. Neither of us can eat more than will fill our bellies. In season you're served sour game stew and I get smoked breast of goose. But I'd rather eat game stew, and your Anna knows and fixes it for me, and for all I know, she slips you a breast of goose once in a while. I don't know and I don't want to know. One shouldn't want to know everything. Each of us has but the one son, and whether we get to keep him is something else we don't know, and both of us suffer from rheumatism, too. Wittkow gives me an injection, and your Anna rubs you down. Your Anna is better at giving a good rubdown; my wife is more interested in dogs. So everything evens out in the long run. And now, Riepe, run up the flag, for heaven's sake. A new life on Poenichen!"

"Which flag shall it be, Baron, sir? The black-white-red or the black-and-white?"

"Put up the Quindt banner, that's suitable for all occasions. The nation is less interested in a girl. Male or female—it's the blood that counts."

A soft easterly breeze ruffled the Quindt family banner flying from the flagstaff. From hour to hour the day grew hotter. The farther reaches of Pomerania. The steady hum of the threshing machine vibrated through the farmyard. In honor of the joyous event of the day Old Quindt had put off until the afternoon his drive across the fields, which he usually took in the early hours. On the threshing floor he spoke with Herr Glinicke, the estate foreman. He was the first Quindt to administer the estate himself, without a manager.

Then he returned to the manor house to write to his son. He took up his pen in the so-called office, his study. His wife was writing to their son at the same moment; she was sitting in the "Ladies' Parlor," which, facing north, was cooler than the other rooms. The new mother, too, had asked Dorchen for paper and ink.

Old Quindt's last statement—"It's the blood that counts"—cannot be dropped without further comment. Was he engaging in irony? Wasn't there always a touch of irony when he spoke of the "the Quindts," when there was any mention of the "heir," the "firstborn male descendant"? What did he know of the events of Zoppot? What did he suspect?

2

Had Joachim Quindt not been forced to take on the responsibility of Poenichen at an early age–his father died in a hunting accident in 1891–he could have spent several decades more following his bent; he had a passion for philology. He might even have turned into an author, a writer of travelogues of the sort, if not the caliber, produced by an Alexander von Humboldt. Later he rarely had time for writing, but he continued to read a great deal, which was unusual for a Pomeranian estate owner. When he wished to go for a drive, he said to Riepe, "Then let the fanfares blow," and the coachman understood him. It was not necessary for him to be familiar with the classics of German literature; it was enough that he was familiar with his master.

Young Sophie Charlotte, née Malo, from Königsberg, at first bore a certain resemblance to the young heroine of Theodor Fontane's novel *Effi Briest*, though subsequently it faded. The most revealing insights into her marriage with Joachim von Quindt can be found in this novel–or, more precisely, in the underlinings and marginal comments in her copy of it. It is hard to determine when these were made. The novel appeared in 1895, and it can be assumed that the Stettin bookseller sent it to Poenichen soon after in one of his regular packages of new publications. That would have been just following

14

the birth of her only son—in any case, after Sophie Charlotte's stay in Zoppot.

In previous years she had gone to Bad Pyrmont and Bad Schwalbach, always with the injunction that her marriage must not remain childless. In the summer of 1896 she refused to travel to one of these women's spas. Instead, she betook herself to Zoppot. Her husband spent those same weeks in the Crimea. Since it was before the harvest, it must have been in May or June, when he and his cousin Max always took an extended trip abroad.

At the agreed-upon time Sophie Charlotte returned home, and early in March of the following year she was brought to bed of a healthy boy. Zoppot achieved what Bad Schwalbach and Bad Pyrmont could not. Was it a place where prayers were answered? Waters taken? In succeeding years she went neither to Zoppot nor to Pyrmont. Zoppot was not repeatable; the one son and no more.

Zoppot, today's Sopot, situated between Danzig and Gdingen, in those days belonged to Prussia and was an elegant, popular seaside spa where people liked to meet again and again in the summers. Wooded hills and then the coast, a landscape about which anyone who knew it raved forevermore.

Sophie Charlotte, twenty-three years old at the time, four years married without issue, was introduced to a young Polish officer at a party or on the boardwalk or at the band concert—we can only conjecture. He was allegedly a descendant of the Josef Wybicki who had fought in the Polish legion during the Napoleonic campaigns and had written the words to "Poland Is Not Yet Lost," the so-called Dombrowski March.

In later years Sophie Charlotte occasionally mentioned "the good beer from Putzig." Every time she had a glass of beer, she made the comparison—"Better than the beer from Putzig" or "Not as fresh as the beer from

15

Putzig that time." She had to bring back something she could talk about from her summer in Zoppot. She was a passionately silent woman. Whenever she heard the Dombrowski March, she remembered her Polish lieutenant, but that happened at most three or four times in the fifty years that followed. On Poenichen they were expert at avoiding discussions—no great feat, given the roominess of the manor house and the extensiveness of the grounds.

Back to Zoppot. An international spa even in those days, where the German Kaiser liked to tarry, as he presumably did in the summer of 1896; subsequently Hitler, Gomulka, Castro—each in his season.

The nights in Zoppot! One word suffices to banish all ideology. It is not far from where the first shot of the Second World War was heard. Historical ground. The young Polish lieutenant and the still younger Pomeranian baroness wandered along the boardwalk, sat in the beach café. They shared a lemonade or the good beer from Putzig. "Pitcher after Pitcher, The Fresh Beer from Putzig." The couple may have wandered as far as the dunes, or they may have gone riding—it felt good to ride horseback along the shore of the Baltic, and there were plenty of trees where the horses could be tethered for a few hours.

The rest of their story can be found in Fontane, except for some details that will and must remain obscure. It is not even certain whether the two Quindts shared the secret that overshadowed the birth of their son or whether each possessed it in solitude, guarding and eventually forgetting it.

The following passages of *Effi Briest* were annotated with a line down the margin, an exclamation point, or a few words. Even the first marked sentence is puzzling. "I am not very much in favor of what is called an exemplary marriage," Effi tells her mother. Did Quindt single out the statement, or did the line in the margin originate with Sophie Charlotte? The couple's handwriting was somewhat similar. Since both of them learned to write at about the same time and belonged to the same social class, that is not remarkable, especially as Sophie Charlotte exhibited male traits not only in her appearance and her way of walking but also in her hand-writing.

If these notes were made by her hand, she was careless to an extraordinary degree. She could not help but know that her husband was in the habit of reading all the new literary works, by the following winter at the very latest. Or was this her way of making him an accomplice?

The following is another conceivable scenario. Sophie Charlotte was given a copy of the novel while she was still in Zoppot. True, that would have meant she had one of the first copies of the first edition. Her affair with the young Polish lieutenant (his home, by the way, was in Congress Poland, the remnant kingdom subordinated to Russia after the final partition of Poland) lasted ten days, not a day longer. If she read for an hour every night, it would have taken her exactly ten days to finish the book. By day the lieutenant, by night *Effi Briest*. When, on the last day, the young Pole handed her a note and vowed faithfully to write to her always, she rejected his promise in horror: Not a word, my friend—goodbye. It is a possible, though not a probable, story.

The next marked passage reads, "For a little hourly distraction and stimulation, for everything that combats boredom, that archenemy. . . ." Later, Sophie Charlotte had her dogs. But in those days, having come to Poenichen at such an early age, far from Königsberg, she had no friends, was without the support of her sister, had no one but her Baron, with his political and literary interests—a man who traveled without her and sent her to women's spas. He may well have borne some resemblance to District Magistrate von Innstetten in *Effi Briest*.

17

"I really married you only out of ambition."
No marginal line; instead, a question mark. In his
handwriting? Hers? "Hereabouts you are stern and self-
righteous. I believe that's the Pomeranian way." Two
exclamation points. "But take care to avoid what is odd,
or what they consider odd; in the end you pay for that
with your happiness." At this point in the novel nothing
has happened yet, but there is a sense of foreboding.
And what does "happen"? The daughter has already
been born, and no one questions Baron von Innstetten's
paternity. Kessin is not Poenichen–both are in Pomerania,
but Kessin is on the coast–and Sophie Charlotte had to
make the trip to Zoppot. The district magistrate was at
home, while Quindt was in the Crimea. And then, in
the Quindts' case, there was the specific desire for a
son and heir.

"It's so hard, everything one is supposed to do and
to leave undone." Not marginally annotated but underlined. "We must be seductive or we are nothing." Was
it really young Sophie Charlotte who underlined, confirmed, thought this statement? By 1918 she had long
since stopped being a seductive woman; she had rejected
her seductive ways perhaps as early as her days among
the dunes. When she returned, she fitted much better
into Poenichen; she was calmer, she gave birth to the
child, she saw to it that there was always a reliable
nanny in the house. When he was ten years old, the
boy was sent to a Potsdam boarding school, and she
dedicated herself to breeding dogs. Since Quindt was
a morning person and she was a night person, there
was an excellent practical reason for their maintaining
separate bedrooms.

"Without recklessness, life isn't worth the powder
to blow it to hell," says Major Crampas, Effi's lover,
and six years later he is worth the powder after all, again
in the dunes. A few pages later, Innstetten remarks of
Crampas that he does not think him a bad man–"on

the contrary, at least he has his good points. But he's half a Pole, not quite reliable, not in anything really, least of all with women." Half a Pole! And the lieutenant in Zoppot had been a whole Pole! With the whole Polish legion in his background. As yet Poland is not lost! Patriotism came into play. One of the Quindt ancestors had gone into battle under a Polish king, but that was long ago.

Transferred to Berlin, Innstetten gets on in the world. The family departs from Pomerania, the scene of the misstep, and a happy ending seems in sight. But then occurs that business with little Annie, who falls down and must be bandaged. They break into the sewing box because her mother is away taking the waters (!) at Bad Ems. The telltale letters are found. Romance turns into drama.

But when could a drama have been played out on Poenichen?

Perhaps Sophie Charlotte did not read the novel until years later. Had Quindt deliberately placed it in her path? Had she read the book up to this point in the hope that things would work out for Effi? Did she rush to her desk, did she pull out all the drawers looking for the telltale notes, did she find them at the very moment when Quindt entered the room? What conclusions would a Quindt have drawn? Would he have been concerned with getting satisfaction? Or would he have said, "Am I disturbing you?" even as he left the room again? And even before she had learned the outcome of the fatal duel, his wife would have burned the letters in the fireplace. In that case she could have been easy in her mind as she went on reading about the banished Effi, who died of a broken heart at an early age.

Or: She hastily scanned the short notes, written in French. At the end of the last one she read, "A Dieu!" No name, no address. She threw the letters into the fire. She pulled the little boy, who may have been three at the time, between her knees and searched his features. He took after her side of the family totally! Not until twenty years later, precisely on November 11, 1918, when the grandchild was christened, would the Pole emerge, but only in the question "Wherever did the child get her eyes?"

It could have happened that way, but then the marginal notes would stop at this juncture. Instead they continue, leaving it an open question whether they were entered by Quindt's hand or that of his wife. "One does not need to be happy, and least of all does one have a right to happiness, and it is not essential to kill the person who has robbed one of one's happiness. If one is willing to continue existing far from the world, one can simply let him go."

The tragic duel follows. "To every side there were thick bunches of beach grass, and around them blue immortelles and a few blood-red carnations. Innstetten bent down and picked a carnation for his buttonhole. 'The immortelles come afterward.' " Who had ordered immortelles planted on Poenichen? Of course they flourished in the loose, sandy soil. Quindt himself? As a sign that he knew the truth? It was true that immortelles also grew in the dunes around Zoppot, but Quindt had never been there. And his wife never paid any attention to landscaping.

"I had to burn the letters, and the world must never learn of them. . . . There are so many lives that are not lives, and so many marriages that are not marriages. . . ." Innstetten's thoughts on his way home from the duel. Underlined! There had been no thought of a duel in the case of the Quindts, though Quindt was renowned as a crack marksman. Who should have been his target? How should he have learned the lover's name? From Sophie Charlotte, whom everyone knew to be passionately reticent? He himself had repeatedly characterized her that way. He had wished for a son and heir; after all, Poenichen was at stake.

Only a few more marginal notations after the duel. One passage from the correspondence between two women friends. "It's truly incredible–first, writing notes and letters, and second, preserving the other person's. What is the point of stoves and fireplaces? At least for as long as this dueling nonsense goes on, such occurrences must not be allowed. A coming generation may be permitted this passion for letters (because by then it may be free from risk), but we are far from that." Perhaps these sentences taught a lesson to many women? Perhaps they saved marriages? Little is known about the effect of books. Did the lady's prophecy come true? No more duels–but no more stoves and fireplaces, either. And no more letters.

One single sentence is marked in red pencil, presumably picked out many years later. Perhaps the line was made by the aging Quindt after the birth of his grandchild. "If I am right, happiness consists in two things: first, in standing entirely in the place where one belongs, and second and best, in the comfortable development of the everyday–that is, in getting enough sleep and having new boots that do not pinch. If the seven hundred twenty minutes of a twelve-hour day pass without particular annoyance, we can speak of a happy day." Characteristic of Fontane in his later years–but of Old Quindt as well. He must have said to Riepe more than once, "The main thing is that one can sleep and one's digestion is in order. One's entire sense of well-being depends on these." Since neither worked smoothly for him, he assigned great importance to both.

A further entry seems particularly revealing. Old Briest and his wife have a conversation about happiness. Briest says, "Well, I know what I mean, and you know something too. Is she happy? Or is there, after all, some-thing standing in her way? From the beginning I had a feeling that she esteemed him more than she loved him. And in my eyes that's a bad thing. Love doesn't always last, of course, but esteem certainly doesn't. Actually, it annoys women to have to esteem a man; first they are annoyed, then they are bored, and finally they laugh at him."

Here a clear "No!" appears in the margin. To judge from it, Sophie Charlotte held a different view when she read this passage. And she was right. Here Fontane is mistaken, or at least old Briest is in error. In our case the couple's regard for each other grew in direct pro-portion to the distance they maintained in their living arrangements. Many years later, when the grandchild was a full-grown woman, their distance diminished, they grew closer, and at their tragic end they were as close as two people can be.

All this must be stated or at least hypothesized so that certain allusions will become understandable. How else to explain the unusual stress in Quindt's utterances "Ah, yes, the Quindts" and "Quindt blood"?

Even the genealogical researches undertaken much later with zeal and precision by a certain Viktor Quint (without the *d*) of the Silesian line did not turn up the heroine's Polish grandfather. Among genealogists, the paternal line plays a disproportionately greater role than the maternal, although in contrast to maternity, paternity must often be characterized as at best assumed.

And now not another word about the dunes of Zoppot. But everything else was a consequence of that affair, even the infant who had just been born. Like her father, this child would grow up on Poenichen and be reared like all the Quindts. Although the child's father bore not the slightest resemblance to either his biological or his nominal father, time and again they said of his little girl, "She's going to end up the spit and image of Old Quindt." Living proof of the remarkable power of environment. In the course of this book, it is true, contrary evidence will also be furnished—everything depends on heredity.

3

In the meantime the three letters to the new father were completed.

"Dear Achim," wrote Old Quindt.

> For the space of two hours Schmaltz furnished us with a male heir, then Wittkow arrived to point out that it was a girl. One would have expected more from an experienced midwife, but we must remember that she's been a widow for many years. The wish was surely father to the thought–or rather, the child.
>
> While the birth was taking place upstairs, I got out the book of Bismarck's correspondence and looked for the letter in which he announces the birth of his first child to his father-in-law. In Bismarck's case, the child's father announces the occurrence to the father of the new mother, which is the most natural course. In wartime everything is unnatural; the grandfather makes the announcement to the father. Bismarck writes: "I'm quite pleased that the first one is a daughter." (And what pleases a Bismarck must please a Quindt as well.) "But even if it had been a cat, I would have thanked God on my knees at the moment when . . . and so on, and so on. . . . It is surely a terrible, despairing matter." So much for Bismarck.

In our case, it's true, your mother would have preferred a dog to a cat. Our handsome Dinah whelped five puppies about four weeks ago, and Cylla is already pregnant again. Your mother will yet manage to achieve world renown for the Quindt bloodhounds, as my grandfather did for the Quindt horses. She has no difficulty disposing of the pups. As with all the products of Poenichen, demand exceeds supply. This last remark applies to the wheat; we have been threshing since day before yesterday. It seems that the weather will hold.

To come back to the child once more. As best I can judge, she turned out a little too small, but it's been a long time since I've seen a newborn baby. I did not see you until you were four weeks old. But that's another story. We will announce the birth in the *County News* as soon as a name has been decided upon. We would like to postpone the christening until after your return.

The regional newspaper arrives on P. only intermittently and with considerable delay, but there's always plenty of time for bad news. I am not worried about the war front. I am about the home front, though. I shall never grow accustomed to such expressions as "the battle for materiel." The politicians are failing. We do not seem to be able to get along without a Bismarck; the Germans require an iron fist. There are too many who want to rule. I no longer participate, though now and then politics still courses in my veins. Right here we must look after the harvest. Our people must eat, whether we win the war or lose it. My mind works like a farmer's. One day you will think the same way.

Yours, Q.

The Baroness wrote,

My dear son,

Now you have become a father, and I never even noticed when you became a man. "A soldier is not the same thing as a man," my father always said. What a pity you did not have a chance to know him. Children need grandfathers even more than they need fathers. The past ten years you have been home only during school holidays and army leaves.

Vera and your father are also planning to write you. Considering that she comes from Berlin, Vera made a good job of it. Schmaltz told them in the kitchen that the baby was born with wide-open hands, though infants' hands are usually clenched into fists at birth. She'd never seen anything like it. "That one won't go far," she said to Anna Riepe. "Well, she won't have to, she already has every-thing," Anna replied. But Schmaltz may be mistaken, as she was mistaken when she thought the baby was a boy.

I'm sure Anna will insist on making a pâté of the last hare still in the ice cellar. You have never gone hunting rabbits. You'll have more practice at sharpshooting now. In future I may breed not only bloodhounds but also dachshunds. Dinah whelped five puppies, a good strain. I've had Cylla studded by the same hound (the one who belongs to the von Kalcks). Everyone says that it won't be long now.

I am writing in the Ladies' Parlor because of the hot weather. When you were a little boy, you could never stand the heat. God willing, we will meet again soon.

Your mother,
Sophie Charlotte v. Q.

Dorchen took the writing paper, inkwell, and lap desk from the young mother, pulled away the supporting

26

pillow, and sat down beside the cradle, where the new-born baby, her head bright red, lay sleeping.

Vera licked the envelope without reading over what she had written. It was months before she saw her letter again, and by that time she was sorry that she had not made an effort to sound more cordial. In extenuation it may be noted that she was still weak when she wrote the following, which had neither salutation nor signature.

There you have it, your child. I'm sorry. It's only a girl. They dressed her in a blue jacket so that it won't show. As it turned out, she wasn't born in the Charité and not in Stettin and not even in your Dramburg. And your doctor didn't make it in time, either. Only that woman from the village. She stinks of goats! Once is enough. Every woman should be made to watch a birth before she agrees to such a thing. Two of my friends named their babies Irene— a Greek name meaning "peace."

Where are you stationed now? Or posted? They say "stationed" for the Somme and "posted" for Potsdam. They say my brother has been wounded. I'm sick of the war. I'll never feel at home on Poe-nichen. The chugging of the locomobile or whatever the thing is called drives me crazy. Promise me that we can live in Berlin in the winter.

None of the three were graceful correspondents, but at least Old Quindt's writing had a touch of originality. The letters were put in separate envelopes, each bearing the recipient's name, rank, and military address. Then they were all put in a large envelope and sent to Military Postal Director Friedrich von Jadow so that he could use his influence to expedite their journey and assure their delivery. Because of the massive troop movements fol-lowing the spring offensive, mail repeatedly went astray. Riepe took the envelope to the railroad station, using the opportunity to pick up the baby nurse, Fräulein Kuhl, who had been summoned by telegram from Stettin.

Anna Riepe had managed to produce an almost peacetime hare pâté for the gentry along with a rabbit stew stretched with dumplings for the household staff, including Veteran Reserve Private Schmidt, who guarded the Russian prisoners. Every holiday she made borscht for the Russians, getting better at it each time, and every holiday they thanked her by singing one of their Russian songs. Her husband translated the words for her; he spoke a little Polish, his mother having come from a village near Posen. This time Anna Riepe added a piece of smoked meat to the pot. Where she had found it in August 1918, although no pigs or cattle had been slaughtered for the last six months, no one knew. The housekeeper always managed to have a little something "extra" in the larder and the ice cellar about which the Baroness knew nothing; except that occasionally she inquired, "Are we managing, Anna? Do you suppose we've got enough for the dogs?"

"We've got it," Anna Riepe would reply.

And the Baroness would say, "Well, then, I won't worry."

The threshing went on in the farmyard until dusk. When the engine spewed out its final puff of smoke, Old Quindt sent Riepe to the distillery for schnapps. "Two pitchers!"

"But, Baron, sir," Riepe said. "The distillery? Schnapps? Now, before the potato harvest? With the jugs empty and the barrels sealed up!"

"Are they empty and are they sealed? Do you think I don't know we've got an illegal still going here? Did we or did we not earn a drink today?"

Riepe returned with the full pitchers, and the men filed into the farmyard one by one. The threshing machine had been parked next to the compost heap to cool off, the barn doors were still standing open, the air was hot and dusty. The old men stood in a group, the women and children formed another group, and the Russians made up a third. Three groups, but all the faces equally sooty, the eyes inflamed by flying kernels of grain. The Russians' heads were shorn, the women's covered by kerchiefs.

"Pour, Riepe."

Riepe served the men first. Then he looked at the Baron.

"The women, too," Quindt said. "Or are there women among us who won't drink our schnapps?"

When Riepe was finished pouring, the pitcher was still not empty. "And what about the rest?" he asked.

Quindt went to him, took the pitcher, walked over to the Russians, and poured the schnapps into their spoons until it spilled.

The reserve soldier protested. "But that ain't fair, Baron. They didn't do no extra work!"

Quindt reddened. "And you, Schmidt? Did you guard the Russians by the sweat of your brow? What kind of work is it to carry a gun around the dungheap? Is it fair that you are given schnapps? You and your idea of justice! We don't practice justice! Here not everyone is given the same. Those who need the most get the most. That's our justice. *Nostrovye*," he said, put the pitcher to his lips, tipped it back, poured the schnapps over his chin, and shook off the drops, not even bothering to wipe the back of his hand over it.

"*Nostrovye*," he repeated and left. No one understood exactly what he was angry about.

That evening the old Quindts sat alone on the verandah. They had eaten some of the cold hare pâté and seen to it that the new mother received a slice, along with a glass of Bordeaux. Old Quindt had poured the wine for her himself. He felt, he claimed, like a "proxy father." He said, "Representing my son, I drink to your good health."

He had nothing more to say about the sleeping infant, and so he spoke about the hare pâté, which Vera had carelessly pushed aside. There was an unusual amount of talk about this particular pâté. Vera closed her eyes, giving Old Quindt an opportunity to wish her a good-night.

At the door he turned back once more. "You did your job well, it seems to me."

There was no answer to this, either.

When he returned to the verandah, he remarked to his wife that a birth did seem to be rather awkward, but perhaps one got used to it.

"Perhaps," she replied.

For the present the infant was referred to as "the baby." There was no need for a name–she was the only newborn far and wide. "The baby didn't even cry"–of course the neighborhood heard about this special trait. But was it true? Why should this child in particular have failed to lodge a loud protest? Was she agreeable to everything from the outset? It seems unlikely. All children cry; they have to cry to clear their lungs and take their first independent breath. In this humankind differs radically from the animals. Never has anyone heard a foal or a kitten cry after its birth. But the widow Schmaltz insisted. "The baby didn't even cry," and there were no other witnesses. The young mother did not discuss the birth with anyone; the process had been unpleasant enough at the time.

When, six months later, her own mother came to visit Poenichen for the first time, staying a full three months, she naturally inquired into the details. Eager to have a woman-to-woman talk with her daughter, she said, "Your father makes demands on me to this day–do you understand what I mean?"

Vera, on whom no such demands were made, whose questions had always been countered by this selfsame mother with "One does not talk about such things," answered irritably, "Let's not talk about such things, Mother."

Therefore: the baby had not cried.

The question of "whether the young baroness has milk" was discussed at length, not only in the kitchen of the manor house, but all through the village. The baby nurse, Fräulein Kuhl from Stettin, quietly but firmly introduced law and order into the lying-in room. She never spoke of the young baroness as other than "the little mother"—what a little mother could and could not do. Most things she could not do, in order not to jeopardize her milk. She never said "Baroness," not even "Frau von Quindt"; she spoke in the third person singular of the little mother, and she was the infant's unequivocal advocate. The little mother's well-being was of interest to her only to the extent that it affected the well-being of the infant.

Vera did not prove herself born to motherhood, nor had anyone expected such a turn of events. She may have been relieved—literally—but she did not seem any happier. Fräulein Kuhl—who was called "the Fräulein," and later, to distinguish her from her successors, "the first Fräulein"—put the infant to Vera's breast. The baby suckled a little but kept falling asleep. The mother's arm grew tired; the baby smacked, slobbered, sucked, slept. In this way the nursing ritual went on for hours, making Vera, who had a tendency to irritability anyway, even more irritable. Whenever she was unobserved, Vera switched the baby from the left breast—where every mother instinctively places her baby, close to her heart—to the right. These changes satisfied neither baby nor mother.

Vera had the record player moved near the bed. Holding the baby with her left hand, she used her right to lower the tone arm over the record and to work the crank. Twice she dislodged the baby, making her fall out of bed. Thereupon Fräulein Kuhl began to operate the record player, though she never changed the record. It happened to be a vapid popular hit, a gift from that

32

young assistant doctor at the Charité Hospital, presented on some long-ago occasion. Unbeknownst to anyone else in the manor house, a furious battle raged between the little mother and the baby nurse. Fräulein Kuhl proved the superior fighter.

Of course the worst apprehensions as to the child's future development arose. Naturally the birth trauma had left the baby with a primal fear, but in the present case the separation of mother and child had taken place long before the birth; the unborn could hardly have felt very comfortable inside her restless and discontented mother. Though she sustained no injury from the horror of being dropped, that was presumably to the credit of the baby nurse, who intervened with firmness and determination. The baby felt secure with her nurse; a protective lap, though an ever-changing one, was always available to the child; she was never left alone in the dark.

Thanks to the privileges the baby enjoyed from birth, several cardinal errors could be avoided during those first crucial months. Later she would be asked, "Were you breast-fed? For how long?" She would not be able to answer even so basic a question. How, then, could she be expected to give any information concerning her mother's prenatal disposition?

Anna Riepe continued to send pigeon broth to the lying-in room, but the young baroness declared that the very smell made her sick. She demanded black coffee and cigarettes but was refused, all the more as it was impossible to get hold of either. She wished to lose weight; her face still seemed bloated. Several times a day she asked for the mirror. With bursts of irritated laughter she disposed of any sentence beginning, "Most of all, the little mother needs . . ."

Was there anyone in this house who knew what she needed? What she needed was not rest but distraction: visitors to admire her tiny baby, especially visitors to admire her for giving birth to a child under such primitive conditions, aided only by a midwife, almost in a manger! Someone to admire the Quindt family cradle, ornamented with a coat of arms and a coronet, as were even the diapers; someone to send her flowers.

But no one brought flowers—flowers grew outside, and what was the point of cutting them? No one brought candy—and just when she had a craving for sweets. Anna Riepe learned of this and personally brought her a dish of tapioca pudding flavored with raspberries and red currants, cooked to the smoothest consistency, thickly sprinkled with sugar, with cool cream to pour over it. Vera did not even taste it, did not even say thank you.

What the little mother was missing was the maternity section of the Charité Hospital, her girl friends, the young doctors, a room filled with flowers, a place where she could have worn her embroidered nightgowns. Then she would have been able to play the role of the young Baroness Quindt, whose husband was fighting at the Western front. She would have been brave in her suffering, her smile hinting at suppressed pain. Before long, by the end of September or in early October, when the Tiergarten and Unter den Linden were particularly magnificent, she would have taken the baby out in a highwheeled perambulator. She would have hovered over it solicitously, plucking at the pillows, and mother and child would have attracted admiration. A baby nurse—preferably a young woman from the country wearing a large hooded cap—would have walked two paces behind, ready at any moment to step in helpfully. On Poenichen they did not even have a perambulator. No Quindt had ever been taken for a walk in a carriage. Where could they have walked? On the sandy paths? Along the rutted clay of the linden-lined avenue? She had no feeling for trees. The hundred-year-old Poenichen linden trees could hold their own with those of Berlin.

Given the situation, the baby could not thrive. Every morning, regularly, she was weighed on the kitchen scale. When she gained not so much as a gram on three consecutive days and on the fourth even seemed to have lost a little weight, Dr. Wittkow was summoned. He palpated the young mother's breasts and found an obstruction of the milk duct, an incipient infection. It did not even involve a fever worth mentioning, but Vera had to submit to damp, cold compresses around her breasts. The baby was weaned, broken of the habit of breast feeding before she had had a chance to acquire it. A wet nurse was not available, for there was no woman on Poenichen who had an infant; all the men capable of procreation were at the front. Therefore it was decided to raise the child on watered cow's milk. Dr. Wittkow gave the appropriate instructions to the baby nurse, and Fräulein Kuhl passed them on to Anna Riepe.

Anna in turn discussed the milk question with the widow Schmaltz, who still appeared daily in the kitchen to inquire about "her baby" and to have a little breakfast. Both women were convinced that goat's milk would be better for the baby.

From then on Dorchen went to the village every morning with an empty milk can concealed in her basket. Later she took the full can into the milking chamber on the farm before carrying it, allegedly brimming with fresh cow's milk, to the kitchen. There, under Fräulein Kuhl's supervision, the goat's milk, masquerading as cow's milk, was poured into a bottle, watered down, and warmed. The Fräulein sat at the window of one of the Green Rooms and held the bottle for the baby. She cradled the baby calmly, she rocked her, she burped her at appropriate intervals, she wiped the bubbles from her lips; she did what she had learned, she practiced her profession. And because she had no one else to talk to, she talked to the baby–which, as we have since learned, is important to the development of infants.

After initial difficulties in readjustment, the baby steadily gained weight, grew chubby, developed dimples. However, she did not get sufficient vitamins or fresh air, and her bones remained soft. She displayed a tendency to pigeon-breastedness that was later diagnosed, in a mass screening, as "typical goat's milk rickets." She was unable to reply when asked whether she had been fed goat's milk as a baby. Her wrists remained slightly thickened, as did her knees, which also protruded somewhat; but both these joints were usually hidden by a subcutaneous fatty layer.

The baby spent the first year of her life in the cradle, sleeping most of the time, rarely or at least only softly crying. A contented baby. She was late in making her first attempts to stand and walk, since no one encouraged her along these lines. Fräulein Kuhl tended to indolence; when the child lay sleeping in her cradle, she gave the least trouble. "An infant needs rest," she declared, and she swaddled the baby tightly because she thought it right. "She's got her share of patience," the widow Schmaltz commented on the baby's behavior.

When Fräulein Kuhl was replaced by a Fräulein Balzer, the baby's health improved markedly; she turned into a crawler. Dressed only in a diaper, she crawled through the summer of 1919. Her delicate spine was favored, her joints were strengthened. She was exposed to sun and wind, on occasion to rain; at night she slept by the open window, even far into the autumn. Fräulein Balzer lasted only the length of the summer; later she was referred to as the crawling Fräulein.

Vera did not meddle in the care of the baby. The nurses and nannies had learned their jobs and could show diplomas; they would know best. She was reluctant to pick the baby up except when the baby was handed to her freshly bathed and dusted with potato flour. Then she held her daughter for a few minutes, rocked her, and gave her back. Her fears that she might drop the baby, smother her under a pillow, or drown her in her bath were shared by the nurses.

5

Ten days after the three letters were dispatched to the child's father, a telegram arrived. It, too, was addressed to "The Quindts on Poenichen" and not directly to Vera. A triple "Hurrah! Hurrah! Hurrah!"– nothing more. The field postal station must have been puzzled or at least surprised by the message; it came from the Western front, after all.

Quindt's fears turned out to be justified. In early August the British, using their new tanks, succeeded in breaking through on both sides of the road from Amiens to St.-Quentin. Our heroine's birthday entered the history of the First World War as "the Black Friday of the German Army." Later, it was remembered simply as Black Friday.

Dr. Wittkow, who considered the infant delicate, made some unspecified references to the state of her health and urged that the christening take place soon. Old Quindt declared, "Just because the child was born without your help doesn't mean she can't survive! Sure I think she's too small, but she's got nothing to do for a while but grow."

After Vera had been released from her lying-in, meals were eaten in the breakfast room: soup, main course, and dessert, served and consumed to the strains of popular hits. The record player stood within reach of Vera's seat. Presumably she was seeking revenge for something or other. A silent battle.

On the third day her mother-in-law decreed that soup would no longer be served on Poenichen. The change of the century, and one that Anna Riepe interpreted as an insult. She was a cook who could still make a tasty soup out of nothing. For days she did not speak to the Baroness, who was unable to explain her true reasons to the housekeeper.

The young father's triple hurrah at hand, the decision was taken to christen the nameless baby. Because of the harsh November weather, the christening would take place at the manor.

Old Quindt had not set foot in the church—nine kilometers from Poenichen, in the next village—for twenty years. He was not a religious man, but he was still church-minded enough to fulfill his duties as patron in the spirit of the Kaiser: Leave the people their religion. He had provided a new roof for the church, as well as a harmonium. Every year as Christmas approached, the Reverend Merzin paid a visit to the manor house. As he left, Quindt walked him to his carriage and always said, "Your visits cost me dearly, Pastor." And Merzin always replied, "You're free to pay me a return visit at any time, sir, and that won't cost you anything but a mite for the collection plate." The return visit was never made. The pew reserved for the patron remained empty.

Early in November Old Quindt sent for the clergyman to discuss the christening. The Reverend Merzin insisted that the little citizen of the world must be christened in God's house, like every other baptismal candidate. "Before God, all children are equal, sir—and not just before God, either." To the patron's face, this was a revolutionary addendum; after all, Quindt accounted for the major part of the church tax.

Even as the Reverend Merzin continued his remarks about the equality of all God's children, Quindt was discussing the condition of the church, noting that of course the child would be christened in the church, in spite of her delicate constitution, were it not that there was no way to heat the church.

It turned out that the Reverend Merzin had precise ideas about a heating system and just happened to have a sketch in his pocket. An agreement was reached. Old Quindt contributed a potbellied stove, and the minister was prepared to take the baby's delicate condition sufficiently into account to perform the christening at the manor. No further mention was made of any connection between heating and baptism, although the thought may arise that at a very early age this child had brought a little warmth into the world.

The circle of guests at the christening was small. Not even the godparents were present. The Berlin grandmother was prevented from attending by the railroad strike. No one else from the von Jadow side of the family could come, nor could the other godmother, Quindt's older sister. She, however, wrote to accept the sponsorship on the condition—as she noted in a casual aside—that the child be given her own name, Maximiliane. She herself had never married, and she lived on Mount Eyckel, the Quindt ancestral seat in Franconia. She was fifty-five years old and farmed her own lands without a manager. Quindt never mentioned her without adding, "My hat's off to her." As a result, the little girl would always think of her aunt as wearing an outsized hat.

The table in the big hall did not, therefore, need to be extended to its full length. The Reverend Merzin and his wife, Dr. Wittkow and his wife, and the neighbors from Perchen estate, the von Kalcks—that was all.

For the past three years Karl Georg von Kalck had had only one arm, having lost his left one in the Battle of Novo-Georgievsk. "Eighty-five thousand Russians captured! What price one measly arm?" he was in the habit of saying after his release from the hospital. Their unmarried daughter, Friederike, was also invited, both because she had to drive the carriage and so the two young women could be introduced to each other. Vera ignored the Quindts' attempts to ease her acclimatization to Poenichen. Age was all she had in common with this hefty young country woman; she referred to all Pomeranian girls as "pompoms."

The big hall, never heated and unused since the last hunt dinner two years earlier, was only moderately warm. Only a little daylight fell through the high glass windows, and a few petroleum lamps had to be lit to provide more illumination. It had not been possible to get candles, but the silver shone, as did the Courland china service that the old Baroness had brought as part of her trousseau—severely classical, smooth, edged with pearl rods and evenly curving festoons, pinecones as knobs on the lids, bouquets of wildflowers as decoration. Frau von Kalck turned the plates over. "Ah," she said, "Royal Prussian manufacture. On Perchen we have Breslau City Castle."

The crystal vases were filled with purple strawflowers, immortelles—more suitable to a funeral but not immediately connected to the dunes of Zoppot. The last roses in the gardens had long since frozen. The palm trees, which had spent the summer on the verandah, were now back in the big hall, so that the sacrament could take place beneath their fronds. The baptismal font on white damask, two white candles brought by the Reverend Merzin, the Quindt family Bible—nothing was missing but the baby's father.

The audience formed a semicircle, Vera and the infant at its center. The Reverend Merzin sent her on life's way with a verse from the Book of Job: "Behold, God is mighty, and despiseth not any: he is mighty in strength and wisdom. He preserveth not the life of the wicked: but giveth right to the poor." In his subsequent sermon he referred to the verse chiseled in stone over the Quindt fireplace: "Your wealth increase! The foe

41

rebuff! Welcome the stranger! Praise God above!" That sentiment, he said, was valid to this day; might it retain its validity in this house for many a day to come. Then he baptized the child in the name of the Father and the Son and the Holy Ghost, bestowing on her the names Maximiliane Irene.

The Baroness took her place at the spinet, which was out of tune by more than a half-note, and played a hymn by Nikolaus Ludwig Count von Zinzendorf, somehow related by marriage to the Quindts. The same hymn was played with Prussian devotion at every Quindt christening. After the third stanza she broke off, since no one was singing along. The message of the lyrics—never to complain, no matter what the hardship—that was the Quindt way.

The Reverend Merzin paid homage to the father, who, far away on the battlefields of the West, was fighting to keep the enemy's foot from treading the soil of the beloved fatherland, and he expressed the hope that God the Almighty might see to his speedy return so that he might take pleasure in his firstborn. Everyone was moved, each in his own way, and yet no one felt compelled to reach for a handkerchief. For the last four years all major events had been prefixed with the word *war:* war wedding, war christening, war death.

The baptismal child followed the events attentively with her eyes, did not sleep, but did not cry when the warm water was trickled on her head. Fräulein Kuhl took the baby from her mother and arranged the long christening gown of white batiste in such a way that the blue embroidered Quindt coat of arms was clearly visible. The Reverend Merzin extinguished the candles and covered the font. All attention was now directed to the table.

Otto Riepe appeared with a tray: a double schnapps for the gentlemen; for the ladies, rose-hip liqueur, a specialty of Anna Riepe's kitchen. Riepe's hands, concealed in white gloves, trembled as he passed the tray. He never got used to serving; he was not a trained footman and had only picked up the rudiments in the army when he had to wait table in the officers' mess. But what he lacked in formality he made up for in solicitude; he placed the lean meat in front of the ladies, reserving the marbled portions for the men. He knew who took black coffee and who preferred cream and sugar.

At this christening dinner, however, he behaved rather more awkwardly than usual. Old Quindt thought it best to take each glass from the tray and hand it to each guest, the first one for his daughter-in-law. "We are not christening a princess here, Riepe. Before God and the law all children are equal—isn't that right, Pastor?" And he raised his glass. The first toast drunk to Maximiliane's health. It should not be forgotten.

Old Quindt did his best to lift the spirits of the assembled company. He asked Riepe to pass the soup. "Women and soup should not be kept waiting or they grow cold, as my cousin Larsson, that old Swede, used to say. We can have the soup right now, and it's to be hoped that the women won't be kept waiting for their men much longer. To your special health, daughter-in-law, and to yours, Fräulein Friederike." Both women blushed, for different reasons.

When the soup tureen was empty, Vera rose, took it from the startled Riepe, forcefully set it down at the center of the table, went to the cradle, picked up the baby, and placed her in it. An unmistakable gesture. This child was her contribution to the festivities; she had nothing further to say. Fräulein Kuhl began to protest, but the Baroness clapped her hands. "Our little star, why shouldn't she be the center of attention?"

Fräulein Kuhl slipped a cloth under the baby, who was not crying even now, but she could not prevent soup stains on the christening gown. Since the tureen was unusually large and the baby unusually small, she fitted snugly. She looked around alertly, her eyes rolling to every side. Of necessity, the conversation turned to these protruding eyes, which demanded comparisons. "Like jet buttons," Frau Merzin suggested. Dr. Wittkow was reminded of black cherries, but his wife disagreed. "More like hazelnuts when they're still a little green." "Like marbles," the Reverend Merzin decided. Aggie eyes, the baptismal child's second husband called them many years later; he was from the Rhineland.

Where did the child get her eyes? Everyone looked at Vera, whose eyes were a grayish blue, light and cool; everyone looked at Old Quindt and looked away at once, so little did his eyes lend themselves to a comparison. And the Baroness? The transmitter of these eyes? She took no part in the discussion and speculation. But it was possible that she had never taken a close look at the eyes that had passed down to her granddaughter, because at the crucial moments she had closed her own.

The baptismal child's eyes were round and large— not fixed, which might have been a sign of goiter, but lively. The ducts gave off plenty of fluid, so that her gaze was damp and glittering. The lids seemed a little too short, the lashes neither excessively long nor thick. In fact the child later complained when she was told to sleep in the large nursery with its three beds, that the room was too bright. "Then close your eyes," she was advised. But when she obediently complied, the best that happened was dusk. Perhaps it was true that her lids let through more light than usual; in any case, it is certain that as an adult Maximiliane would take great care that dark curtains were hung in the windows of her own children's bedrooms.

"As a man I must say," Herr von Kalck noted, "that eyes like those are an inestimable fortune for a girl."

Baroness Quindt drew the guests' attention to the portraits of the Quindt ancestors, and Dorchen, who

44

was helping serve, reported in the kitchen while she was having the bowls of red cabbage refilled, "They're talking about the baby's eyes." Anna Riepe and the widow Schmaltz agreed: the child had beer eyes. Now light, now dark, more brown than yellow. "What she sees, she sees," the midwife added.

In the big hall they had begun to talk about the ancestors, whose portraits hung along one of the long walls eyeball to eyeball with the rulers on the wall opposite. There was William I, white-bearded, paternal, a sovereign still deeply venerated by the Quindts. Next came Frederick, the ninety-nine-day emperor, in whom such high hopes had been placed. Next came the portrait of Frederick the Great, an effective copy. A picture of Bismarck with a Great Dane at his feet had been acquired by the present lord of the manor. The only woman was Queen Louise, also a copy of a contemporary oil painting. Conspicuously absent was William II, the present emperor of the German Reich. Instead there was a steel engraving of Hindenburg, the victor of Tannenberg, wearing his field marshal's uniform; it had been added to the gallery only two years earlier. This time too he was remembered with a toast.

The far wall of the room contained the fireplace in front of which, protected from flying sparks by a fire screen, the baby was sleeping once more in her cradle. "Please clear the baby off the table, Riepe," Old Quindt had ordered, whereupon Fräulein Kuhl had risen to rescue the child. The opposite wall contained the windows, and between them the arrangement of potted palms with the table that had served as an altar.

The ancestors' gallery: seven Quindts in oil, all in heavy gold frames, all well along in years, most of them wearing their regimental uniforms or hunting outfits, with gun and booty, stag or pheasant or, in one case wild ducks. Next to last in the series came Old Quindt himself, high on his horse. A Quindt horse in front of a pale-blue Pomeranian sky. The incorrect position of the horse's legs–right front and right rear both raised and pointing forward–annoyed Quindt whenever he looked at the picture. The portrait had been painted eight years earlier, before he grew his beard.

Next to his image, a child's portrait: Achim von Quindt, barely twelve years old, wearing pale-blue velvet with a white lace collar, in the manner of an English lord. The painter had spent several weeks on Poenichen one summer. Quindt had met him in Naples, and the opportunity was favorable, so the boy's portrait was commissioned as well. The painter had been more successful with the two pointers than with the boy; the brown of their pelts complemented the blue velvet. Frau Merzin, who came from Dresden, spoke of "painterly delicacy," of "German impressionism."

The father's health was drunk while everyone thought of him as a twelve-year-old boy with a lace collar.

Quindt asked Riepe to pass the potatoes one more time. "Speaking of delicacies, Frau Merzin, please have some more of Pomerania's finest."

The main course was roast boar with preserved vegetables, mixed pickles, red cabbage, and boiled potatoes. Herr von Kalck shoved his plate over to his wife so that she could cut his meat for him. There was no longer any talk of the eighty-five thousand Russians who were worth one measly arm.

There was no printed menu, but while they ate, Quindt passed around the menu from his own christening dinner in 1867. On the cover, a photograph–now faded– of the baptismal child surmounted the Quindt coat of arms. The inside listed the sequence of courses: turtle soup; smoked pike with dill sauce; saddle of venison in cream sauce. Seven courses in all, ending with demitasse– printed on handmade paper. What was remarkable about the document, and the reason he showed it: his grand-

46

father, born near the end of the eighteenth century, had completed the listing in his own careful though already somewhat shaky hand by adding next to the demitasse, "Cookies and cheese straws." These four words represented the single handwritten testimony to the present baby's great-great-grandfather. Cookies and cheese straws as proof of existence. The deeper significance of the anecdote escaped the guests. Only Maximiliane, who was later presented with this menu, understood what was meant. All her life cookies seemed to her something special, something personal.

When all the guests had been offered a second helping of roast boar and red cabbage and Fräulein Kuhl had refused with "No, thank you, that's quite enough," Old Quindt rose to make his speech. In consideration of the kitchen, he never spoke until the last hot course had been finished. Everyone was contented, full, and sleepy.

First he spoke about the baby's name. It might appear too large for so small a little girl, he said, but if his knowledge of Latin had not been altogether bogged down in the Pomeranian morass, *maximal* meant "most" or "greatest"; and a maxim, surely that was a fundamental principle adopted by the French moralists as the basis for practical conduct. Now, if this child were to live out her days according to the laws of practical conduct, the name would seem to him a good omen, with intimations of greatness clinging to it; one was inadvertently reminded of Emperor Maximilian, the last of the knights, on whose realm the sun never set.

At this point the Reverend Merzin allowed himself to clear his throat and interject that the speaker was surely confusing Maximilian with Charles V. Quindt, who did not appreciate interruptions–a trait that at one time had gained him a reputation as an undemocratic diet delegate–replied with a certain acerbity, "If a story

47

is good enough, it's true," to which Dr. Wittkow responded, "The delegate can still carry the day."

"As far as my granddaughter's eyes are concerned," Quindt continued, "I'm sure there are many testators. Goths and Wends and Swedes, perhaps a Pole—who can be certain, and who cares? The main thing is to be Pomeranian—that's always proven to be the strongest. In the long run the Goths, Slavs, Wends, and Swedes, all of whom settled here at one time or another, turned into good Pomeranians. Nationality has not always been so very important, or a Quindt could not have become a provincial governor in Poland. Only with the Berliners does it take a little longer, though they're so quick in other ways." He looked at Vera. She held her ground.

He turned to generalizations, touched on conditions at the front and at home, and noted that by the time the news reached Poenichen, it had lost some of its fire but that even tepid it was hard to digest.

"Among us Germans, everything is always 'too far to the left' or 'too far to the right.' This German *too*, if I may call it that for once—it will give us a lot of trouble yet. Nietzsche and Krupp, these are the names of Germany's nemesis—we could have managed one or the other." Another of his "Quindt-essences," which he considered popular and graphic. His after-dinner speeches did not materially differ from the speeches he had given as a delegate to the regional diet. Now and again he allowed his listeners to let off steam with a little laughter, but he was no buffoon or populist, even if he occasionally concealed his intelligence behind a kind of peasant cunning.

A form of rhetorical knight's move brought him to Bismarck this time as well, and his hand flourished a glass of red wine in the direction of Bismarck's portrait. The guests, in suspense whether the wine would spill, did not devote the requisite attention to his performance.

48

"A man such as Bismarck reverently bowed his knee to the man you seek in vain among these men. Presumably Bismarck was not even aware that he was a Bismarck." He reminded them that he, Quindt, had refused to kiss the Kaiser's hand. "A Quindt kisses no one's hand, nor does he allow anyone to kiss his hand. That is no one's due. The splendid times of William the Second are past, and we should not grieve after them; we have enough to grieve over. So that you won't have to correct me, Pastor, I've noted down a passage from one of the Kaiser's speeches."

Taking a page from his pocket, he read, " 'Open your eyes! Raise your heads! Turn your gaze upward and bend your knees to the Great Ally Who has never yet deserted the Germans, no matter how hard He has tested and humiliated them, Who has always raised them out of the dust. Hands on your hearts, eyes trained on the distance, and from time to time a glance of remembrance for strength to the old Kaiser and his time, and I am firmly convinced that–' And so on, and so on. 'Our fatherland will lead on the road to enlightenment, the road to clarification, the road to practical Christianity, a blessing for mankind, a bulwark of peace, an object of admiration for all nations.'

"Thus spake the Kaiser, who on another occasion enlarged upon the German essence, which must cure the world–a statement we will surely be reminded of often. On this eleventh day of November in the year 1918 it should be worded instead that the world must first be cured of the German essence! We have made our contribution to the history of the twentieth century. The Great Ally did not fight on our side. Whether Ally or Almighty, Pastor, he always seems on the side of the victors."

The Reverend Merzin jumped to his feet. "May He be merciful to us all, Baron."

"Yes, He and the victors as well," Quindt concluded his speech.

And Riepe added, "Amen."

Herr von Kalck retorted sharply, "Naval revolt, what? Conditions such as they had in Kiel. Have we come to this in Pomerania? Will you allow that to happen, Baron Quindt?"

So the reprimand was addressed, not to Riepe but to Herr von Kalck. "In my house anyone may say, 'Amen.' " Quindt was looking at Riepe as he spoke, his chin jutting out, a twitch in his face. Then he regained control. "Hand me the bottle, Riepe. I'll pour."

Everyone rose and drank silently. Dorchen placed the caramel pudding on the table; there was no coffee. Frau Wittkow said, "So—not even coffee this time. I do hope the child will not be without the little luxuries all her life."

Dr. Wittkow added, "As long as she can eat her fill of roast boar."

And the Reverend Merzin noted that on his travels through his parish he hardly ever saw game anymore. "The forests are as empty as the lake. We've come to the end."

That statement, too, was hardly calculated to raise the general mood. Dr. Wittkow once more alluded to "the error in the matter of the baby's gender," expressing the hope that even as a grown woman the child would always manfully do her duty.

Then the Baroness rose, putting an end to the christening dinner. The guests, she said, would surely want to get home before dark. She asked Riepe to harness their horses. The men retired for as long as it took to smoke a cigar. Vera also lit a cigarette and joined the gentlemen. "Now this little bit of nicotine can't harm the baby anymore," she said.

"Perhaps not biologically," Fräulein von Kalck said, "but morally it may."

50

To which Vera replied, "Then presumably a cigar is ten times more immoral than a cigarette. Surely an object doesn't become moral just because it's held by a man?"

Quindt agreed that there was something illogical in the argument and handed her the ashtray. Dr. Wittkow expressed the sentiment that, given the general shortage, any cigar given up to a friend was another sacrifice occasioned by the war. Revolutions in Munich and Berlin, soldiers' and workers' councils—those were not topics one could ask ladies to listen to. That the Kaiser had abdicated and already left the country, that Scheidemann had already declared the republic—no one on Poenichen had had the news yet. The armistice negotiations had been completed. One world war was at an end.

When the two carriages drove up, Quindt, as always, stood at the top of the steps leading to the verandah. Dorchen flipped down the running boards, and Riepe helped the guests to get in before buttoning up the oilcloth covering. The carbide lamps were already lit, the November day was coming to an early and foggy end. The von Kalcks were the first to drive off. Dr. Wittkow was taking the Merzins in his carriage. A lash of the whip in farewell, Quindt's shout of "Good night" in response, and then there was silence.

The baby had long since fallen asleep in her cradle. Vera had gone to her room, as had the Baroness. On Poenichen everyone retired as early as possible.

"Show me," Quindt called to Riepe.

Riepe stuttered. "Oh, Baron, sir."

"Riepe, you were never a good footman, but you're a worse actor."

"But you gave no sign, sir."

"I do have to be a little more clever than my coachman, Riepe."

Quindt extended his hand. Awkwardly Riepe pulled the telegram from his pocket and smoothed it out. He knew the contents, since the local postman had pressed it into his hand saying, "It affects everyone on Poenichen—and now, after such a long time."

Old Quindt read the telegram, folded it carefully, and put it in his pocket. "When did you pick this up, Riepe?"

"This morning, around ten o'clock it might have been, Baron, sir. I thought the baby should have her christening first."

"And she's had it. One thing at a time. This way, at least, we didn't baptize an orphan."

"May I–"

"Let's not talk about it now. Do they know in the kitchen?"

"Only Anna."

Quindt turned around, walked into the house, and asked Dorchen to tell his wife and his daughter-in-law that he was waiting for them in his study. One of the two housemaids was always called Dorchen, Quindt deciding which. The maids accepted this order of things. It was a title, and they felt honored.

So Dorchen scurried to the Baroness's room. She was wearing her Sunday best, like everyone on the estate. When there was a feast in the manor house, they celebrated in the cottages too, only more modestly. Goose breast and sour game stew. They shared joy and sorrow; though it was true that the manor usually had the larger share–of sorrow as well.

At the same time, the death of the young baron seemed sadder to the estate hands than the death of a son of their own. All of them had several children, and new generations were always springing up. Though they hardly knew the young baron, they had all thought of him as the next lord of the manor.

A few days after the telegram the regimental commander's letter arrived. It announced to the sorrowing parents and the young widow that Second Lieutenant Achim von Quindt had fallen at the head of his unit. A bullet had penetrated his chest. For centuries the Quindts had died the same way: always at the head of their unit, their company, their battalion, always a bullet in the chest, always a simple shot through the lungs. For mothers and widows, that had proven the most bearable form of heroic death.

In the obituary that appeared in the regional and local papers, Quindt had the word *proud* deleted–not "in proud sorrow" but only "in sorrow." Second Lieutenant Achim von Quindt, born on Poenichen in 1897, died in France in 1918. Followed by the names of the bereaved survivors, last of whom was Maximiliane Irene.

It took several weeks before the package containing the dead man's personal effects arrived–the gold pocket watch Achim had been given for his confirmation; the iron watch chain that had been traded for the gold one in 1917 and that bore the legend "For arms I gave up gold, With pride I iron hold"; the seal ring with the Quindt crest; and the Iron Cross Second Class, which was awarded him after the battles on the Lys; further, Vera's last letter. The package also contained a plan of the cemetery indicating the spot where Second Lieutenant Quindt had found his temporary final resting place. Quindt appropriated the map. He intended having his son's mortal remains transferred to Poenichen as soon as possible so that they could be interred in the family plot.

The fallen hero's mother placed these last things in an ivory box, adding the only photograph of her son; it showed him as a wartime volunteer standing next to his dugout. She also put in the telegram with the triple hurrah, his last living communication. She asked if Vera would like to have the box, and when Vera said no, she placed it on the mantel in the big hall, where similar caskets and cases were already standing. When Maximiliane later began to ask about her father–she must have been around five years old–her grandmother showed her the contents of the box, item by item. But her explanations must have been inadequate, for the little girl came to believe that her dead father was in the box. She grew afraid of it and for years did not dare approach the fireplace.

The death notice caused dismay but no visible mourning. No wound was torn open. For several months Quindt wore a black ribbon in the buttonhole of his coat, and the two women dressed in black throughout the winter. The succession had been broken, but it was not the first time this had happened to the Quindts. Quindt himself had only just turned fifty, and he could count on administering his estates for another twenty years. A child was growing up, and in the end what mattered was blood. Though eventually it would become impossible to mention the estate owner "Quindt on Poenichen," the name of Poenichen would surely always remain. The young German Empire, the old Kingdom of Prussia: all shattered. How could Poenichen have emerged unscathed from the catastrophe?

The Reverend Merzin sent to ask whether a visit from him was desired and whether the family was considering a memorial service in the church or the house of mourning; but Quindt gave him to understand that he saw no occasion for a ceremony. To his wife he said, "Those who believe in God have an easier time of it— at least they know whom to complain to." While speaking, he had placed his hand on her arm, which was not his usual practice; and for a moment she covered his hand with hers. Then they went their separate ways again.

All that winter Quindt stayed in the woods for half-days at a time. He had Riepe drive him there and back in the closed coupe or the sleigh. As Riepe, stiff-legged and stooped with rheumatism, prepared to climb on the block, Quindt ordered him to take a seat inside, which caused Riepe to protest every time. "But that's not right, Baron, sir."

"I can order you to get into the carriage, Riepe, but I can't order you to feel at ease in it," Quindt answered, awkwardly climbing on the box. Once he quoted a Christmas carol—" 'He'll be a lord, and I a servant'—or is it the other way around?"

"It goes, 'He'll be a servant, I a lord, What changes there will be,' Baron, sir."

"All right, then, it fits."

And Quindt, wearing his heavy fur coat, tramped off through the woods. When the snow was too high, he remained on Poenichen and walked up and down the avenue, his hands folded on his back. He worked off the event with the help of trees, his wife with her dogs. Vera felt connected neither to trees nor to dogs, not even to the sleeping little baby. Her restlessness seeped through the walls.

7

How could Vera have raised her child in the spirit of the fallen father? No one on Poenichen knew the dead man's spirit. The usual model of upbringing prevailed, in which the mother need not necessarily play the central part. For some time the phonograph stood in a corner, covered with a black cloth, until one day it was returned to service. Vera used the old popular hit like a protest song and acted as if Poenichen were a Prussian Siberia.

She treated the housemaids like personal attendants, as she did the housekeeper and even Riepe. In her rooms she dropped whatever she had just taken off—dresses, underwear, shoes. That was not the way of Poenichen, where everyone poured out his own wash water, no one left rings in the washbowl, everyone put away his own belongings. Though each room was provided with two bell pulls, they were never used. Only Vera rang, demanding hot water, demanding that a blouse be ironed. She became annoyed when Dorchen did not appear immediately. The daughter of a dairyman! Not even clean hands! Nor did Dorchen apologize when she had kept the young lady waiting. Vera complained.

"That uncouth thing!"

"You have to know how to take her," Quindt explained. "Then she's quite docile."

"Are you trying to say that I don't know how to handle servants?"

"I meant to say no more than what I said."

"Does that mean that the Jadows—"

"Let's drop it." Quindt tried to end the exchange.

But Vera played her trump card. "At least during the war my father was military postal director, and my grandmother on my mother's side was born—"

As soon as she said, "At least"—and she did so frequently—Quindt rose, sketched an uncertain bow in her direction, reached for his cane, and made off.

The verandah had always been the Quindts' favorite spot. At the beginning of May the palms from the dining hall were brought out there. Quindt's mother had grown them from seed, a memorial to Quindt's father's trip to German East Africa. By now the palms were six feet high and could easily withstand the slight frosts that occurred in May and often into early June. The verandah offered a view across the lawn, with its round flower bed where the immortelles grew, down along the linden-lined avenue to the farmyard and the outbuildings, barns, and cottages. The sounds from the stables, the smithy, the wheelwright's shop, gave an impression of bustle without being disturbing. With each noise Quindt looked at his watch: now the scythes were being whetted, now it was time to feed the pigs. From this vantage point one could welcome guests and see them off; this was the place to sit and read the newspapers—not inside, not outside, affording plenty of fresh air but not exposed to the inclemencies of the weather.

For some time Vera made this favorite spot unlivable. There were no discussions, let alone confrontations; instead, everyone went his own way. Quarrels arise when there is not enough room for people to avoid each other, and such was not the case on Poenichen. When they met after hours of separation, they took their places at table, passed bowls back and forth, and managed to make do with please and thank you. One silence led to another. Questions were generally addressed to the baby nurse and concerned the child's well-being. "She's sleeping." "She's cut her first tooth." "She's crawling." The answers were always satisfactory.

Vera could not grasp the tone of Poenichen. At the Jadows' house there had been one girl to do it all: she cleaned, mended, cooked, shopped, used the servants' entrance, and after ten years no one knew when her birthday was. After their only meeting, Quindt's oldest sister, Maximiliane, commented on Vera: "An apartment-house child." What could you expect? Vera's ancestral acres consisted of a seven-room third-floor apartment in the Charlottenburg section of Berlin.

One morning she came to breakfast in pajamas. Quindt made no comment, but when she was still wearing the same outfit at noon, he ordered Dorchen to take the food back to the kitchen. To Vera he said, "I see you're not ready yet. We'll wait."

"I assumed you never noticed what people wore around here."

And Quindt retorted, "We just don't talk about it, that's all."

That same evening he proposed that she spend some weeks in Berlin. He was sure, he said, that she was in need of Berlin air, not just the air that came from the funnel—by which he meant the phonograph. He had set up a bank account for her so that she could come and go as she pleased.

From this first trip to Berlin Vera returned with a shingled haircut that was extremely becoming to her. She was still wearing black, no longer as a sign of mourning but because she had been assured in Berlin that black suited her—black strap shoes, black silk stockings, black all the way to the ebony cigarette holder, the hem of her skirt just clearing her knees.

Quindt inquired, "You don't think that your skirt turned out just a little short?"

"No, I don't think so."

"You don't?"

"No."

Such lapidary exchanges could hardly furnish the proper soil for family feelings. Nevertheless Quindt was impressed with his daughter-in-law. "She's got a certain something," he declared more than once.

To give her pleasure, he subscribed to the *Berliner Illustrierte*. On Thursdays the magazine was delivered in Berlin, on Fridays it arrived on Poenichen. The cover of the first issue they received showed Friedrich Ebert and Gustav Noske at a meeting in the seaside resort of Haffkrug near Travemünde, both wearing short bathing trunks. "So that's what the world looks like underneath," Quindt noted. "It must be republican, that showing off. A Bismarck has no need of such displays. We've got a lot to learn yet."

The things one had previously only read about in the regional and county papers now appeared illustrated and photographed: Berlin without lights; Berlin without water; Berlin without newspapers; street brawls and barricades. Long after Vera had left Poenichen for good, the subscription was continued.

Among the neighbors, long before the war, a group of estate owners had joined in what they called the *jeu*, among them the von Kalcks, the Pichts, and Dr. Wittkow. This *jeu* was now revived. Quindt, who did not care for card games and had no intention of either winning or losing money in this way, had never shown his face at these gatherings. To offer Vera some distraction, he proposed that she go to take a look, which she did several times. While the gentlemen had their game in the den, the ladies played rummy in the salon.

60

The Jadows came for a visit, "to regale themselves in the Pomeranian fleshpots"; each evening they checked their weight on the scale in the barn. "My God, but they still eat high on the hog here," the Berlin guests exclaimed.

Quindt qualified the statement. "Let's say halfway up the hog."

A certain reserve persisted; they did not use first names but called each other "my dear Quindt" and "my dear Jadow," with more stress on the formality than on the cordiality. Herr von Jadow proved to be a sociable type just as long as the conversation did not touch on politics and on what he termed "social conditions." When he had spent a week "thoroughly inspecting the situation on one of these Pomeranian estates," he said at dinner, "You, my dear Quindt, with your carriages and horses, with your oil lamps and water pumps! You're living as if the industrial revolution had never happened! By now people drive cars! We have electric light!"

His wife agreed. "It's medieval. The Dark Ages!"

In point of fact dusk was falling, and the oil lamps had not yet been lit. Quindt cut his meat and listened.

Herr von Jadow resumed the conversational lead. "Patriarchal conditions, my dear Quindt—please don't mind my saying so. Things can't go on like this much longer. Let this be said by a man who thinks of himself as a progressive. You can't stop progress! It won't come to Poenichen by horse-drawn carriage but by rail, at express speeds, and by telephone! There's a new wind blowing!"

"Here the wind still blows from the east, my dear Jadow, and presumably it will go on doing so for quite some time. And for as long as I'm the person who knows best what wind is the right one for this land and these people, things will be done as I say. When someone else comes along who knows better—fine, then I'll step down."

The Baroness saw to it that the dumplings were passed again and inquired as to her guests' current weight gain.

She no longer needed to fear for the baby's weight. The little girl thrived under Fräulein Balzer's care. She lay on her stomach on a blanket in the dappled shade beneath the copper beech until the Fräulein got her going again. Then she obediently started moving, left her blanket, crawled in the grass, used her hands and sometimes her mouth to pick daisies in the spring and beech leaves in the fall, and generally incorporated whatever came within reach. Fräulein Balzer chased away frolicsome puppies and forcefully pleaded for a playpen. Quindt refused. He was convinced that such an appurtenance was hardly worthwhile for an only child. He explained carefully that the acquisition of a nanny to supervise the child made any further acquisitions superfluous; would she therefore please see to it that the child remained on her blanket.

His answer also expressed annoyance that Fritz Schwarze, the wheelwright, had left Poenichen soon after his return from the army. He just couldn't stand conditions on the farm any longer, he allegedly said. Three months later his wife and two daughters, all of whom had worked on the farm, followed him. The wheelwright had been influenced by Willem Riepe, who turned up two months after the end of the war—just to pick up his duds, as he said.

"You won't see me here again anytime soon. Sometime you can send me a goose," he said to his mother. She sent him that and more, especially in the years of the inflation, but he was not seen again all the same. In the farmworkers' common room he had explained that he wouldn't get wet in the Baron's rain anymore. "Those barons are finished! Bloodsuckers—every last one

62

of them. The estates are gonna be split up, but me, I don't want any part of them, not even if you paid me. Regular working hours–that's what I want. A regular salary, not an allowance." At night he broke into the distillery, seized several bottles of spirits, and distributed them to various of the men. Besides schnapps, he also passed out leaflets. "War on the palaces, peace to the cottages."

But in spite of its five white pillars, the manor house was no palace, and though the cottages were built of clay, they did have tiled roofs. Willem Riepe's leaflets and speeches cut no ice; but the schnapps did. With five men in tow, shouting, he marched on the manor house and tried to put it to the torch. But this act of arson, which should not be taken too seriously, was further complicated by the fact that his parents and sisters inhabited that selfsame "palace," though only its basement.

The following morning his father took him to the railroad station, using the gig to speed things up. Willem Riepe set off westward in a freight train. "Like a head of cattle," his father said when, two hours later, he and Quindt had one of their laconic discussions. "As if this place was nothing." And he added, "This way is harder, Baron, sir. Death, that's something else, that you've got to accept–but this!"

"The differences,"Quindt replied. "I've said it before, Riepe, it's the differences. They want to do away with them now. Everybody equally rich, that won't work, so–everybody equally poor, that's what it comes down to. Except that by sharing, nobody gets to the top. It has to be in the person."

"And what's in Willem? An arsonist, that's what's in him."

"Stuff and nonsense, Riepe, somebody else put that in him. And now let's stop the 'Baron, sir' business. We're living in a republic, so you'll simply call me Herr

Quindt—or, if you prefer, Herr von Quindt, because the *von* is part of the name."

Baron Joachim von Quindt had turned into Joachim Baron von Quindt. A change of priorities, the title of nobility now no more than an element of the name. It was Quindt's opinion that democracy had to trickle down from the top before it was seized from below in the form of socialism. Therefore, no more table service! In the kitchen Anna Riepe put the full bowls in the dumbwaiter, which Frau von Quindt personally hauled up, removing them and placing them on the table. Dorchen, who until this time had been able to report to the kitchen, "The Baroness praised the sauce," no longer furnished a connection between upstairs and downstairs.

The staff was deeply offended by these changes, so that they had to be countermanded.

The dinner conversation about progress coming by rail did result in the purchase of an automobile. Not a limousine, which would have been the obvious choice, but a closed sedan where the driver was not separated, even by a glass screen, from the passengers. Quindt referred to it as a "republican motor vehicle," and he took his place in the seat next to the driver. When Frau von Quindt was driven to Dramburg or Arnswalde, she cried, "Otto! Otto!" whenever Riepe drove faster than twenty.

Though the car was not specifically assigned to Vera, it was available whenever she wanted it. Riepe imparted to her his limited driving skills, and she turned out to be a born motorist with a surprising instinct for automobile mechanics. She drove out in the car even more frequently than she had ridden out on horseback.

During the summer she invited her Berlin friends to Poenichen; these women found life in the country "heavenly." The rowboat was caulked, freshly painted, and launched on Poenichen Lake. Boat trips alternated with carriage drives, the latter in the "vis-à-vis," which could hold six, in an emergency eight. Vera arranged picnics at the lake, and Anna Riepe filled the hampers with game pâté and fish aspics. Occasionally someone glanced at the baby, who was asleep or pretending to be asleep. The cradle was rocked, but then it turned out to be more fun to play with the puppies–Dinah had already had another litter–for the thickly bunched diapers were not an appealing sight. Fräulein Balzer was in favor of letting children develop naturally, without interference. No sitting on the potty for hours, no slaps–nothing but diapers, and sometimes not even those.

Fräulein Balzer's father practiced nudism faithfully; he was a fanatic who espoused reverence for unclothed nature, "pure realization of the body as the vessel of moral forces." Himself naked and chaste, he preached to his followers in a leafy arbor in the Lichterfelde suburb of Berlin. Fräulein Balzer's papers listed her father's occupation simply as bookkeeper. She played "pushcart" with the baby, exercised with her, kissed every one of her dimples, and stinted in no other department either. Every day, however, she took two hours off at noon to satisfy her needs for pure realization of the body at the Blue Pond.

Then, too, the child could not boast curls that might have aroused the young ladies' raptures. Her hair was neither light nor dark nor wavy. No one paid any attention to her evenly tanned skin; pallor was still considered a sign of good breeding. As soon as footsteps approached, the little girl closed the eyes that might have evoked exclamations of admiration; she made herself as invisible as possible.

One of the young ladies discovered the family coat of arms on the diapers. "Real batiste! You should have it made into a blouse, Vera!"

When the laughter faded away, the baby opened her eyes.

The days grew shorter, and the oil lamps were lit in the evenings. Vera's brother, Franz von Jadow, came for a visit. He was a trained warrior, as Quindt put it.

The young Herr von Jadow also inquired, "You don't have electricity yet? No gas for cooking? No steam heat? Not even running water?"

"That's how it is," Quindt allowed. "Water must be carried from the well to the house by the sweat of Dorchen's or Frieda's brow—at least the drinking water. The lamps are cleaned and filled by Priska, my former coachman, and the fire in the hearth is tended by Anna Riepe, our housekeeper."

"But technology! It makes all those people unnecessary!"

"I've got the people, but I don't have the technology. And what would become of old Priska? He can't be coachman anymore, he's too old to work in the fields or in the barns, but he can still take care of the lamps. And in the summer he can weed the paths. If a storm knocks out the overhead wires or lightning hits a generator, you sit in the dark. Priska's lamps burn even during a snowstorm. Water pipes break, but it's not so easy to break Dorchen or Frieda if you treat them properly. And in your Berlin apartments you won't find fresher water than what you get on my table. As for heating, no one ever has to be cold on Poenichen. On the other hand, I've been told that people are cold in Berlin and that the gas isn't always turned on. In my woods there's plenty of fuel, and each year brings new growth!"

"That may be all very true here in the manor house," Herr von Jadow objected. "But the cottages? I notice they're all dark."

"The people are asleep now, Herr von Jadow," Quindt pointed out. "They're tired because they got up early and worked twelve hours. None of them is cold and none of them is hungry. All receive their allowances of wood, potatoes, and wheat; they keep pigs, goats, geese. If they're ill, they're cared for, and when they grow old, they aren't thrown out of their houses; there's always room, always something for them to do. It seems to me I've read that such conditions don't always obtain in the cities. And now good night, ladies, sir. Dorchen, please take my lamp upstairs. You see, Dorchen isn't only Poenichen's water pipe, she's also the one who conducts the light, and as you can tell, she's in good shape even if you can't switch her on and off."

This last remark took the sting out of the conversation. Dorchen blushed under a glance from young Herr von Jadow, who became aware of her for the first time.

"A charming argument against electricity, Baron," he said in his snappy officer's tone, raising his glass. "If I may take the liberty of drinking to your special good health."

Her father-in-law had once been a parliamentary delegate, Vera explained on another occasion.

"An archconservative, I bet."

"Not at all," the Baroness replied. "A liberal—even a progressive liberal." And she rose to signify the conclusion of the meal. She rarely intervened in a conversation, but she was always ready to put an end to one if she considered it desirable. Few people realized that she headed the household. She had been taught that a house should be kept without fanfare. No visitor was allowed to notice that the lady of the manor performed any chores, and it was this air of effortlessness that set her apart from the workers. Complaints and perspiration belonged in the kitchens and the maids' rooms. Sophie Charlotte was an East Prussian of the silent type by nature. Besides, early in their marriage Quindt must have said, "Stay out of it, Sophie Charlotte"—an injunction strong enough to last five decades.

Outsiders assumed that the Baroness pursued her hobbies exclusively, breeding dogs and, in winter, weaving. During the final winter of the war Klara Slewenka, the smith's wife, had taught her how to use a loom. She wove rugs of sheep's wool, and lately she had taken to making thick vests of the stuff, both long-sleeved and sleeveless. So that currently everyone on Poenichen wore this peaceable uniform, which concealed all differences: men, women, and children, with the exception of the Baron, who continued to wear his green shag jacket. Material was scarce, and no one could pay the inflated prices. Sheep's wool was readily available and kept on replicating itself on the backs of the sheep, especially after the new assistant foreman began to breed the sheep specifically for wool.

During the afternoons the Baroness sat in the breakfast room weaving with Dorchen and Frieda. A cottage industry: one carded the wool, the other spun, the Baroness wove. When Anna Riepe was finished in the kitchen, she joined them. At first the jackets were stiff with sheep sweat, later with human sweat. Vera had refused to work in the weaving chamber; she turned up her nose. "It's like Hauptmann's play *The Weavers*."

From time to time Anna Riepe let the hot jacket slide from her lap, clutched her throat, pushed her graying, damp hair from her forehead, and rested her hands in her lap. The Baroness cast her a searching glance and made an effort, if not to prevent, at least to keep from showing the wave of heat collecting in her own body. She wore inserts of tulle and lace to hide the rising flush at her throat. Anna Riepe undid the top buttons of her dress to get some air. One menopausal, the other going through the change, but without any possibility of communicating their discomfort, except perhaps through mutual consideration and the shared need for a cup of mint tea.

The weaving chamber was well-heated and smelled of sheep; the even clatter of the loom made Anna Riepe sleepy. Her chin sank to her chest, she snored, repeatedly reducing the two maids to giggles, and when the Baroness became entangled in the warp threads, as happened frequently, they could barely remain in their seats with laughing. Toward evening, when the nurse brought the freshly bathed baby to the weaving chamber, they all sang. The baby was placed on one of the piles of wool, where she burrowed like a mole and emitted gurgles of well-being while her little hands plucked at the fuzz. Fräulein Hämmerling began to edge the jackets with cording.

Then the little girl demanded to be taken on Anna Riepe's lap. Loudly and distinctly she called, "Mama," holding out her arms and rolling her eyes. She was corrected, first by Fräulein Hämmerling, then by all the others–"Anna." Still she insisted on Mama, though she was eventually willing to say "Amma." And so matters remained for years. She sat on Anna Riepe's soft lap, pressed against her warm breasts. Her own mother could offer her neither and did not even try. The child was rocked, and under Fräulein Hämmerling's direction the maids sang, "Sleep, baby, sleep," an injunction quickly obeyed.

By February everyone knew why Dorchen had stopped giggling and singing: she was pregnant. She was not sent away; that was not how things were done on Poenichen. Quindt wrote a letter to young Herr von Jadow, but the letter was never acknowledged. Instead the young man wrote to his sister, "You ought to be pleased that someone is bringing new blood to your farm. They're all running away from you into the factories." An army buddy had found him a job in banking, but he was not used to handling other people's money. Some things could be hushed up, and twice his father helped out at considerable sacrifice to himself. Finally the only solution was a steamship ticket to America–a gesture that exhausted the Jadows' modest fortune.

Quindt tried to find a husband for Dorchen, an attempt that also failed. Vera was the only one who objected to her staying in the house; her distaste for pregnant women was rooted in her own pregnancy. "For God's sake, send her away! She can have her baby anywhere! You're so stingy! You don't want to pay! She has to work for you to the very end!"

Dorchen was again called Luise Priebe, which was equivalent to a demotion: that's what happened to a girl who did not think enough of herself. After her delivery she went to the city; the infant, baptized with the name Helene, was brought back to Poenichen village and raised by her grandparents; later she was called Lenchen. Luise Priebe regularly sent small sums of money, not to her parents, but to Baron von Quindt, who put the funds in the savings bank and each year added a little something of his own.

Riepe inquired whether his youngest daughter, Martha, might now start as the latest Dorchen; though only fifteen years old, she was thoroughly employable. Quindt rejected his appeal. "No infiltration, Riepe. The lower house is growing too strong."

"But Martha isn't at all like Willem," Riepe objected.

"I don't mean that, no. But there's too much back and forth. The matter is settled."

For days Riepe did not speak to his master; both of them had the Pomeranian stubbornness.

Unlike her mother-in-law, Vera had not been raised to be the lady of the manor. She lacked every prerequisite, but she went to great lengths to lead the life she considered proper. When she went to the kitchen to fry herself an egg, Anna Riepe took the frying pan from her and defended the stove with her own broad backside. "Let's not even start that, madam." Belowstairs was Anna Riepe's domain. Upstairs and downstairs remained separate; downstairs they had their rights too, rights that must be honored.

So Vera spent most of her time on horseback or behind the wheel of the car, rushing along the roads, her throat wound with a long black mourning scarf that billowed in the breeze. "Flags at half-mast," as Old Quindt put it. The teamsters had difficulty managing their horses, which were not used to howling engines. The crazy young lady was on the road! Geese and chickens could not scamper fast enough. Vera did not even turn around when she ran over a chicken. The bird would end up in the stewpot anyway, and why not today instead of tomorrow.

The Quindt horses were named for the winds: Trade Wind, Monsoon, Sirocco, Typhoon. When Vera went riding, her favorite was Mistral, a lively five-year-old mare. Her black scarf tied to her hat, Vera leaped over ditches and fences, returning home only after many hours, hot and exhausted.

"Have them rub down the horse," Quindt would say. "And you too, if you'll take my advice."

Usually she took a route that passed Poenichen Lake. For some time a new assistant foreman had been living in the foreman's house by the lake. When he looked at her, his gaze drove the blood to her face. Though hers was not a passionate nature—she tended more to coolness—she was nearing the end of her twenties and was unsatisfied. Her husband, as inexperienced as herself, had probably demonstrated more awkwardness than ardor during their few nights of wedded bliss.

During those October days on Poenichen Lake a Lady Chatterley type of affair might easily have been played out, but Quindt sensed the way the wind was blowing in good time, though no work of literature gave him a hint; Lawrence had not yet written his novel. In answer to Vera's question about the new man at the lake, Quindt gave her the facts and at the same time proposed that now, when there was no denying that autumn had come and the good months on Poenichen were over, she go to Berlin again for a long visit. Horses, dogs, and country gentlemen were surely not fit company for a true Berliner.

72

9

Anna Riepe filled sacks with wheat flour and dried fruit, wrapped sides of bacon in cheesecloth, packed smoked goose breast and sheep's-wool jackets. The maids tucked the foodstuffs among the young madam's clothing, and then Riepe took her and her hampers to the railroad station in Stargard, where, with the stationmaster's help, in exchange for a cigar "with the Baron's most respectful compliments," he found her a seat. She remained immune from the customs check for hoarders.

At first she stayed with her parents, sleeping in the room with the white furniture suitable for a young girl. Her father was writing a paper on "Advances and Difficulties in the Transmission of Communications Between Home and Front," supporting his argument with precise figures: 17.7 billion letters from home to the front! Before he could complete his dissertation, he died of pneumonia. Vera, who was on Poenichen at the time, once more took her hampers to Berlin, this time staying several weeks. But two widows in the same apartment, of whom the older knew precisely what a widow should and more importantly should not do–that could never work. Vera rented a furnished room.

Often they had no news of her on Poenichen for weeks on end, until a telegram came to announce her arrival in Stargard. From one of these stays in Berlin she brought back a camera, a simple plate instrument.

At first she only took pictures of whatever stood still. Then she graduated to dogs and horses, and finally to her daughter: a small, round little girl with a big white bow in her hair. "Stand still," Vera would command when she wanted to take a picture. Then the little girl would hold the pose her mother had placed her in, perhaps before one of the white pillars of the verandah. But as soon as her mother began to trip the shutter, the child would raise her hands to her face. After several repetitions, Vera gave up.

One of these failed photographs was preserved. It reveals the whole incongruity: the pillar ten times taller than the child. And one day she was expected to carry it all and to pass it on—what a burden for such a little girl!

Quindt had adopted the practice of standing Maximiliane up against this selfsame pillar on the morning of her birthday, placing a book on her head, and drawing a line. In the course of ten years, less than a full meter was added to the original 42 centimeters, and each year her grandfather commented, "Hurry up, now. You're doing it too slowly." If she tried to stand on tiptoe while he was measuring her, he pushed her back down.

For the present Vera's photographs were ordinary, amateurish. She sent the exposed plates to Stargard, where an optician developed them and made prints. Horseback riding, driving the car, photography—all were considered useless and expensive hobbies on Poenichen. There people only rode and drove to get to a particular place, never for the sake of the activity. Relations worsened.

During one of her stays in Berlin Vera had become acquainted with an editor of the *Berliner Illustrierte*, and she showed him her most successful pictures. At first he was more interested in the applicant herself and the smoked goose breast from Pomerania, but soon he recognized a certain talent and saw to it that she was taken on by Vogt, a photographer in Steglitz, who trained her for six months. They knew nothing about this on Poenichen. When she returned from Berlin, they asked at most whether she had had a pleasant journey; no one pressed for details.

Vera developed a sure eye for picture sequences. She was even among the inventors of the photo series. She took pictures of the same tree at various times of day or year, or of a foal, a mare, an old nag long in the tooth, proving herself capable of a surprising amount of patience. Later on she grew bold enough to photograph human beings–not posed portraits but snapshots, objective and revealing, mostly of people who believed themselves unobserved.

On a Friday in early October Quindt was sitting on the verandah innocently flipping through the *Berliner Illustrierte*. His eyes fell on four large photos under the collective title "Images of Pomerania." He started. First picture: a country gentleman in his gig, the coachman standing on the step behind his master, both observed from the rear down a long avenue ending in a light, castlelike building. Second picture: a man on horseback, also observed from the rear, his whip raised in command, and to the right and left, between the legs of the horse, a column of potato pickers–"The Foreman." Third picture: a woman stooping over straddle-legged, wearing thick skirts, picking potatoes. Finally: a child struggling with a basket of potatoes that was much too heavy for her. In the bottom right-hand corner, "Photographs by Vera v. Q." The initials were enough. The photographer's meaning was equally clear. Certainly each of the figures was recognizable–Quindt and Riepe, Foreman Palcke, Marie Priebe, and little Erika Beske.

Besides Quindt, no one on Poenichen looked at the *Berliner Illustrierte*, not even Herr Palcke. But the neighboring estates also subscribed to the magazine. The telephone never stopped ringing.

Quindt began by bringing the matter up with his wife. "What do you think, Sophie Charlotte?"

"I'm staying out of it."

Next he sought out his daughter-in-law in the Green Rooms. This confrontation was of somewhat longer duration. Vera was lying on the sofa, smoking and listening to the phonograph. "Yes, we have no bananas, we have no bananas today."

Quindt held up the magazine. "The photographs are good. They reflect the situation—though one-sidedly. From behind, as it were. It would be possible to face the problem, wouldn't it? But let's forget about that. I don't want you to put Poenichen in the press a second time. It's better for you to look for your subjects in Berlin. That's where you belong; you don't belong here. Which I regret."

"Really?" Vera cranked up the phonograph and once more put the needle to the edge of the record: "Yes, we have no bananas." "Tell me, has the word *eman-ci-pa-tion* ever penetrated to Poenichen?" She had a way of scanning certain words, just like her mother.

"Verbally and in writing, yes," Quindt said, "but I've never seen any of it. You think of yourself as an emancipated woman. All right, then, you ought to live like one. You'll have to do without the monthly allowance you've been drawing. Instead, I'll set up a photography studio for you—I'll find out what it should cost. The child remains here."

He paused. "I see that you have no objection. If you are not willing to shoulder the responsibilities of a mother, there is no reason for your further presence on Poenichen. In spite of what you seem to believe, everyone does his duty here. If you wish, you can spend your holidays here—your friends, of course, are not welcome. In a few years the child will be old enough to visit you in Berlin by mutual arrangement. I would prefer that you acquire some kind of pen name for your photographic

76

endeavors. I do not care to see the name Quindt in a picture magazine. Whether you will use the name Jadow is up to you—or to the Jadows. But then, the Jadows appear in the press in quite another context." This last was an allusion to Vera's brother; it would have been better left unsaid, but presumably the bananas had inspired it.

Vera stubbed out her cigarette. "Are you quite finished? You can practice your tyr-an-ny on Poenichen. Leave me and my family out of it. And please—don't turn your obligations to me into charity. If you do, I'll engage a lawyer to arrive at the proper estimate for the manufacture of an heiress."

"I most sincerely apologize," Quindt said. He went to the door, where he turned back. "And I hope your memories of your guest engagement here are not all bad."

Quindt's prophecy—"She's got a certain something"—turned out to be true. Though he had to pay for furnishing her Berlin studio in the new reform currency, which required taking out a loan at a time when interest was high and money was tight, the investment paid off. Vera became independent and made no further claims. Once a month the *Berliner Illustrierte* featured a major photo series under the name Vera Jadow; she was a regular contributor, though she never joined the staff. Her sequences had such titles as "Unter den Linden at Half-Past Four" or simply "Music"—Wilhelm Furtwängler, the conductor of the Philharmonic Orchestra, his baton lowered, juxtaposed with a solo entertainer in a corner bar, followed by an organ grinder in the courtyard of an apartment house. Soon she achieved recognition: a woman looking at Berlin, touching a contemporary nerve. She photographed balconies on art nouveau buildings supported by caryatids. Palms and oleander in brass buckets. Western Berlin. And balconies in the north of the city, where diapers were hung out to dry.

These sequences made her a celebrity with access to journalistic and artistic circles. The twenties were very flattering to her. She appropriated the Berlin tomboy look, even helped shape it. She wore pantsuits, usually of black velvet, shirtwaists, and red silk ties. She was at ease with homosexuals without herself being a lesbian. She smoked, drank scotch, drove a black roadster convertible, usually a man's car, a two-seater, her Leica at the ready. She was skilled at dancing the Charleston and had the quick, sharp wit of the Berliner. Although her photographs revealed social injustices, she was apolitical and gave no thought to changing conditions. She discovered the "poetry of poverty," but she was no Käthe Kollwitz; at most she was "the red princess." It was said that somewhere in the farthest reaches of Pomerania she had a little daughter, all perfectly legal.

During a reception at the headquarters of the magazine she was photographed, and the next issue introduced her visually to the readers of the *Berliner Illustrierte*. Maximiliane cut the picture out and put it in the box on the mantel. Sooner or later the separation between mother and daughter had to happen; Vera had decided on sooner, before they had had a chance to grow used to each other.

"The worry about my children gnaws at me," Grandmother Jadow wrote to Poenichen. Her only son was missing somewhere in America, her only daughter was emancipated, whatever that meant. The letter was read out loud and discussed. Maximiliane listened but asked no questions.

A second letter arrived some time later. "I have shrunk." The grandmother had moved to a four-room apartment in the same section of town. Maximiliane formed a mental image of her grandmother, shrunken and gnawed. When they asked if she would like to visit her grandmother, she said no without giving a reason.

78

Grandmother Jadow regularly received a Christmas package from Pomerania, and she invariably wrote a thank-you note some time in January. Each year she sent a toy "for my only grandchild." Once it was a jumping jack, another time a celluloid doll dressed in the habit of the Kaiserswerther Deaconesses, and once a toy store complete with cash register, scales, counter, and shelves, the boxes of noodles filled with candy. But Maximiliane did not play with the store; for years it stood in the nursery, tidy and covered. She had no passion for buying and selling, nor was there anyone to promote such a drive. Nothing was ever bought on Poenichen. The kitchen used whatever came from the gardens, woods, and lakes; there were no bananas, and no candies except homemade ones. Clothes were sewn by Frau Görke, who twice a year spent a week in the breakfast room to lengthen and alter dresses.

Though it had not come to an open break between Vera Jadow and the Quindts, there was distance. This spatial and temporal separation also gave rise to a spiritual one. Each Friday Quindt approached the latest issue of the *Berliner Illustrierte* with foreboding, for which there was no occasion. Vera stuck to the agreement: no more images of Pomerania.

10

Once Quindt had hired a new foreman to look after the estate proper–that same Herr Palcke, who lived in the foreman's house with his family–and once the outlying farmland along the lake was being worked again, he had more free time and occasionally let it be known that he was not averse to another fling at politics.

The German National People's Party was the first to send a delegation to Poenichen, but the Center Party also dispatched two men to see him; they were looking for a suitable politician in East Elbia, and at least this Baron von Quindt did not seem committed to any religious sect. Even the Social Democrats would have liked to see him in their ranks: a country squire with parliamentary experience, by no means conservative, who might represent in the Reichstag the concerns of agriculture, which employed at least half the Pomeranian population. He should be persuaded to begin by running for the regional diet. But first it was necessary to ascertain the political ideology of this estate owner, who was presumably something of a maverick.

Quindt received them all, let each explain the party program, and thus acquired a political overview. He himself learned a great deal, the party agents much less.

The conversations took place in his study, where the gentlemen were served a simple snack. They began by talking about agriculture in general, then more specifically about the large landed properties, which were in a regrettable state—all parties were agreed on that.

Quindt himself saw to the drinks: spirits from his own distillery, doubles. In this way they could remain undisturbed, unhampered by an audience. The only other presence was Maximiliane, Quindt's little grand-daughter, who sat under the big oak desk playing with her dolls. Because of some special circumstance, no governess was in residence on Poenichen at the time; it was harder and harder to find help in the country, for the younger people drifted to the cities in spite of all the obvious advantages of country life—this too was a point of general agreement.

The conversations turned into discussions. Voices were raised, and even Quindt grew louder. Names and slogans were dropped—Scheidemann, Friedrich Ebert, Noske; Versailles Treaty; reparation demands; policy of fulfillment. And again, Ebert and Noske. Quindt asked for time to think it over.

Before the gentlemen took their leave, they bent down to the little girl and patted her head or pulled her hair ribbon. "And what's your name? How old are you? But your doll is much older than you are. What's your dolly's name?"

Maximiliane readily held up her doll. "That's Ebert." She held up her other doll. "That's Noske."

The gentlemen laughed. "Adorable! You see what you're creating, my dear Herr von Quindt? You're raising a little Rosa Luxemburg. What a darling child! Your granddaughter, is that right?" They asked about the child's father and were told that he had died in the war.

"Ah, yes, the war. All the more reason for the right men to put themselves at the service of their country. Life goes on."

Maximiliane's dolls dated from the 1870s: museum pieces. Their torsos were of leather, the parts below the chest encased in a sack stuffed with sawdust, sexless and concealed by women's clothing. The leather arms were bendable, the heads painted and covered with real hair parted in the middle. Ebert's braids were wound double around her head. Maximiliane, a model mother, faithfully smeared her grandfather's rheumatism salve thickly on the sawdust bodies, washed it off after allowing it to penetrate for a while, and rearranged the dolls' clothing. Then she aired their bed linen, placing Ebert and Noske in boxes she had transformed into canopy beds by raising the lids. She did not a have doll carriage— it would not have been worthwhile to acquire one for an only child. The dolls were leftovers from the years when Quindt's sisters had played with them.

Another delegation appeared, this one from the National Liberals. Again the discussion touched on the Treaty of Versailles.

"This treaty was not agreed upon, Herr von Quindt, but dictated."

"And what would we Germans have done under the same circumstances, gentlemen? Would the Kaiser or a man such as General Ludendorff have granted more favorable terms to the powers of the Entente? I see no reason for making such an assumption. The Germans are no better simply because they're Germans."

General outrage. "Surely that's carrying liberalism to an extreme."

"Gentlemen, you're dreaming of a time before 1914. Are you hoping to recapture those days? I was present when Januschau-Oldenburg declared in the Reichstag, 'The King of Prussia and the Kaiser of Germany must be able at any moment to say to a lieutenant, "Take ten men and shut down the Reichstag." ' Would you want to be a delegate to such a Reichstag? Perhaps you are not aware that at the time, a reserve officer in full uniform, I walked out of the hall. In protest!" He began to speak of Reich President Ebert, and finally of Noske. "*Vox populi*," he said. "One must listen to the people, one must pay attention to what the people have to say, because tomorrow they will translate into action what today they're only talking about."

"What exactly is your position, Herr von Quindt?"

"As long as the right thinks I'm on the left and the left thinks I'm on the right, it's just fine with me. We must learn democracy, gentlemen! Each of us, in private tutorials. Democracy is the name of our endeavor. And everything else—national and liberal and social—those are only modifiers."

A week later several more gentlemen arrived, these from the Social Democratic party. It was a beautiful day, so they decided to hold their meeting under the copper beech. Maximiliane joined the delegation, dragging along her doll boxes and settling in under the tree; then she ran off again, returning with a shovel. She dug a hole between the exposed roots of the old tree.

In the light of the afternoon sun the manor house appeared particularly classical. One of the men promptly remarked, "Altogether Greek! Seeking the land of the Greeks with all its soul!"

Quindt explained that one of his ancestors had been to Greece, but apparently not long enough.

"Never at a loss for an answer, Herr von Quindt. Always ready with the witty saying."

Old Priska, out of earshot, could be seen weeding the paths, furnishing an occasion for a few sentences about old-age pensions for agricultural workers.

The locust trees were in full bloom, emitting clouds of scent that the east wind drove across the lawns. The men from the city were in raptures. The song of an oriole was heard—a rarity even on Poenichen—the hunting dogs chased each other around the house, and a little girl was peacefully playing under the old beech; the scene could not have been better arranged. The usual questions of "What's your name?" and "How old are you?" had been put and answered. What a successful excursion to the country. City people had no idea of the beauties of Pomerania. Sandy? Not for a moment. More like Switzerland. This expanse, so pleasing to the eye! A carriage ride to the lake was considered.

On the political level, it had not been possible to reach agreement on every point—but given such a self-willed, strong type as Quindt, that could not have been expected. He had been assured more than once that there was need of politically prominent men and had arrived at his favorite topic—democracy, which had to be learned. "And that," he said, "will take some time; one can't skip a grade. That wouldn't speed it up, it would just lead to dictatorship." There, too, there was universal agreement.

"A man like yourself, Herr von Quindt, who voluntarily gave up his title, who ought to be a conservative by birth and social class but who nevertheless thinks like a democrat—even like a socialist—is more important to us at this time than someone who turned into a socialist from his own social needs. May we count on you, then?"

Quindt was not ready to give a definite answer, but it was in the air, like the scent of the locusts. The men had already risen to take their leave when Quindt began to clarify his position once more. "As far as political judgment is concerned, I'd like to say, 'First think, then speak, then act.' In Germany one group takes care of the thinking, others do the talking, and those who end up acting have generally neither thought it through nor talked about it; they simply present the people with accomplished facts."

The gentlemen applauded. "How true! The oratory at the Reichstag! You don't hear much there."

"It isn't necessary for a politician to be a good speaker,

gentlemen, but he must know how to keep silent when he has nothing to say."

"Bravo! Such 'Quindt-essences' are known throughout the country!"

But Quindt was ready with another qualification. "In order to feel independent, one must be wealthy enough to resign at any moment without having to consider one's economic situation. As yet I'm not plagued by debts, but what if the prices for agricultural products continue to fall and the prices for chemical fertilizer continue to rise?"

"That's another reason you should exert your influence on political and economic developments."

"Are you aware that on most questions I have at least two opinions?"

The men laughed and started to walk away. In passing, one of them patted the head of the little girl, who was still playing contentedly under the tree. "Charming! An idyll! What game are you playing? Surely you don't want to bury your pretty dolly in the hole?"

"Yes, I do," said Maximiliane. "Ebert stinks." She opened the coffin one last time, took the doll from the box, and held it up in her grubby hands so that the man could see for himself.

There was no point in attempting to explain. Quindt did not try. In any other household the child would have been forbidden to name her dolls after important statesmen or to treat them with ointment and water. The little girl was right: Ebert stank quite blatantly, you could smell it.

A sense of humor could not be expected. The gentlemen reached for their panama hats and coolly departed. They gave up the idea of lunch and a carriage ride, and they gave up the thought of the Pomeranian country squire as a member of the Social Democratic Party.

For some years this story of the end of his political career was among Quindt's favorite anecdotes. He liked to recite it at the drop of a hat at a late hour during every hunting dinner.

"Quindt, my good man, tell us how you did not become a politician."

11

None of the governesses stayed on Poenichen longer than a year. When she was three years old, the little girl was looked after by a Fräulein Arndt from Stolp. Quindt, who hired her by mail, had neglected to find out how she felt about religion. As it turned out, she had no use for it whatever. She felt responsible solely for the child's physical welfare, and in that respect she neglected nothing. Never again was the little girl washed so thoroughly, never again were her nails cleaned and trimmed every morning and night, during which activity Fräulein Arndt frequently spoke of the family in Köslin where she had been employed for three years: four children, meaning eighty fingernails and toenails every morning and every night.

"And your own nails, Fräulein Arndt?" Quindt inquired.

Following his eyes, Fräulein Arndt replied, "I'm responsible only for the child." Since there were other reasons why the turnover in governesses was rapid, Quindt merely said, "Let me make a suggestion. On even-numbered days, the child's nails; on odd-numbered ones, your own." After that, he rarely interfered. On Poenichen everyone did as he thought right, even if it was often wrong.

Until she was three years old the little girl constantly carried around a piece of balled-up silk, which she sucked on before falling asleep–perhaps one of her mother's handkerchiefs but no longer recognizable. Fräulein Arndt, giving every sign of disgust, promptly relieved the child of this fetish. After she had left Poenichen, it turned out that the little girl bit her fingernails, and even–a rare occurrence–her toenails. Was this a case of cause and effect? Was she expressing her dislike of the governess? Was she attempting to prevent having her nails cut? By now child psychologists have realized that nail-biting is a form of repressed aggression. Some damage remained from this oral stage of development, but it was more of an aesthetic nature. Maximiliane would grow into a woman who all her life bit her nails.

Since no one on Poenichen ever referred to her as anything but "the child," she too called herself "child" for an unusually long period; even when she was five, she still spoke of herself in the third person singular. Thus she discovered her ego late in life.

Fräulein Arndt, however, has to be credited with promptly breaking the little girl of another habit, even a bad habit–taking off her clothes for no good reason. Most of the time it happened on the verandah. Without warning, the child took off her dress, shoes, and stockings, carefully folded and piled them, and started off for a naked walk. She was quickly apprehended and dressed all over again. Perhaps the influence of the crawling Fräulein with her nudist tendencies was greater than had been realized at the time. Unlike her predecessor, Fräulein Arndt taught the little girl a feeling of shame, at least temporarily.

That year the grandparents had to see to the child's spiritual development. Every night at seven Fräulein Arndt appeared to announce, "The child is ready for bed."

Quindt looked at the grandfather clock. "Is it that time again?" Rising, he went to the Ladies' Parlor and said, "Sophie Charlotte, we've got to pray the child."

Twenty years earlier they had adopted the same posture before the same bed—just as embarrassed then as now. Then, the only son; now, the only granddaughter.

"All right, get going," her grandfather commanded.

The child folded her hands, closed her eyes—for which her grandparents were grateful—and prayed: "Our father, kingdom come, Amen."

"She seems to have the gist of it right," Quindt decided. One could hardly call it a prayer—at best a prayerlet. The seed of devotion planted in this child was small. Even before her grandfather and grandmother had left the room, she was asleep, curled up like a dog. As soon as the little girl was bored, she rolled up in her bed, in an armchair, or in the corner of the carriage and went to sleep. The ability to fall asleep anywhere and anytime remained with her and turned out to be a blessing. What others have to teach themselves laboriously she was given at birth.

When Quindt looked for the next governess, he informed the agency in Stettin that the spiritual as well as the physical care of the four-year-old would be in her charge. This condition was more than met. The father of Fräulein Hollatz was a Jehovah's Witness. During the war and especially in the years immediately following, this sect found many adherents, most particularly since it vigorously attacked not only the established church but also the state. While she remained on Poenichen, Fräulein Hollatz was regularly supplied with *The Watchtower*, courtesy of her father; she took the paper to the village, where it was passed from household to household. She taught the child that the end of the world was near, and she crammed her with Bible stories. Her response to disobedience was not scolding or even spanking but a recital of the verse "Blessed are the meek: for they shall inherit the earth."

Quindt was preparing to run for the regional diet and had handed most of the administration of the estate over to his foreman, who made a complete report every morning between nine and ten. Herr Palcke was not aware of the meetings Fräulein Hollatz held once a week at the house of Jäckel the carpenter, and by the time Quindt learned about them, much of the damage had been done. Unexpectedly he appeared at one such gathering. Fräulein Hollatz was just reading aloud about the golden age. Quindt did not allow her to finish the sentence. He declared that the golden age was not at issue on Poenichen and that it was best not to rely on prophecy; times of want had a long way to go on earth. He did not believe in golden ages on principle—rather, he preferred to put his faith in iron hard work. It was none of his business what those present thought of heavenly splendor, but here on Poenichen they should leave biblical studies to the pastor, who was trained in them and was being paid to engage in them.

When he left, he took Fräulein Hollatz with him. "Your train leaves tomorrow morning at ten. Herr Riepe will drive you to the station. I'll pay you for three months; it's worth it to me."

Fräulein Hollatz proclaimed the imminent end of the world to him, but Quindt replied that he had survived a world war and come through the economic depression, so presumably he'd manage the end of the world as well.

Later on, Fräulein Hollatz was referred to as the Fräulein of the Bible; each governess had earned a soubriquet in place of a name.

Since governesses were apt to leave Poenichen from one day to the next, there were frequent interruptions in the little girl's upbringing, times when she was left to her own devices and those of Frau Riepe, "Amma," who slipped her tidbits, homemade caramels, a supplement of affection. During the Fräuleinless months, Maximiliane gained weight steadily. What else could

90

you do for the poor little mite? For years the farmworkers referred to her as "the poor child" or "the poor kid."

Anna Riepe gave her cooking pots and wooden spoons to play with. She was allowed to stir the big pots on the big stove. She playfully and wantonly threw cups on the stone floor because the clatter was so amusing. Frau Riepe spanked her for it and immediately comforted her for the pain. She was allowed to pull red currants off their stems and shell peas, and she was praised for her efforts. She was given a knife to cut rhubarb stalks into pieces, and she cut her finger. She early learned the kitchen measurements: a handful of sugar, a pinch of salt, a shot of vinegar.

When the kitchen chores were finished, Frau Riepe pulled a chair over to the stove, stoked it with a few more slabs of wood, propped her feet on the top, and took the little girl on her lap.

"Tell about the pigsty, Amma."

The child's every wish was granted. Frau Riepe gave no thought to broadening the mind. So, over and over, she told about the fisherman and his wife. Before she could finish saying, " 'Well, what does she want, now?' said the Flounder," the child was already shouting, "Flounder, flounder in the sea, Come, I pray thee, here to me; for my wife, good Ilsabil, Wills not as I'd have her will."

Assigned parts in the telling of fairy tales. Outside, night was falling. Herr Riepe came, ran his hands over the toasty stove top, warmed his back, and sat down with them. Frau Riepe took off one of the stove rings, which made the kitchen light enough again, and the child curled up in her soft lap to wait for the next cue. A fisherman's hut, a stone castle, a king's palace, the kingdom of heaven for Ilsabil. And at the end–"You will find her again in the pig-sty"–the child crowed with delight. Milk was warmed up, white bread crumbled into it, sugar strewn over it: for Herr Riepe a big bowl of bread and milk, for Maximiliane the brown cup.

The grounds, the manor house, the rooms, the halls, the stairs, even the bed in which Maximiliane was sleeping by now—everything turned out to be too large for such a little girl. She built nests and caves for herself; she established hiding places, bringing her dolls along. She crawled between wardrobes standing in the half-light of the long corridors and cowered there, unmoving. She played hide-and-seek in the garden. But no one found the little girl because no one was looking for her. Only when darkness set in did the question arise, "Where can the child be?"

"She's probably hiding again."

The search was joined, not only by whatever governess might be in charge at the moment, but also by the housemaids and Frau Riepe, often by the child's grandfather. Carrying lamps, they walked the grounds, calling the child's name loudly. When they eventually found her, she did not speak, did not answer their questions—"Didn't you hear us calling you? Why didn't you answer?"

Fräulein Eberle had instructed the child to call Grandpa "Grandfather" and Uncle Riepe "Herr Riepe." The child complied by avoiding any direct address, but there was no budging her from "Amma." From now on, too, the child was called by her rightful name, Maximiliane.

"Maximiliane is stubborn," Fräulein Eberle announced to the child's grandfather. In reply he said what he always said when he was told about difficulties in child rearing: "She'll grow out of it." As a rule he was right.

Fräulein Eberle patiently explained that at this age a child's education outside the home must begin. Maximiliane was living in a world of adults; the proportions

92

of the house were quite unchildlike. Though she was right, so was Quindt in his objections.

"Just because of one child, are we all supposed to sit in high chairs and spoon up porridge?" he asked.

Fräulein Eberle stuck to her principles. "Try to imagine, Herr von Quindt, that you had to climb up into your chair. Or, what's even harder, onto the commode."

"I have no desire whatever to imagine any such thing, and I do not wish you to imagine it either, Fräulein Eberle. The child will grow, don't worry." He looked at Maximiliane, who was standing by his side with her legs apart, her hands folded on her back. He added, "Slowly, I must admit."

"The child belongs in nursery school," Fräulein Eberle insisted, explaining to Herr von Quindt down to the last detail the advantages of child rearing in such an environment. She used the current term—*kindergarten*—making Maximiliane think of a garden with children tied to stakes like pole beans.

"I see no possibility of establishing a kindergarten on Poenichen, Fräulein Eberle," Quindt said. "Why don't you send the child to the village for a couple of hours? She'll find somebody to play with."

Maximiliane was dispatched to the village, but she promptly returned.

"Don't you want to play with the nice little boys and girls in the village? Aren't they good enough for you?" Fräulein Eberle inquired.

"But they don't want to play!"

Taking Maximiliane's hand, Fräulein Eberle said, "We'll see about that," and walked to the village with her.

Outside the cottages a few old women sat on benches, and two boys watched the geese on the green. There was no one else in sight.

"Come here, boys," Fräulein Eberle called. "You may play with little Maximiliane."

No response.

"Wouldn't it be more fun to play than to watch the geese, boys?"

"No!"

Fräulein Eberle had a word with the old women.

"We ain't used to that."

"But little Maximiliane would like some playmates."

"Work comes first."

"But Herr von Quindt has agreed to it."

"Here in the village. . . ."

In the end, Riepe assumed the negotiator's role. Walter Beske, the son of the grocer; Klaus, the oldest son of Klukas the fieldhand; and Lenchen Priebe—these three were assigned to special duty. Klaus and Walter were a little older than Maximiliane, Lenchen a good two years younger. Though the latter was some sort of cousin, no mention was made of her parentage.

"We'll play if we get paid."

Fräulein Eberle hovered. "What game do you have in mind, children?"

Klaus Klukas decided. "We'll play Father and Mother. Where's your mother?" he asked Maximiliane.

"In Berlin."

"And your father?"

"He's dead."

"Then we'll play Father's Dead. Walter will be your father, and I'll shoot him dead."

"Children!" Fräulein Eberle objected. "Wouldn't you like to play something else? There are so many really charming games! Do you know Farmer in the Dell?"

"Nah."

Fräulein Eberle assigned the roles. She herself would be the cheese. "Lenchen, you be the farmer."

"I won't!" Lenchen began to bawl.

94

"Then you'll be the farmer, Maximiliane. Stand in the middle."

The others stood on the grass, arms linked. Maximiliane stood inside the circle. All of them sang at the top of their voices, "The farmer in the dell, the farmer in the dell."

Klaus entered the circle. Before anyone could intervene, the farmer had thrown her arms around his neck and kissed him square on the lips. The slap in the face meant for the wife of the farmer was received by the farmer from her wife as soon as he had overcome his initial shock.

Fräulein Eberle was outraged. "What do you think you're doing?"

That was the end of the game. The children walked out. Fräulein Eberle called to them, "Be sure to come back tomorrow."

Klaus Klukas turned back. "I won't let nobody kiss me, not for all the money in the world."

Herr Riepe had to be consulted again.

At the next attempt, the children were left to their own devices for pedagogical reasons. Barefoot but with neatly combed hair, they stood at the bottom of the verandah steps. Maximiliane took off her shoes and stockings as well. Walter Beske and Klaus Klukas brought a small cart from the shed. They played Horse and Carriage. Lenchen Priebe was put at the back of the cart to act as a brake. Maximiliane climbed inside and made herself comfortable. Walter Beske pulled off a linden twig and made it into a whip for her. The boys put themselves on either side of the shaft. "We're a pair of horses! Let's go!"

Maximiliane flourished the whip, and the boys trotted down the avenue. Maximiliane shouted "Gee" and "Haw."

Quindt was reading the paper on the verandah while Fräulein Eberle observed the children at play. "Now look at that, Herr von Quindt," she said. "She plays the princess every time unless someone stops her."

"It must be that the other children turn her into one," Quindt answered. "That sort of thing goes deep. We all play out our parts, my dear Fräulein Eberle. Some pull the wagon, and others try to put on the brakes. Only one sits inside and is pulled. The main thing is that the cart runs."

"Surely you're taking too philosophical a view of it, without regard to pedagogy. One day it will change. You'll be surprised."

"Oh, my dear, surprised? It's not that easy to surprise me. Someone else will sit in the cart, and others will pull it—and then you'll be surprised."

In the meantime Lenchen had taken a spill and was lying in the dust bawling. With Maximiliane still shouting "Haw" and "Gee," the horses changed gait and broke into a gallop. Maximiliane too was thrown from the cart and landed in the dirt not far from Lenchen.

"Hey, will you look at Maxi," Klaus Klukas yelled.

From then on Maximiliane stood at the top of the steps every day, waiting for the children to come. If they stayed away, she left the grounds and headed for the village. A few minutes later Fräulein Eberle also left the grounds but in the opposite direction, headed for Poenichen Lake and the assistant foreman's house. There was no more talk about her late fiancé, killed at Arras.

Maximiliane took off her shoes and stockings, untied her white hair ribbon, and fastened rubber bands around the short braids that stuck out from her ears. She hid the remnants of the manorial heiress under the last rhododendron bush before running down the dusty village street, looking in the houses and behind them, in the kitchens of the Klukases, Jäckels, and Griesemanns, at the smithy and at Finke the schoolmaster's and at the widow Schmaltz's, until she found the other children. They were hunting thistles for the goslings, catching ducklings that had waddled away, gathering chamomile blossoms for drying and rose hips for tea. They drove the geese to the stubble fields and beat the hazelnut bushes with sticks.

In less than four weeks she was chattering away in the local dialect and whistling between two fingers. Though by the end of the summer her hair was still not flaxen like the other children's, her arms and legs were just as tanned and scratched. When she put her shoes and stockings back on at the gate to the grounds, she resumed her normal speech as well. When her grandfather rode through the village in the carriage, she ran toward him through the mire and the goose flock and jumped up on the running board.

"Grandpa, I wanna lot of kids."

"Later," he said.

There were no further declarations of love toward Klaus Klukas, but she hung around him. When the sun was high in the sky and the old women had abandoned the benches outside the cottages to sit in their cool kitchens, the children withdrew into their nest among the hazelnut bushes. Nothing could penetrate it, not even the sun. There they played Doctor, at Maximiliane's suggestion. Klaus Klukas was the doctor, Maximiliane the nurse, and Walter Beske the doorkeeper who had to make certain that no one entered the operating theater. Lenchen Priebe was the patient who had to be given a thorough examination, always in the same place. She was placed on her back, then turned over, and then her skirt was lifted. She did not wear underpants. A long-stemmed ribwort leaf served as the surgical instrument. Lenchen lay very still, screwed up her eyes, and giggled.

Maximiliane suggested that they exchange roles, but Klaus Klukas refused. "I won't." Walter Beske was willing to play the patient, but Maximiliane wasn't interested in him. For a change, they sometimes tried Having a Baby, which was played by shoving a ball under Lenchen's dress. But Having a Baby was over too soon and quickly grew boring. They stopped playing Doctor, too. It did Maximiliane no permanent damage. She forgot all about it.

All winter long Fräulein Eberle played educational games with Maximiliane. The toys progressive educators considered proper for her age were not available on Poenichen and were not acquired. Such toys as there were, among them three fifty-year-old hobbyhorses and a few tin soldiers, were out of the question. Fräulein Eberle paid a visit to the wheelwright's shop and procured blocks and rods for building. She also made the little girl paint. Maximiliane always began by painting a large sun at the center of the sheet of paper.

"Now paint your grandmother and grandfather," Fräulein Eberle ordered, and Maximiliane painted a sun. Next to it, standing on two giant legs, she placed a head from which dangled two arms. Then, on the other side of the paper, as far removed from the first figure as possible, she put another of the same size, with three legs–obviously Grandfather with his cane.

"You shouldn't paint the sun, Maximiliane," Fräulein Eberle remonstrated.

"But if there's no sun, you can't see Grandfather and Grandmother."

Fräulein Eberle was deaf to the child's logic. "Now paint the house."

But again Maximiliane began with the sun and then added a house that resembled the fisherman's pigsty more than it did the manor house, with a door and five windows and a path running straight to the door.

"But the house only has holes," Fräulein Eberle objected. "You have to put in windows and doors."

"The windows and the door are all wide open."

In the autumn Fräulein Eberle brought back rushes from Poenichen Lake, as well as acorns and chestnuts.

98

She worked with Maximiliane to tie the acorns into chains, she whittled little baskets out of chestnuts, she braided chairs and tables from the rushes. Maximiliane gave all these products to her grandfather, who placed them on the bookshelves. Every Christmas package her grandmother sent to Vera and the grandmother in Berlin always contained one acorn chain and a chestnut basket.

The next governess Herr von Quindt hired was a Fräulein Eschholtz, who had lost her home in West Prussia and was not, as she wrote, suited to life in the city. She had been through hard times and would consider herself fortunate if she and her little boy could find a home on Poenichen. After a short discussion, the grandparents agreed that it might be good for Maximiliane's future development if she were not an only child anymore. Besides, the illegitimate son would protect Fräulein Eschholtz from further follies. The little boy, whose name was Peter, was the same age as Maximiliane and was called Peterkin. All her life Maximiliane would retain her dislike of the name. As soon as she was supposed to play with the boy, she ran away and hid. To her surprise, Peterkin did not come looking for her but went his separate way. He chased the dogs and threw stones at the pigs, chickens, and ducks. The dislike was mutual.

Fräulein Eschholtz bathed the children together in one tub, a practice of which the grandparents remained unaware; presumably they would not have approved. It was, however, part of the educational process: instruction with a real-life model. Fräulein Eschholtz was prepared for the familiar children's questions, but they were not put. Maximiliane simply inspected the boy closely and rather reluctantly. In return, the boy was all the more inquisitive. Fräulein Eschholtz talked about a womb and pointed to her stomach. "That's where babies grow," she explained.

"And where do they come out?" Peterkin asked.

"Do you know, Maximiliane?"

99

"The navel," she said curtly and climbed out of the tub.

As it turned out, the illegitimate child did not protect Fräulein Eschholtz from further follies. She too left Poenichen prematurely.

Occasionally there were still outbursts of passion, when Maximiliane vehemently embraced her grandfather's leg and pressed her face with all her might against his stomach. Once she even appeared at his bedside during a storm. In the dark she had felt her way out of her room, then along three long corridors filled with monstrous wardrobes and giant coffers that the lightning magnified in front of her, then onward past the big mirrors. Twice she picked the wrong door, until she finally found Grandpa.

"Can I get in bed with you, Grandfather?"

He had shared his bed with no one for decades, and only rarely before that; now he was confronted by this child, shaking with fear. What was he to do? He raised the blanket and moved aside, although the little girl was seeking his closeness. Maximiliane made herself comfortable, pushed her cold feet against the warmest spot on her grandfather, and fell asleep. As soon as the storm was over, Quindt woke the child and sent her back to her room. But he put on his robe and escorted Maximiliane to her bed through the nocturnal corridors. He even smoothed the covers over her. Then he said, "We don't want to make a habit of this, understand?"

Whenever there was a storm after that, she took her dolls to bed with her, held them tight, and comforted them. "There's nothing for you to be afraid of. I'll protect you. We'll just pull the blanket over our heads."

At breakfast the Fräulein declared that she was not a night nurse. She locked the door to her room; not always, it must be noted, from the inside.

After she had outgrown the cradle, Maximiliane slept in the so-called nursery, where her grandfather and his sisters had slept when they were children. The room still contained three beds, six feet of space between each. A dormitory. In the course of a night Maximiliane changed her bed several times. When one grew too warm, she sleepily wandered to the next, cooler bed. She loved cold beds, a preference many would exploit in later life. Her body temperature was high from birth.

Now, Quindt might have learned from his experience with young, generally pretty governesses and engaged an older woman. And he did so—with disastrous results. Fräulein Gering was unmasked as a vegetarian and a devout follower of one Dr. Kneipp, who believed in the curative powers of cold water and mud baths. When, on the evening of her arrrival, supper was served as usual just before eight o'clock, she announced, "Late meals fill coffins." She extended her educational efforts to the entire household.

The young governesses had been more loving to the child the more in love they were themselves. When they returned from their furtive outings, they made up for every moment of neglect, they hugged the little girl, they played with her. This child was the occasion for their happiness; but for her they would never have come to Pomerania, would never have experienced such a summer! And now this Fräulein Gering with her diet of raw vegetables. She chewed her salad while emphatically pointing out to the Quindts the damage they might sustain if they continued to eat meat, fats, and sweets.

"In the menopausal years, Frau von Quindt, a raw-vegetable diet is especially beneficial. The body must be purged." She went on to discuss obesity, which characterized neither Herr von Quindt nor Frau von Quindt, except possibly by comparison with her own scrawniness.

"A meatless diet is the only salvation from your rheumatism, Herr von Quindt. It's quite evident that you suffer from costiveness–what we call constipation."

"We are not accustomed to discussing disease at table, my dear Fräulein Gering," Quindt said.

"But you should," the Fräulein insisted. "The modern science of nutrition–"

Quindt interrupted. "Would you be so kind as to leave the choice of topics to us, Fräulein Gering? You are charged with the child's upbringing, not that of her grandparents." From then on he referred to her as the constipated Fräulein.

On her own initiative, Fräulein Gering put buckets in the bathrooms and filled them with cold water. Every morning she ran barefoot through the grass with Maximiliane, always around the round flower bed, always accompanied by barking dogs. She was the only governess who did not insist that Maximiliane wear shoes, since going barefoot strengthened the human foot.

In the evenings, uninvited, she joined the Quindts in the study and read them extracts from Kneipp's book on healthful living. She gave Anna Riepe Kneipp's laxative pills and insisted that every morning she make grain coffee instead of bean coffee for everyone, including the Quindts. Anna Riepe fell deeply under her influence– as did Friederike von Kalck, who eventually became a convert to vegetarianism. The helpings of meat that arrived on the table grew smaller day by day, the vegetables were barely steamed so as not to cook the nutrients out of them.

One day Quindt appeared personally in the kitchen, an event that had not taken place for years, to declare that about three decades ago, if his memory did not fail him, he had hired Frau Riepe to be the cook. Surely the word *cook* derived from *cooking* and was a professional designation. If he wanted to eat raw food, he could go straight to the barn.

He gave full vent to his anger, went back upstairs, and gave notice to the governess. Fräulein Gering proved that her concern for the Quindts' well-being was genuine. She left behind her copy of the book *Child Care in Health and Sickness*. On the flyleaf she wrote, "A healthy mind can live only in a healthy body, or, in Latin, *Mens sana in corpore sano*," thereby giving Maximiliane her first and only instruction in that language.

The constant succession of governesses had taught Maximiliane painting, singing, flute playing, reading, embroidery, and good manners, depending on what the governess of the moment considered most vital. Her education was therefore more wide than deep. But on the whole the frequent change affected the little girl favorably. Remarkably, it tended to occur as summer drew to a close.

Later, when Quindt talked about "the time of the Fräuleins," which he liked to do—there were not too many topics of conversation on Poenichen—each of the Fräuleins came out a caricature. The Fräulein of the Bible. The constipated Fräulein. And then there was the crawling Fräulein, who tried to drown herself in the Blue Pond.

In the autumn of 1929 a wedding announcement arrived on Poenichen. Vera had married a Dr. Daniel Grün. Two days later they were able to see a picture of the event: a reception at the magazine headquarters in honor of Vera Jadow, the photojournalist. Quindt remarked to his wife, "I'd be surprised if this Dr. Grün weren't Jewish."

How was the child to be told about what had occurred? It was probably best to let her read the announcement for herself. Maximiliane, eleven years old at the time, retired with it to her mother's Green Rooms, read what there was to read, and took the occasion of saying good-night to her grandfather to inquire, "Is that my father now, this man Grün? Is my name Grün now?"

"No, you remain a Quindt."

Thus reassured, Maximiliane placed the announcement in the box with the relics of her father, which still stood on the mantel in the big hall.

The Quindts decided to send Vera one of their two silverpoint drawings by Caspar David Friedrich as a wedding present. What else could they give her? If their memories served, she was interested in art, but no one really had a clear recollection. *Pomeranian Landscape*—a little dull, but that was how it looked to people who had no feeling for the region. A good-bye present; presumably they would not hear from her again.

The Green Rooms remained unchanged and unlocked. Maximiliane often spent time there, opening the wardrobes and taking out the old-fashioned dresses, hats, and shoes her mother had left behind. She put them on and looked at herself in the mirror. At the age of eleven, she already had a thicker waist than her mother had had at twenty-five. Only the maternity dress fit her.

Maximiliane stuffed a pillow in over her stomach and stood before the mirror for a long time.

12

Even before the monetary inflation, another sort of devaluation had already set in: the inflation of heroism. The men who fought in the war and returned home after defeat turned out to be very much less heroic and admirable than those who did not return home but remained victorious on the battlefields of honor. Vera once called them "the lost warriors."

Quindt met one of these depreciated officers soon after the end of the war, when he was looking for an assistant foreman to handle the outlying tracts near the lake.

"The assistant foreman's job hasn't been filled for a long time," Quindt explained to the applicant. "The cottage has been empty for years; it's right on the lake. The sheep farm and the fishery are part of the outlands. Try it and see how it goes. Dealing with sheep and fish is work for an eccentric. The main thing is to manage the loneliness. Everything else can be learned. Do you have any family—a wife or something of the sort? What did you say your name was?"

"Just call me Fisher," the man answered, "or you could call me Shepherd, but I'd prefer Fisher."

He seemed to be a little off his rocker, but at the time that was true of many—off their rockers in the literal sense of the phrase: out of place.

The man sitting across from Quindt, blue-eyed and with a high forehead, explained that it was necessary to make a new start. "The year zero. The baker is called Baker again because he bakes the bread. There is no longer a Herr Kaiser, any more than there is a Kaiser; the end of the imperial era has dawned. And as for any wife of mine, she gets my pension. She knows nothing. She hasn't a clue." That was all he had to say on the subject. He was evidently tired of war, tired of people. What he needed was quiet—and fertility after so much dying; increase instead of waste. Spawning fish, lambing ewes.

There were many lives like his during that period, but not everyone had the chance to escape inward. Not everyone could turn fear and helplessness into the virtues of the simple life, be content with returning to the true forces of nature, to reflect. Not everyone encountered a Quindt.

At their subsequent meetings the two men never had another such basic conversation. They spoke only about the weather, and sometimes about the world situation, but they never touched on personal matters again. It turned out that the man's name was Blaskorken—Christian Blaskorken. When he talked with Quindt, he omitted the von, said simply "Herr Quindt," but with the proper respect.

Two weeks after that first interview, which took place in the waiting room of the Stettin railroad station, Herr Riepe met the new foreman in Stargard. Three officer's footlockers stenciled "Lt. Blaskorken" comprised his luggage. He brought nothing else except a hunting horn, an old French *trompe de chasse* in a leather case. The foreman settled down in one room of the house on Poenichen Lake, the rest of the house remaining uninhabited. The absolute essentials in domestic furnishings were brought from the manor attic. Quindt handed him a book on raising fish in sweet-water lakes and another about the importance of sheep for meat production, as well as the current edition of the sheepman's pocket calendar.

Since Quindt had stopped working the outlying farm, anyone who could make his way there fished Poenichen Lake. "See to it that there's no trouble," Quindt said. "At present we're under something like common law—or common lawlessness. But on Poenichen no one deprives another of anything once there's somebody to stop him."

Next to the house was a shed full of fishing gear, creels, seines, rods, tackle, nets, all in poor condition. After the sheep pen was repaired, the sheep, which had formerly been kept on the main farm, were herded into their new home—at first twenty ewes and one ram, Hampshires, short-haired, easy to care for but meaty. The new foreman learned, grasping a woolly head with his right hand and the instruction manual with his left, to tell a sheep's age by its teeth. He absorbed information about bathing and shearing sheep, about setting up a summer pen, about unrestricted grazing on the heath, the advantages of lambing in the summer, and the dangers of lambing paralysis. All that remained to be learned was how to kill lambs and how to kill fish. Soon word got around the village and the farm that the new foreman was shooting the lambs instead of slaughtering them, that he shot at the fish instead of sticking them. But that may have been no more than a rumor. Legends began to grow around "the man at the lake," especially when he began to blow his hunting horn in the evenings and the sound drifted over the fields.

Blaskorken had the use of a horse and carriage so that he could take fish and lamb to market in town. Twice a week he appeared at the manor house to supply the kitchen with fish: perch, tench, and pike. "He's got a calm hand," they said of him in the village. He was a good fisherman and a good shepherd. In the course of very few years the herd increased, and Blaskorken was even able to supply the neighboring estates with ewes. Without doubt a useful man for the outlying farm. The only possible cause for criticism was the business with the governesses—but who was to say whether the young ladies from the city would have lasted more than a month in farthest Pomerania if it hadn't been for the pale-eyed foreman? The extent to which the governesses were considered members of the family was limited to joint meals, use of the library, and occasional participation in a hunt dinner.

Of course Quindt could have had a talk with his foreman, but he did not care for man-to-man discussions, least of all on the topic of women. Anyway, it was easier to get a new governess than a competent foreman; damages in the sheepfold were harder to repair than damages in the nursery, where so much was outgrown eventually. There were more than enough war widows and abandoned fiancées. In Quindt's view, which was the general view, a woman had to look out for herself; it was a man's business to keep her from doing so. "He won't be here forever," they said in the village. As long as the foreman left their daughters alone, no one thought to interfere.

Only the Reverend Merzin felt called upon to do so. One day he set out for Poenichen Lake. He did not find the foreman in his house but came upon him at the lakeside, where he had been sitting for hours in a reedy backwater waiting for a pike. Blaskorken made it clear to the clergyman that the utmost silence was required but motioned him to sit down. He played his fly, but the fish seemed to be sated and lazy; nothing stirred.

The matter at hand was so delicate that it was hard to bring it up at all; certainly it could not be discussed in whispers. On the other hand, the Reverend Merzin was reluctant either to abandon or to postpone his mission. He hinted that he had the greatest understanding as a man—if he might allude to himself that way; after all, he, Blaskorken, a hale and vigorous person, was deprived of the protection against temptation afforded by a regulated married life, and the young ladies themselves were alone and equally healthy, and it was not good for man to be alone—even in the Bible it said that man was given woman—but as the spiritual leader of the parish he felt responsible for the spiritual welfare of all, as well as for questions of ethics and morals.

For an instant Christian Blaskorken turned his blue eyes fully on Merzin, raising his eyebrows questioningly. "Spiritual welfare? Did I hear you right?"

"Yes," the Reverend Merzin whispered. "Souls, too, can ail. Surely we understand each other?"

Again the raised eyebrows. "Ail?" Surely there could be no question of ailing; let the pastor ask Fräulein Warnett, the current occupant.

The Reverend Merzin admitted that it must be easy for Herr Blaskorken to attract women, but surely things did not have to go all the way at once. Whispering, he repeated, "All the way."

At that moment the fly jerked down deep under the water. Carefully and with a light hand, Blaskorken turned the reel. Merzin, himself no mean pike fisherman, excitedly reached for the creel, losing sight of his topic. For the next few minutes both of them had their hands full getting the pike in the net and the net on shore. Merzin took charge of killing the fish.

When the job was done, the men talked a while longer about the problems of catching pike, swapping anecdotes and stories. Then, carrying the four-pound fish, Merzin took his leave, without returning to the matter that had brought him to the lake. He only said, "But the hunting horn, my dear Herr Blaskorken. If you'd only leave off blowing it." Of course there could be no objection if he blew the signals when the Quindts went hunting. He knew from the other estate owners in the vicinity that Baron Quindt was envied for his trumpeter. "There's no one far and wide who can blow the signals as cleanly as you. A real coup for Quindt. But there's a time for everything, including the signals. Even my wife—she comes from Dresden, by the way, and is musically talented, like all Saxons—seems made uneasy by it; she goes to the window every time."

Blaskorken replied that he used the hunt signals for communication since there was no telephone in the assistant foreman's house. The four-pound pike remained the only result of the interview. There was no further intervention on the part of the clergyman.

You did not have to be a twenty-year-old governess driven to Pomerania from Stettin or Berlin; when, at dusk, the hunting horn sounded from the lake across the fields, it roused the blood of even the calmest natures— even of little Maximiliane, who was still a child, or at least half a child. Many years later, in France, when she heard the horn signals drifting across a field, she was seized by a vague, vehement longing: on to the hunt!

Of course the trumpet calls also disquieted the dogs, especially Dinah. In the village they said, "He's chasing his amours again." In the manor house they were usually gathered around the oval supper table at that time of day. Quindt glanced at the governess, who invariably blushed. The nature of the signal and the deepness of the blush allowed Quindt to gauge how matters stood from day to day.

About halfway between the grounds and Poenichen Lake lay the Blue Pond, almost concealed by reeds and rushes. It reflected the blue of the sky and the white of the summery clouds. On a nearby rise grew little clumps of juniper and dwarf birches—a lovely landscape, but hard to put to agricultural use. During the summers Blaskorken was in the habit of setting up his shepherd's cart near the Blue Pond. There he bathed and sheared the sheep. When summer was over, he dismantled the

110

summer pen and drove the cart to the winter site. The land around the Blue Pond had been grazed clean; it was time to blow taps, the end of the hunt.

Fräulein Balzer, the crawling Fräulein, whose addiction to nudism no one suspected, was in the habit of sunbathing at the Blue Pond. One evening in September her seat at the supper table remained empty. The lamps were already lit. "The Fräulein must have had another tryst with your foreman," Frau von Quindt said.

"Once he has the sheep back in the permanent pen, there will be an end of it," Quindt answered. As it turned out, there was rather a bad end of it.

Taps had been sounded two days previously, but it was not until this evening that Fräulein Balzer walked into the water. She probably threatened her lover with the action, and he probably did not even try to stop her. He knew what she may well have suspected, at least subconsciously: the Blue Pond had formed in a place where the passage of the glacier had left a hole no deeper than a foot and a half.

Wet through and through, Fräulein Balzer sneaked back to the house under cover of darkness. But her return did not go unnoticed–the dogs barked, and before she could reach the stairs, shoes in hand, Herr von Quindt appeared. He examined her from top to bottom and said in conclusion, "Herr Riepe will take you to the ten-o'clock train tomorrow, Fräulein Balzer."

This same ten-o'clock train always arrived on schedule to carry away whatever difficulties might arise on Poenichen in the course of the years. There were as yet no laws prohibiting the firing of expectant mothers, and Quindt felt responsible at most for the girls from the village, but not for the governesses. In those days no man relied on a woman's precautions in the matter of contraception. To forestall any false hopes, the foreman would surely have mentioned "a Frau Blaskorken," who

111

not only existed but consumed his pension. Nevertheless, every governess would naturally have believed herself the exception. Such is the nature of love and of women.

In the case of subsequent governesses, precautions were taken long before taps sounded and the Fräulein could return dripping from the Blue Pond. Herr von Quindt made it a point early on to mention at table that the blue of the lake was deceptive as to its depth, which should not be allowed to fool anyone.

The foreman had made himself indispensable through more than his achievements as a shepherd and fisherman. There was an additional reason why Quindt did not wish to lose him: Blaskorken was a chess player.

The relationship was mutual, perhaps even in the spirit of a sublimated father-son bond. Once a week, for years on end, the two men played chess. In the summer Quindt rode out to the lake at night or sometimes took the carriage, driving himself. Blaskorken had laid planks and boards on a spit of land extending a short way into the lake and set up a place to sit; when it got dark, he lit lanterns. Both men were deliberate players. Each game went on for hours but was finished the same evening, mostly in silence. Only during their very first encounters did they discuss opening moves and end games; later even this much conversation was superfluous. Blaskorken was more skilled at openings, Quindt at end games, a situation that did not change in all the years they played.

They used pieces of carved, painted ivory. The king bore an evident resemblance to Frederick the Great, the knights and bishops also had individual features perhaps modeled on those of court officials in Potsdam, and the pawns wore tricorns, more courtiers than vassals. Quindt sometimes considered the figures "amazing," sometimes "scandalous," but he never asked how Blaskorken had come by them, any more than he asked about the fore-

112

man's English china tea set or the old, presumably valuable hunting horn. In the winter they played in the manor-house study on a gaming table in the "Pomeranian classical" style–marquetry with six columnar pearwood legs, more or less Doric.

Maximiliane–six years old, seven years old, eight and nine years old–stood wordlessly nearby, her hands folded on her back, and watched the players. She asked no questions, and neither man explained to her the meaning of the various pieces. When she was a few years older, Quindt took her along to the lake on summer evenings; she swam as the men played, moving her arms and legs so gently that she made no noise that might disturb them, only a gurgle or a splash no louder than the jumping of the fish. Afterward, wearing her father's beach robe, she stood next to the table and watched. She had long since learned about the Queen's Pawn opening, as well as castling. She even knew the Sicilian gambit. When Quindt was confined to his bed with lumbago–she was eleven at the time–she carried the gaming table to his bedroom to play with him. Her grandfather looked at her in surprise. "Do you know how?"

"Well, I could try." She never said, "I can do that," much less, "I can do it well." All her life she would say, "I could try." It made people like her.

It was inevitable that Maximiliane, too, would fall in love with Blaskorken. He was the only man far and wide who was in any way a suitable object for her longings. One day she rode her bicycle to the lake, hid in the reeds, and waited until Blaskorken cast off in his boat to spread the nets. Then she swam after him, but he paid no attention.

Of course she had noticed that her governesses spent their nights away from the house, and she had guessed where they went. That particular summer it was a Fräulein Warnett from Königsberg, who liked to teach the little girl sentimental, fake folksongs with lyrics full of birch trees, brambles, larks. Whenever Maximiliane saw flowering broom in later life, she was reminded of Fräulein Warnett.

One night the child, unobserved, followed the governess all the way to the foreman's house; the lights were lit, and the windows uncurtained—no human eye for miles around. Maximiliane fetched one of the chairs from the spit of land, placed it under a window, and climbed up. Whatever she may have seen, it did not cripple her psyche in any way. Of course she was ashamed, and she wept too; but she was not cured. She did not lose her head. She returned the chair to its place, mounted her bicycle, and rode home.

A few days after this occurrence, at high noon, she got on her bicycle once more and pedaled to the lake, barefoot as always and wearing a dress with a low neckline. It was the first summer she had something to display. She lay on her stomach on the landing, right in the foreman's line of vision; he was sitting outside his house repairing an eel trap. A few minutes later he rose, put aside his gear, and disappeared into the house. He had given only a fleeting acknowledgment of Maximiliane's greeting.

It was June, and the wheat was in blossom; you could smell it all the way to the lake. In among the reeds the first water lilies were blooming; a bittern called nearby. Smoke rose from the chimney: the foreman was cooking his dinner. Maximiliane got up and moved into the reeds at the spot where they grew most sparsely, so that one could see through them from the house. There she did an elaborate striptease, turning, bending over, looking around shyly with every garment she shed; then, naked, she slid into the water, emitting short, frightened gurgles. When none of this worked, she let herself sink, waved her arms in the air, dove down,

114

rose once more, gulped water, and finally called loudly for help.

Blaskorken hurried from the house–after all, he could hardly let the girl drown right before his eyes. He jumped into the water from the landing, grabbed her, and carried her to shore. Almost fainting from excitement, fear, embarrassment, and swallowed water, she dangled from his arms. Blaskorken set her on her feet on the landing and slapped her face twice. "Never do that again."

In reply she threw her arms around his neck. She could barely stand, and she cast him a beseeching glance from her cherry eyes damp with water and tears. What was he to do with the child? He gave her another vigorous slap on the rear, then freed himself and left her swaying, wet and naked, in the sunshine. He went back to his house, making sure to lock the door, but then he stepped to the window and calmly watched. Maximiliane gathered up her clothes, disappeared behind the nearest alderbush, and hurriedly dressed. Then she picked up her bicycle and pedaled away, loudly ringing her bell.

The next time she and her grandfather drove to the lake–he had let her take the reins more frequently of late–she smiled at the foreman from the coachman's box, and he smiled back. The twinkle in his eye decided Quindt to have a man-to-man talk with his foreman after all–something he had managed to avoid in the matter of the Fräuleins. But even now there was really no necessity for it; Blaskorken had a "more than passing" acquaintance with the penal code, as he assured Quindt. Quindt asked no further questions. He had long harbored the disturbing suspicion that his foreman had good reason for disappearing into the depths of Pomerania.

13

Maximiliane wanted to learn to ride. Her desire was understandable, nor was there any dearth of horses, but it turned out that her legs were too short. Other families with other children might have bought a pony, but on Poenichen such an acquisition was not considered worthwhile for an only child. No one ever said that the horses were too tall; it was always "Your legs are too short." For an only child it was not worthwhile to acquire a sandbox or a swing, a scooter or picture books.

One day, when she was present during one of the Reverend Merzin's visits, the conversation turned to her future. Quindt announced, "We'll have to start looking around in good time for a husband for her, someone who can take over Poenichen one day." Unbidden, Maximiliane asked, "Do you really think that acquiring a husband is worthwhile for an only child?"

Quindt added this question to his collection of anecdotes, repeating it at her confirmation, her engagement, and her wedding dinner. His grandson-in-law never saw the humor in it.

So no pony, and of course no new bicycle; Grandfather's decisions were irrevocable. A circumvention of the child's will. A stunting of personality development.

Though there were no parents to make mistakes in bringing up their little girl, there was a grandfather. And instead of an Oedipus complex, she developed a fixation on her grandfather. A super-superego. Barely three years old, Maximiliane already aped him, took a broad-legged stance, folded her hands on her back. At table she handled her napkin as he handled his when he awkwardly wiped bits of food from his beard. "What a resemblance" and "Her grandfather all over again," every visitor said.

The course was set from the day of her birth. Maximiliane had been and was and would be: the heir of Poenichen. This situation conformed completely to her own desires. She never wanted to be anything else. Was the congruence due to environmental influences? The projection of Quindt's will onto his granddaughter? Heredity? But this latter factor remained an imponderable. Little was known of the Jadows, less of the Polish lieutenant.

Maximiliane's deepest, most unshakable faith was Poenichen and Quindt. It could be given a name.

So she continued to ride the same old clattering bicycle that had already served "the young baron." Because its saddle, too, was too high for her short legs, she pedaled standing, rattled down the village street, which had been paved by now but still had to be weeded, rode over the planked bridges and through the ruts of the sandy paths.

Her favorite activity was following her grandfather at a distance when he went on horseback through the fields or to the tree nurseries. She proved herself persistent, a quality her grandfather liked: the child knew what she wanted, and in his experience most people did not know what they wanted.

One day he said, "Come with me," told her to get into the carriage, and drove to the fields. At some point they got out and continued on foot. He learned all the joys of teaching as he showed her rabbit tracks, crow's-feet in the snow, fox droppings. He explained the difference between winter and summer wheat, he told her that the crested diver was called crested diver, he gave names to the birds and the trees. Each of their walks across the fields became days of the Creation. Geography lessons and history lessons, both extending through the ages of the world, but with everything referred back to Pomerania.

"Everything mine!" Maximiliane exclaimed when they climbed the hundred-foot Innicher Hill and looked around. "Is Riepe mine, too?" she asked.

Her grandfather's hesitation lasted only a moment. He believed in always answering questions with an unequivocal yes or no rather than qualifying. So he said, "Yes."

"Why?"

Quindt told her of Goths and Slavs and Swedish invasions, of colonization and Christianization, knights and vassals.

"I could have been born in one of those pigsties?" Maximiliane inquired.

"Where?"

"Like Lenchen Priebe, in one of the cottages?"

Again the answer was an unequivocal yes.

"You're responsible for everyone, Grandfather?"

"Yes."

"That must be hard for you."

"Yes."

Once he took her along when he paid a sick call on his fieldhand Klukas. "No shamming, now," he said. "You're going to be good as new. A proper piece of meat in the soup; I'll let Anna Riepe know. Every day a shot of brandy, and then–up and at 'em. Not back to the fields right away, though. Start off slow and easy on the bench outside the house." His bits of advice were all similar, but they had their result and were almost as efficacious as Dr. Wittkow's prescriptions.

Six years after the end of the "war to end all wars"– Quindt had taken this description from Wilson's peace

118

mission–he could start implementing the plan he had long harbored. He reforested a thousand acres with a "peace forest," as he called it, which he expected to last until *"anno Domini* 2050."

"Then it will have to be cut down. If you want to achieve something that will last beyond your lifetime, you'll have to plant trees rather than make babies."

He taught Maximiliane to read a tree's age by the rings. "One ring a year. Every ten years the trees will have to be pruned."

As yet he had to bend down to his trees; as yet even Maximiliane was taller than they were. The peace forest was still in the nursery stage, surrounded by a chain-link fence to protect it from wild game.

By the time Maximiliane was ten years old, the trees had caught up with her. By the time she had to leave Poenichen, the peace forest was exactly twenty years old, and the trees were thirty feet tall. By that time they could rightfully be called a forest, though peace no longer had anything to do with it.

To get to this newly forested acreage, one had to pass the paddock. There the Quindt horses grazed. They were a little too heavy for the light Pomeranian sandy soil, but Quindt's father's attempt at crossing them with a different strain indigenous to East Prussia had not resulted in any improvement. The "Quindt trotters" were raised only for private use.

Grandfather and granddaughter witnessed a stallion mounting a mare in heat. Quindt stopped, pointed his cane at the scene, and asked, "Do you understand about all this?"

Maximiliane did not reply. Her face showed awe. After a long time she said, "But that's wonderful!" She was breathing heavily.

Of course her grandfather was surprised; he had been expecting embarrassment. "That's one way of looking at it," he said, adding, "This is the basis of the whole Creation story."

The mare, neighing loudly, galloped away while the stallion ran in the opposite direction. Quindt, saying, "Well, that's that," was about to walk on, but Maximiliane stopped him. "Wait." The horses returned, rubbed their bodies together, and licked each other's nostrils.

That was the extent of the sexual information imparted to the girl, with the possible exception of the biology course she later took in school.

Eleven months later Quindt took Maximiliane along to the stables. "Come," he said. "I want to show you something." He stopped before one of the stalls.

"Any minute now, Baron," said Griesemann, the head teamster.

"Is that the mare the stallion straddled last year?" Maximiliane asked.

"Mounted," Quindt corrected. "Mounted, not straddled."

"May I help?" Maximiliane asked, and again her breath came faster. When the foal's head appeared, Maximiliane jumped into the stall, squatted in the straw, and received the damp newborn. Instructed by Griesemann, she rubbed it down. Afterward she spoke only of "my foal," "my horse," acting very much like Schmaltz the midwife. She decided that the foal should be named Falada. Her grandfather explained that the name was suitable only for a mare.

"How do you know?" Maximiliane asked.

"You mean, how do I know the foal isn't a mare?"

"No—I can see that for myself. The name, I mean."

"Falada has a feminine ending."

"That doesn't matter," she declared. "Fräulein Friedrich has a man's name." And so her horse was named Falada, though a male. When, a year later, it was scheduled for castration, Maximiliane burst into

120

tears. Falada should be allowed to jump! Falada should sire foals!

Occasionally Quindt took Maximiliane along when he went stalking deer in the evenings. She learned to walk soundlessly and to see in the dark. "A child of nature," as would be said of her on a later occasion. "She is and remains a child of nature." On that other occasion, in that place, it amounted to calling her a prodigy.

One evening grandfather and granddaughter sat side by side in the blind near Poenichen Lake. Riepe was waiting for them with the horse and carriage some distance away. Quindt was smoking his pipe to discourage the mosquitoes. The waning moon rose over the pines, bringing light to the clearing. In the reeds the toads rustled. At each new noise Quindt pointed to the appropriate quarter, but neither of them spoke. They were waiting for a royal stag that Quindt had been observing for weeks. If all went well, this would be Maximiliane's first experience of a shoot.

The stag appeared, and Quindt exchanged his pipe for his gun; everything happened without a sound except for the buzzing of the gnats. The light was good. The stag turned his head and splendid antlers. Quindt's finger was already on the trigger, but as he was about to squeeze it, Maximiliane, with an unexpected and spontaneous gesture, pushed the muzzle aside. The shot misfired and hit a tree trunk, setting off a multiple echo. Her grandfather rose, put the gun aside, and raised his arm to give his granddaughter her first and only slap in the face. He intended it to be a memorable one. There was little room to maneuver; he stepped back and into emptiness. No stag and no unforgettable slap. Instead, a broken thigh.

This Quindt, too, came close to losing his life in a hunting accident. As he lay recovering, he told every visitor—and of course all the neighbors drove up, Dr.

Wittkow came daily, and the Reverend Merzin came once a week–"I intend to be the first Quindt to die a natural death. Not on the hunt and not in war, but very peacefully. But not just yet, Pastor. The heavenly hunting grounds can wait a while longer."

He resisted any suggestion that he be taken to the hospital, and so the fracture was not treated properly. Thereafter his right leg was shorter. This time, too, Quindt said, "I'll be good as new," but he was not good as new. Since no one mentioned it, however, he was unaware that he dragged his right leg. He never accused his granddaughter, and she did not feel in the least responsible. Presumably she saw no connection between her knocking the gun aside and her grandfather's fall. In future he rode in the carriage alongside the hunters, and from that vantage point he shot an occasional buck.

After his accident he taught Maximiliane to shoot, giving her a thorough course of lessons–small-bore rifles, shotguns, pistols. She learned to hit targets and wild pigeons. She became a quick, sure shot.

Two years later he forced her to shoot Dinah, the bitch, who had grown old and almost blind. "One must learn to kill what one loves. Aim carefully! Do not torture the animal."

Nevertheless Maximiliane needed three shots.

"An animal must be killed by the person who loves it most," Quindt repeated. "He will have the most compassion. The stag that time, he was going to be shot down anyway; his number had come up. If I didn't do it, Palcke would. The depredation they wreak in the forest is too much. One must never lose sight of the larger picture."

One after another, Maximiliane had conquered the manor house, the grounds, the village, and the ten thousand acres of land belonging to the Quindts–annual rings. As far as her feet could reach, nothing but Poenichen, and never a person who did not know her. "Aren't you the little Quindt girl?" and in the next breath, "The poor child, she hasn't got a father or a mother." But she had a home, she grew up fearless, she had this grandfather. The Baroness, it was true, continued to be more interested in her dogs than in the child. She had begun to breed dachshunds along with the hunting dogs, she telephoned and corresponded with breeders and buyers, and she went on long trips to find proper mates for her bitches, Herr Riepe behind the steering wheel. "Otto! Otto!" she called as soon as he speeded up to pass one of the few cars on the Pomeranian roads.

Life on Poenichen went on, endless winters, endless summers. Time and again the flax bloomed, the larks rose, white and pink garlands wound to the right and left of the roads across the green wheatfields when the apple trees flowered in late May. Time and again spring erupted in Pomerania, sudden as the autumn that took summer by surprise and rushed off in storms. Joy and sorrow took turns on Poenichen, as they did in the old farmers' sayings. On joyous occasions Anna Riepe fried a fish; it was a time for something light. On sorrowful occasions she roasted game, preferably a boar, which lay heavy on the stomach and made you sleepy. In October the scent of fruit filled the house for days: Anna Riepe was putting up pears, sweet and sour, spiced with cloves, ginger, and cinnamon.

In spite of Herr von Jadow's prediction, progress had not arrived in Pomerania by express train; many of the prophecies uttered after the war did not come true. Nevertheless, by now there was electricity on Poenichen, not only in the manor house, but also in the cottages. There were streetlights, but they were turned off as soon as Merck, the mayor, went to bed. The kitchens of the farmhands burned forty-watt bulbs, the manor used hundred-watt bulbs. In the village the last light was extinguished no later than nine, in Quindt's room the lights often stayed on past two o'clock in the morning. He slept badly and read a lot. At times rainstorms and snowstorms bent the poles, and therefore the oil lamps were kept at hand.

Though water mains had been built, the women continued to go to the village well because the water was not metered. The tin pails of wash water were still emptied in the gutter of the village street, for a sewage system was out of the question. The outhouses in the barns with the goats and pigs were still in use, and what Quindt called "the differences" had not been abolished. Steam heat had been installed in the manor house, but the big furnace in the cellar was fired by wood, supervised day and night by old Priska, grown older still and widowed besides. He hardly ever left the furnace room. Anna Riepe brought him his meals in a bowl. "Polish conditions," a man such as Herr von Jadow would probably have said. Priska wore out his master's old clothes; the green jacket hung loosely from his bones. He was the only one who reached for the Baron's hand to kiss it. But they met at most twice a year.

When he hired Herr Palcke, Quindt had struck it lucky. Palcke had owned an estate himself, almost five hundred acres near Wronke on the Warthe. Forced to leave it when West Prussia was ceded to Poland, he had become a Poland-hater; under his management, the Polish farmhands soon disappeared from the Poenichen farm. When Palcke began to speak about Hitler, Quindt turned a deaf ear.

"German space in the East," Herr Palcke said. "Only one man can help us there—Adolf Hitler! He'll make room for the German people."

At most Quindt might say, "We really aren't pressed for space, Herr Palcke; our case is that we have rather too much of it."

The mechanization of Poenichen agriculture proceeded slowly. The transformation of the teamsters into

124

expert tractor drivers could not happen overnight. Quindt counseled patience. "It took hundreds of years to turn a wild horse into a good plowhorse. A tractor has to be tamed like a trotter."

Herr Palcke's determination to introduce the eight-hour day shattered against his master's resistance. "In July, during the harvest—eight hours of work? During potato digging? And the early snows? And why should the people work eight hours in January when the ground is frozen solid? Work has to be done when work needs to be done."

"The people grumble about having to work on Sundays," Herr Palcke insisted.

"I'll be the one to decide when it's Sunday on Poenichen, Herr Palcke. Is that understood?"

Herr Palcke understood the Baron less completely than Quindt assumed, a fact that would become evident much later.

Of course the Baron's final utterance was reported to the pastor, who arrived unannounced to discuss the Lord's day with Quindt.

"Pastor," Quindt said, "if God had insisted on resting on the seventh day, he would have seen to it that on that day the grass stopped growing and the cows didn't give milk and there were no storms."

"On Sundays man must prepare for life after death, Herr von Quindt."

"I'm not concerned with life after death but with life before death, and for that man needs more than a coffin. He needs a roof over his head and a goat in his barn and a piece of land so that he knows where his home is."

"There is yet another home, Baron."

"Let us hope so, Pastor."

"We must believe so, Baron."

"Just hoping is hard enough."

Maximiliane had stood to one side during this discussion. When the clergyman had left, Quindt told her, "All my life I've had to think about how I was to get new seeds, how I was to finance the new machines, how I was to raise the interest on my loans. New barns. Cottages for the farmhands. The price of potatoes. How old are you now, anyway?"

"Twelve."

"Since there are laws against child labor, I presume there are also laws against child marriage. And yet you look ready. Sixteen is probably the earliest. You have to go away to school."

"No!"

"I'm not asking you, I'm telling you."

"Can't we discuss it, Grandfather?" Her eyes were brimming with tears. "You can't just send me away."

"Of course I can. More than that—I have to. The education authorities are asking questions. Arnswalde isn't far—it's on this planet."

"Not on mine!" A claim that corresponded to Quindt's own views. Arnswalde was not on his planet, either.

"When the new school year starts in the spring, you'll go to Arnswalde."

It sounded like a threat even before the fact, though it was softened by comparison with "the shock of your life," which had already been promised her by Fräulein Hollatz as soon as she attended a regular school. Fräulein Eberle had said, "Are you going to be surprised, Maximiliane," and Fräulein Gering used to say, "Wait until you're in school—that'll be a whole other story."

Maximiliane's expectations of school consisted entirely of such promises.

126

14

Her problems started even before the school year did. Frau Görke, who usually did not spend her week on Poenichen until fall, appeared out of season in early April to sew three school dresses for Maximiliane. Their concepts of what constituted a school dress were diverse in the extreme. Maximiliane wanted tucks, lower necklines, shorter sleeves, longer skirts. But Frau Görke declared, "At the age of twelve, a girl does not need tucks."

Frau Görke sewed on all the estates in the immediate neighborhood, for the von Kalcks on Perchen, for the Pichts and the Rassows. She had also sewn for the Kreschins, who had moved to Berlin; for them, she even made evening clothes.

There were tears. Not only did Maximiliane cry, but so did Frau Görke, who could be persuaded to stay only with difficulty; she had already packed up her pincushion. "And all because of that miserable chest." She was a Pietist. When she was excited, she forgot to speak her elegant German. When she said "miserable chest," she meant the same thing as Ecclesiastes' "All is vanity."

Quindt had to come to the sewing room and talk soothingly to her. "If the tailor can't make the dress fit, the surgeon will have to alter the body to fit."

This statement touched Frau Görke's pride. A surgeon! She could make anything fit, especially on a twelve-year-old girl. She put tucks in the bodice, explaining repeatedly that it was quite inappropriate for a twelve-year-old girl to be fully developed.

The final result of all the tears and effort was unsatisfactory. Maximiliane looked pudgy in her school dresses. The stance she took in front of the tall mirror during the fitting was the same stance she would assume on a similar occasion when forced to buy another dress: shoulders held stiffly, protruding kneecaps pushed back, arms extended. She had to become habituated to every new item of apparel, which often took years. All her life she remained a hard person to clothe. It was her Aunt Maximiliane who finally realized that the girl should wear dirndl dresses. For decades she would keep her firm, round figure, always more pleasurable to behold unclothed than clothed, a credit to every nude beach, an object of envy in any sauna. But when she was young it was not yet fashionable to wear skin, and by the time the fashion changed it was almost too late for Maximiliane.

Prior to entering the girls' high school in Arnswalde, she had already taken a year of English lessons given by one Miss Gledhill from Liverpool on Baron Picht's estate. But the school in Arnswalde initiated her in the truest sense into life that was serious, that was earnest.

Though Arnswalde was no more than twenty miles from Poenichen as the crow flies, it was hard to reach by train, and even cars had to take several roundabout routes, making for about thirty miles of driving. On a bicycle, against the wind, the trip took half a day. To celebrate her enrollment in school, Maximiliane was given a girl's bicycle, but only to ride between the school building and the house of the widowed Frau Schimanowski, who had boarded schoolgirls since her husband's death. It was agreed that once a month Riepe would fetch her on Saturday to spend Sunday at home.

128

Until this time Maximiliane had never presented any serious behavioral problem. Rather, she had proved to be tractable and adaptable. But of course she had grown up as the village princess, a very special person from the first. In Arnswalde that was no longer the case; there she saw nothing but strange faces—her fellow students, the teachers, the principal, the custodian, and Frau Schimanowski, whom Maximiliane addressed the very first night as Frau Schimpanski, not with evil intent but out of ignorance, causing endless giggles among the five boarders. The widow sent all of them to bed hungry after saying to Maximiliane, "Hurry up, out with whatever your housekeeper packed up for you. You're too fat anyway." Frau Schimanowski made her hand over everything—from the goose breast, the ham, and the currant buns down to the cream toffee Anna Riepe had cooked before Maximiliane's departure. The only things the new boarder was allowed to keep were the wrinkled apples.

Maximiliane knew no one in Arnswalde—and, what was worse, no one knew her. Until now everyone had known who she was—Maxi to some, Maximiliane to others, but always at the very least "the little Quindt girl." No one had ever had to ask, "And who do you belong to?"

Now she was constantly asked her last name, her first name, her address. "Poenichen," she replied, without street name or house number. "Manor," she eventually added in order to complete the information.

"Another one of those manor-house children," said Herr Kressman, the principal, a Social Democrat, and then he inquired as to her father's occupation. Maximiliane was not prepared for such questions. Therefore she said, "Second Lieutenant."

"His occupation in private life."

"Secondary-school graduate."

The question was rephrased once more. "His current occupation."

"Dead," said Maximiliane.

For a few days it seemed as if she had forfeited not only Poenichen but also her name. "Ah, the new girl."

"Who'll sit next to the new girl?"

"Shall we listen to what the new girl has to say about that?"

"The new girl will lead us in prayer this morning."

The new girl had to come up to the dais in front of the class. Her face turned red, but no prayer emerged.

"Let us hope that you were not brought up outside the church?"

Her silence continued.

"Don't you know any prayers at all?"

"No public ones," Maximiliane admitted.

"You have a lot to learn. Return to your seat."

She had to line up to go to the schoolyard for recess, she had to line up to return from the schoolyard to the school; she had to get to her feet in order to answer a question, and she had to get to her feet even if she did not know the answer.

"You, the new girl. Stand up when I call on you."

Always, over and over, in every class—the new girl. In the needlework class she replied to Fräulein Blum, "You're just as new to me, ma'am." Not even "Fräulein Blum," only "ma'am."

What a rude answer! Fräulein Blum, already suffering from an inferiority complex because she did not have a craft degree, was the first to complain to the principal about the refractory new girl.

In music class she was asked to come up front and sing a song. She sang her favorite popular ballad. Closing her eyes against the twenty sets of eyes that were turned on her, she visualized the foreman's house, its bright window, Blaskorken and Fräulein Warnett on the bed. As she continued to sing, she reopened her round eyes,

130

and tears glittered on her lashes; her gaze still held Blaskorken, fish scales on his hairy arms. She tried to erase the image by blinking, and vaguely she recognized the classroom. A few tears, far apart but all the larger for it, ran down her cheeks.

Music lessons were given by a male instructor. Her cherry eyes had their effect. Herr Hute approached and placed his arm around the girl's shoulder. "There's no need to cry. You have a nice little voice. You'd best do harmony, though; you'll never reach the heights."

Her eyes damp with joy, Maximiliane looked at him. He took his arm away and never touched her again.

Of course Maximiliane compared herself to the other girls, for it was the first time she had ever had anything to do with people of the same age and rank. The same Pomeranian strain, dusky blond and vigorous, but she herself was the smallest save one although she was the oldest save one.

In physical-education class it turned out that she was clumsy at gymnastics. Like a mule, she stopped dead at the approach to the springboard. At home she had jumped every ditch, had used a beanpole to leap the brook at its widest point, had flashed past any obstacle with a side-vault; yet here she shied at a gymnastic horse, a piece of equipment that was even upholstered. She had been quicker than Dinah and almost as swift as three-year-old Lucky, and here she finished last in the race. No tree had been too tall for her, and here she was quite unable to climb the ladders. She could not understand the purpose of physical education: running for the sake of running, jumping for the sake of jumping, climbing for the sake of climbing.

During math class, which was given by Herr Kressmann himself, she performed like the seven-year-old to whom Fräulein Eschholtz had tried to teach simple addition of two-place numbers. She was able to add a specific number of apples, but not pure numbers; she could not separate the number from its object. She could not know that later she would be asked to do arithmetic with letters, which meant even less to her.

Was it possible that she could not recite one single poem among all the great German classics? Maximiliane stood on the teacher's dais, prepared to recite a poem by Goethe. She was carried away by the rhythm, the rapid gallop of the horse, away from the classroom straight to the last stanza—where, still betrayed by speed, she missed the rhyme and said "lust" instead of "love." Almost a scandal for an innocent girls' school in Arnswalde.

After class Fräulein Tetzlass had a word with the principal about the precocious new girl.

In her lessons with Miss Gledill, Maximiliane had learned to pronounce the English *th* and *r* perfectly, but neither sounded like the English spoken by Fräulein Wanke. "Whoever taught you to speak like that?" She called Maximiliane up front to practice her *th* before the whole class until it sounded more like what Fräulein Wanke considered correct. Her tongue pressed against her palate, Maximiliane repeated, "She thinks that someone. . . ."

During recess her classmates played secret paper-and-pencil games, counting-out rhymes for adolescents; they drew squares on a piece of paper, wrote initials in the squares, and called off, "This one loves me, This one adores me, This one will leave me, This one bores me." The name that remained when all the others had been crossed out was the name of one's future husband. Maximiliane wrote the initials *C.B.*, thinking of Christian Blaskorken; she wrote *K.K.*, thinking of Klaus Klukas, who would have said, "I won't"; and *W.B.*, Walter Beske. There were no more. The other girls made fun of her. "You only know three boys?" It never occurred to her to invent names, like they did.

Repeatedly she was made to stay after class for a whole hour, and sometimes she had to memorize poems as a punishment, omitting not a single stanza. After school she paced up and down the boxwood-lined gravel path in the widow Schimanowski's garden. Twenty steps forward, twenty steps back, espaliered fruit trees to the right, espaliered fruit trees to the left, remnants of snow on the vegetable patch, her book held in numb hands; in thirty-degree weather an hour of high emotion in the garden before she knew all six stanzas by heart. Along with the poem, she devoured six wrinkly apples.

As another form of punishment she was made to copy out poems, even hymns—all the stanzas, five times. School as penal institution. Her store of apples dwindled.

After only three weeks she had had enough. As they were climbing the stairs in double file after recess, she told one of the other girls that she had to go. The toilets were in the schoolyard, right next to the bicycle shed. She got her bicycle and took off, not even bringing her schoolbag. She arrived on Poenichen late in the afternoon, threw her bicycle down on the round flower bed, and ran to the kitchen to Anna Riepe, who warmed up some milk and broke raisin bread into it, saying, "First, eat." Maximiliane sat down at the big kitchen table and spooned up the soaked bread, sobbing and telling about the principal, Herr Kressman, about the teachers, about Frau Schimanowski.

Anna Riepe listened, her hands folded across her body. Then she said, "They're only human." Her single sentence imparted a whole lesson in psychology. "It's because they don't know anything about you and you don't know anything about them. Each one of them has a story."

"Do you think so, Amma? Everyone? You too?"

"Me too."

"Because of your Willem?"

Anna Riepe shook her head. "He's working for Siemens. But because of this." She pointed to her swollen stomach.

"Are you going to have a baby?"

"What's growing in there—that's not a living thing, that's deadly. But don't talk about it. Nobody has to know. Just let the others think that Anna's getting fat."

"Does Grandfather know?"

Anna Riepe shook her head again. "He'd send me to the hospital. I just told you because of the stories."

"What are you going to do, Amma?"

"I'll do nothing. I'll act as if nothing's happening. Go upstairs now. I'll make you some toffee to take back with you."

"They won't let me keep it. They take everything away."

"Then hide it."

The following day Quindt woke his granddaughter at four in the morning. "If you ride hard, you'll make it by eight o'clock."

It was early May but still cold and windy, and rainwater filled the potholes. Quindt had written her an excuse. Because of urgent family matters, his granddaughter. . . . He requested that the child not be interrogated further. A horse that is harnessed for the first time occasionally shies or runs away.

Nothing in Arnswalde changed: extra assignments and detention.

Memory albums became a fad in her class. A polite curtsy to the teacher after the bell had rung: "Please, would you write something in my book?" The albums made their way from one schoolbag to the next, little shiny pictures were traded and pasted in, the pages slowly filled. Maximiliane was the only one who did not join in.

"Don't you have an album?" they asked her.

"Sure I do," she said. "Of course I do. I just didn't bring it with me, that's all. It's at home."

Secretly she went to the stationery store in town and bought an album. Her pocket money managed to stretch enough for a linen-bound one as well as two sheets of decorative pictures to paste in, one of angel's heads and one of forget-me-nots. On her next visit to Poenichen she placed the book before her grandfather.

"Please write something in it."

"Later," he said, laying the book aside and reaching for his account ledgers.

"No, Grandfather, please–now."

"Where's the fire?"

"Right here."

"What is it supposed to be when it's finished?"

"A memory album."

"Does it have to rhyme?"

"That's the best kind."

Quindt sat down and copied out the saying chiseled over the fireplace–"Your wealth increase . . ." –concerning the proper attitude toward foes, strangers, and God. He signed with his title, which he was in the habit of remembering or forgetting, depending on his mood.

Then Maximiliane took the album to her grandmother. "Please write something on the next page."

Her grandmother was playing solitaire in her private sitting room. Maximiliane fetched her writing utensils and set them down in the middle of the rows of cards.

"Do girls still do that, my child? A memory album!" Something like emotion tinged her voice. She reflected for a moment before writing, "For we cannot shape children in our spirit; the way God gave them to us– that is the way we must keep them and love them, that is the way we must raise them as best we can and let each grow his own way." And underneath she wrote, "This sentence from *Hermann and Dorothea* was copied out for you, my dear Maximiliane, by your grandmother Sophie Charlotte von Quindt."

Maximiliane thanked her with a kiss and rushed downstairs to Anna Riepe. "Write something in my book, Amma."

Anna Riepe was about to make the egg drops in the egg-drop soup, a moment that would brook no interruption. "What do you want me to write, child?"

"A sentiment, Amma."

"Oh, sentiments, child, sentiments." Then, on the third page, she wrote what had proven true in her life: "A rolling stone gathers no moss."

Foreman Palcke also added a sentiment—more of a meteorological rule than a guideline for life—to her book. Then she dashed off to the village, making her first stop at the widow Schmaltz's. It was some time before the midwife found pen and ink. After much debate, they agreed on the motto embroidered in blue on the towel holder. " 'Home is where the heart is.' Emma Schmaltz, midwife on Poenichen."

She could not find Walter Beske, who had bicycled to the neighboring village to play soccer, and Klaus Klukas declared, "I won't." Negotiations took precious time. "Go to hell," he said finally.

Lenchen Priebe had an album of her own and had only to copy off its final page, "Here at the end I stand strong and stowt, to keap the others from faling out. Helene Priebe." Three spelling errors, but Maximiliane could hardly be choosy when it was a matter of filling the book as rapidly as possible. Lenchen received a whole row of angel's heads in recompense.

Maximiliane ran home, arriving late for dinner. Her grandmother raised her eyebrows. In explanation, Maximiliane laid the book in front of her. "I've only got seven pages! What am I going to do?"

Quindt pointed to her chair. "You will eat your soup. First things first."

136

"Why didn't you write that in my book, Grandfather?"

"There's still time."

"But you're already in it."

"Then I'll just have to sign a different name."

"Is that allowed?"

"In this case it's a must."

"But Quindt," his wife admonished.

"You'll have to do the same thing." He turned the pages of the album, stopping to read the second one. " 'And let each grow his own way.' So typical of Sophie Charlotte von Malo from Königsberg. These albums are more revealing than I realized."

That afternoon the three of them sat at the round table in the library. Quindt had a book of famous quotations in front of him, while Maximiliane's grandmother was consulting her own memory album. She took from it not only verses but also pressed and faded bouquets of forget-me-nots. Quindt pulled over the Königsberg album, scanned some of the entries, and looked at his wife. " 'Such, dear Pia, are the wishes of your eternal friend. . . .' Why Pia?" he asked.

The Baroness put on one of her cautious smiles. "That's what I was called as a girl."

"I never knew about that."

"There's a lot you don't know, Quindt."

"Pia, the mystery girl from Königsberg." Though he had always been properly attentive to her, he had paid her little attention. Now he gave his wife a searching look, noticing for the first time that in the course of the years her hair had turned a whitish gray and that she wore glasses. Her eyes were no longer Prussian blue, as Quindt had called them once, decades ago, but East Prussian gray-blue.

"Pia! It's too late for me to get used to it."

"Why should you, Quindt?"

"You're right, why should I?"

Quindt brought out three different kinds of ink as well as several steel nibs, broad ones and narrow ones. They thinned down the blue ink. Disguising her handwriting, Maximiliane wrote, "Live as you will wish to have lived when you die. Your loving friend, Amalie von Seekt." She pasted shiny pictures in all four corners. "Write something in English, Grandfather," she begged. "Not everybody has something in English."

Quindt wrote, "Early to bed and early to rise, Makes a man healthy, wealthy, and wise. Best wishes, Yours, Benjamin Franklin."

The Baroness sent to ask Anna Riepe to make coffee and send up the rose-hip liqueur.

Dusk descended and the three were still sitting around the table. Quindt took more books from the shelves and leafed through them, and Maximilane's grandmother told anecdotes about her old schoolfriends while using a damp sponge to loosen the pictures from her album.

"Today we're like a real family," Maximiliane said.

"A gangster family," Quindt corrected her, writing, "Want knows no laws."

Then Riepe appeared to announce, "It's high time, or the little miss will get back too late, and Frau Schimanowski's gonna make trouble again."

Anna placed the official hamper, which had to be turned over to Frau Schimanowski, in the car and tucked toffee and raisin rolls into the schoolbag. Thanks to Lenchen Priebe, who had made a grease spot on the linen binding, the album no longer looked brand new.

The following day Maximiliane left the album lying on her bed, where it was immediately found by Marianne and Gisela. "Amalie von Seekt? Josephine? What old-fashioned names! Benjamin Franklin—who's that?"

"One of my uncles," Maximiliane said.

"And what does this mean, here?"

138

"That's Swedish. *Lyckan kommer, Lyckan gar, Lycklig den, Som lyckan far.* Lars Larsson from Uppsala, that's another uncle. 'Happiness comes, Happiness goes, Happy he Who happiness knows.' "

The teachers wrote their pearls of wisdom into Maximiliane's book, the other girls wrote pearls of foolishness. In later years these would be supplemented by the sayings of the Führer, Hermann Göring, and Baldur von Schirach.

The agreement that every four weeks Riepe would come to fetch her in the car on Saturday was breached. After another three weeks Maximiliane again appeared at home on her bicycle.

Quindt saw no way of robbing Maximiliane and himself of the pleasure of these visits but to deprive her of the means of flight: her bicycle. She must learn the consequences of her actions; from now on she would have to walk to school in Arnswalde. Riepe returned her without the bicycle. On Poenichen they were relieved. The child would get used to it.

Then the call came from the girls' high school in Arnswalde. "Kressmann speaking, the principal. I call to inquire about Herr Quindt's health." Quindt, who had answered the phone himself, thanked Kressmann for the inquiry, for which he saw no occasion.

It turned out that Maximiliane had been absent from school for a full ten days. "A serious, fatal illness–her grandfather. Right to my face, with tears! The girl seemed quite desperate. No reason to disbelieve her! But I must say–with the best will in the world!"

The widow Schimanowski did not have a telephone. Therefore Quindt had Riepe drive him to Arnswalde, where he learned from the boardinghouse keeper that his granddaughter had packed a few thing in her suitcase and left for the railroad station. "Ten days ago. I didn't suspect a thing. After all, anything can happen to grand-parents."

Quindt had Riepe drive him to the school, where he waited for recess. Watching the girls get into line and silently file into the building, he formed his own opinion. He spoke in the hall with Fräulein Wanke about Maximiliane. A reserved child with a tendency to un-controlled outbursts of feeling, he was told. She, the teacher, had not yet arrived at a clear picture of the child, but girls who had been tutored at home always had a harder time adapting. It was so much better to send them to a regular school from the outset.

Quindt replied that he had not visited the school in order to receive instruction. He asked to be directed to the principal's office, but Herr Kressmann had retired to his private apartment for his midmorning snack. Quindt sent Riepe to the house with the visiting card he had had made up at the time he was a parliamentary delegate. It was engraved with his title of nobility and the designation "Member of the Reichstag." In his own hand he had added, "Requests the courtesy of an in-terview."

Dr. Kressmann acceded and initiated the discussion. "With the best will in the world, Herr Quindt. Your granddaughter has to adapt, just like all the other girls. But I assure you, we have shown her a great deal of understanding and patience—and we will continue to do so. Bring her back to us!"

"We'll have to find her before we can bring her back, Herr Kressmann. A child who feels well does not run away without provocation."

Kressmann, himself a man of choleric temperament, strode up and down behind his desk with his hands folded on his back and his head lowered, dragging his wooden leg. "My students are not supposed to feel well but to behave well."

140

Quindt, on the other side of the desk, also began to pace, also dragging his shortened leg, his hands on his back, his head lowered. As they could not help but come face to face rather frequently in the course of the ensuing conversation, they exchanged mistrustful looks, each suspecting the other of making fun of him by aping him.

"Behaving well instead of feeling well. Is that the pedagogical principle by which you run your institution?"

"Please! You are free to withdraw your grand-daughter at any time, Herr Quindt."

"If we had her, Herr Essmann."

"Kressmann, please."

"Von Quindt, please."

"That girl's in for a shock or two. Especially when you send her to boarding school."

"I have no intention of sending her to boarding school, Herr Kressmann, and she's already experienced the shocks of Arnswalde."

"Our state has certain regulations dealing with the obligation of schooling, Herr von Quindt."

"There are many regulations in our state, but surely a twelve-year-old child has a right to a little happiness."

"Obligations in school, happiness at home. I'll just repeat that I'm prepared to give your granddaughter one more chance if you can guarantee—"

Quindt interrupted. "I can guarantee nothing, Herr Kressmann."

"You are siding with the child? Against the school?"

"*In dubio pro reo*, Herr Kressmann. When in doubt, side with the weaker one."

As principal of this renowned—yes, he felt entitled to call it that—this renowned school for girls, Herr Kressmann had heard a number of complaints, more's the pity. He rejoiced in this opportunity of discussion with someone entitled to an explanation. "Tears at the drop of a hat! With the best will in the world—the girl is twelve years old. Surely she should have been broken of the habit of crying before this!"

"Should she have? And laughing too? And you intend driving both out of her? This child's reaction to your renowned institution is tears and flight."

"I repeat, Herr von Quindt, an educator is a very patient man. He does not throw in the sponge at the first setback."

"Nor would I advise that course of action, Herr Kressmann."

"How am I to understand that statement?"

The two men came to a stop, facing each other.

"There are better uses for sponges. I know."

"Is that meant to be a joke?"

"My last one."

Herr Kressmann repeated, "With the best will in the world."

But Quindt was already closing the door behind him.

In the empty schoolyard he met the music teacher. Hesitating at first, Herr Hute tipped his hat and stopped. Though he was reluctant to become involved, he said, and though music was only a secondary subject, he was nevertheless one of the few male members of the teaching staff, and of course he might be mistaken, but Maximiliane looked at him—how should he put it?—looked at him as a man in a far from childlike way; he was tempted to use the term *precocious*. "There's something in her eyes, Baron—but a pretty voice. Might a man already. . . ?" Herr Hute grew even more vague. Some days ago a capsized boat had drifted to shore near the municipal baths. No one had attached any immediate importance to it because at the time Maximiliane was believed to be visiting. . . . Just a hint, a suspicion . . .

"Any suspicions concerning my granddaughter's whereabouts you will kindly leave to me. We are, after all, talking about a Quindt."

142

He returned to the car and ordered Riepe to go back to the widow Schimanowski's. During the drive he asked, "Tell me, Riepe, do you believe the child drowned herself?"

"No way, Baron, sir, no way at all. She's not far away."

They made Frau Schimanowski give them Maximiliane's belongings.

"But the rent, Baron! I won't be able to find anyone to take the room for what's left of the school term!"

"We're talking about a third of a room, Frau Schimanowski. I will send you what I consider the proper amount."

One of the boarders was just returning. Quindt looked her over carefully before asking, "What kind of girls are you that people have to run away from you?"

"They found a capsized boat, Herr von Quindt—a week ago!"

"Then it's high time to turn it right side up."

"She left unpaid bills behind! At the stationery store and the confectioner's."

Quindt directed Riepe to drive to these two establishments before proceeding to the railroad station. There he learned that ten days before, a parked bicycle had been stolen, a man's model. "We think it was a fat girl. Around eleven years old."

On the trip back to Poenichen, Quindt asked Riepe, "Do you have any idea?"

"Yes, sir, I do."

"Then take me there."

Smoke was rising from the chimney of the assistant foreman's house, the wind driving it eastward. The rain call of the quail came off the lake.

Quindt got out of the car and approached the house. There was no need for him either to knock or to call.

The door flew open, and Maximiliane jumped down the steps and threw her arms around his neck.

Quindt had not counted on such behavior. He pushed her back a little way, looked her over, and could not see anything remarkable about her–though he had no idea what changes he should be looking for.

"Is he inside?"

· "No, of course not. You know he stays with his sheep."

"Come with me."

"First I have to close the stove top and move the kettle. I've been cooking turnips with mutton."

"All right. I'll be waiting in the car."

When she was sitting by his side, he began enumerating. "Fifty chocolate eclairs, the same number of angel's heads. An overturned boat in the reeds. And a stolen bicycle. I think that's rather a lot. Look at me. What's the matter with your eyes?"

Maximiliane kept her lids lowered. When she finally raised her head and opened her eyes, her irises glistened with tears. Her gaze was imploring.

"Good heavens!" Quindt exclaimed. "Is that the way you look at everybody? That's presumably what they mean when they talk about a woman's weapons. Don't wear them out too soon. Who knows what you might need them for in the future."

As a rule to live by, this was insufficient; he realized it himself. He had never considered himself a suitable educator. Whatever he had to say about the events in Arnswalde he had already said there and then; he did not like repeating himself. In addition, he was pleased as punch to have the little girl back with him.

They were driving over the plank bridge past the paddock, where the horses had gathered under the pines. It was raining. Quindt asked Riepe to stop the car. "Did anybody ever tell you anything about the theory of natural selection?"

144

"No."

"About Darwinism?"

"No."

"It has to do with nature's way of picking the best." He explained to her the origin and evolution of species, the advantages and disadvantages for new mutant forms of particular environmental conditions. "The horse has preserved its kind through millennia purely by its speed, not its strength. It's a runaway."

Maximiliane listened attentively. "You think I'm a runaway?"

"Yes."

"To preserve the Quindt species?"

"In a way."

Maximiliane pushed her hand under his. Riepe drove on, and Quindt decided to teach the child himself, at least for the coming winter.

That same winter Assistant Foreman Blaskorken appeared unbidden at the manor. The Baroness, her embroidery in her lap, sat with the men.

"Well?" Quindt initiated the conversation, though he did not ask the foreman to sit down. "No details in the presence of the ladies!"

Maximiliane, too, was present. She asked whether she should leave the room. Quindt decided. "You'll stay. If you are capable of doing something, you are capable of talking about it. Words are never worse than deeds."

The Baroness looked up from her embroidery and raised her eyebrows. Blaskorken said that the girl had done the cooking and the cleaning, that she had helped spread the nets, and that on the whole she had made herself eminently useful. There was nothing more to be said on the subject. The sheep trailer was still parked at the Blue Pond; in the summer it was his, Blaskorken's, habit to sleep out there and "guard the flocks." He hoped that he had proven himself a good shepherd, but now his time was up. Everything was in good order on the outlying farm, with the sheep and the fish. It seemed that a new era was dawning, that the years of disgrace were at an end. "The horizon is growing bright over our German fatherland."

Quindt looked at him carefully, just as he listened carefully, before saying in conclusion, "Then it's best if Riepe takes you to the ten-o'clock train tomorrow morning."

So this time it was the foreman who left Poenichen at summer's end. The rift was deeper than at the governesses' parting. He had lived in the house by the lake for many years, and a friendship had flourished. But there was no room on Poenichen for a man who saw a new day dawning. His three footlockers and the hunting horn were loaded in the car. The foreman departed as he had arrived, a few more gray strands in his hair, his forehead an inch higher. He still wore corduroys.

That night Quindt asked his wife whether she thought they ought to cross-examine the girl. She did not consider it necessary. "At her age a girl can learn even from experiences she doesn't have."

This time the Quindt-essence issued from the lips of the Baroness.

15

Herr Kressmann's remark—"When you send the girl to boarding school . . ."—had fallen on fertile soil. Until now Quindt had never considered the idea of boarding school, but by the end of the winter it had become a certainty: Maximiliane had to be educated in the company of girls her own age; he himself could not give her an education. At most he could impart a little knowledge, and only a limited amount of that. After the experiences of Arnswalde, a nearby school was out of the question, since the risk of running away would remain. Quindt had sent off for a number of prospectuses, and he had made inquiries from neighboring estate owners who had also sent daughters to boarding schools. Friederike von Kalck had attended one of the institutions run by the Mathilde Zimmer Foundation. The oldest daughter of Klein-Malchow had spent three years on Hermannswerder. Both establishments were on Quindt's final list.

The three Quindts met in the sitting room for discussion. The first prospectus Quindt examined was from the Mathilde Zimmer Foundation, since a second cousin of his wife's had been enrolled in one of their schools before the war. By now the student had become the mother of seven. Frau von Quindt remembered her vividly—though she also remembered that one of her sons, while still a minor, had shot himself over gambling debts.

Quindt declared that this incident could be blamed on neither Mathilde nor Friedrich von Zimmer, and he recited from one of the founder's writings in his own way, shortened and sprinkled with glosses of his own.

" 'All genuine education is education for life—that is, education of the person for life and through life. The entirety of popular education activity must be seen from this point of view.' Well, that Zimmer bit off quite a bit there—the entire population! 'If education is to be education for life, then it must wrest from life the laws by which life teaches and shapes. Education promotes the growth of what has already been predestined in the germ. Therefore, away with uniformity, with drill, and on with conscious nurturing of the individual, the personal. Not everyone can be everything, but what he can be, let him be to the utmost. A human being is not only an individual but at the same time a member of society.' There seems to me to be rather too much wresting and germinating, but his mixture of individual and society— what do you think, Sophie Charlotte, alias Pia from Königsberg? Or are you staying out of it? And you, Maximiliane?''

Maximiliane sat on the edge of her chair, her knees, her hands, her lips pressed tight, looking exactly like a thirteen-year-old girl about to be sent to boarding school.

Quindt pulled out the illustrated prospectus of the Evangelical Parish School of Potsdam-Hermannswerder. " 'Spacious and surrounded by water, hemmed in by reeds rustling in the wind, Hermannswerder is situated in the delta of the Havel. Formerly confined, the river has just left Potsdam to spread out around the island into delightful lakes and bays.' Look how they impute intention to an innocent river. 'Like a unique jewel, the island lies outside the treasure of the nation, the city of Potsdam, and the chimes of the garrison church with their admonitory tones waft across every half-hour. . . .' And so on, and so on. 'The goal of education is to develop responsible German housewives and mothers. . . . Poultry runs, accredited landscaping, student kitchens, infant and toddler care, practical and theoretical training . . . meet the needs of the present day for intensified ties to the soil.' I prefer my soil less clinging, I must say. But here, there's a good Potsdam ring to this. 'But it is not mental and practical work alone that mold the young person of our day; the truly complete formation of a healthy and strong generation is additionally brought about by athletics and physical exercise, for which the richest possibilities and a highly trained teaching staff are at hand. Genuine education presupposes constant striving for wholeness and penetration of the body by the mind.' What did the constipated Fräulein used to say? *Mens sana in corpore sano.* I guess education is not possible without adages. 'Each day's work begins in the auditorium with a Lutheran morning celebration.' Well, it can't hurt the child, at least. 'Anyone who has ever lived in the magic realm of this island will never forget it, though life may prescribe quite other roads. Precious seeds planted in the youthful soul bear the sweetest fruits in later life.' "

In spite of soil and precious seeds, the decision was made in favor of Hermannswerder; Grandmother Jadow in Charlottenburg was nearby, Berlin itself not on the moon. Besides, Vera was living in Berlin—though this was a subject on which silence was scrupulously preserved on this occasion as well, as it had always been since she had married Dr. Grün.

Four years of Hermannswerder!

The island did turn out to be a "magic realm" and a "unique jewel," and the admonitory airs of the Potsdam chimes penetrated Maximiliane's susceptible soul: a prospectus come true. If nothing unforeseen arose, she would get her diploma in 1938—although it would be nothing more than a so-called kitchen diploma, not acceptable for admission to advanced schooling. But there had never been any plans for that anyway. English would be her only foreign language, but on Poenichen that was considered quite adequate for worldly wisdom.

Whenever, in later years, Maximiliane met Magdalene or Bella, the friends with whom she shared a room for years, her heart would glow. At those meetings catchwords sufficed, duets of short exclamations evoking endless laughter. "Our housemother, Old Fritz." "Our solstice fires." "Our hot jelly doughnuts when we went ice skating." "Our braised chard." "The ice-cream cake in our café." "Father Lehmann, our ferryman." "Our boat rides by moonlight." "Our store, where we bought chocolate kisses." "The Jute ditch, we called it the Jew ditch"–a fleeting shadow, even years later. "Our ensigns, who rode up on hobbyhorses at Carnival time." *Our* being the only possessive pronoun in use. What an education for an only child! For a lifetime she used "Hermannswerder" as a badge of merit.

"Our housemother, a deaconess, though of noble descent, has us address her by a bourgeois name, and yet she is of the highest nobility," Maximiliane wrote in one of her weekly letters to Poenichen. She learned to curtsy more deeply when greeting the housemother, and a "Good morning, my dear child" was the reply– every single morning. Regularity, reliability, cordiality. They lived in a house that, like all the houses, was named after a tree: Birch House. Beech, Chestnut, Oak– a mixed forest of neo-Gothic brick buildings, all flatteringly entwined in ivy. Infant center, nursery school, teachers' training college, girl's high school–an island of women, except for the male infants.

In the classrooms and dormitories the walls were adorned with pictures of Jesus and the apostles. In Maximiliane's room it was *The Road to the Last Supper*. Soon these had to make way for pictures and sayings of the Führer. But they lived on an island. The spirit of

150

the times stopped at the white bridge, at least during the early years of the National Socialist seizure of power.

Maximiliane was assigned to a rowing crew, took recorder lessons, and during German class was made familiar with Ludendorff's views. She was asked, "What would you like to talk about?" Ever conscientious, she answered truthfully, "Actually, I don't want to talk at all."

Such answers were tolerated, even smiled at. The head of the school, who officiated at her confirmation, gave her a verse from the Fiftieth Psalm to speed her on life's way: "The mighty God, even the Lord, hath spoken, and called the earth from the rising of the sun unto the going down thereof." This verse strengthened her feeling that the sun was her personal star.

For garden work she wore a green linen apron, and for athletics a pair of blue shorts with a white jersey, and one afternoon a week she donned the uniform of the League of German Girls–black skirt and white blouse. At night she rolled her obstinate hair in curlers, combing it out in the mornings into a pageboy. She turned into a contemporary girl. According to the numerous surviving photographs the uniform was becoming to her, especially the short jacket, a present from Vera.

Now and again Vera drove up to the white bridge to call for Maximiliane. Her outward appearance put the housemother on alert. Maximiliane was called in. "Who is that person, my dear child? We do not care for such associations. Remember the spirit of our house. Keep yourself pure." Maximiliane concealed the fact that they were talking about her mother. The association came to a speedy end anyway.

During the winter Party meetings were held indoors, during the summer they met at the tip of the island. Campfires and scouting games, choral recitations, and song: "Behold the dawning in the East."

Maximiliane heard speeches by Goebbels and Hitler on the radio, sang the German national anthem and the Horst Wessel song. She developed the muscles in her right arm more than those in her left through energetically raising it in the Party salute and keeping it raised for the length of a song. She learned by heart the twenty-five points of the National Socialist Party program, as she did the details of Hitler's rise from unknown wartime dispatch runner to leader of the German nation. She won the Reich Sports Badge–for which she performed everything that could be done in water; because of her short legs, she was less accomplished on the track or at the jumps. She wore her badge like a medal; her grandfather called it a bluebottle fly.

For the first two years that Maximiliane was at Hermannswerder, Quindt had to go to Berlin once a month on business. Each time he invited his granddaughter and any two friends she chose to a pastry shop. Back on Poenichen, he claimed that the famous Berlin air you got to breathe must already have been inhaled and exhaled at least three times–but he never gave up his trips. Occasionally he confessed to Riepe that he missed the child.

In addition to the academic subjects, which were taught in the mornings, Maximiliane was tutored in the practical arts during the afternoons. Sewing lessons initiated her into the various kinds of seams and stitches; she learned that vegetables should be cooked only briefly, in order to conserve their vitamins. She learned to make green-rye dumplings and chard. On Poenichen she would have no need for either lap seams or chard, but she would know enough to admire the quality of the lap seams manufactured by Frau Görke. She would never forget any of it, though life would lead her on quite other roads. The prospectus had promised no less. They tried to teach her to make a simple white sauce according to a complicated recipe–not "a few tablespoons of flour"

152

but "50 grams flour," not "a slab of butter" but "20 grams vegetable shortening"; Anna Riepe had already spoiled her for recipes. In cooking as in other classes she remained an average student, though willing, often eager, and on the whole well-liked.

She was taught that poems and hymns are just as important to humankind as daily bread. During those years she nourished herself primarily on poems and apples, the latter arriving in a hamper from Poenichen every other week from August to April, one variety after another, carefully packed by Anna Riepe. This chewing of apples provided her with strong white teeth and rosy gums. In later life, whenever she ate apples she was overcome with a longing for poetry, which then effortlessly surfaced in her memory.

As often as could be managed, she retreated with a book, either to one of the attic staircases or behind the rhododendron bushes on the grounds, where there was a smell that reminded her of Poenichen. She read whatever she could get her hands on, indiscriminately, even the blood-and-soil literature of the Nazi period. She was a child of her time, and she satisfied her hunger for literature with the creations of her time. It all had little influence on her later thinking—except that whenever she came across a poem, she unconsciously put out her hand for an apple.

She grew more slender and a little taller; she matured: a young woman. She became used to subways, elevators, escalators; she became capable of cosmopolitanism and learned what every young woman must learn.

For the most part her fellow students came from families with a lot of land and very little money. This was the Prussian and especially the Pomeranian way of life. It was said of Pomeranians that they were easily satisfied, patient, a little self-willed, and stubborn. They were thought to be level-headed besides. Was Maxi-

153

miliane level-headed? With her zeal for camping, solstice fires, and torchlight parades, her passion for poetry?

The human animal is not just an individual but at the same time a link in a chain, claimed the prospectus. She liked to march with arms linked, loved the parade step, the fanfares, the drummer boy up ahead! Carrying a collection box for the people's welfare or the winter relief, she stood outside movie houses or walked through the Potsdam pastry shops; she gave badges to the donors, cornflowers and daisies, persuaded of her high purpose.

"She'll grow out of it," Old Quindt said to Riepe as they were driving home from Berlin.

Once a month Maximiliane paid a visit to her grandmother Jadow in Charlottenburg. For an hour she sat among the antique furniture and antique etchings. An aging maid from the country brought tea. "A girl must never be allowed to be idle," her grandmother declared, and taught Maximiliane to crochet lace doilies.

Even in dancing school there was a new, fresh spirit. The Charleston had yielded to new dances, new tunes— German marches, German country waltzes. But the tango survived, and once again Maximiliane's legs proved too short. The slow foxtrot was more suited to her Pomeranian temperament. She was in demand as a dancing partner, and for her part she adored the young ensigns. For the graduation ball in the Potsdam Palace Hotel she got her first permanent wave and a dress of stiff white organdy embroidered with flowery wreaths, both a present from Grandmother Jadow, who sat among the parents, small, white-haired, aristocratic, and always a tiny bit offended.

"I'm dancing my way into heaven with you, Into the seventh heaven of love." Of course she fell in love again: Siegfried Schmidt, cavalry ensign. With the utmost difficulty she succeeded in meeting him once or twice for a walk in the woods. She copied out long poems for him, one of which used the word *love* four times in each stanza. Of course it had to be this particular poem that was intercepted by the housemother before it could reach its intended recipient.

"My dear child! Do you have any idea what you're saying?"

"Yes," said the dear child, opening her eyes wide. The damp gaze of the cherry orbs served to reinforce the housemother's anxiety.

"You are only sixteen years old, Maximiliane!"

Where did the deaconess draw the line? She could just as easily have said "already sixteen."

Even now Maximiliane sometimes came up with answers in class that were surprising and made the others laugh. She took words all too literally. The only girl who came from the far reaches of Pomerania, "east of the Oder"—cause enough for hilarity in itself.

"He served the King of Prussia," the history teacher said, and Maximiliane asked, "Served him what?"

Naturally her inquiry aroused astonishment and laughter. Everyone knew that people served not things but others. The question was answered not with philosophy but with grammar. A German serves with the sword, with the weapon in his hand; he serves his king, his emperor, his Führer. With God for Führer and Fatherland! Universal compulsory military service had already been reestablished, but in spite of her fervor Maximiliane was unaware of the words engraved on her ensign's belt buckle.

Occasionally, when she was daydreaming out the window, she had to be called to attention. But what did she care about the interior of Asia, Katmandu, Nepal, the Kirghiz steppes? Instead she dreamed of Poenichen Lake and of the hedged paths she walked with her Siegfried or wished she were walking with her Siegfried. She had no suspicion of the importance India would one day play in her life, or the homeland of the Kirghiz.

In German class they read Ernst Jünger's reminiscences of trench warefare. Compulsory material. In conclusion they were assigned an essay in which they were to take a position on the book's statement "Here war, which usually takes away so much, turns into a giver. It trains us in manly community and restores to their rightful place values that had been half forgotten because there had been no opportunity to express them. Once more we feel blood in our veins, destiny and future bound up together—the country will find out later on. Such years do not go by without a trace."

Sentences like tossed stones. One of them lodged in Maximiliane's heart. She stared out the window into the oaks and replaced them with the oaks growing above the graves of the Quindts, graves marked by erratic rocks, one of them for her father. She wrote and crossed out, stared out the window some more, began again, and after four hours, like the other girls, placed her exam book up front, where they were collected. "Our neighbor lost his right arm in the war. Our foreman lost his home in the war. I lost my father in the war. Poenichen lost its heir. All of us lost the war. Our country has found out. The years did not go by without a trace. I do not see what a war can give to a people."

There it was, in black and white—at the height of reawakened national sentiment and German fighting spirit. It was not possible to assign a grade to the essay, nor was it suited to class discussion. The history teacher did not want to hurt the girl, and so he held the exam book out to his dog. "Here, Fido." The dog snapped at the paper, tore the booklet out of the teacher's hand, bit and chewed until it was in shreds.

A week later the essays were handed back. Dr. Stöckel held out the tattered one and explained that there had been an accident; his dog had taken a special liking to it even before he had had a chance to correct and grade it. "We'll have to consider the essay unwritten.

156

You better acquire a new composition book, Maximiliane." Laughter in the classroom. No private dressing-down. Even Maximiliane had to believe that the situation was as the teacher had presented it.

If you heard Maximiliane talk about Hermannswerder in later years, you would think that all they had done there was laugh. Everything floated on a wave of hilarity. Almost everything.

The Potsdam chimes ring on the hour to this day, though now they come from the tower of the little forest church of St. Peter and Paul in West Berlin.

16

Vera–who called herself Jadow after her return to Berlin–had met Dr. Daniel Grün under unusual circumstances. At the time, she was working on a sequence of photographs subsequently published under the collective title "The Bench in the Park." She snapped her camera in the Tiergarten, in Tegeler Park, in the Lustgarten: women flanked by their shopping bags, retired old men, people out of work, lovers; some sitting at the edge of the bench, others sprawling at its center. In the Lustgarten she was observed by a man whose attention was also focused on two men sitting on a bench. Without further introduction he said to Vera, "Have you noticed how one of them keeps inching over and the other edges farther away? Any minute now he'll get up and leave. It's a duel."

They walked alongside each other for a few steps and talked about gestures–children's gestures, adults' gestures.

"Did you ever watch people cross a street? Straight or on the diagonal? Or the way a shy person waits until a car is close by and then runs as fast as he can? Or the way a woman sits down? Fishing for the chair leg with her foot? Smoothing her skirt or pulling it up? Or the way people get into bed? Some–mostly women, by the way–stand straight up, pull up the covers, and then lower themselves down."

158

Vera listened and watched the man, attentive and amused. It seldom happened that a man's comments amused her.

"People give off signals! The different dialects of body language! Jusk take the radius people claim for themselves. How close does a person let another person come? Have you ever noticed that there are touchers, people who grasp others by the sleeves, the shoulder, the coat button? A continual offense against the zone of distance, for which mass society is to blame–for example, in public vehicles, in waiting lines, at public gatherings. Is it that humans are seeking something like the warmth of the hearth because they have lost the warmth of the nest? Why do they suddenly put on uniforms in the midst of peacetime? Why do they put on disguises? Are they seeking camouflage?" Even at this first encounter he sketched for her the outlines of his field of research.

A short time later she met Dr. Grün again, dressed as a rabbi, the prayer strap across his forehead, his shoulders draped with a prayer shawl. It was a costume ball given by the Berlin Academy of Fine Arts. All the guests had come as famous, for the most part Expressionist, paintings. Dr. Grün was portraying Chagall's *Rabbi of Vitebsk*–a painting then still on exhibition in the Crown Prince's Palace. Because of its authenticity, his costume was alienating. Though he knew hardly anyone in the crowd, he immediately recognized Vera. He danced with her "at a distance." Their topic of conversation was obvious: how do people dance with each other? Both found themselves constantly searching for subjects, the one being concerned with the background, the other with the surface–the subject and the subjective. Both were mistaken when they agreed during their conversation that they shared a common point of view. Though the view was the same, Dr. Grün saw a deeper level.

Vera was dressed and made up like one of Jawlensky's women—harsh, almost brutal. She and Dr. Grün made a spectacular couple. That night she learned that he had only recently arrived in Berlin from Vienna—a skilled Viennese, but still an amateur Berliner, as he put it. A student of Freud's, he had established a psychotherapeutic practice in Berlin. Depth psychology. Analysis. He pointed out to her a number of potential patients in the crowd of gaily costumed dancers, though they were presumably unaware of their illnesses. "Do you see that man, the way he points his toes inward? An anxiety symptom. He's possessed by the constant fear that someone might step on his toes—literally."

They spent the greater part of the evening together. They danced the rumba, the paso doble, the Charleston. Vera drank a lot, was in high spirits, sang along with the music. She knew that her partner was Jewish, for he had told her when he introduced himself. But Semitic, anti-Semitic, those terms had no meaning for her; she attended no church, Dr. Grün set foot in no synagogue, and both considered themselves free of prejudice. They were modern-thinking people.

In the weeks that followed, they saw a lot of each other. Dr. Grün was convinced that Vera, a dyed-in-the-wool Berliner—"true blue," to use Vera's phrase—could turn him into a Berliner too. Besides, he expected that she would help him expand his practice.

Vera must also have drawn up her balance sheet. By now she was in her mid-thirties. Her age must have played an important part in her second marriage, as it had done in her first. Dr. Grün was a good-looking man, and Vera was a visual person, someone who valued appearances. He did not look Jewish; if anything, he resembled an Arab.

The two sums did not, as it happened, come out even. In the early months of their marriage they sometimes worked together. At Grün's request, Vera photographed people as they ate, shoveling in food, poking about on their plates, devouring their forkfuls. He scrutinized the pictures at length and took notes. She also shot leg positions, but neither study resulted in a publishable photo series, and both consumed a great deal of her time. Though she was highly regarded by her publisher, she was by no means indispensable. She could not afford any lengthy interruption in her work. Always new ideas, always witty, always solid—no one could be allowed to be better than Vera Jadow. She had to remain at the center.

And as an observer, Dr. Grün had to remain on the periphery. He continued his researches into human behavior and made notes for eventual publication. Hidden by the drapes, he spent hour upon hour standing at the window of his apartment, watching. When he went for a walk, he stalked his prey, and when she was with him, Vera felt herself constantly under scrutiny, which became irritating. He was less interested in his patients' tales than in their behavior: the way they lay on the couch, the way they moved their hands, their legs, their heads. How did this patient hang up his coat—the front or the back to the wall? None of it was much use to the patient, but it was crucial to Grün's studies. A true Freudian, he could recognize in almost every gesture that deviated from the norm a form of repressed sexuality.

For a time it looked as if Vera was in a position to free her husband's sexuality from its repression—until the observations and notes he would not stop making even in bed robbed even her of her self-assurance. Neither of them wanted children; the question had been discussed and settled before the wedding.

Their constant preoccupation with people had turned both of them into cynics. No church wedding, no wedding supper. "I've had all that," Vera said. "I had it when I was no more than a baby." When Dr. Grün asked if she would like to meet his father, who lived in Lodz, she said, "A father-in-law is something else I had before."

They bought a beautifully appointed house in the Steglitz district, near the Teltow Canal. But Vera did not give up her studio and darkroom in Tempelhof, nor did she give up her friends. Her husband continued to live in the zone of distance afforded him by his profession: a psychoanalyst, both attractive and repellent.

Once a month Vera held an open house. At the beginning fifty or more guests came, some to eat their fill, some because it was considered chic to be on Vera's guest list, some to enjoy the genuine bourbon she favored, and some attracted by her jazz records. But even before Hitler's seizure of power a number of the regulars became conspicuous by their absence. Now it was the observer, Dr. Grün, who became the subject of observation. Did he not really look very Jewish? Was it true that he had his women patients lie down on a couch? It was said that some of their sessions lasted over two hours. His practice, rather than growing, began to shrink. In the end he was left with a mere four patients, two of whom he was treating without charge. He spent his afternoons at the movies, where he carried on his researches both with the audience members and with the characters on the screen, which necessitated repeated viewings of the same film. That, too, aroused suspicion. Later, when the box offices began to display the sign "Jews Not Welcome," this field of observation was also closed to him.

When Maximiliane arrived at Hermannswerder, Dr. Grün expressed a desire to meet "this issue of a Berlin woman and a Pomeranian country gentleman." Maximiliane was sent an invitation. She came, and Dr. Grün put her through a series of tests. He asked her to make a fist, a request with which she complied innocently, her thumb rigidly sticking upward—she was still in her phallic phase. He watched her detach a bite of cake with her fork, twist it a little, and guide it to her mouth. He asked her to show him her hands, the hands with the chewed nails. Dr. Grün was well satisfied with the visit. "Come back soon." But on subsequent occasions Maximiliane could always think up reasons for refusing.

When she had time, Vera met Maximiliane at the white bridge in her car, drove her to the Wannsee, bought her ice cream or clothes. If they ran into someone Vera knew, she said, "This is Maximiliane, a little baroness from Pomerania," never "This is my daughter." When Maximiliane reported that she had joined the League of German Girls, Vera bought her a uniform.

"Why don't you wear it out of the store? It looks wonderful on you," she suggested.

"But I'm not on duty now, Vera!"

"What difference does that make?"

A few times Vera was able to arrange things in such a way that she could pick Maximiliane up after her League meetings and drive her in the open convertible to the magazine headquarters before taking her home. "My husband is in his room. We'll sit on the balcony. I'll fix us some iced chocolate." Contrivances Maximiliane was unable to see through. For some time her mother used her like a Party badge. At first Maximiliane did not know that Dr. Grün was Jewish; when she found out, she tried to suppress the knowledge.

One day Maximiliane was called in to see the housemother. "My dear child. Please sit down." She opened a newspaper, laid it in front of Maximiliane, and went to the window, allowing the girl time to look at the picture. Then she asked, "Do you know that woman?"

"No," Maximiliane said. No cock crowed.

"Isn't it the woman who called for you here a couple of times in her car?"

"No."

Maximiliane did not move. Her knees were pressed together, her elbows tight against her sides. She sat staring at the picture, which took up half a page of the newspaper. Eight uniformed men, and at their center a woman with a sign around her neck. The sign read, "I'm the biggest pig you ever knew, I'll do anything with a Jew." Next to the woman stood a stout man, no longer young, hat in hand, tie askew, also with a sign around his neck. His read, "The German girls are what I like–me, a Jewboy and a kike."

"You won't reconsider your answer, Maximiliane? We only want to help you."

Maximiliane repeated her denial without giving it a second thought, but her face was beet-red and her voice trembled.

"All right, then, go to your room."

That afternoon, during her free period, Maximiliane left the school without permission. So as not to arouse suspicion, she sauntered to the bridge, past the gatehouse. Catching sight of the gatekeeper, who was reading the newspaper, she broke into a run. She got to the bus stop, took the suburban line into Berlin, then rode the streetcar as far as the Teltow Canal. Everyone was reading the newspaper, everyone was staring at her. After an hour and a half, out of breath, she reached the Grüns' garden gate.

She rang the bell. When no one answered, she left. The trip back took her three hours. It had grown dark, and suppertime had passed. Again she was called in to see the housemother.

"Where have you been?"

Silence.

"You did not have permission, Maximiliane von Quindt." The housemother used her full name for the first time.

Still Maximiliane made no reply.

"Then go to your room."

164

At the door Maximiliane turned back and asked if she could take the newspaper.

The housemother handed it to her. "But hide it carefully." A deep breath, and then "My dear child." She would have liked to hug the girl, but such was not the Hermannswerder custom.

Maximiliane continued to march though the streets of Potsdam and sing, "Behold the dawning in the East." She danced with the ensigns and sang, "I'm dancing my way into heaven." At evensong she sang the hymns current during those years: "The sun has set, the night is drawing nigh." All with equal zeal—she was seventeen years old.

One day, after the infamous photograph had made its way through all the newspapers, Quindt turned up at the house near the canal. Looking it over, he estimated its cost and the year of its construction. He examined the pines and arrived at an age of forty or fifty years. High windows, bright brass—a residence for the well-to-do. But the sign next to the bell at the garden gate was smudged with dirt, barely decipherable. "Daniel Grün, M.D., By Appointment Only." Quindt rang repeatedly and finally thought he saw a curtain twitch on the second floor. He took one of his cards from his billfold, those same cards on which his name was followed by the initials *M.P.*, and scribbled a message to Vera that he would be waiting for her in the café across the street.

He had waited half an hour before Vera arrived—changed, but invariably elegant, striking, haughty.

Quindt rose, held out a chair for her. No greeting. Both omitted the nonessentials.

"And now?"

Vera shrugged as she inserted a cigarette in a long ebony holder—the same she had used on Poenichen. Before Quindt could locate his matches, she had wielded her lighter. She waved the matches away.

"He's already left?"

"Yes."

"When did he go?"

Vera did not answer.

"Where did he go?"

Again she did not answer.

"You're right. If you don't know, you have no secrets to keep. Do you love him?"

"What does love have to do with it? I'm a Jadow, if you know what that means. Presumably we would have separated sooner or later, but the way things are, that's impossible. Look at me! Is there still room for me in this country? A German woman does not smoke. A German woman presents the Führer with children. If she's not a blond, that's enough to arouse suspicion. It's enough to make her resemble a woman who has an affair with a Jew."

"Do you mean . . ."

"It's not me. The woman in the newspaper must be someone who resembles me. But it could be me—do you understand?"

"It's not hard to understand. Do you have any money saved?"

"Do I look like a woman who knows how to save? I don't lead my life with an eye to the future. I had a couple of good years."

"And he?"

"By the end he had hardly any patients left. A good German has no psychological illnesses."

"So you want to leave as well?"

"Yes. I just haven't made up my mind whether in the canal"–she pointed to the Teltow–"or across the canal with my camera and an overnight bag."

"Did you ever consider Poenichen? You could go underground there for a while. This state of affairs can't go on much longer."

166

"Poenichen? I've had that. No one can swim twice . . . How does it go?"

"In the same river. Is that what you mean?"

"Yes."

The waitress brought their tea in glasses. They broke off their conversation.

"It will take me a couple of days to liquidate some assets. Surely you remember–though the Quindts have plenty of land, they're hardly rich."

"Why would you do that? You're under no obligation. It will cost you. First you got me out of Poenichen–that wasn't exactly cheap either–and now you're prepared to get me out of Germany?"

"It seems so, Vera."

"It seems so, Baron von Quindt on Poenichen."

"And the child? Did she come?"

"Yes, when it was nearly dark."

"And?"

"I wouldn't let her in. Satisfied?"

"We'd best keep her out of it"–he paused–"as my wife likes to say. What about your mother?"

"I married into the middle class, the first Jadow to marry below her station. First a baron and then a Jew. We've had nothing to do with each other for years. I have no talent for motherhood, and I don't have any talent for wifehood, either. It takes too long for us to understand ourselves. I see the whole world only through the lens of my camera, through the viewfinder. That changes your point of view. I live like a one-eyed person."

"In my heavy-handed way I always thought a lot of you."

"Me you too."

The hint of a smile. Then Vera stubbed out the cigarette she had just lit.

"You took care of everything?"

"My car is parked outside the publishing house with the keys in the ignition. Sooner or later someone will take a shine to it. My cleaning lady will be given the house key, as she always is when I go on a trip. I have a commission for a series about the Dutch. I won't come back. That's how easy it is. It's surprising that more people don't take a trip when it's so easy."

"Here is an address for you. Learn it by heart. It would be best if we did not speak or write to each other again. A country where people have stopped speaking. They only shout. Send news when you've landed somewhere."

"Speak softly." Vera rose.

Quindt also got up. "What name will you be using."

"Grün. Quite simply, Vera Grün. No stain will blemish the name of Quindt or the name of Jadow. I'll send my press pass back to the publisher."

"You're bitter, Vera. Couldn't you look at it as a chance for a new beginning? In freedom?"

"I'm forty years old!"

"When you're pushing seventy, that seems very young. Pomeranians aren't emigrants. Nothing but sand— and we get stuck in it."

"Maximiliane will be getting married before long, and then you'll—" She broke off. "I can't care about the future of Poenichen!" She pulled down the veil of her little hat, pointing at the tea she had not finished. "Will you take care of it?"

"One week—that's the most it will take by my reckoning. In Amsterdam, make inquiries at the Mejer en Van Hoogstraten Bank. And Vera—thank you for the child."

"We're even, then."

She did not put out her hand. She did not look back. Quindt sat down again and finished his cigar before beckoning to the waitress.

When she came, she pointed to the door. "Do you know who that was?"

"Yes, miss, I know very well."

168

"Someone like that—you can only spit at her."

Quindt looked at her. Repeating her words, he decided to return to Poenichen as quickly as possible and to return to Berlin as seldom as possible.

Vera's doorbell rang only a few minutes after she had returned home. It was a man in civilian clothes who did not introduce himself and had clearly observed both her departure and her return. The Reich Ministry for the People's Education deeply regretted the incident, he said. A denunciation. An overzealous, rash person. Presumably an act of revenge. Someone like herself must have enemies. Unfortunately there was no way to recall the photograph. The authorities knew, of course, that her Aryan credentials were impeccable. The researches that had been initiated had resulted in the discovery that she was the widow of a deserving frontline soldier. Furthermore, she had never adopted the name of the Jew Grün. According to the new laws for the protection of German blood and German honor, divorce was a mere formality. To the best of the authorities' knowledge, the Jew Grün had already decamped. Presumably to Vienna. Or Galicia.

Vera listened in silence. They were still standing in the front hall, where it was dusky.

Of course the authorities knew that she was one of the best German photojournalists. Nor would the magazine be forced to do without her services in future— provided, of course, that she would cooperate. A series about the new German woman, for example. Of course her photographs would henceforth have to pass inspection.

When the man stopped speaking, Vera raised her right hand in the German salute while opening the front door with her left. She did not tell him that the whole incident had been a case of mistaken identity.

Twenty-four hours later she was on a train headed for the Dutch border, armed with her camera and an overnight case. As soon as they had crossed into Holland, she placed the newspaper picture in her passport, intending it to legitimize her claim that she was a political refugee. It turned out to be worth less than she supposed. From that day on she was the wife of a Jew, and destitute Jews were not in demand anywhere in the world.

Quindt used his stay in Berlin for the additional purpose of checking into the whereabouts of Willem Riepe. Next he went to his bank. The negotiations took two hours, and he had to mortgage Poenichen to the hilt. Presumably the matter would not be resolved without the sale of some land. Since he needed the money immediately, the interest was disproportionately high. Because of the currency freeze, it was not possible simply to transfer the sum from one bank to another, so he had to find a middleman to smuggle the money into Holland; that, too, was costly.

He denied himself a reunion with Maximiliane.

On the way to the railroad station Quindt spotted a unit of men in brown uniforms marching toward him, singing, following the flag. The pedestrians stopped on the sidewalk, saluting with upraised arms; a few quickly turned down the side streets. He saw no alternative but to take refuge through the handiest shop door. He had entered a lingerie store. Recognized as a wealthy man from the country, he was shown a selection of corselets, some flesh-colored and some extravagantly black. He decided to buy one of the flesh-colored kind.

When Riepe met him at the train, Quindt was tired. "What times we live in, Riepe."

Riepe agreed. "Yes, Baron, sir, what times indeed." Then he asked, "And what about Willem?"

"Oh, well, Riepe, what can you expect? Oranienburg Concentration Camp, I'm told. And for how long, nobody knows. He couldn't quit handing out fliers. His wife is

170

allowed to bring him something once a week, when she has it."

"If only he'd stayed on Poenichen!"

"We can't all bury our heads in the sand, Riepe. I take a different view of a number of things today. Until now I always thought that it would blow over. After all, on Poenichen we have only Priebe, and we can handle him."

"And Palcke the foreman, Baron, sir. And Meier. And others."

"You're right, Riepe. They sang 'Germany, Awake,' and now the wrong sort have awakened and the right sort are asleep."

Before a week had passed, Palcke, the estate foreman, appeared unbidden in Quindt's office. "Just one question, Herr von Quindt."

The question turned into a discussion, and the discussion into a resignation.

Until now Quindt had not taken his estate foreman seriously enough. To his wife and occasionally to some of his neighbors he had spoken of "pushy Palcke," because the foreman stuck his nose in things that did not concern him. Repeatedly he had insisted on "inspection of the books," which were kept by Herr Meier, the distiller.

"Why another mortgage?" Palcke now demanded. "How do you intend investing the borrowed funds on the land?"

Quindt refused to explain. Herr Palcke promised to investigate, and since Priebe was not a sufficiently weighty threat, he threatened the intervention of the Party head for the whole county.

"And there is a Regional Office in Stettin."

Quindt suggested that the incident be reported straightaway to the Führer.

Both men grew sharper than was necessary.

"The time of the great landed estates is past," Herr Palcke asserted.

Quindt retorted that he'd heard the same sentiment from the Communists, though that had been some years earlier. At the moment the time of his chief foreman was past. What he needed on Poenichen was a farmer, and he had hired him, Palcke, because he was a good farmer–an opinion he still held. What he did not need was a politician, good or bad.

The period of formal notice had to be respected. Palcke could not be rushed to the ten-o'clock train by Riepe, as Quindt would have wished.

Herr Palcke used his remaining time to foment sentiment against Baron von Quindt; he created bad blood among the farmworkers and stirred up the people in the village. "The German nation," "sturdy German peasantry," "blood and soil"–the catchphrases were delivered to his house with the newspapers.

For the time being Quindt asked Riepe to take his letters to Stargard and post them in the mailbox at the railroad station. Soon even that procedure did not seem safe enough. He stopped writing letters altogether.

Quindt had regularly suffered an attack of rheumatism every single May Day, thus being prevented from participating in the festivities and singing held in the workers' mess. This year he suffered a severe attack as early as March, just in time for the Reichstag elections. Confined to bed, he was in no position to go to the polls.

At eleven o'clock in the morning on election Sunday four men appeared at the mansion. They wore brown shirts and swastika armbands–election volunteers, two of them farmworkers. Their boots clattered up the stairs, marking the first time either of them had set foot on the staircase; they had never been allowed beyond the front hall. The dogs, accustomed neither to boots nor to uniforms, began to bark; no one calmed them.

172

"We'll help you." Herr Griesemann's offer sounded like a threat.

"I'm an old, sick man," Quindt replied.

"The local Party leader desires a hundred-percent turnout at the polls."

"Then I have no choice? I notice that you gentlemen are in uniform. May I ask you to wait in the hall and send Riepe in to me?"

Quindt asked Riepe to fetch his uniform coat. With his own hands he removed the mothballs from the pockets, saying grimly, "Let's show them, Riepe." He also asked for the "the box—my wife will know what I mean."

He put the "box" on the coverlet, took from it all the Quindt medals, and attached them to the coat one by one: the Distinguished Service Medal of the Prussian Crown; the Military Distinguished Service Medal First Class; the red Imperial Medal Second Class, awarded posthumously to his grandfather after the Battle of Vionville; the Prussian Medal of Honor; the Iron Cross First Class, which Hindenburg had personally pinned on him after the Battle of Tannenberg; and the Order of the House of Hohenzollern, earned by his father. Everything down to the Pour le Merite and the Order of the Crown. Almost the entire panoply of Prussian medals across his chest. It took him half an hour to dress.

His wife came in. "Quindt, don't go too far."

Quindt was a heavy man, and obstinacy doubled his weight. It took all four men to carry him down the stairs in a wicker chair, through the front hall, down the steps, and place him in the Plaid, which was still used on special occasions. He begged the Party members to join him in the carriage. "You'll walk, Sophie Charlotte." Two horses drew him to the polling place, the local inn.

"Given such cooperation by the Party, surely one has no choice but to acquiesce," he said to Local Leader Priebe, who was standing next to the ballot box. Priebe came to attention before the Baron's cavalry captain's uniform, raising his arm in the German salute. "Heil Hitler, Herr von Quindt."

Quindt tried valiantly to raise his arthritic right arm but failed. He begged one of the volunteers to help him. "Heil," he said. "Heil Hitler."

When Quindt had dutifully exercised his franchise, he pushed the uniformed men aside, grimly left the polling place, sent Riepe and the carriage on ahead, and walked down the village street and through the grounds before disappearing inside the mansion.

The election results showed that of the ninety-two eligible voters in Poenichen, ninety-two had voted for the National Socialists. In Pomerania free elections had always run into snags anyway. When Quindt himself had been a candidate, his estate foreman had stood beside the ballot box while Quindt personally poured a drink for each voter—two for those where the outcome was not absolutely certain.

Herr Palcke had to depart, but so also did Anna Riepe. The past winter she had pulled her chair over to the stove more and more frequently, but she had never complained. She had lost weight, and only her stomach seemed bloated. Frau von Quindt had repeatedly suggested sending for Dr. Wittkow, but each time Anna Riepe had declared, "Nobody's gonna touch me. It's nothing. I'm just old." Finally she stopped eating almost entirely, except for cottage cheese and chamomile tea.

"That's not enough to do your work on, Anna. That's not enough to keep a bird alive," Riepe said.

"There's no need to, Otto," she answered.

She lasted in bed for a week. Dr. Wittkow was summoned. He prescribed opium drops against the pain.

When Maximiliane came home during her next vacation, Anna Riepe was already buried. A new housekeeper had taken the place of her Amma.

174

And the farm was supervised by the former manager of Perchen estate, a Herr Kalinski. The von Kalcks had their troubles, too. Old von Kalck no longer looked after his affairs, and his son had to get along without a manager; they had had to sell off land. "I'll see him broke and landless yet," Quindt said. During recent years several of his neighbors had had to give up their estates.

He himself had struck it lucky with Herr Kalinski. He understood about Pomeranian soil, he understood the local people, he had worked his way up from milker to dairyman to estate foreman, and as far as politics went, he generally said, "I have full confidence in the Führer." That statement made any further political discussions unnecessary.

Maximiliane arrived wearing her uniform. "Notice anything, Grandfather?"

He had noticed nothing.

"Can't you see? I've been made a troop leader. And I bet next year I'll be promoted to group leader."

Quindt made no comment. It could not hurt for Poenichen to see her in her uniform now and then.

He did say casually one night, when the three of them were at long last sitting together at the supper table again, "By the way, I've heard from Vera. She is in safety. Her house at the Teltow Canal has been officially sealed off."

Maximiliane lowered her eyes. Where this safety lay–in Holland, England, or the United States–he did not say and she did not ask.

17

Following the Olympic Games, which were held in Berlin in the summer of 1936, a family reunion was to take place on Mount Eyckel, the Quindts' ancestral seat in the mountains of Franconia. The idea had been conceived by Quindt's older sister, the same Maximiliane Hedwig von Quindt who had in absentia accepted the godmother's duty for Maximiliane. Unmarried, she lived in Eyckel Castle and worked the land.

The castle, which had retained very few acres, had been passed down for several generations in an unusual way: it was handed on from one unmarried Quindt woman to the next unmarried Quindt woman. This method of inheritance proclaimed not only the under-developed sexual drive in at least some branches of the clan–exaggerated in a few female members to the point of animosity toward reproduction–but also the Quindt women's striving for emancipation. When a daughter was born on Poenichen in August 1918, thus assuring further progeny, the old baroness on Mount Eyckel secretly hoped she had found her heir.

The family reunion was in the hands of a young Quint from Breslau who was interested in genealogy in general and Quindt genealogy in particular. People would be housed in those parts of the castle that were still livable, some of them sleeping on mattresses in dormitories; the young people would be quartered in tents.

More than a hundred relatives were expected. The most aristocratic representatives of the Quindt clan, such as Ferdinand von Quindt, a former panel president with the Reich Administrative Court, refused to attend after they learned that the participants would be for the most part middle-class–"Quindts who have come down in the world," as they put it. They feared that the reunion might degenerate into a kind of folk festival.

The flags of all nations were still waving over Berlin, outstanding among them the two flags of the victorious German nation. In consideration of visitors from abroad, the signs reading "Jews Not Welcome" had been temporarily removed from shops and movie houses. The world was impressed by the new Germany.

Reflected Olympic glory was shed on the Quindt family reunion. Both the Swedish and Alsatian branches had seen the Führer at the closing rally. "With our own eyes!"

Maximiliane, the only child, suddenly found herself at the center of a huge family. No sooner had she arrived at the railroad station than she was met and hugged by quantities of unknown Quindts. Uncles and cousins kissed her for no other reason than that they were Uncle Max or Cousin Ingo. She was by turns confused, happy, and embarrassed. She had never traveled so far before, had never seen the mountains before, was not familiar with market squares surrounded by half-timbered houses, with burbling fountains, with rocks, caves, and river valleys, with lady's slipper and carline thistle. Nor was she used to romantic castles, to wells and drawbridges. From the wooden guardrail around the tall tower three distant castles could be seen. And always Ingo Brandes from Bamberg was at her side, ready to explain everything, making jokes about everything. He was a high-school student in his final year and explained that his father was merely a Quindt by marriage.

In the courtyard tables and benches had been set up. In the stew kettle green-pea or goulash soup bubbled. And in the old keep several barrels of beer reposed, a donation from Herr Brandes, the brewer from Bamberg.

Like her Pomeranian brother, Aunt Maximiliane had a predilection for stairs. She always stood a little higher than the others, usually near the front gate where she could control them—an old-fashioned figure, as if woven by hand, her graying braids wound around her head. Maximiliane faced her, speechless, curtsied too late and too deeply, and stared reverently at the head of the ancestress, her grandfather's "Hats off" still ringing in her ears.

"You must be a Quindt," her aunt said.

"Yes." Maximiliane blushed. That was exactly what she must be.

"Where did you get your eyes?"

Maximiliane could answer this question only by lowering her lids.

"Anyway, you don't have the Quindt nose." This was true but seemed a distinct advantage for a young girl. "You should wear dirndl dresses, part your hair in the middle, and knot it at the nape."

Though these sounded like commands, Maximiliane did not follow them until some time later; and they determined the way she looked for a number of years.

As other arrivals had to be greeted, Maximiliane stepped aside. She had looked forward to sleeping in one of the tents that had been set up in the small castle garden, but her aunt had already decreed that Maximiliane should sleep in the bedchamber next to her own. The decision was based on Maximiliane's eyes, the succession, and Ingo Brandes. For the rest, Maximiliane was assigned to kitchen duty. She made up jelly-and-dripping sandwiches, which were passed around on tin plates.

All sorts of Quindts arrived, some with names ending in *dt*, some with a final *t*, and some with *ten*. Quindts from East Prussia, Quints from Lusatia, from Hessen, from Alsatia. Estate owners, high-school teachers, farmers. One eighty-year-old August von Quinten from Lübeck, symbol of the life expectancy of all the Quindts and a four-year-old from Strasbourg, bearer of the name, good-looking, blond, healthy, worldly wise: the embodiment of the continuity of an old line. Poor and rich relations, wealthy or land-proud, blond ones and dark-haired ones, even two redheads; some Protestant, some Catholic. Much getting acquainted and reacquainted, exchanging news of deaths and births. Those who could not come were present as photographs carried in wallets and pulled out of pockets. All had one name and, for three days, one mind. Laughing, they washed in tubs and at the well. "Visions of the Middle Ages," one Nuremberg newspaper wrote.

The aristocratic Quindts–among them many impoverished ones–were housed in bedrooms; the middle-class Quindts–among them many high officials, well-to-do merchants, and their wives–were put up in the mattress dormitories. As a result, some of them left the very next morning. The others expressed their approval of all the arrangements after Max von Quindt, Maximiliane's great-uncle from East Prussia, said forcefully, "To participate means to agree." He had come by ship; he would never take the train through the Polish Corridor, traveling through German lands in a closed compartment!

The first night's introductory ceremony took place in the courtyard by torchlight. As added illumination, the moon rose over the top of the towers. Adolf von Quindt, a military historian from Friedberg in Hessen, delivered the welcoming address. "A family that can trace its history back six hundred years has every reason to face the future with confidence. Not demands and rights but devotion and willingness to serve secure man's

179

liberty and future. Once the Quindts conquered, settled, and defended the East in their role as knights. Quindts in East Prussia, Quindts in Pomerania. In 1917 they were expelled from the Baltic region, but not for all time!"

He expressed everyone's feelings; applause greeted every sentence. One by one he welcomed the visitors by name, and each stood at the appropriate moment.

"The Quindts on Poenichen in Pomerania." Maximiliane rose, standing alone—an additional reason to welcome her with special warmth. She was urged to step up on the bench so that everyone could see her, which gave those at the farthest remove the impression that she was an unusually tall girl.

The four-year-old was lifted up on the table. "Je suis Maurice de Strasbourg, le plus petit Quinte," he said, blowing kisses in all directions.

Then it was the turn of Viktor Quint from Breslau, the young man who had so efficiently organized the event. In the light of the torch he was holding stood a young man in the uniform of a Labor Service leader, modestly fending off all thanks and applause.

"Lars Larsson from Uppsala, with his wife, Louisa, the sister of our esteemed chatelaine, if I may so call her in this exalted hour." The Larssons, with their four grandchildren, rose and shouted, "Hej" and "Hejsan."

"Let it not be said, as I've heard repeatedly, that the women are 'only born Quindts' or 'only Quindts by marriage,' " the speaker continued. "Quindt daughters vanish. Quindt wives come into being. Women marry in and marry out: the family's lifeline. Because of them, there is a constant renewal of—yes, I may be allowed the phrase here—of the Quindt blood; no less. The men lend the name, the women fill it with blood."

Goblets of beer and apple juice were raised to toast the women, and the speaker went on. "In his great call to the youth of Germany, in Berlin on the first of May after the assumption of power, the Führer said, 'Because it is our will, it must succeed.' That is the spirit of Immanuel Kant. 'We live in a time of the greatest historical upheavals, such as may overtake a people only twice in a millennium. Fortunate the young who cannot only witness but also help shape and embody this mighty historical movement.' With these words of Adolf Hitler I welcome all the young Quindts, the flowering of the many-branched tree of the Quindts."

After this welcoming address they stayed together a while longer, drinking and exchanging stories. The moon rose higher, the crickets chirped in the meadows. Finally the Quints from Lusatia struck up one of the folksongs of their region, and those who lived along the North Sea responded with one of theirs.

Gradually weariness set in, and the wooden benches began to feel hard. Most of the Quindts had made a long journey. Everyone agreed to join in one final song. The waning moon stood over the battlements and was only half visible, and from the valley white mist rose most wonderfully–it was clear that they should serenade the moon. But the front tables had decided differently. "Deutschland, Deutschland über alles" carried the day, and because it had become the custom, it was followed by the Horst Wessel song, with its line about closed ranks. Perhaps some thought about the ranks of the Quindts and Quints, whose family flag was unfurled on the tower next to the black-white-and-red and the swastika.

The following morning a special service was held in the castle chapel. It, too, could be led by a Quint, this one a deacon from Lusatia named Johannes Quint. His thirteen-year-old son played a hymn on the trumpet he had brought along.

The sound of the trumpet had the same effect on Maximiliane as the call of the hunting horn; although she had had the particular features of the various brass

181

instruments explained to her over and over, she was not able to distinguish among them. A shudder ran through her body. Ingo Brandes had made sure that he was standing next to her, closer than necessary–shoe to shoe and elbow to elbow. Deacon Quint based his sermon on a verse from the Gospel of St. John, "This is my commandment, That ye love one another, as I have loved you." Ingo Brandes heard it as an invitation to move even closer. In his concluding prayer the deacon expressed the hope that God might guide the Führer of the German people. After a final hymn, during which Ingo Brandes raised his voice beside her, Maximiliane was moved and elated and in love.

Right after the service an exhibition, Six Hundred Years of the Quindt Family, was opened in the Stone Parlor. This display, too, was the work of Viktor Quint from Breslau. It was mostly given over to charts of ancestors and their descendants. Then there were variations on the Quindt coat of arms: photographs and book plates, woodcuts, paintings on glass. No matter how much the coats of arms differed in detail, all carried in their lower field five leaves or five blooming roses–the number five standing for *quintus*. The upper field was always occupied by a bird, in one case even five birds, interpreted as a goldfinch or a hoopoe; for the Pomeranian Quindts it was geese marching from right to left, three in number. The baptismal gown of the Pomeranian Quindts was among the more admired exhibits. Uncle Max from Königsberg pointed out the coat of arms at chest height. "What a charming place for a coat of arms."

Viktor Quint contented himself with a short speech of explanation.

We will have to pay careful attention to this young Labor Service leader from Breslau, since he will play a major part in Maximiliane's life. His father, a high-school teacher of history and geography, had returned from the war wounded and bitter and had soon thereafter

182

died of his injuries, leaving a wife, five children, and a tiny civil-service pension. Viktor, the second-oldest, had endured a hard childhood.

In addition, for many decades a taint had attached to the Silesian line of the Quints, not because they lacked a title of nobility, but because in 1910 Gerhart Hauptmann had published a novel called *The Fool in Christ, Emanuel Quint*, the story of a religious fanatic who preached repentance in the marketplace, performed miracles, was scorned, and took to the road, always close to madness. The illegitimate son of a minister, he went on to shout, "I am Christ" in his father's church, destroyed pictures and altar fixtures, was suspected of murdering a gardener's daughter, and finally perished in a snowstorm in the Alps. Viktor's grandfather, Leopold Quint, a grain dealer, had sued Gerhart Hauptmann for defaming the name of an old German family, but he lost the suit on all counts.

Viktor Quint had inherited his grandfather's animosities, which extended to religion, tramps, and illegitimacy, as well as to snowstorms. The years of his life had been lean until now: world war, inflation, emergency measures, high unemployment. Since university study was out of the question, he volunteered for the Labor Service, where he had already risen to divisional leader for Central Silesia. He was ambitious and had made up his mind to achieve great things.

Brief though it was, his speech made considerable mention of the Germanization of the Eastern territories, alluded to the matter of proof of ancestry and Aryanism, and proclaimed that no Quindt need worry about his Aryan descent; one glance at the genealogies—and at those present on this occasion—was quite sufficient.

Ingo Brandes asked if he might interrupt for a moment. He had the impression that in the Quindt family there were more ancestors than in other, more ordinary families—as if each of them had a greater number of grandfathers and great-grandfathers. Everyone except the speaker laughed.

The speaker continued, holding up in illustration a family tree artfully arranged in the form of an oak. The original ancestor was the trunk; children, grandchildren, and great-grandchildren were shown as branches and twigs, and so on down to the leaves and acorns. Viktor Quint read out the final entry on one of the acorns: " 'Achim von Quindt, born 1898 on Poenichen, Pomerania. Married 1917 to Vera, née von Jadow.' Perhaps there is someone from this family among us?"

Maximiliane gave no sign.

"A casualty of the war," the chatelaine said.

"Then the line has died out," Viktor Quint noted. "It's unfortunate that the tree has not been brought up to date."

Ingo Brandes pushed Maximiliane forward, whispering, "Go ahead, Pomeranian acorn!"

Maximiliane stepped from the crowd. "Maximiliane Irene von Quindt, born August eighth, 1918, on Poenichen."

Viktor Quint looked at her and saw all there was to see. His eyes were opened.

Wondrous are the ways of love–not to mention the detours. Viktor Quint fell in love at first sight with the marvelous family tree of the Pomeranian Quindts, who had been settled for centuries in the German East, a dying line with a single daughter of marriageable age! He had certainly not set out for the family reunion to find himself a landed Quindt heiress, but suddenly all his plans for the future were made incarnate in Maximiliane: a genetically healthy family; a blond, sturdy woman of the Nordic type, perhaps a little too short, but he was tall enough for both of them. He was not entirely sure of the color of her eyes. Were they blue or brown? Under his searching glance Maximiliane naturally kept her lids lowered. His wish that her eyes be blue

184

was so strong that in the end he persuaded himself and others of Maximiliane's blue-eyedness. He further believed that he loved life in the country, that he felt in himself the spaciousness of the East. There was no blood relationship, only a relationship by name. This, too, he foresaw: Viktor Quint, Poenichen. All this at the very first moment.

Maximiliane did not suspect what was happening in the soul of this Labor Service leader who took such an interest in her family tree. She readily answered his questions, explaining her relationship to the chatelaine and to the Larssons from Uppsala.

"And your mother?" he inquired. "I hope that she has not also passed on?"

"No." Maximiliane blushed again. "She remarried. She lives abroad."

Viktor Quint was nonplussed; he was clever enough, however, to ask no further questions and to content himself with "Aha." She was of Aryan descent; that would have to suffice. "Don't you have a photograph of your estate? It must be splendid country."

Maximiliane showed him the etching of the manor she had brought.

"Our next reunion should be held there."

The afternoon's program consisted of an excursion into the surrounding countryside. On the way they sang; there was much singing throughout the reunion, there being less to talk about than they had supposed when they first assembled.

The air was rather heavy, and clouds were beginning to gather across the blue sky. Maximiliane felt the scenery too narrow and small, the fields like handkerchiefs, and nowhere for her eyes to roam freely; always they stumbled on rocks and mountain chains. But the grain was heavy in the ears, and it had never been more golden. On the flat, grazed mountaintops grew low juniper bushes, crippled birches, and along the path grazed a flock of sheep. There was even a shepherd's trailer!

Ingo Brandes stayed close to her, caught grasshoppers for her, picked a cornflower and a poppy–both bloomed in profusion in the field of oats they were just passing–held them experimentally against her hair, decided that the cornflower suited her better, tucked it behind her ear, and quoted poetry.

What a romance might have had its beginnings here! What letters Ingo would have written her, with dried flowers between the pages, for years on end. If only Maximiliane could have waited. If only it had not been for Poenichen. And Viktor Quint from Breslau.

They arrived at their destination, a stalactite cavern. it was not one of the major caves–quite negligible, really–but one of the visitors, a high-school teacher from Mergentheim, was able to share a number of significant geological facts. They shivered in the cool interior. Ingo was about to draw Maximiliane into a side corridor to show her a stalactite even older than the Quindts when little Maurice from Strasbourg, who was afraid of the dark, began to cry. Maximiliane turned to him, picked him up, and carried him outside–a vision that became indelibly etched in Viktor Quint's mind. The blond boy in the arms of the young woman at the entrance to the cave. Motherhood and security. One's own sacrifice and future security: this girl would make a splendid mother.

But on the way back it was Ingo Brandes who walked by her side again. He proposed a plan. At midnight, when the moon rose and the castle had fallen silent, he would call beneath her window–"Hoo-hoo-hoo," like the owl that frequently hooted at that time of year in that part of the world. The ground under her window was soft, he said. Though the window was narrow, it was wide enough to climb through; he had checked it out that very morning. She'd have to jump no farther

186

than two yards. "And then we'll go swimming in the river by moonlight."

Her objection that she had not brought a bathing suit was met with laughter.

But first they had to get through supper, which meant that three hundred sandwiches had to be made. Supper was followed by a lively evening spearheaded largely by Max von Quindt from Königsberg. A talent for public speaking, and most especially a desire to speak in public, he said, must be a hereditary Quindt trait. His words elicited his audience's laughter. The title of his address was "From Quintus to the Quintillions." "Quintus, the fifth among the feudal lords, the Latinized form of the name; quintillion, a one followed by eighteen zeros, envisioned as the monetary unit beyond the billion during the time of the inflation, a time the older ones among us remember with horror."

He went on to speak of the fifth in music and of musical quintets. During the 1880s there had been a Quindt Quintet in Königsberg. For ten years its members had struggled dutifully to strum the strings, whereupon the Quintet fell victim to the family's proverbial lack of musical talent. A different fate awaited the periodical his grandfather had founded, *Quintoles*. Regrettably, it had been a casualty of the war, like so much else. Now it was up to the young Quindts to bring it back to life. The same Quindt had, in 1880, founded the Quindt Circle, an organization that existed to this day. The present chairman of the Königsberg contingent, which met on the fifth of each month, was his oldest son, Erwin by name and major by rank.

Finally he mentioned "quintessence," according to Aristotle "the true essence of any matter"—the ether, the fifth and highest element. "Unfortunately the famous formulator of Quindt-essences is not present. My dear cousin Joachim von Quindt on Poenichen, former member of the German Reichstag, who had the courage during

187

the war to speak of fields of peace. But he has sent us his charming and only heir."

Again all eyes turned to Maximiliane.

"In the course of the centuries," the speaker continued, "the Quindts increased not only in number but also in stature. Nevertheless, the number of Quindts remained limited–more quality than quantity. Whole parts of the country without Quindts!"

The speech was repeatedly interrupted by laughter. At its conclusion, its author grew reflective. "What a strange emporium is a family! At the moment of conception, the past and the future intersect along real and metaphoric paths. The meeting point of tradition and progress, biology and history, nature and spirit! The life of the individual has its natural boundary: death. But a family does not know the natural law of dying. As a family member, the individual is a link in the chain and thus immortal. In the second part of *Faust* Goethe writes, 'Each one is immortal in his place. One is contented and whole.' That is how we feel on Mount Eyckel– contented and whole." He awaited the applause, which was meant for the chatelaine.

"In this exultant hour I may be allowed to conjure up a vision; a man of the Quindts together with a woman of the Quints conceives a Quindt son, who in his turn joins with another Quint woman to conceive still another Quindt son. A world of Quindts–women, men, children, ministers, doctors, farmers, and brewers." In each case he pointed to the appropriate Quindt. "We're on our way! If conception–"

The chatelaine pounded the ground with her cane. "Enough of conception, Quindt from Königsberg." By which she dictatorially put an undisputed end to his speech.

Even as he concluded, darkness was falling. There was sheet lightning to the west. They cast worried eyes to the skies, but it was too soon to think of dispersing and going to bed. The deacon's son still had to play his
188

trumpet, the Quints from Holstein had to sing one of their dialect songs, and the Larsson grandchildren had to perform a Swedish folk dance. Then Maximiliane stayed to help straighten up. The torches were extinguished, and the smell of tar drifted through the yard. In the dark she bumped into Ingo, who whispered, "Hoo-hoo-hoo." And the voices kept on, the laughter and closing of doors, the sheet lightning.

Maximiliane went to her room, opened the window, and stared out. She put her shoes within easy reach and lay down on the bed fully clothed. Gradually the world fell silent. Only the night song of the crickets, the beating of her heart. A window blew shut, steps sounded on the floor above her room. She was feverish with excitement. Which did not prevent her from falling asleep.

She slept through the owl's cry, slept through the moonlight dip in the river, even slept through the two-hour thunderstorm at dawn. The Swedish grandchildren had to come and shake her to get her up for breakfast; they were surprised to find their Pomeranian cousin sleeping in her dress.

Breakfast was served buffet style in the Stone Parlor. They had to eat standing, since the tables and benches were still wet with rain. All of them talked about the storm and about the lightning that had struck nearby. They also discussed the owl that had hooted near the castle: "A bad omen?" Ingo Brandes caught Maximiliane's eye; she blushed to the roots of her hair.

During the reunion Viktor Quint had been able to persuade the chatelaine that Eyckel Castle was ideally suited to be a youth hostel; all the areas of the castle that now lay idle could and must be renovated so as to pass on to German youth a concept of the German knightly past.

In parting he said to Maximiliane, "I shall come and see this Poenichen for myself."

It sounded almost like a threat.

18

As early as October a letter from this same Viktor Quint without the *d* arrived on Poenichen. He inquired whether he might be so bold as to pay a short visit to Poenichen to further his genealogical researches; polite, determined, and specifying the train by which he would arrive. Maximiliane was on Poenichen at the time; it was her autumn vacation.

"Who is this?" Quindt inquired. "Divisional leader in the Reich Labor Service. Do you recall meeting him?"

Of course she remembered, but she could not think of more than two sentences to say about him. But Quindt's sister Maximiliane had already written two other sentences when she informed him about the renovation of Eyckel Castle into a youth hostel. A young Quint from Breslau was taking care of all the arrangements, she said. Her exact words were, "A sere branch of the Silesian Quints seems to be sprouting mightily. I'll be very surprised if he doesn't make it big."

"Well, then, let that promising Quint without a *d* come," Quindt decided, thinking back to her prediction.

Riepe met him at the station with the car, and Quindt received him on the verandah steps.

Viktor Quint looked handsome in his jodhpurs and riding boots. For the rest he was dressed in mufti: a trenchcoat and traveling cap. He leaped from the car,

190

sprang up the three steps, came to attention, and saluted. "Heil Hitler."

Baron von Quindt used his left arm to raise his right a little way, giving the salute an air of effort and embarrassment. "Yes. Heil Hitler."

Viktor Quint was quick to add, "Please don't trouble yourself. A war wound? The Battle of Tannenberg, wasn't it?"

"Tannenberg, yes. Wound, no. Pomeranian rheumatism." He gave the young man his left hand and bade him welcome, turning himself into an instant left-hander; but that became a nuisance after a while, and he reverted.

In the library a fire was burning in the fireplace. The ladies were expecting the gentlemen for tea. Maximiliane was wearing one of the two dirndl dresses Frau Görke had run up since the reunion—a skirt of forget-me-not blue, a bodice of violet blue, a white embroidered apron, dimples in the hollow of her throat, dimples in her elbows, a dimple in her chin. Her hair was still too short for a proper knot, but it could be made into a kind of low ponytail with a center part, just as her aunt had advised.

Maximiliane herself had set the tea table, demonstrating what young girls learned at Hermannswerder: at every setting a tiny bouquet of blue, late-blooming asters carefully arranged, the napkins folded beautifully, and the china service from Königsberg laid out perfectly. The new housekeeper had baked a Crown Cake. Quindt broke off a piece with his left hand, saying, "A relic from a former time, Crown Cake. It takes a while for outdated forms of government to disappear from the cookbooks. Our previous housekeeper—Anna Riepe, the wife of my coachman, the one who drove you—used to bake a Prince Frederick Cake, better still than this royal concoction. What does that make of precedence? Or take a man like Bismarck. The only thing named after him is a modest pickled herring. One day they'll name a cake, a fish, whatever, after our present–"

"Excuse me for interrupting," the Baroness said, "but our guest's cup is empty. Maximiliane, would you please pour more tea?"

"What I was going to say–" Quindt attempted to pick up where he had left off.

"Surely you were finished with that subject, Quindt?"

There ensued a silence during which Quindt did not speculate that perhaps someday a soup would be named after Adolf Hitler.

Their guest began to speak. He had little skill at tea-table small talk and quickly reduced the conversation to the essentials–the German farmer, who was finally being properly valued again, rising to the station to which he was entitled. " 'For if it were not for the farmer, we would have no bread.' At last that truth is restored to the consciousness of our countrymen."

"Would you say that it applies to the landed estates as well?" Quindt inquired. "In Pomerania we seem to deal more in potatoes than in bread."

It seemed that the visitor was using *bread* in the figurative sense: our daily bread. He began to discourse on political realities. Quindt let him have his say, commenting at the end, "Young friend! Allow an old member of parliament to tell you. There is no such thing as political reality. Politics is fifty percent rhetoric–pure rhetoric–thirty percent speculation, and twenty percent utopia." Quindt was willing to negotiate the percentages.

Young Quint declared that such a way of thinking was reactionary. "It may," he said, "have been true for the Weimar Republic and its demoralizing spirit. In Pomerania, it seems, they are a little–well, if not exactly in the Middle Ages, still. . . . But the National Socialist movement–"

192

"Buried in the sand. Oh, if it were simply a movement, my dear Quint without a *d*! But, to keep things in perspective, in recent years this movement has turned into a gale. Our Local Party Leader Priebe, my dairyman, to take but one example. Or County Leader Kaiser. We have them here, too; they sing along pretty well. We really aren't lacking in National Socialist movement. Rather—"

The Baroness asked Maximiliane to pour the tea once more.

Quindt enjoyed the debate, including his wife's tactful interruptions. On Poenichen he often longed for skillful opponents in argument. He did not need people who shared his opinion—he was well enough acquainted with it himself—but he also did not need men like Priebe, who ducked when the Baron walked through the barns and who put his foot down when he was wearing his armband with the swastika.

By the end of the tea party Old Quindt had taken full measure of the young Quint, who had also gone on to talk of the purpose of his visit—or rather, the means to his end.

They rose, and the Baroness rang for the maid to clear the table. They went to the big hall to look at the ancestors' portraits. In the light of the electric bulbs that had long since replaced the candles in the chandelier, the ancestors stood out more clearly than they did by daylight. But first a respectful look at the rulers. The guest recognized them, named them—"Frederick the Great. Emperor William I. Bismarck. Former Reich President Hindenburg."

Quindt corrected him. "He hangs here as the victor of Tannenberg, not as Reich president."

"And there?" A questioning look.

"You mean the last empty place? You're right, that will have to be carefully considered."

"Surely there's nothing to consider."

Frau Quindt poked her husband.

"Yes, yes, surely there is," Quindt replied. "I ask myself if Hitler would come out better in copper, steel, or oil. Or would you advise a photograph to begin with? For the transition? I have seen one picture that features children handing the Führer bouquets of daisies. Do you consider that typical?"

The Baroness pressed her hand to her aching gall bladder. "Quindt, would you help me to my room? I must lie down for a little while. Excuse me, Herr Quint. My granddaughter will introduce you to our ancestors."

Quindt and his wife left the room. The two young people were alone.

"Do you always have to live with these old people?" Viktor Quint asked.

Maximiliane had never thought of her grandparents as old people. "I'm here only during vacation time, and I spend most of it outdoors. I know my way around better out there. Shall I show you the estate tomorrow? Our lake? Our heath? Our meadow?"

Viktor Quint would not be distracted so easily. His genealogical research had first priority. He made a few notes, retired to his room until suppertime, and read through the documents Herr von Quindt had turned over to him. Then he added to his notes and outlined some questions he intended asking, realizing as he did so that a day and a half would not be enough to finish off the Pomeranian Quindts. He announced as much at supper.

"Why don't you come back at Christmas? I'll be here then, too." Maximiliane blushed as she spoke.

"If you think that's possible? Madam? Herr von Quindt?" All three times a quick bow in the proper direction.

"And your family?" the Baroness asked. "Aren't they expecting you at home? In Breslau? I'm right that you live in Breslau?"

"Yes, Breslau. But I've grown beyond my family. I have an urge to go into the larger world." He was thinking, he said, of establishing a family of his own; he added a few sentences about his background, his childhood and youth, his mother's life, the difficult years of the Weimar Republic.

His description had the desired effect. Especially on Maximiliane. "Five children?" she asked. "Sisters, too?"

"Yes, three sisters."

Though her gall bladder had relaxed, the Baroness drank chamomile tea as a precaution. Quindt, awkwardly using his left hand, noted in passing that during the war to end all wars his neighbor von Kalck on Perchen estate had lost an arm. "During the Battle of Novo-Georgievsk. For a few years he said, 'Eighty-five thousand Russians captured. What price one measly arm?' His wife was his left hand, as it were, and by now he's lost her, too. The son won't be able to keep up the estate. He'll have to take up the white cane, like several of our neighbors."

"White cane?" Viktor Quint asked. "What does that mean?"

"The white canes stand ready inside every front door," Quindt explained. "The Junkers use them for support when they have to leave their estates because of indebtedness."

The young genealogist argued with his host. "On the contrary," he protested. "The German East! The Corridor, an outrage and a humiliation. East Prussia separated from the Reich!"

The Baroness declared supper at an end, and they retired to the library for another hour or so. Maximiliane squatted on the floor by the fireplace, adding pine logs to get the fire going again. Quindt offered doubles. "Pomeranian brandy. Homegrown." But their guest never touched alcohol. He needed a clear head. It was not always an advantage, Quindt objected, to see too clearly.

"What do you mean by that?" the guest asked, but the Baroness interrupted quickly. Quindt had to keep starting the conversation anew, a tiring effort.

"Perhaps you play chess?" he inquired.

"No. I don't have the time."

"Of course," Quindt said. "You have great things ahead. I've heard about that. I myself have rather more time. I retired from public life at an early age. I leave the farming largely to my foreman, Kalinski, a good, sensible man. In the morning a ride through my fields, mostly in the car, in the afternoon a stroll through the barns. The only thing I take care of personally is handing out the allowances and the wages. Actually I see to all the financial affairs personally. Well, even a good foreman can't keep all debts at bay. And who knows? The other way around—a bad foreman and no debts—might be worse."

Again a silence ensued. Using one of the spills Maximiliane made up in great quantities, Quindt lit his cigar. Viktor Quint regretted that his official duties left him so little time for leisure activities. As a leader in the Labor Service, he was occupied with the formation of a new generation of young people. "It can't all be achieved in an eight-hour day—regulations, training, ideals!"

"Is it really possible to achieve those through example and drill? Isn't it a question of biology?"

Thus Quindt provided a new topic. Viktor Quint began to declaim on blood—Nordic blood and inferior blood—the new master race, the genetically sound man. "What is inferior must be eradicated! Mercilessly!" Each of his sentences was so terse and so fraught with meaning that it could be punctuated only with an exclamation point.

Since the biological objectives of young Quint and those of Adolf Hitler could not be realized in the twelve

196

years at their disposal, there is no need to burden the reader further with Viktor's sentiments. It is enough to mention that in his argument Viktor made reference to the speech he had delivered at the family reunion on Mount Eyckel.

Maximiliane, who had been listening with only half an ear while she busied herself with twisting more spills, did not become alert again until their guest began to speak of his personal future. The Reich Labor Service, he said, important as it was in molding the populace, could not fulfill his need for a professional goal. He had been invited to join the Reich Genealogical Office in Berlin. "A new post! A new field of endeavor! Responsible directly to the SS Reichsführer! New territory!" He would begin his new job on January 1, and therefore he might be able to continue in a professional capacity the researches he had just initiated concerning the Pomeranian Quindts. "So if the young lady's invitation . . ."

Old Quindt looked at his wife, who was pressing her hand against her gall bladder in a way that allowed no misunderstanding. "What do you think, Sophie Charlotte? Or are you staying out of it?"

"Must we decide tonight? I'm sure our visitor is tired from his journey."

"I can't imagine such a thing, Sophie Charlotte. What did Napoleon say? 'Five hours' sleep for an older man, six hours for a young man, seven for a woman, and eight for fools.' If sleep is to be the criterion, I must be either very old or very smart."

Viktor Quint, who already suspected hidden meanings behind the Baron's words, rose. Although, he assured them, he personally did not know what it meant to be tired, he would welcome a few hours to lose himself in his researches. He bowed, expressed his thanks, and wished everyone a good night.

The following day was Sunday. A one-dish-meal Sunday.

They had mutton with turnips, underdone in the Pomeranian style. Quindt could not forgo an insinuation. "What was the name of that French king again, one of those Henris?" he asked Maximiliane.

"*Quatre.*"

"That's right, *quatre*. He promised his people a chicken in every pot on Sundays. That was an empty promise. A people needs orders, not promises. The Führer gave an order, and an entire nation began to spoon up one-dish meals. When it comes to mutton and turnips, I share Hitler's taste."

The visitor explained that the dish was new to him but that he found it delicious. He sketched a bow in the Baroness's direction.

Without transition Quindt went from the casserole to farming. "I've been asked to cede a tract of more than a thousand acres to the state. Training grounds for the artillery corps." The land in question was inferior, the roads along it in poor shape, and repairing them much too costly. "The wild boars harvest all the potatoes, though it's true that I myself prefer a good haunch of boar to potatoes. Too bad, Herr Quint, that you did not come on some other Sunday for a piece of the haunch—but the conversion of potatoes into wild boar probably cannot be justified in agricultural terms. We're talking mainly about meadowland right next to the forest I planted just after the war." He had, he added, been an officer in the cavalry, and he realized that the army needed land for maneuvers. "A country must be prepared for war."

Viktor assured Quindt that the Führer wanted only peace, and Quindt assured Viktor that he had no doubts on that point.

"To be prepared for war means to prevent it."

Viktor Quint could only agree.

198

Right after dinner a carriage was brought to the door, a two-seater drawn by two horses. Maximiliane drove with a light hand. At the height of the day the roads were still damp with dew, the wheels ground through the sand, the horses went at a walk. They drove over planks and through the heath. The October sun intensified the gold of the birch leaves. Maximiliane stopped the carriage, jumped over the wheel, and loosely knotted the reins around a birch trunk.

"Come along," she called to Viktor, running ahead toward a large hill. At the top, she stopped and pointed in a sweep across the land. "From here you can see only Poenichen. To the north, the east, the west, the south," she announced.

They drew up at the boat dock. In the bog a stork was stalking frogs. Wild ducks rose from the reeds, assuming a formation in the air.

"Did you see that? They're making a giant *V* in your honor!" Once again she stood with open hands and open arms–this time at the edge of the lake–and her face was wide open as well.

She showed him the best place for pike. "Do you know how to fish?" she asked.

"No, I don't."

"Pike like that"–her arms indicated the length, exaggerating by at least a foot and a half, although any size should have been enough to impress someone who grew up in an apartment–"and eels like that."

"What's that house over there?" Viktor Quint wondered.

"That's where our assistant foreman used to live. He could row the boat standing up. At night he always blew an old hunting horn."

"And where is he now?"

"He left."

"And the house?"

"Empty."

Overcome by memories, she would have liked to tell him all about herself. But she glanced at his expression and fell silent, dropping her arms to her sides.

After some time she asked, "Shall we visit the departed Quindts? After all, you find ancestors much more interesting than living people. Once I'm dead, you can visit me." She flirted in the manner of a child of nature, though one with a "South Pomeranian temperament," as Old Quindt was apt to put it.

"Aren't you cold?" Viktor Quint asked.

"No! I'm never cold. Just feel." She laid her warm hand against his cool neck; he felt a slight prickling of his skin, and she felt it too.

The Quindt necropolis was situated on the slope of Innicher Hill. Since there was no carriage road, one had to walk up. The horses spent the time grazing, the reins hanging loose.

Ten oaks grew above the gravesite, the only ones far and wide, and also sporting autumnal colors; they were about a hundred and fifty years old, sturdy maturity for oaks. No graves beneath them, no rows, only rough stones, erratic rocks from the Ice Age, moss-covered by now. No flowers, only thin, tall wood grasses.

Maximiliane showed her guest the stone that had been placed as a memorial to her father. "He fell in France."

"Where?"

"I don't know." She pointed to a smaller stone without an inscription. "That one is mine. One day I'll lie here."

The wind rustled the leaves, rattled the branches, tossed acorns into the grass. Maximiliane picked up one, rubbed it shiny, and handed it to him. "I am the last acorn on the tree of the Quindts."

Viktor, used to living among men and in barracks, was momentarily overwhelmed by the expanse of the countryside, by this old place of worship, by this gilded child of nature. He took Maximiliane by the arms, shook her, lifted her up until she could look straight into his uncontrolled face. But then he set her back on her feet, regained possession of himself, turned away. He had a plan, and he meant to abide by it. Neatness! Keeping things under wraps! It must have been one of those moments when he felt the Emanuel Quint rising in himself.

Maximiliane stood still, her empty arms dangling. Then she ran to the nearest oak and embraced its trunk. She pressed her cheek, rosy with wind and emotion, against the bark.

They got back in the carriage and covered their legs with a blanket.

"Do you know how to drive?" Maximiliane asked.

"No. But I'd love to try. The horses are as gentle as lambs."

He reached for the reins, but Maximiliane did not give them up at once. Her small, round hands disappeared under his large, bony ones.

She gave him a few instructions. "Your touch must be light but firm. You have to call the horses by name—Monsoon, Mistral."

The horses stopped and turned their heads.

"Now lift the reins, give them a quick shake, and slap them lightly on the horses' backs. The horses need only the slightest hint. They must be made to feel that you're smarter than they are."

Viktor laughed out loud. Maximiliane joined in, showing her wide, sturdy teeth. Viktor assumed that she was laughing at him, and he grabbed the reins harder.

"Can you ride?" Maximiliane inquired.

"I've had no opportunity "

"Good," she said. "Me neither. My legs are too short, and it's not worthwhile acquiring a smaller horse for an only child. We have a tennis court, too, but none of us plays tennis. Do you play?"

201

"No. It appears that here it's important to know how to play chess, ride, drive, play tennis, and fish."

Laughing, they drove along at a light trot. Neither spoke. The sandy Pomeranian soil fell away to either side of them, autumnally bedecked with rose hips and wild plums. Spiders had spread their webs in the juniper bushes, dewdrops glistened, and the air smelled of rotting potato greens. Poenichen meadowland, fallow, slightly undulant, beautiful to look at in the October light, but of course no steaming sod, as Viktor had imagined the German East to be and wanted it to be. Rather, it was an ideal site for maneuvers.

The horses came to the wooden bridge leading across the Drage. Maximiliane threw off the blanket, left the reins to Viktor Quint, and jumped down over the wheel. She broke off a few stalks of reed grass, letting the long, reddish-brown spikes glide through her hands. Then she got back in the cart, and they drove on.

"Don't pull so hard," she commanded. In response, he tightened the reins still more and even used the whip. The horses reared and broke into a full gallop. The cart began to skid, threatening to overturn, and it cost Maximiliane some effort to bring it to a stop. Viktor wiped the perspiration from his forehead and left the reins to her.

"You have to show the horses who is master," he asserted.

Maximiliane corrected him. "Not who's stronger but who's smarter."

They came to the village and drove down the cobbled street with its clayey paths branching off to end in the fields. Outside the low houses the old women sat on benches, their shoulders shrouded in black shawls. The children had staked the goats on the village green and were using sticks to drive the geese into flocks. Ducks quacked and dogs barked. Maximiliane nodded to the right and left, calling out, "Good evening" and "How

202

are you feeling?" and explaining now and again, "That was my midwife, she brought me into the world" or "That was Slewenka, the son of the old smith. Over there, that's Lenchen Priebe–I always played with her. There, under the juniper."

Viktor Quint was astonished. "You played with the village children?"

"Why not? Now, though, I'm here only during my vacations."

"How much longer do you have in school?"

"Two years more. If somebody doesn't take me away sooner." Then, as they passed Priebe, the local Party leader, she called out, "Heil Hitler," her head thrown back, the reins in her lap, a village princess still. Viktor Quint also saluted. The widow Schmaltz said to Klara Slewenka, "He'll take the reins from her soon enough."

They drove through the manor gate at a light trot. At the end of the avenue the manor glowed. Night was rapidly falling over the countryside.

"You like living on Poenichen?" Viktor Quint asked.

Maximiliane nodded, looking at him with damp eyes. "In three days I have to leave again! I won't be allowed to come home until Christmas!" She was suffused with homesickness. As others are overcome by anticipations of pleasure, she fell prey to anticipations of sorrow. Whenever she was to leave Hermannswerder for home, she endured the same suffering for three days. She had trouble with all transitions. She loved Hermannswerder–the school, the island, the lakes, Potsdam, the Party meetings, her girl friends, her teachers–but she loved Poenichen more.

It was arranged that Riepe would drive the visitor to the ten-o'clock train the following morning. While Riepe stowed the luggage in the trunk, Viktor Quint stood by the car with Maximiliane.

The older Quindts came as far as the verandah, where they said good-bye. They waited on the steps, watching the young couple. "That young Quint without a *d* is a man with ideals and principles," Quindt said. "The only question is if they are the right ones. But I prefer someone who is committed to a wrong cause to someone who has no convictions at all."

They saw Viktor Quint place his hand on Maximiliane's shoulder. A hand like a lid. "Did you see that?" Frau von Quindt asked. "He's putting his hands on the child! But what he means is Poenichen!"

"Yes, Sophie Charlotte, that's what he means. And so do I. And so does the child. All of us mean the same thing, so it will have to work out. And now I'll give those fellows the thousand acres for their maneuvers, and I'll use the money to pay off the mortgage. Thirty pieces of silver. A piece of Pomerania for the wife of a Jew who had to flee."

"But does she love him, Quindt?"

"Are you talking about Vera or Maximiliane?"

"I mean our child."

"At eighteen, a girl loves anyone who comes near her. She's like a freshly plowed field clamoring to be seeded."

"Quindt!" She raised her hands to ward off worse.

"Pia from Königsberg. Did anybody ask you if you loved that Pomeranian hayseed Junker? You see! And the two of us have done pretty well. In fact, we keep doing better and better. Now, don't give me that East Prussian blue-eyed look. You've frightened me with it often enough."

Now the car was driving down the avenue. Maximiliane went on waving.

"Aren't we letting the fox into the chicken coop, Quindt?" the Baroness asked.

"Probably. But the fox will be in Berlin most of the time. And we get to keep the chicken coop."

204

19

On the morning of the wedding there had been a brief though wordless disagreement. Herr Riepe had inquired whether the flag should be raised, and Viktor Quint had been forced to realize that in the year 1937 Poenichen did not yet own a swastika. Thereupon it was decided to do without benefit of flags.

This time the whole congregation joined in the traditional hymn. No one from the village wanted to miss the occasion when "the child," "the little Quindt girl," to some still "the little baroness," got married—not even the local Party leader or the Party agrarian leader. The wheat had been reaped, though a few more weeks would have to pass before the potatoes were ready for harvest.

A beautiful morning in late summer. The altar was decorated with bunches of dahlias, the bride and bridegroom were bedecked with myrtle wreath and myrtle bouquet. The bride, in all innocence, was fully entitled to wreath and veil.

The Reverend Merzin performed the ceremony. The old Quindts sat in their patrons' pew, the Baron in the seat to which he was entitled and which had stood vacant for decades. The bridegroom wore a borrowed tailcoat since he considered his uniform unsuitable for a church wedding. But everyone knew: he worked for the Party—and in Berlin, to boot! What he did there they were not entirely certain, but they knew it was "something big." Four of the village children scattered boxwood twigs, two others carried the long Quindt family train.

The Reverend Merzin chose his Bible passage with care this time as well. A selection from the Epistle of James. He addressed his sermon not only to the bridal couple and the Quindts but also to his whole congregation, which had seldom assembled in such numbers at his altar. "What doth it profit, my brethren, though a man say he hath faith, and have not works? can faith save him? If a brother or sister be naked, and destitute of daily food, and one of you say unto them, Depart in peace, be ye warm and filled; notwithstanding ye give them not those things which are needful to the body; what doth it profit? Even so faith, if it hath not works, is dead, being alone. Yea, a man may say, Thou hast faith, and I have works: shew me thy faith without thy works, and I will shew thee my faith by my works. . . . But wilt thou know, O vain man, that faith without works is dead? . . . For as the body without the spirit is dead, so faith without works is dead also."

At the end of his sermon the clergyman turned to the bridal couple. "Substitute the word *love* for the word *faith*. To speak love is useless. To tell love is useless. It is important for both of you to live love at every moment. What you do, you do henceforth for love of one another. Each in the other you love your God. In the other you love the world. Let each of you shoulder the other's burden."

This last was the only sentence Maximiliane heard and remembered and did not understand. Why shouldn't everyone shoulder his own burden?

"Until death do you part." Which it would do.

Both said loudly and honestly, "I do."

During the exchange of rings the congregation sang a hymn. Maximiliane sang along, though it was not the custom on Poenichen for the bride to sing. "I nothing lack if I am His, and He is mine forever." She meant the man at her side rather than the Lord above; she was chock-full of goodwill and had always sung most of her prayers anyway. Subsequently, whenever Viktor spoke of "Him" and "His Realm Will Come," meaning Hitler, Maximiliane applied the words to God. She confused these matters, being more clever than she appeared.

The church wedding did not, of course, meet the bridegroom's expectations; he had conceived of something more like a rite of consecration. But with all due respect to Poenichen, the ceremony could not have been avoided. Besides, he was just as eager as anyone else to preserve tradition. He had not yet come far enough to create new traditions, but he was firmly determined to do so. He thought of nothing else during the ceremony.

The Reverend Merzin said the Lord's Prayer, the congregation supplying the final lines in unison: "For Thine is the kingdom and the power and the glory. Amen." And the sun shone through the windows in the nave, and the bell tolled.

The old Baron stood to the right and the old clergyman to the left of the portal, shaking hands with all the congregation. Quindt said, "You should include another request in your Lord's Prayer, Pastor. 'Give us this day our goodwill.'"

"If it really were my Lord's Prayer, I'd give it some thought, Baron."

Priebe, dairyman and local Party leader, came up to the Baron, pushing his granddaughter Lenchen before him. "The girl is sixteen now, Herr von Quindt. You should engage her as a housemaid. She can wait on the young lady. The two of them used to play together as children, and she's a member of the household in her own way."

"Not exactly, Herr Priebe," Quindt replied. "You have other ways of finding out what's going on in the manor; it'll just take a little longer. And the charges you've been lodging with the county administration—

you can just stop those from now on." He pointed to the golden Party badge on the bridegroom's tailcoat.

The widow Schmaltz, stooped, almost eighty by now, reached for the bride's hand to kiss it, but Maximiliane was startled and drew back. Thereupon the old midwife reached for her child's bridal gown and kissed the hem. Moved, Maximiliane took her hand from her husband's arm, stepped away from him, and kissed the old woman's wrinkled cheeks.

The wedding dinner was held in the large hall using the Courland service, with immortelles for decoration. This time the meal was cooked by Frau Pech, the new housekeeper from Arnswalde, who kept a more frugal kitchen than Anna Riepe had ever done: clear consommé with royal custard, roast loin of veal with braised beans, followed by a dessert of raspberry ice made with the last raspberries from the garden. With the remark "The child only gets married once," Frau von Quindt had had to persuade Kalinski, the estate foreman, to slaughter a calf. He answered all the Baroness's requests and questions with reference to the "four-year plan." Keeping to it made enormous difficulties.

None of Maximiliane's school friends from Hermannswerder had been able to attend the festivities: the school could not shut down for a Pomeranian wedding. Maximiliane was the first to marry out of the schoolroom. But the girls in her class had written her a rhymed poem that she read over and over, weeping each time.

Uncle Max from Königsberg was the first to toast the young couple, recalling his prophetic words at the family reunion—"A man of the Quints together with a woman of the Quindts conceives a Quindt"—and making some of the guests laugh out loud. The joke would probably have gone on if the old Baroness had not focused her lorgnette on him. Later, during the soup, he said to Frau Louisa Larsson, who was seated across the table from him and with whom he was discussing the bride's looks, "That's all baby fat, dear Louisa. She's got a way to go. I know this type of girl–their time comes later. Wait until she's thirty! She'll grow another five centimeters once she's had her first baby, I'll vouch for that." Because Frau Larsson was hard of hearing, Uncle Max had to repeat each sentence twice, until everyone at the table had heard it.

In his after-dinner speech–it was to be the last major speech the old Baron ever made, which is why it should be faithfully recorded–Quindt began by reminding his audience of the field-gray wedding of 1917, now twenty years in the past, to which the bride owed her existence. He mentioned Berlin, the Hotel Adlon, the mock-turtle soup. This time, too, he had little to say about the bridegroom of that former wedding, the father of today's bride, and he was excessively silent about the earlier bride. So there was nothing left except Bismarck and the letter in the family's possession.

"Its contents are sure to be of interest to today's bridegroom," he said, turning in Viktor's direction. "In our nation it is not always easy to be a patriot. . . .' So says the letter. Such a statement from Bismarck may perhaps not always seem appropriate in our circle at a time when there is nothing more splendid than to be a patriot, a German patriot. Two hundred years ago a Quindt was still provincial governor in Poland! Unfortunately we no longer have any ties to the Polish Quindts. Bismarck brought nationalism into politics. The soil hardly cares whose feet walk across it. The important thing is that it be tilled.

"At my last visit to Dramburg–you, Merzin, or if not you then your dear wife, can confirm this–I saw a shopwindow–it was Schacht's butcher shop on the main street–displaying a blood sausage of considerable size. It was in the shape of a swastika. That's what they sell there by the slice. The symbolism is clear to the naked eye–or the naked tongue. Today the best way to patriotism is through the stomach!"

The laughter was hesitant. All eyes turned to the bridegroom, who lost no time in clarifying the situation. Such aberrations, he explained, had by now been successfully prevented by a law against national bad taste. The regulations might not yet have made their way to the farther reaches of Pomerania.

Quindt–chin still firm, clean-shaven now, gray hair cut short, once more attired in one of his green cloth coats from which dangled his pince-nez–firmly stuck to his topic. For his part, he thought mainly of Poenichen when he thought of patriotism, just as Bismarck–quite properly, be it noted–had said in describing Quindt's father.

"When we are young, we want to change the world. I myself had the same desire, and for that reason I became a member of the German Reichstag. Well, I did not change the world; it changed without any help from me. For special reasons that, in consideration of the bride, I do not wish to clarify here–let it only be said, 'Ebert stinks'–I did not run again after the war. At the time I still believed it was my duty to care about Pomerania, and in the end I did no more than care for Poenichen. As a man of seventy, I have no other wish today than that there be no more changes. I further wish that Viktor Quint never lose sight of the welfare of Poenichen, even if at present he is still at the stage of changing the world. 'The dawn is rising in the East,' or however it goes. Let us raise our glasses to Poenichen. Quindt with or without a *d*–that does not matter; all that matters is Poenichen."

The company rose. Everyone looked at each other, which took some time. They drank, looked at each other again, and sat down.

Next Quindt turned to the day of Maximiliane's birth, that "Black Friday" of 1918 when another new bride had made a grandfather of him–a very happy grandfather, as he freely admitted. Of course he alluded to the widow Schmaltz's error, which was greeted with hearty and undisguised laughter. "Then our dear Dr. Wittkow declared, 'The boy is a girl.' Our good midwife Schmaltz went to the kitchen and reported to the house-keeper–for many years the beloved 'Amma' of our bride– 'The baby was born with open hands! Not with fists!' "

"With eyes like that, she doesn't need fists," Uncle Max interjected.

"It was meant differently, dear Cousin Max," Quindt corrected him. " 'That one won't go far,' the midwife claimed, and in answer our Anna Riepe, who had to die far too soon, said, 'Well, she won't have to, she already has everything.' "

Everyone laughed again and took another sip, and Riepe was invited to drink along.

"In the event, the name Maximiliane turned out to be too big," Quindt continued. "One meter fifty-nine. I checked it out only last night. The gradual growth rate can be read off by anyone who likes on the right-hand pillar. The bridegroom will have to make do, but–and perhaps not everyone at this table is aware of the fact– Frederick the Great was the same height, which did not prevent him from being the greatest man in Prussia. What was enough for him must suffice for my grand-daughter."

Briefly and anecdotally Quindt recalled all the "Fräuleins," mentioned the school in Arnswalde, and added a few sentences about Hermannswerder–a bio-graphical summary such as is commonly offered at wed-dings by the father of the bride. He also reported the conversation during which Maximiliane, still a child, had wondered, "But is acquiring a husband really worthwhile for an only child?"

"That, my dear Viktor Quint without the *d*, is what you must determine from this day forward."

The Baron performed his task wittily, providing plenty of opportunities for laughter and drinking. His wife had already leaned back in her chair, relieved; there was no further need for her to ply her lorgnette. He'll come to his conclusion now, she thought, and Riepe can serve dessert. Riepe, also seventy years old, was standing ready at the door. He had acquired a paunch over which his coat barely buttoned, but according to Louisa Larsson, he looked "more baronial than the Baron." This was the last time he would serve at a gala dinner, the last time he would wear the white stockings and cotton gloves, "only for the child."

The guests were comfortably enjoying the speech—at least most of them. Dr. Wittkow, a widower by now; Walter Quint, Viktor's younger brother; Uncle Max; the Reverend Merzin and his wife; the Larssons from Uppsala with the giggling twins, Karen and Britta, who went unreprimanded as they played with their yoyos at the table; Kalinski, the estate foreman, and his wife. All of them were mentioned by name. Nor did Quindt forget to thank the pastor for his beautiful sermon, though he added a few thoughts.

"What we do matters. What we say matters. But what matters just as much, my dear Pastor—and both of us know it and so do the others—is what we don't say and don't do. That counts just as much."

Sophie Charlotte von Quindt found herself forced to reach for her lorgnette after all. Quindt caught her look, which reminded him that he had not yet mentioned the widow Jadow from Charlottenburg and especially the widow Quint from Breslau—omissions he undertook to repair at once.

If only he had not! In this connection he began to speak of the Silesian Quints, a branch of whom he knew very little so far, he said, but a German writer had chosen a Silesian Quint as the model, the hero, for one of his novels. He himself, he continued, was unfamiliar with

212

the book, but to the best of his knowledge it was a work of merit.

"Emanuel Quint! Also without the *d*. Whether he appears in the Quint family tree is something we can surely learn from the bridegroom, a specialist in the field. The epithet 'Fool in Christ'–"

Rising, Viktor supported himself on the table with two clenched fists and struck it repeatedly so that the silver and the crystal tinkled. Without his being aware of it, Maximiliane placed her hand on his arm–the selfsame gesture the Baroness had used for a lifetime when trying to calm her husband.

"Let it be, Quindt," Sophie Charlotte said gently even now, placing her hand on her husband's arm.

But it was too late. A disagreement broke out in front of the assembled company. Viktor, at first controlled and more or less objective, explained that his grandfather had taken Gerhart Hauptmann to court for defamation of character; but as he went on, he grew more and more agitated, speaking of religious fanaticism, and adding a reference to the "Christian mumbo-jumbo" he had had to endure this very day. "In my house"–here he banged the table with his fists–"a new spirit will be installed. At my table a different language will be spoken."

This sentiment struck everyone dumb. The raspberry ice was never served. The Baroness declared the dinner at an end.

An hour later the young couple set out on the wedding trip. They left behind a disturbed party that broke into two camps: the Quindts with a *d* and those without, with a few turncoats.

Grandmother Jadow allied herself with the Quint mother-in-law. Two widows, as they noted–even widowed the same year. The differences were that one had been made a widow at thirty, the other at fifty, and one had led a sheltered life, the only recipient of a civil-service pension in Charlottenburg, while the other had had to raise five children. One did not know or did not want to know where her children were. What an exchange of miseries. What a contest to see whose fate was the more trying. Loss or sacrifice?

"I've raised five children! I've forgotten how to laugh," the widow Quint said.

"My children deserted me," said the widow Jadow.

Two kindred wounded souls. Even on Poenichen they felt neglected, even here. They were only widows. You could do what you wanted to a widow—put her in the smallest, most remote bedroom. The widows retired, "resentful," as Old Quindt noted.

Uncle Max from Königsberg, taller than his cousin by a head, grabbed Quindt by his coat button. "You're going to talk your head into a noose one day."

"A noose? How old-fashioned! In this Reich they have quite other methods," Quindt answered. But he was tired and depressed. Maximiliane had not said good-bye to him. His wife had retired and was sure to have another attack of colic; the housemaid was already on her way upstairs with a hot-water bottle. Dr. Wittkow and the Merzins had left. Walter Quint asked to see the barns and the stables; he was a nice young man, less steely than his brother. Louisa Larsson showed her grandchildren where she had played when she was a little girl. Everywhere there were people who did not belong. Quindt wished he could drive to his forest with Riepe in the Plaid, but the two old men could no longer get into the high-wheeled carriage, and the automobile was not used for such drives.

"I'd rather talk to the trees than to people, Riepe. People's answers annoy me, but the answers of the trees always soothe me."

When Erika Schmaltz returned to the village that night, she had to face a barrage of questions. "What was dished up at the manor?"

214

She began to recite. "Soup, and then loin of veal with—"

But that was not what they wanted to know. "The fight."

"Because of the name," she said. "First they wouldn't stop talking about Quindt, and then suddenly they talked about the Führer."

"What did they say? Were they against him?"

"More like for him," Erika opined. "The young gentleman from Berlin is for, definitely."

But they already knew that.

They could not get anything out of Otto Riepe, either. It used to be that by way of Anna Riepe a tidbit or two reached them. Since Riepe had gone to live with his daughter in the apartment over the distillery, hardly any news got through.

Once again they said in the village, "They've got their troubles, just like us."

20

Kolberg in Pomerania, seaport and ocean spa, located at the point where the Persante flows into the Baltic. In those days it was, and presumably still is, a favorite family resort, with a cathedral to the Virgin Mary and other historic buildings in brick Gothic–in which, however, Maximiliane and Viktor took no interest. They stayed at a hotel near the little woods, where they experienced the usual awkwardnesses of a honeymoon.

The day they arrived, they took their first walk before supper, strolling along the boardwalk on the dunes to the ocean pier. Other resort visitors were doing the same. A few fishing boats were still on the water, and couples pointed them out to each other with quick shouts. "Look at the ship." "There's the lighthouse."

An evening in late summer. The air was clear, the wind blowing from inland was cool. The sun was fast approaching the horizon. Maximiliane had never seen a sunset at sea before. "Let's wait," she begged.

They stood at the end of the pier for almost a quarter of an hour, staring into the west. Viktor did not like to wait, especially not for natural phenomena. Nevertheless, he did not refuse Maximiliane's request. He lit one cigarette, he lit another.

"We could leave," Maximiliane suggested. "We don't have to wait. We can see the sunset from the road."

But once he had made up his mind, Viktor did not retreat. Maximiliane stared into the water, remarking that ever since the Ice Age the waters of the Drage had flowed into the Baltic. But Viktor had no idea what she meant by the comment.

Finally the sun was close to sinking. Maximiliane snuggled her hand into her husband's, but he did not understand her emotion. Not even at this moment did he put his arm around her.

Could it have been that Maximiliane equated the dying of the sun with the death of her innocence? For Viktor it was a sunset like any other, seen a hundred times before, but Maximiliane had grown up in the interior and was used to the clear demarcation between sky and land. Until now the sun had set behind trees or fields, at most behind a hill, and now this alien sun fell into the sea, never to return. The lack of shoreline frightened her. She needed limits. She was married, and she was afraid.

Viktor did not notice her tears because he had already turned to walk back to the hotel. "It's time for supper. We have to change."

It grew dark rapidly. Viktor took two steps for every three of hers. He veered off the paved path, stepped in the sand, and had to take off his shoes and empty them out.

Maximiliane, too, took off her shoes, but she carried them in her hand so she could walk barefoot through the damp sand. "You're not a little girl anymore," Viktor said, and she put her shoes back on. She would never again go barefoot in his presence—though in his absence she did.

Maximiliane called her husband's attention to the evening star. At that time of year it was probably Venus; neither of them knew the names of the stars. "Look," she said, stopping to grab his sleeve and point to the sky. The star gave her renewed courage. There was no lack even of shooting stars, although the time of the Perseid showers was past. There was no lack of wishing or of goodwill.

The word had gone around the small hotel: a newly married couple on their honeymoon, the bride a member of the nobility. There were felicitations, and toasts were drunk to them, all highly embarrassing to Viktor. He had by no means forgotten the incident that had taken place during the wedding dinner.

When Maximiliane, years ago, had watched the stud mount the mare, she had exclaimed, "How wonderful." She had spoken in all innocence and anticipation. And on the evening of her wedding day, too, she looked forward with pleasure to the night to come, though with a girlish admixture of fear as well. She had confused but exciting images of a wedding night, though in her mind she had never thought of night but of woods, grasses, reeds, a cornfield, an open sky, Mother Nature's time. When Viktor paid a brief visit to Poenichen in June, she had been ready to realize her fantasies. In vain. The fact that she went chaste to her bridal bed was purely and solely Viktor's doing. "After we're legally married," he had said to her at the time—and now the time was come.

And he went right to work, managing to deprive her of her innocence. The act was rather like a rape, in spite of her desire to give herself. He was a conqueror who claimed, not devotion, but submission.

As we know, the Quindts' sexual drive had gone underground generations ago. Maximiliane represented erotic virgin soil. Eroticism and sexuality—or rather, sensuality—were dammed up in her and erupted—or rather, could have erupted, given a different lover. In Viktor she came up against a man who took the business of propagation seriously. It was impossible to attain mutual enjoyment with him. But at least they had one thing in common: both were dedicated to continuing the line of

218

the Quindts or Quints. Maximiliane, too, had quite un-consciously chosen this Quint from Breslau for breeding so that the name could remain "Quint on Poenichen." Neither had any right to reproach the other, and neither ever did.

Viktor remained true to his idea of how the marriage was to be consummated. "Did you take the necessary precautions?" Only a few minutes later he was sitting on the edge of the bed smoking a cigarette. He merely took off his pajama bottoms. He did not need to point out to his wife that she was to wear a nightgown; she adapted to his principles. But when she was alone on Poenichen, she continued to sleep in the nude and even returned to the old nursery with its three beds.

As for the act of procreation, for the duration of this marriage she considered her husband's part in it insignificant. Conception and birth were a woman's business, as were raising and training the children. No one had ever tried to give her a biological explanation of the act. The Hermannswerder deaconesses had skimmed lightly over the subject, which at the time still required the utmost delicacy.

Viktor adopted the rhythm method of birth control. In his application of it, however, he departed from its inventors' intentions. The days he chose to perform his marital duties were not those most unlikely to result in impregnation but those that most favored it. The flaws of the rhythm method are well known, and these flaws worked to Maximiliane's advantage; her husband might have contented himself with a single act of intercourse a year if he could have been certain of achieving his objective. He was no saint; it was simply that he saw marriage as the way to realize his eugenic ideals. After all, an entire people believed in the chastity of its Führer. Most of the time Viktor managed manfully to hold his carnal feelings toward his wife in check.

219

That very first night in Kolberg he spoke to her about her "menses," a word with which she was not familiar but whose meaning she suspected. She blushed although the room was dark. At Hermannswerder the girls had spoken of their *"petites malades."* Subsequently Viktor kept a running account of his wife's biological cycle and arranged his visits to Poenichen accordingly. Maximiliane referred to his notebook as "the studbook."

Viktor was one of those men who always wake up at the same hour and immediately leap with both legs from the bed into the new day. That first morning in Kolberg he tried to be quiet as he washed, shaved, and dressed—an unnecessary measure, since his wife was a heavy sleeper. She lay on her back, her arms thrown upward; her hair was loosened and damp with the exertions of sleep, but her face and body were relaxed; her mouth was slightly open, as were her hands. This posture, which would have been of great interest to Dr. Grün, is known nowadays as "the submissive position." She no longer slept curled up like a dog; she had stretched out—burst from the cocoon. It was her best time of day. She was never more beautiful than just before waking.

Viktor had never before seen a sleeping woman—which is not to say that he went into marriage without previous experience. The situation seemed to him improper, and he called her name, first softly, then louder—"Maximiliane." When she did not stir, he drew back the curtain to let in the full light of day. The sun's rays fell on Maximiliane's face. She raised her arm, laid it across her eyes, and went on sleeping. Viktor took hold of her shoulder and shook her.

It was then that she opened her eyes, recognized him, and smiled. Taking his hand, she placed it on her bare breast and lightly stroked its back so that his skin contracted and the hairs stood on end. A physical reaction, beyond his control and therefore unpleasant.

220

"You get goose pimples when I touch you," Maximiliane said, elated.

But Viktor did not appreciate being laughed at. He moved away from her, tugged at his suit, and said, "It's broad daylight." He managed to make her feel ashamed, as he had last night when he asked, "What are you doing?" and she answered truthfully, "I'm saying my prayers." "For heaven's sake." He had laughed out loud. That, too, was never repeated. She never prayed in his presence again.

From the first day of their marriage Viktor treated his wife like a Pomeranian goose, and consequently she behaved like a Pomeranian goose.

The planned five days of the honeymoon seemed long to both of them.

Never again would Viktor go for so many walks as he did in Kolberg. As they walked, he took pains to explain his political views and aims to Maximiliane. He spoke without cease, addressing an inattentive and therefore uncontentious audience. With one foot he stood in the great German past, with the other in the great German future, while Maximiliane stood with both feet firmly planted in the present, with no talent except for the present. Her short sentences–which mostly began with "Look!"–seemed to him simple-minded. He spoke of the earth that He would alter, meaning the entire planet, and what did this Pomeranian goose do? She bent down, buried both hands in the freshly plowed soil they happened to be passing, held out her full hands to him, and said, "That is the earth."

"You'll only get your hands dirty," he replied.

He did not see that the gulls, searching for grubs behind the plowing teams, looked like white flowers, although she pointed directly at them.

"You must break yourself of the habit of pointing at everything."

221

At night they went dancing at the Casino. Since Maximiliane liked to be led, this activity presented no further difficulties. They had always gotten along best when they were dancing. The only problem was that she reached only to his shoulder, which made them look less attractive.

On the way home he even put his arm around her shoulders. She tilted her head back, looked at the stars, and imbued with a desire to please him, recited some lines from a poem: ". . . And 'gainst the stars he brushed his soul, And yet remained a man, as are we all." She stressed the words *he* and *his*.

"And who committed that one?" Viktor was wary.

"Baldur von Schirach." The Reich youth leader.

Without replying, he took his arm from her shoulder and walked on. He was in a bad mood.

On the final morning, when it was barely dawn, Maximiliane jumped out of bed, tore open the curtains and the window, and roused her sleeping husband. "The wild geese! The wild geese are flying past!" she called. "Now autumn will come!" There was a rustling sound, the whistling noise of beating wings, occasional restless caws.

The cry of a bird could waken her though her husband's voice could not.

"Put on your slippers. You'll catch cold," he said from the bed.

21

Every month Viktor handed his wife a sum of money appropriate to his income. Maximiliane passed it on to Martha Riepe, who had been engaged as estate secretary. At Old Quindt's request, Viktor brought the money in cash. "Money can't ever be cash enough," the old man claimed.

Certain domestic changes proved necessary. Shortly before the wedding Viktor had asked to see every room in the manor. "Who lives here?" he said when he and Maximiliane stood at the door to the Green Rooms.

"My mother used to live here," she explained.

"Aha."

Once more there were no questions. The two rooms satisfied his requirements. The smaller one would serve as his study, the larger one would be promoted to marital bedchamber. At dinner he inquired, "Surely somewhere in this house there must be something like a family bed where babies were born and people died through all the generations of Quindts living here. I request that bed for future family events."

The old Baroness lowered her gaze, as did Maximiliane, blushing darkly. Quindt was thoughtful for a long time. "A deathbed? To the best of my knowledge, the Quindts never died in their beds." He mentioned his grandfather and the Battle of Vionville, his father and the duck hunt. He himself, he said, was determined to die neither on the field of honor nor during the hunt, both of which the Quindts had heretofore clearly considered a natural death.

"There is, as far as I can see, no tradition of a bed to die in. And as far as births are concerned, my sisters and I, as best as I can recall, were born in the bed in which I have been sleeping, though badly, for decades. As the arena for the marital act, however–" He interrupted himself to turn to his wife. "Don't listen, Sophie Charlotte." Then he continued, "–it has seen no duty in the past fifty years, and all Maximiliane's parents had was a hotel bed in the Adlon, though they used it with great success."

"Quindt! That's quite enough," his wife objected.

"But no, Sophie Charlotte. Such matters must be discussed. I admit that there hasn't been much conceiving and dying on Poenichen in this century. I myself consider this a deficit, but if my bed represents sufficient tradition, I'll be happy to make it available to you for your marital observances. I can always borrow it back to die in."

Viktor, unable to summon up the least feeling for Quindt's ironic undertone, was silent.

For the moment they were content with the Green Rooms. Once again, the phrase was "for the moment." Though no one said so, now it could only mean until the older Quindts were dead.

New wallpaper, yellow-and-white-striped, and new curtains, white dotted swiss at Maximiliane's request. Not a touch of green anywhere except in the name–the Green Rooms. At Viktor's next visit, the armoires and bureaus were empty. He hung his hunting outfit in the wardrobe, laid a few pieces of underwear in the drawers. What else should he have brought? Everything was already there, even guns and writing materials. Vera's arrival may be recalled; at least she had brought a few hampers into her marriage.

As soon as Viktor was back in Berlin—and he was in Berlin most of the time—Maximiliane took her sheets and returned to the nursery with the three white beds. She went bicycling barefoot and ran barefoot through the grounds. She led two lives—a Sunday life with Viktor, a workaday life without him.

The Baroness retreated more and more to the Ladies' Parlor and left the duties of mistress of the estate to Maximiliane. "Ask me when there's something you don't know, but think before you ask. Later on, there won't be anyone to ask."

So Maximiliane carried on discussions with the gardener, with the housekeeper, with the downstairs maid, with Frau Görke. She became semiresponsible for the linen closet, the laundry shed, the smokehouse, the ice cellar. Raspberries had to be picked and boiled down into jelly, potatoes had to be stored for the winter.

She gave orders for tasks that had already been performed, that had been routine for years. Everything simply went on the way it had always gone on. In November, when it came time to kill the geese, the women sat in the barn and plucked the fowl while they were still warm. Feathers flew, down separated from half-down; the wings were kept for sweeping out the fireplaces. At dinner there was sour game stew with almond dumplings and stewed fruit for the Baron, smoked breast of goose for the young gentleman. There was no need to give orders for this arrangement either; the new young gentleman did not look like anyone who would eat sour game stew. He had come to visit from the city, and he was treated like a visitor and delivered back to the railway station like a visitor.

His letters, which arrived regularly in the middle of the week, contained a brief summary of events in the capital, though these were already familiar from the newspapers. Maximiliane could have left the letters lying around openly had it not been for their postscripts, which made her blush even when she read them alone in her room. Before his visits he wrote, "Please keep me informed about your 'm' so that I will not come at an unsuitable time." After his visits he simply added, "Well?"

After only his third visit Maximiliane could give him the desired news. Fertile soil, where the seed flourished.

During the early months of her pregnancy she did not feel expectant; rather, she was depressed and devoured more apples than usual while reading Rilke's *Book of Hours*. Dr. Wittkow advised diversion. A trip to Berlin would work wonders. Pomeranians always expected wonders from Berlin.

Maximiliane arrived in Berlin on a Friday in the early evening so that Viktor could meet her at the station. He stood on the platform holding flowers; he neglected none of the niceties. The boardinghouse where he lived was near his office. Maximiliane had to content herself with sleeping on the couch, which would have been too short for Viktor. Of course, in every other respect he was extremely considerate of his wife's condition, and there were no caresses aside from the kiss at the railway station. His wife's pregnancy was sacred to him, as was his entire marriage. The first evening they spent in a restaurant. Viktor stinted on nothing, but alcohol might have harmed the baby: apple juice for Maximiliane.

For the first time he had a chance to compare his wife with other women—a comparison that left her at a disadvantage. Maximiliane made an impression only by herself, not among others of her sex.

"You should have your hair done tomorrow," he said in passing. "I hope you brought a change of clothes. Don't you ever wear a hat?"

He did not notice that his wife turned pale, that she did not touch her dessert; he noticed only that she chewed her nails—right in the restaurant. He reached for her hand and looked at her fingers. "Don't ever do that again," he said; not another word. Maximiliane was frightened and ashamed, not of chewing her nails, but of her husband, just as her embarrassment had always been for others and never for herself. She curled her fingers like claws, starting a habit that would persist whenever she was with him.

They walked back along the Spree River. It began to rain. Viktor observed that Maximiliane did not have an umbrella. "Didn't you bring an umbrella? In November?"

"No," she answered, wiping drops of rain from her face. "No one on Poenichen carries an umbrella. We put sacks over our heads if we have to go out in the rain."

"Of course," Viktor said. "On Poenichen."

The following morning he went to his office as usual. That night he would introduce her to some friends. He planned to take her to the movies on Sunday, to the biggest movie palace to see a film with Zarah Leander, Hitler's favorite actress.

As soon as Viktor had left, Maximiliane traveled to Potsdam, listened once more to the carillon in the garrison chapel, crossed the little white bridge to the "island," walked through the damp grounds, entered the school building, and waited in the hall for recess. People called her Frau Quint.

She was no longer part of the class. The school benches formed a barrier between her and her former friends, who had just finished writing a mathematics paper on third-degree parallels.

They asked Maximiliane about her wedding and about her husband, and then they fell into an animated discussion about the story they had had to read for the upcoming German class. "Nothing is more various than the ways of love," quoted Magdalene. "The temptations

227

of the mighty and the easy seduction of the powerless,"
Nettie quoted in return.

Maximiliane, standing to one side, had no idea what
they were talking about. Abruptly she said, "I'm going
to have a baby."

For an instant there was surprise, silence, embarrassment. Then the girls returned to their discussion.
Final exams were coming up.

When recess was over, Maximiliane said good-bye
and left. She went to the little store on the island to buy
some chocolate kisses, as she had in the old days. Seeing
a jar of sour pickles, she bought two, ate them greedily
right out of the package, and just managed to get to the
bushes before she was sick.

On her way back she stopped at a large department
store in Berlin and bought a smocked Georgette blouse
that was highly unbecoming to her. She also bought a
pair of high-heeled shoes in which she could not walk
and a flat, broad-brimmed hat that made her seem even
shorter. Then, after buying the book the girls had been
discussing, she returned to the boardinghouse, where
she passed the time reading while she waited for Viktor
to return.

A screen concealed the washing facilities. She intended no more than to freshen up a little. Perhaps her
husband would like her better if she plucked her eyebrows? She looked for tweezers. Instead she found three
hairpins. A short blond hair was caught in one of them.

The thought of leaving a note never occurred to
her. But at least she changed her shoes, put on her coat,
and replaced the new shoes in the box, which she left
lying beside her suitcase, the smocked Georgette blouse,
the hat, and the new book. Putting her wallet and return
ticket in her pocket, she left the boardinghouse unnoticed
and headed for the railway station.

She spent three quarters of an hour in the third-
class waiting room before catching the train to Stargard,

228

where she had another wait. For the first time no one met her at the station, nor did she telephone. Rather, in spite of the dark, she began the long walk to Poenichen. It took an hour and a half; she ran the last stretch up the avenue.

The lights were still on in the study. Her grandfather rose from his chair; her grandmother merely raised her lorgnette and her eyebrows. Maximiliane closed the door and leaned against it breathlessly, her hair loose on her back, her shoes and the hem of her coat muddied.

"Frau Pech can make you some chamomile tea," her grandmother said.

Maximiliane shook her head. "I'm a runaway, Grandfather."

And Quindt said, "Let's assume you had a good reason."

In a little while the telephone rang. Maximiliane refused to take the call although Viktor claimed that she owed him an explanation.

He made the same demand in a letter that arrived two days later. "You're acting like a child! First a lot of foolish purchases! I'm going to have to be very patient with you. It must have something to do with your condition. You must learn to think for two." Because of her "condition," he wrote, he was prepared to forgive her. He did not hold grudges but thought it best not to come to Poenichen for a few weeks.

Nothing was ever said about the three hairpins.

22

Every year the end of the Ice Age was replayed in Pomerania. The melted snow and ice filled every hollow and depression; new lakes came into being and disappeared only gradually.

The spring of 1938 was not just any spring, replicable. The Thousand-Year Reich lasted twelve years, so each one counted for a lot. Once again the narrator and the reader can feel superior; they know how the story will end. The people on Poenichen did not know, though Old Quindt may have had some premonition. German troops marched into Austria. Two days later the Anschluss was complete. Torchlight parades throughout the entire Reich, now the Greater German Reich.

No torchlight parade was arranged on Poenichen, though Local Party Leader Priebe had asked Dramburg for torches. Finally the Baroness had the attics checked, and some Japanese lanterns were found. They were fitted with candle stubs, and at dusk a group of children wandered down the avenue and through the village streets with the lanterns. Of course the adults refused to carry these childish lanterns, and so they did not participate; instead, they stood outside their cottages, spectators. The children were not even wearing uniforms, nor did anyone know the appropriate songs. Those who did not have lanterns waved little paper swastikas. None of it properly reflected the grandeur of the moment.

Maximiliane paid no attention to the proceedings; she was carrying her child. Humming and singing, she carried it all through that momentous German spring. Her condition did not disfigure her. She rounded out into a complete woman; starting in the fifth month, she felt better and no longer thought of the child as a foreign body but as a human being to whom she could talk. Her girl friends sent her snapshots that showed them doing their Labor Service, posing by the flagstaff at reveille.

In April Aunt Maximiliane's wedding present arrived: an electric incubator for a hundred newborn chicks, to be heated from below and covered with a black iron roof. Quindt examined the monster. "It's so like her," he said. "An artificial chicken." Two days later two baskets of chicks arrived, mid-sized Rhode Island Reds, though for the present light as a feather, all alive. The most exciting day of that spring! Finke the wheelwright built a chicken coop and run, securing both with dense chain-link fencing to protect the little birds from hungry foxes and hawks.

From then on Maximiliane was engaged in poultry raising. Formerly the main growth on Poenichen had been first horses, then dogs.

"We're going downhill," Quindt said. With a glance at his granddaugher's midsection, he qualified his remark. "Unless you decide to add human breeding to our production line."

It was Maximiliane's job to raise the hundred chicks. She had no time to care about the Greater German Reich. She wore a green linen apron to protect her round stomach and a kerchief to hold back her hair, as she had been taught at Hermannswerder. At night and during the cold April showers the chicks sought the protection of the artificial hen. As they grew, it became easy to recognize the roosters by their larger combs; aggressively they fought each other. Whenever a chicken did not reach the incubator in time, Maximiliane scooped up the sopping creature, held it in her cupped hands, and breathed on it softly until its little feathers puffed up. Then she put five or six of them into her apron, warming them against her body like a hen. We cannot help but think about her mother, Vera, who during her pregnancy could not bear the sight of the sucking, smacking lambs, piglets, and puppies.

One night Maximiliane woke up with a start. The cranes were returning, flying so low that they seemed to brush the treetops. She felt the heavy beating of their wings weighing down her heart. Closing the window, she went to a different bed. She never returned to a bed already warmed by sleep. As soon as she awoke, she changed beds in a daze. Often the maid had to make three beds in the morning.

Under the copper beech the violets bloomed, dark-blue ponds in the green lawn. Early in May Hitler traveled to Rome and paid Mussolini a state visit. Parades and ceremonies! Viktor reported in detail by mail about the stability of the Berlin-Rome axis and inquired, as always before closing a letter, about the exact day of Maximiliane's confinement. He assured her that in her most difficult hour he would be by her side.

He was not, as it turned out, by her side; even later, when it would have been necessary, he was not present. At the given moment Maximiliane retired to the marital bed. On this occasion Dr. Wittkow arrived in time, and old Frau Schmaltz staggered around the house until finally Frau Pech took her to the kitchen and gave her a brandy. Her baby was having a baby!

The birth was a long one. Maximiliane had prepared herself for a difficult hour but never counted on eight. Finally Quindt stuck his head in the door. "Get going," he said. "You can't keep it inside forever, you know."

That helped. Ten minutes later the birth was accomplished. The son met all the demands made on him.

232

Fifty-two centimeters long, slender, blond, blue-eyed. He screamed and made fists.

The confinement room became the center of the universe. Historical events, at a great remove at the best of times, retreated even further into the background for some considerable period. At last: the male heir to whom Old Quindt could assign Poenichen–*fidei commissum*, in loyal hands. He did so the very same day–the undivided inheritance to a single male successor, as dictated by the law of entailment, which was still valid on Poenichen.

Viktor Quint, who had naturally informed himself in good time about the conditions of possession and inheritance, had never thought of administering the estate himself, nor had he even considered taking up permanent residence on Poenichen. Greater things needed doing in Berlin. He saw Poenichen as a kind of breeding ground, fertile soil on which his children would flourish.

Dr. Wittkow departed, the lawyer–Dr. Philipp from Dramburg, who had taken over the practice of Dr. Deutsch, the Jewish lawyer–arrived, and the power of attorney for the estate was assigned to the boy's mother until he attained his majority. Two generations skipped, the name changed insignificantly. "It's the blood that counts," Quindt repeated, but this time he said it to the lawyer without a double meaning.

By comparison, what weight could be attached to mobilization in Czechoslovakia, Chamberlain's trip to Berchtesgaden, Daladier's trip to England, Chamberlain's second trip to Germany? Old Quindt occasionally mentioned that there was too much talk of peace for his taste–a bad sign. Too many nonaggression pacts. Between England and Poland, between Poland and the Soviet Union, between Germany and France. And Poenichen only thirty-five miles from the Polish border!

Following family tradition, the boy was named Joachim. The christening and the christening dinner were held in the great hall in compliance with the father's wishes: no hymns, no sermons; nothing but the baptismal ceremony.

Also in compliance with the father's wish, an oil painting of Hitler was hung on the long wall of the hall on the morning of the christening. The Führer's left hand rested lightly on the head of a German shepherd while his right hand vigorously grasped the belt buckle on his uniform coat. The last in the series of rulers' portraits.

When the picture was installed, Viktor announced that they would have to make a decision about whom to remove to make more room.

"After Hitler, there won't be any need of more space," Old Quindt replied.

His words were received with a look of suspicion.

Quindt did not abandon the subject, but he changed it slightly. "You should start giving some thought to when you yourself will want to take your place up there on the wall. You won't have any trouble finding a painter in Berlin. I'd suggest a family tree as your emblem."

Viktor considered the offer an honor but nevertheless said that he would hardly be able to get to it in the near future and that there was plenty of time.

"You know best," Quindt said.

At least the two men were on speaking terms again— one with caution and the other with mistrust, to be sure, but they no longer avoided each other.

For the length of one day Poenichen was resplendent with the full complement of flags. This, too, Viktor had seen to. He was convinced that with the acquisition of a swastika and a portrait of the Führer he had significantly affected life on Poenichen, and no one robbed him of his illusion. Quindt was present when the flags were raised. "Two flags and two national anthems! Not even the British Commonwealth has so much. As far as I know, even the United States of America makes do with one flag and one song."

234

Twenty years earlier Quindt would not have passed up the opportunity to discourse on the word *too* in an after-dinner speech: too big, too much, too high. This time he made no speech in honor of the baptismal child, but at least the baby was the beneficiary of a new custom inaugurated by Quindt: he was served up in the soup tureen of the Courland china. Crying gently, he participated in the dinner as the centerpiece.

Viktor declared that he was not an orator but rather a man of action. Agreement from the foot of the table, where Old Quindt was seated. "Bravo! The Quindts always knew how to speak, drink, and shoot, but they also knew how not to. Let us drink to the hope that at the appropriate moment this child will have the same talent. It's a matter of commission and omission."

Viktor had been able to get leave, and after the christening he remained on Poenichen for a whole week. He spent most of his time in the study bent over the desk, mapping out the family tree of Viktor and Maximiliane Quint, née Quindt, on a large white sheet of paper. Ancestors and descendants all in one, two intertwined trunks growing from the intricate root system of the forebears. On Maximiliane's side the roots reached deep into the sixteenth century, one tendril even burrowing down to the thirteenth century, to the abbess Hedwig von Quinten. At the top Viktor left room for a mighty branch. What a glorious moment for him when he sketched the first limb and wrote in the name of Joachim Quint. One shoot a year, he was firmly determined.

There will be more details to be reported about the shoots.

The sketch was bold; Viktor was skillful at drawing. Sometimes Maximiliane sat beside his desk in the same rocking chair her mother had favored. But she sat quietly; she was nursing her son. A picture to warm the cockles of Viktor's heart! When their glances met, Maximiliane turned the smile intended for her son on his father. Then Viktor returned his undivided attention to the complicated Quindt root system.

Never again would Viktor spend so many days on Poenichen. The work on the family tree was interrupted by his departure. The drawing remained incomplete on the desk top and was carefully dusted. For obvious reasons his visits grew shorter and fewer. In later years he could no longer give himself over to the roots of the Quindts and Quints, though he could still attend to the new shoots.

In the meantime he had learned the skills a Pomeranian country gentleman must master: driving the horses, riding, hunting, fishing. Kalinski, however, felt that the young master from Berlin had a hard hand and ruined the horses. Nor, in Kalinski's opinion, was he a huntsman, merely a marksman. Viktor Quint had the steady eye and firm hand of a sharpshooter. He never missed his prey. When on occasion he brought other men from Berlin for the hunt, they admired him. But Pomeranians did not regard the purpose of the hunt as the bumping off of game.

"Five of that sort, and our woods will soon be bare," Kalinski declared.

When Viktor played a game of chess with Old Quindt, it was the same way: he struck and cleared the field, "without a thought to the losses."

Little Joachim slept in the old Quindt cradle, which was placed on the verandah every morning. The first sound he heard was that of the palm fronds moving in the wind; not a roaring, more a rustle. In later years this sound would remain deep in his consciousness, and he would feel comforted when he heard it, without knowing the reason why.

Rustling of palms, rustling of reeds by the lake. Primal sounds.

236

23

Storks stalked on red legs behind the harrow, clacking their beaks and driving away crows that were also on the lookout for grubs. No other sound except the occasional snorting of the farm horses, coming closer and then moving into the distance again. The horses were harnessed in threes; clouds of sand rose behind them. The grain had been harvested, in the farmyard threshing was under way, in the fields they were plowing and harrowing. The potatoes were in dire need of rain, but there was no rain.

First thing every morning Old Quindt went to the hygrometer to check the humidity. Then he rapped against the barometer, which did not budge from its reading of dry, and finally he looked up at the sky searching for clouds.

Right after this ritual Erika Schmaltz put a bowl of steaming milk soup before him, a salty poor-people's dish but easy to digest. Soon after, Maximiliane appeared, carrying her little boy. She also went straight to the barometer and rapped on it, but she was hoping that it would not rain.

She had already scanned the sky early in the morning, just after sunrise, at the time when her son asked for his first feeding and she, quite naked, sat down with him in the cool of dawn on one of the window seats in the nursery. Never before had detonations been heard with such a happily beating heart. Never before had there been such ardent longing for the rising puffs of smoke from the muzzle flashes.

Maximiliane worried that it would rain. Old Quindt hoped for rain.

For the first time Poenichen Heath was the site of shooting maneuvers for the light artillery with its 10.5-centimeter weapons. The officers had called on the former owner of the tract. Before they could be requisitioned, Quindt had put five riding and coach horses at their disposal. He was greeted with respect: one of the heroes of Tannenberg. On the verandah home-distilled brandy was served, "Pomeranian country wine." The mood was jovial. The ladies asked to be excused, so only the heir was present, sleeping peacefully beneath the palms.

No further disagreeableness except for the discharge and impact, which were impossible not to hear, but the guns were silenced for two hours at noon. Firing practice was necessary, but old Baron von Quindt refused to appear on the practice range. At night the sound of taps could be heard, but at a greater distance and less sharp than Blaskorken's signals had been.

Right after dinner, when her grandparents retired to their rooms, Maximiliane placed her baby in one of the chicks' baskets, added books and diapers as well as a few apples, tied the basket to the handlebars of her bicycle with leather straps, and pedaled to the lake. There she leaned the bicycle against the trunk of an alder, undid the basket, and set it down near the shore in the shade of the tall reeds. Then she took off her dress and lay down on the warm wooden planks of the landing stage, books and apples within easy reach. Rilke and unripe fruit. Without looking up from the page, she banged the unripe apples on the wooden pier until they were soft and the skin broke, allowing the juice to spurt out. The snorting of the horses, the clatter of the storks' beaks, approached and receded again. When she

238

was hot through and through from the sun, she stood up and stretched: sun and mother love and poetry! She moved the basket with the sleeping baby deeper into the reeds, placed her books and the rest of the apples in it, and jumped into the lake.

A slight wind had arisen, rippling the surface of the lake and bending the reeds deeper over the basket. The waves splashed against the leaky skiff that was moored at the pier, keel uppermost. Maximiliane swam far out into the lake, writhing in the water, turning somersaults, her head bobbing above and below the surface until she was dizzy. Then she let the current carry her. A loon kept her company for a while, dove, and disappeared. In the distance she could hear the snorting of the horses, a familiar sound that increased her feeling of well-being.

But at that very moment the plowhorses were disappearing behind a rise in the ground, along with the harrow, storks, and crows. It would be at least an hour before they reappeared. The snorts she heard came from a saddle horse at the shore.

The rider was leading his mount to a shallow cove for a drink when he became aware of a strange sound. It might have come from a kitten that was meant to be drowned. His eyes searched the cove and discovered a basket floating on the water a few feet from the shore, softly rocked by the waves. He jumped from his horse and waded through the water, which did not even reach to the tops of his boots. Seizing the basket, he raised it out of the water and inspected his find. Then he carried the basket with the weeping foundling to shore. The pillows were dry, but the little shirt felt warm with dampness.

The young officer was perplexed. He examined the rest of the basket's contents and found two diapers, several apples, and two books. Hard, green apples for a toothless baby? Rilke and Binding for reading matter?

The baby had stopped crying by now. He put the basket on the sand, sat down next to it, reached for an apple, tapped it softly against his boot before biting into it, and read a few lines.

A sound from the lake caused him to look up, and he saw a head nearing the shore. Then, before his eyes, a young woman rose from the water, wrung out her long hair, and brushed the drops of water from her arms, chest, and hips before catching sight of her audience. She evinced no surprise or startlement but left both of these to the man, who jumped up and pointed to the basket.

"I saved the little weeping Moses from the water," he stuttered.

Maximiliane did not even thank him. She must have taken it for granted that someone would appear to save her child from drowning. Instead she asked, "Moses? Did you say Moses?"

She did not wait for an answer, since the baby had begun to cry again. Expertly spreading a diaper on the sand, she folded it into a triangle, unwrapped the baby, picked him up by the feet and blew away the grains of sand, then swaddled him in the clean diaper and laid him back in the basket. When he had been taken care of, she took the last apple and brought it to the horse, which was cropping tough grasses at the bank. She patted his neck and called him by name: "Falada!" The horse neighed as his shiny teeth crushed the apple. The juice dripped on Maximiliane's shoulder, and the horse licked it away.

Should he have asked, "Does the baby belong to you? Do you belong to the manor?" After all, he had seen the coronet embroidered on the diaper. Should Maximiliane have asked, "Are you associated with the maneuvers?" After all, he was riding Falada. No questions and no introductions were necessary, only comments.

240

"Your eyes are green like the reeds." But by the time he said that, considerable time had already elapsed.

They lay side by side in the sand, swam side by side in the lake. Before they went swimming, he tied Baby Moses' basket to one of the piles of the pier, and the horse to the trunk of an alder. They dove under the surface and rose again, a performance that was not executed without contact. On the horizon the two teams appeared, followed immediately by the sound of the horses' snorting. Falada neighed in answer. And nothing else except dragonflies, loons, and herons. The noontime quiet. Mother Nature's time, accruing no guilt.

They leaned over the pages of the book, wordlessly pointing out sentences to each other like deaf-mutes. The man's finger underlined "As yet they were ignorant and happy. When he looked into the innocent golden ground of her eyes, he sank into unfathomable depths of bliss and knew there was nothing else in the world like this." And Maximiliane's finger replied, "A sweet, heavy scent ran through the nights, and everything made the time hard to bear for those who were in love." High noon, and yet as if it had been written just for the two of them—a legend of chastity.

He took her foot between his hands, using her toes as piano keys to play the theme from Mozart's Sonata in A Major. He had to resort to her right foot because the toes of her left were not enough. He hummed along, but very softly; nothing was really voiced. Nor did Maximiliane ask, "What is that tune? Where does it come from?" Only many years later, at a chamber-music concert, would she recognize the melody.

Like every woman, she was discovered piece by piece. This man discovered her feet. For this, too, she found a verse in Rilke: ". . . And did not believe and named that land the well-situated, the always-sweet, and felt along it for her feet." Maximiliane picked up his officer's cap, which was lying in the sand. "The black cap with the death's head." Falada neighed, demanding another apple.

These days, before leaving for the lake, Maximiliane gathered up enough apples for three.

Joachim did not scream at the crucial moment. As his mother's protector he showed no aptitude. Berlin was far from Poenichen Lake, Viktor seldom present; she was not depriving him of anything. He had neither comprehension of nor use for mermaids and Mother Nature. The baby Moses in his basket on the Nile, the daughter of the Pharaoh: Jewish legends. You would not have got far with him there. "Mose," said the horseman.

Conscience and Mose were fast asleep, and the horseman was not one of those men who say, "But it's broad daylight!" or "But not outdoors!"

Is it important to know the man's name? His age, rank, and unit? His life-span, a short one, would run a mere year more, until the battles around Lemberg in Poland. He would never appear in Maximiliane's life again, and his role in it was almost at an end, but like Blaskorken, he belonged to her mental image of Poenichen Lake. In later years Joachim would call himself Mose, the only confirmation of the dream of a summer's day that lasted for a week in September 1938. How was she to have lived without dreams?

At their second meeting he asked, "Why don't you ride? Why do you use a bicycle?"

"My legs are too short," Maximiliane answered.

His eyes examined her. Legs, knee, thigh. "Try."

She put her foot in his hand, vaulted onto the horse, and sat firmly in the saddle, her toes reaching down to the stirrups. She leaned over the brown mane and spoke with Falada.

That night she stood by the pillar on the verandah. "Measure me again, Grandfather."

He did so and found her taller by five centimeters. Another prophecy had been fulfilled. Every morning Maximiliane washed her hair, rinsed it with chamomile, and dried it in the sun.

On the fourth day they went to the foreman's cottage. "It would just suit us," the man said. "I'd be the fisherman and you'd be my wife. I could go fishing and hunting for you and Mose. But 'I must ride, ride, ride. . . .' "

As soon as he had galloped off, Maximiliane straightened the center part in her hair, which made everything neat again. Once more her hair had turned a little lighter and her skin a little darker. In the shade of the reeds she nursed her child, in the distance Falada neighed, and soon the first bursts of gunfire sounded.

The clouds were still and white against the sky, great towers of cumulus clouds, and over and over plumes of dust rose behind the plowing teams. Thirty acres of Pomeranian barley, seven days' task for two teams. On the last noon the clouds thronged together, rimmed with sulfurous yellow. The wind swelled to a storm, blowing the lovers apart.

That afternoon the sun did not come out again. The storm did not move on until nighttime, ending in sheet lightning. Maximiliane stood on the verandah while her grandfather checked the rain gauge.

"And night and distant riding; for the train of the entire army draws past the park." End of maneuvers.

The following summer more maneuvers would take place on Poenichen Heath. Others would be taking part in them. The following summer. Maximiliane, infused with tenderness, remained behind. The tenderness profited little Joachim, a breast-fed baby. It rarely happened now that she embraced a tree trunk. Instead she looked up when a horse neighed or when the radio emitted piano music.

That September, too, Viktor was unable to come to Poenichen. Instead, he wrote letters. "You will have heard His speech in the Sports Palace over the radio. The cession of the Sudetenland represents His final non-negotiable demand."

Only a few days later the whole world looked to Munich, where Hitler, Mussolini, Daladier, and Chamberlain were meeting. "He has succeeded in preserving world peace," Viktor wrote.

On October 1 German troops marched into the Sudetenland.

Viktor did not come until mid-October, and he had eyes for nothing but his firstborn son. He appeared satisfied with the baby's development, although the little boy cried throughout Viktor's examination, pressing both fists to the drooling mouth where his first tooth was just breaking through. Maximiliane had to soothe and rock him. "Mose," she said, "Mose."

"What are you calling my son? Mose? That's just another way of saying Moses—Moses, of all names!"

"It's such a beautiful name," Maximiliane objected. "But if you don't like to hear it, I won't use it again." Viktor never would hear it again, though she would go on calling her son by that name.

She said, "I ride horseback now. I've grown five centimeters."

"Good for you!" Viktor looked her over searchingly, his gaze coming to rest on her thighs. "You've also grown prettier since your confinement." He gave himself the credit for it. Looking out the window, he saw that it had gotten dark. "Come," he said. "Let's hurry. Surely the maid can give the baby his bath for once."

She resisted him for a moment, but that was exactly what he needed—her resistance. "Close your eyes," he ordered.

Dutifully she closed her eyes. And only now, when her eyes were shut and could not see him, was she unfaithful to him with another man.

Afterward, as always, he sat on the edge of the bed smoking a cigarette. He sucked the smoke in forcefully, expelled it forcefully; after only a couple of minutes he stubbed the cigarette out with his middle finger. "During the maneuvers you didn't invite the officers to dinner even once?"

"No," Maximiliane answered truthfully.

"And you weren't even aware that the Führer spent a whole hour on the maneuver site—on your Poenichen Heath?"

"No."

24

Maximiliane was still nursing her firstborn; that was the only reason she had not conceived again. She did not reply to the expectant "Well?" with which her husband closed his letters.

In Paris a member of the German embassy staff had been murdered by a Jew! Viktor's letter gave a detailed account of the event but contained not a line about the acts of vengeance of the Crystal Night.

"Crystal?" Quindt asked. "Broken glass is more like it, nothing but broken glass. Until everything is broken."

Even in Dramburg and Arnswalde the few remaining Jewish stores were said to have been looted. In the home of Deutsch the attorney, the pillows had been cut open and the feathers shaken out the window! All through the Reich the synagogues were reduced to rubble and ashes. A week of terror. On Poenichen the silence about Vera and her husband became even more pronounced. And Viktor wrote that events were coming to a head.

Advent season rolled around. In the breakfast room Maximiliane ironed straws until they were flat, cut them, and sewed them up into stars—among them six-sided stars of David—as she had learned to do at Hermannswerder. She sang the old Christmas carols as well as the newer ones. She decorated the house with fir and pine branches in which she stuck homemade red paper roses. Of course the four weeks of Advent were not long enough for her to adorn the entire house, but she even produced a gold tinsel angel, in its dimensions and appearance more a figurehead than a harbinger of heaven. With the help of old Frau Pech she braided an Advent wreath. Everywhere there was a smell of pine needles and candle wax. The aroma of gingerbread and cinnamon cookies wafted up the dumbwaiter through the house, and for the first time on Poenichen even the smell of a Liegnitz torte, baked carefully according to handwritten instructions from the Silesian mother-in-law: "half a pound of almonds for every pound of honey." It was eight inches tall and was intended as a surprise for Viktor.

By now little Joachim had, against his will, been weaned. He drank warm, watered-down cow's milk from a bottle, and his father wrote that matters were continuing to come to a head.

Which was particularly true for himself. His girl friend, owner of the three hairpins, a salesgirl in a department store, three years his senior, began to make demands she had never made before. "If you go away again over Christmas, I'll write to your wife." She could no longer be pacified with gifts. "If you won't spend this Christmas in Berlin, then—"

Whereupon Viktor wrote another letter about the situation that was coming to a head—for once a situation Old Quindt had not yet read about in the papers.

He further informed them that he would not be able to get to Poenichen until the day after Christmas, when he would arrive on the usual afternoon train. "It is best in any case if I am not present until then. You know how unpleasant all this is for me." This time he managed not to use the phrase "Christian mumbo-jumbo," but he added, "During the days of my visit, we will jointly have to give some thought to how to celebrate a proper seasonal feast with our children in future. It should be possible to combine it with the Germanic tradition of the winter solstice. The Christian element overlays the old national characteristics like a fake patina, and it is important to scrape it away."

Maximiliane sat beside the Quindt cradle playing a carol on her recorder, and the old Baroness even sat down at the piano while Maximiliane sang her way through the songbook. The child in the cradle under the Christmas tree was busy manufacturing further teeth, and he was whiny. A successful Christmas Eve, a silent night that satisfied them all.

As in every other year, Christmas Day was spent taking gifts to the farmworkers. Viktor was expected the following day.

Maximiliane herself drove the automobile to the railroad station. She had put on her grandmother's heavy, fur-lined suede coat since there was no way to warm the car. Frau Pech had heated a brick and filled a thermos bottle with hot coffee. Though some snow had fallen the roads were clear enough. The wind did not rise until Maximiliane had arrived at the station.

The train was an hour late. Maximiliane spent the time in the unheated waiting room. No one else was there; no one else was afoot in such an out-of-the-way place on the day after Christmas. When the train finally steamed into Stargard station, Viktor was the only passenger to get off.

By that time it had grown dark, it had begun to snow, and the wind had increased to a gale. A snowstorm—just what had befallen Emanuel Quint! If the road had not been lined with trees on either side, they would not have been able to find it. The ditches were already drifted over, and the windshield was covered by a thin layer of ice and snow.

After a distance of a mile and a half, Viktor declared, "It won't work this way," and took Maximiliane's place behind the wheel. But he had even less experience with automobiles than she, and no experience at all of Pomeranian roads and Pomeranian snowstorms. Nevertheless he rejected her advice, and when the car swerved into a snowdrift he stepped on the accelerator, with the result that the wheels began to spin. Maximiliane unscrewed the top of the thermos and handed Viktor a cup of steaming hot coffee. Irritably refusing it, he tried once more to work his way out of the drift. He turned the wheel with all his strength to the right and again floored the accelerator, but the car would not budge by so much as an inch. He swore, using a Silesian dialect word that was new to Maximiliane and charmed her.

Maximiliane got out and tried to push. She put all her weight against the bumper, but it was no use. She suggested that they break off some branches from the nearby pines and place them behind the wheels, but Viktor, in a rage against snow and gale, Pomerania and Christmas, ordered her back in the car. He intended to sound the horn until such time as someone arrived to tow the car away. Alas, who could be expected to pass by this god-forsaken spot on the night of the day after Christmas?

Maximiliane asked, "Shall I try once more?"

Her reply was prolonged tooting of the horn.

"We'll walk," Viktor commanded.

They set out on foot, the wind in their faces. Flakes of snow crept into their collars, shoes, and gloves, made them blind and deaf. A few times they came close to losing their way, but Viktor, experienced in night marches, grabbed his wife by the arm and pulled her along behind him, each time managing to find the road again. His boots and long legs allowed him to advance more easily than she could in her grandmother's trailing fur coat. Once or twice they rested in the shelter of the trees and caught their breath, then Viktor dragged her onward. Finally they spied lights. Viktor was triumphant. "You see?"

They walked toward the lights, and as they came closer they realized that they were back at the railway station.

Maximiliane telephoned her grandfather, but by the time Griesemann arrived with the sleigh and horses, two more hours had passed. These Viktor and Maximiliane spent in the living room of the stationmaster, Pech, a brother of the housekeeper on Poenichen. His wife made "Turkish milk" for the unexpected guests—hot milk with rum, ginger, and beaten eggs. The Pechs lit the candles on the Christmas tree solely for their guests, and their two little girls were summoned to sing "Silent Night, Holy Night."

When the sleigh finally pulled up at the manor, the old Quindts had already retired for the night. The housekeeper served the young Quints a pitcher of hot Turkish milk and carp à la Polonaise, prepared after the fashion of what the cookbook swore was a traditional Christmas delicacy in Silesia. She apologized for the fact that it was dried out; she had put it in to bake at the time the train was supposed to get in. The greatest cooks in the world—and Frau Pech could not be counted among them—could not have kept the carp from becoming too crusty on the outside and too mushy on the inside after four hours in the oven. Viktor, who had lost his appetite in any case, turned on the electric light, put out the candles with the flat of his hand, and angrily said to Frau Pech, "Polack carp," and to his wife, "Come."

Frau Pech burst into tears, and Maximiliane got to her feet. Whenever Viktor entered the house, she changed owners.

That night their second child was conceived. Even at the time Maximiliane was so sure she could "feel it" that she was ready to put out the flags. What a child this was, conceived in anger! While still in the womb he kicked his mother, and in the fifth month he tried

250

to reach freedom by pushing his head through her abdominal wall.

In March Willem Riepe suddenly turned up on the estate. There had been rumors for a long time, but no one had known for sure except old Riepe and Old Quindt. Siemens, his old firm, had refused to rehire Willem. Who would take on a man who'd been in Oranienburg as a political?

Old Riepe appeared at the manor, unbidden and in his stocking feet. As usual, he had left his boots on the verandah.

"How do, Riepe," Quindt said. And "Oh, Baron, sir," Riepe replied. Their form of greeting never varied.

At first Old Quindt was firm. "No." But then he was annoyed with Riepe for not repeating his request. "Whatever did you have in mind, Riepe? How is it supposed to work? Here, where everybody knows him!"

"That's just it, Baron, sir. Everybody here knows him." He'd been thinking of the foreman's cottage, empty and decaying for years. "Let's face it, Willem grew up in the country. He won't have forgotten everything in the city. He's a metalworker. He could repair the machinery. His health isn't the best."

"And his wife? And his children?"

"Two of them are already out working, and they won't be coming along."

Of course the arrangement had to be discussed with Kalinski, the estate foreman, nor would it work without Priebe's consent. Once more Old Quindt had to wave his son-in-law's Party card, and the son-in-law had to be informed as well. Maximiliane assumed the responsibility of asking him; but her strategy was not clever. "Do it for me," she begged him. "If you love me."

He had heard enough of such pleas. Nevertheless he agreed. Let them see that the Party could be generous when it was a matter of helping someone who had stumbled to get back on his feet.

In May the Berlin contingent of the Riepe family moved into the cottage by the lake, suspect and pitied. No more sheep as during Blaskorken's term, and the fishing rights had been assigned elsewhere as well. Every morning Willem Riepe arrived on his bicycle; he soldered, hammered, and filed in the workshop; he repaired tractors and threshers. Whenever anyone whispered to him, "Tell me, Willem. Oranienburg. What's it like there?" Willem asked in return, "Can you keep a secret?" And when the questioner assured him that he could, Willem said, "Well, so can I."

His father was the only one to whom he had told some details. The old man passed them on to Quindt, and for two days the Baron did not eat, spending his time in the library with the shutters closed.

Willem Riepe's two little children made the bathing beach unusable. They built dams, threw stones at the fish, and destroyed the loons' and herons' nests.

Artillery maneuvers were held on Poenichen Heath again. The officers paid their duty call, and horses were ordered for them. The same process was repeated every few weeks. However, Hitler never again visited the site—at most the unit was inspected by a corps commander.

Little Joachim learned to stand on his own two feet, and then he learned to walk, but whenever possible he clung to his mother's skirt. She was in no condition either to bicycle or to ride a horse; she was carrying her tempestuous second child.

When a horseman appeared on the horizon at noon, when the mares neighed loudly and amorously, she remembered and was seized by the same desire. Pregnancy could not protect her against that—on the contrary. Once more she was compelled to embrace tree trunks and press her cheek against the rough bark.

In the chicken coop the artificial hen for artificial chicks was not installed a second time. One hen after the other sat down to hatch, twenty hens and eventually twenty chicken families populating the chicken coop, fluffy and reddish-brown.

A nonaggression pact was concluded between the Greater German Reich and the Soviet Union.

"You see," said Viktor, who was on Poenichen at the time. "A renewed confirmation of the fact that the Führer wants peace."

"Yes," Old Quindt said. "Yes, Hitler." He had adopted this manner of speaking, which could be interpreted as either praise or contempt. "Yes, the law." Was he applauding it or calling it into question? He spoke of the "Third Reich" in the same tones.

"You make it sound," Viktor said, "as if a fourth might follow."

"I can't help but agree with your correction," Quindt replied. "After the third, it would be hard for there to be a fourth."

But in general he had grown more cautious and even avoided Willem Riepe as best he could. Once, when he did not succeed, he stopped the car and got out. Willem Riepe put on his withdrawn expression.

"Come now, Herr Riepe, cheer up," Quindt said. "You've got no place to go but up. You're starting from the bottom–though it's not as far under as you always claimed, either, but that's a whole other story. The Quindts are on their way down. Well, we had it our own way long enough, don't you think? At heart I tend to agree with you. But none of us are responsible for where we were born. That's what it is."

Willem Riepe did not even take off his cap, and he said not a word in reply. All the same, Quindt felt relieved when he got back into his car.

He spent more and more time with the Reverend Merzin, to whom he declared, "If you don't say it in the first place, you don't run the chance of being misunderstood." Sometimes they talked about "the eternal," and sometimes they kept their silence on the subject. The Reverend Merzin had acquired a wig the color of a red fox, because his bald head was cold otherwise. When he grew warm sitting by the fireplace, he took off the wig. After Baby Joachim had put it on his own head one time, Merzin regularly clapped it on the child's skull–to keep the wig warm, he said.

"The boy always reminds me a little of your own son, by the way," he told Quindt. "He was a quiet one, too. This one doesn't take after our dear Maximiliane very much, but sometimes I think I see little Achim standing there. Yes, my dear Quindt, the war."

And both fell into a deep silence about the "war to end all wars" and the war to come.

During the final nights of August, Poenichen heard the sound of troop transports, light and heavy artillery. "Night and distant driving." Maximiliane stood at the window of the nursery and listened, and on the other side of the house Old Quindt stood and listened. Then there was an end to the troop movements, and the nights grew quiet again.

Aunt Maximiliane wrote of the "waves of a great epoch, which break against Mount Eyckel as well," and Quindt replied, "In the course of the centuries Mount Eyckel has withstood many things."

Though he normally got his news not from the radio but from newspapers because his ears were not yet as case-hardened as his eyes, he too spent the morning of September 1 sitting by the radio, listening to the broadcast of Hitler's speech from the Kroll Opera House.

"And I have therefore decided to reply to Poland in the same language Poland has been using to us for months. Beginning at five forty-five this morning, their

254

fire is being returned. And from now on it will be a bomb for a bomb. I will carry on this battle, no matter against whom, until the safety of the Reich and its rights are secured. I now want to be nothing but the first soldier of the German Reich. Therefore, I have once again put on that uniform which was always so sacred and dear to me. I shall not take it off until after the victory—or I shall not live to see the end!"

The Quindts sat in the study. Old Frau Pech had pulled a chair over by the door. The maids and Riepe, all in stocking feet, stood beside her. Even before the triple "Sieg Heil!" had made its way from Berlin to Pomerania, Quindt switched off. He went to the dogs' room, fetched the brandy bottle from the rifle cabinet, and poured triples all around.

Viktor wrote that old accounts would now be settled and that what was at stake was the extension of living space in the East and the preservation of the German people's food supply. For the time being he would be unable to come to Poenichen; it was obvious that he would immediately and voluntarily put himself at the country's service. Maximiliane read his letter out loud. "From now on only one thing matters for us all: the Führer commands, we follow!"

"But where?" Quindt asked. "Does he tell us that too?"

Viktor's letter spoke of "rushing to the flag," no longer of the "Reich Party Congress of Peace," which had been scheduled to take place in Nuremberg and which he had planned to attend. Nor was there any mention of his wife's imminent confinement. The letter carried no postscript.

Great Britain declared war on Germany and was followed by France. Quindt, who never came to the study until after the news, inquired each evening, "So who declared war on us today?" The time of army reports and special bulletins had begun: "Heil Hitler" and a triple "Sieg Heil." Ration coupons, induction notices, priority vouchers for textiles. And only thirty-five miles as the crow flew to the Polish border–which, granted, moved farther away by the hour.

Given these circumstances, Maximiliane's confinement lost much of its significance. At the first signs she pulled little Joachim close and told him, "Mose, we're going to bring out your little brother." She pressed Joachim's head to her stomach. "Can you hear him?"

But little Joachim was frightened; turning on his wobbly little legs, he eagerly sought the care of Frau Pech.

Maximiliane fetched a basket of apples and a volume of poetry, retired to the marital bed, which had been covered with clean linen, and awaited the arrival of the doctor.

Of course this impetuous child was born too soon and too quickly. In spite of the telephone and motorcar, young Dr. Christ from Dramburg, successor to Dr. Wittkow, did not appear in time. The birth even happened too suddenly for the old legs of Schmaltz the midwife. She put her head through the door and exclaimed, "Mother of God!"

At his birth, the baby broke his collarbone.

25

The final skirmishes took place in late October; then the Polish campaign ended. More than half a million Polish prisoners of war were made available to the German economy, among them ten agricultural workers for Poenichen.

Soon thereafter Anya arrived to be employed as a housemaid; Quindt never called her anything but "the Polish girl"—dark-haired, dark-eyed, quick, friendly, always ready to lend a hand. Even before the sky grew light in the morning, she ran through the house in hand-knitted socks and took care of the tiled stoves. By the time the Quindts got up, the rooms were warm—a comfort they attributed directly to the Polish girl. Erika Schmaltz, who had been firing the ovens until then—the steam heating system had not been in use for some time—had always managed to wake most of the members of the household but had produced mostly smoke and little heat.

Every afternoon the Baroness now found a hot-water bottle in her bed. As soon as she had lain down, there was a knock on her door and she was given a cup of chamomile tea and a shy smile. Whenever anybody met Anya on the stairs, she stepped aside and dropped her eyes. She knew how to deal with small children, for she herself had three little brothers and sisters.

"Where?" Maximiliane asked.

Anya shrugged her shoulders.

"Your father?"

Another shrug.

"Your mother?"

Anya made the sign of the cross.

Since they could exchange no more than a couple of words, they laughed together. Along with little Joachim, Anya learned her first words of German. She owned only a single dress, which she wore constantly, so Maximiliane passed a dress and a jacket along to her. They were the same size. They were the same age, too. After Quindt had seen Anya in his granddaughter's dress and had momentarily mistaken her for Maximiliane, he said at dinner, "Let's hope that Viktor never makes the same mistake."

His wife and his granddaughter looked at him questioningly.

"A man can make a mistake. And if I'm not totally wrong, that's a very pretty little Polish girl. But perhaps I'm past the age where you can tell that sort of thing. I never did understand a lot about it. I know, Sophie Charlotte."

"I didn't say anything, Quindt."

"No, you didn't say anything."

They continued to play their accustomed roles, but the tone had changed; something like a secret understanding had crept in.

Quindt's fear proved unfounded and inappropriate. Viktor did not waste so much as a glance on the housemaid; his racial awareness preserved him against the charms of a Pole. He even went so far as to request that any attempts at intimacy or fraternization be discontinued.

"The poor little thing," Maximiliane said. "She doesn't even know if her family is still alive. She lost her home."

"Poland lost the war."

258

Anya, sensing the hostility of the young Herr Quint, avoided him.

When he was visiting on Poenichen, Viktor went horseback riding right after breakfast. But usually he returned quite soon, without looking to the sweat-soaked horse, throwing the reins to some worker in the yard without so much as a please or thank you. A man born to rule. Old Quindt was respected by his men; that he was loved by them is unlikely, though no one ever inquired. There was no doubt that young Herr Quint was feared. He could not nor did not wish to adapt, any more than Vera had in her day. In spite of his "love for the German East," Viktor remained a foreign body.

At irregular intervals he was seen in the stables or made an appearance in the village inn, so that people felt spied upon. Old Quindt had never shown his face in the inn, and he made his tours of inspection at prescribed times. Sometimes Viktor Quint even turned up in the basement, inspecting the pantries and the ice cellar, asking questions. Was consumption excessive? Were they, as subsistence consumers, setting a good example of frugality? He left behind an offended housekeeper.

He also went to the office to look at the books—an inspection, it must be admitted, that Martha Riepe was only too happy to allow. She had conceived a crush on the young master the first day he had arrived on Poenichen, and by now she had turned into an old maid. In her late thirties, she had no prospects of marriage. She was an irreplaceable and unselfish worker, devoted to the Quindt family but even more devoted to her German fatherland. In her presence they had to be careful not to make any critical remarks.

Only once during these early war years did Viktor try to play chess with Old Quindt again. But even more than before he proved to be an impatient player, turning the gameboard into a battlefield; it took less than fifteen minutes to checkmate. Quindt waived a return match, for all time.

At his christening the baby was given the name Golo. Several of the Silesian Quints bore that name; Viktor showed his wife the appropriate entries on his certificate of ancestry.

Following Quindt tradition, he had volunteered for the tank corps, the successor to the cavalry. But the Second World War was not a war of volunteers. Besides, he was considered indispensable in his job. He was rejected, and from one campaign to the next he feared that the war would end without him. As a substitute for the uniform of his country, he wore a rubberized trenchcoat; when he turned up the collar, it gave him a military air. Joachim seemed to take a dislike to the rubber smell that always clung to his father; he started to cry whenever Viktor wanted to pick him up.

In his wife's presence Viktor entered his second-born son on the Quindt oak, once again in the shape of an acorn. A great moment–even Maximiliane could sense as much. Viktor was more talkative than usual and lectured his wife at length on the necessity of the Polish campaigns that had just concluded. Unfortunately this conversation did not take the desired turn, either. Maximiliane put one of her questionable questions.

"Why do they call it a declaration of war?" she wondered aloud. "It isn't as though it clarifies anything for anybody."

Viktor could not follow the workings of her mind. "It is not a matter of clarifying something. Rather–"

"Why 'rather'?" Maximiliane asked.

"Are you really so stupid, or are you only pretending?" He gave her a suspicious look. "You ask the wrong questions."

"They told me the same thing in Arnswalde and at Hermannswerder."

260

"You see! You don't have to bother your pretty little head with such questions. It's enough for you to do your duty."

"And what is my duty?"

"Aren't you aware of it at every moment?"

Maximiliane shook her head.

"But you do bring children into the world."

"So does Cylla the dog."

"Do I really have to explain the noble concept of motherhood to you?"

Maximiliane laughed out loud.

"What's so funny?"

"Another declaration, not a clarification," Maximiliane said.

No one raised any objection to the baby's being named Golo. Only Maximiliane harbored some fears, but she did not voice them. At one time Fräulein Eberle had read her the legend of Saint Genevieve for pedagogical purposes, to make her understand at an early age what could happen to the rich. She remembered very clearly the steward Golo, who unjustly accused the countess of adultery–a sinister figure. But the count believed him and banished his consort, who was forced to give birth to her child and raise him in a cave. She named the baby Rich-in-Sorrow. During a hunt a doe led the count to his wife's hiding place, and he could see her touching innocence for himself; then he had the steward Golo pulled to pieces by four oxen.

Maximiliane wondered whether to tell the legend to her husband. But Viktor had a low opinion of literature, and he had surely never heard of Genevieve–a story for little girls with romantic longings. And Maximiliane did not feel quite as innocent as Genevieve, either! Hardly a year had passed since the ardent interlude by the lake. Viktor was sure of his wife's unconditional fidelity.

The baby's christening was the first order of business. The small celebration supper took place in the breakfast room since the large hall was no longer heated. Quindt, who did not like to follow orders that had not originated with him, had personally established as soon as the war broke out conservation rules that went beyond what was necessary. The christening dinner was frugal by the same measure. No ceremony and no "mumbo-jumbo."

After the christening Maximiliane played a selection on her recorder, to no applause. During the meal there was talk of a trip to Breslau; Maximiliane had not yet been to her husband's home, nor had she met his younger sister, Ruth, who had agreed to be Golo's godmother but was unable to attend because she worked for the Red Cross and could not get away. Being unable to get away lent a great deal of prestige to absent guests, dwarfing the prestige of those present.

In the fourth generation the eyes of the Polish lieutenant turned out to be a dominant trait. Golo was endowed with them on his rocky life's way. How much better it would have been if a daughter had the use of those eyes! For her, as for her mother, they would have made life much easier. This time no one asked, "Where did the child get his eyes?" One glance was enough. They were the mother's eyes. And with them the long, curling lashes of his grandmother Vera.

It was impossible to let Golo be part of the dinner in the soup tureen. His mother had to hold him on her lap and keep him quiet as best she could. She dipped her finger in the dill sauce for the unrationed smoked pike and let the infant suck it. She did the same with the caramel pudding.

No lofty sermon or worldly after-dinner speech—or so it seemed at first. But in the end Viktor toasted the Führer and victory, whereupon Old Quindt, who had no intention of ever again making a christening speech, felt impelled to utter something resembling a christening speech, if only a short one, containing a Quindt-essence that Maximiliane committed to memory, though not word for word. Excused by age, rheumatism, and his badly healed broken leg, he did not get to his feet. He only tapped his glass, raised it, and said, "Long life especially to the mother of this child and to his father."

At that moment he recalled a statement Bismarck had made to the German Reichstag—in February 1886, to be precise; he himself had been seventeen at the time. He explained that he did not wish to deprive the guests at his table of this particular recollection. " 'We Germans fear God, and nothing in this world.' My father was in the habit of quoting the remark, but with the following changes. 'We Pomeranian estate owners fear nothing except severe storms, runaway horses, hoof-and-mouth disease, the pine moth, and war on two fronts—and nothing else in the world.' "

He had wanted to say this out of respect for tradition, he concluded. He took a sip of wine, put down his glass, and pointed his pince-nez at Viktor. "You will have to learn our Pomeranian ways. To swallow, not your anger, but smoked pike."

26

Maximiliane was pregnant. Because this was her third time around, it had lost its specialness. And her husband had replied to the news with only the sentence "Accept this instance of my desire for progeny as proof of my unshakable faith in the future of our Reich."

She had also had a clear intimation of this conception, and the night was engraved in her memory for another reason. At his express wish, she had visited Viktor in Berlin. In the evening, following a mass meeting in the Sports Palace, she was introduced to the Führer. He shook her hand, and for a moment his eyes bored into hers.

Later Viktor asked, "Well, did I promise too much?"

"No," she answered. And she really had been impressed, though she had imagined Him to be taller; it had always been easy to impress her with height. Even thirty and forty years later they would mention that she was someone who had seen Hitler close up and had shaken hands with him; it is noteworthy that in these later stories it was she who had shaken his hand, not the other way around.

During the first months of 1942 Viktor was stationed at an infantry school near Berlin, having received his induction orders early in January. After the actions on the Eastern front had exacted unexpectedly heavy casualties and the United States had joined the war, his request–supported, as he relayed to Poenichen, down to the smallest detail, by the head of the Army Personnel Office himself–was granted. "Don't count on a visit from me anytime soon. You will have realized in these, the first few years of our marriage, that I am not an armchair soldier but a frontline fighter. I shall stand my ground and prove myself. My several years' activity as a leader in the Reich Labor Service will stand me in as good stead as my work as department head in the Reich Genealogical Office."

Maximiliane accepted the events of the war as she did sun and rain, though she never expected storms. In the same way she reacted to Viktor's visiting or staying away; both suited her equally well. Old Quindt became aware of his granddaughter's physical condition only later but noted all the more dramatically, "So you're broody again."

Since the outbreak of the war Grandmother Jadow from Charlottenburg had come to visit on Poenichen more frequently, staying several weeks each time to warm herself, eat her fill, and catch up on her sleep. She resented the fact that these things were still possible in Pomerania, and she held it against the Quindts. As there was always something for her to resent, she kept to her room most of the time; of course, the fact that no one invited her to come out of it furnished another source of resentment.

The Quindts from Lübeck announced their arrival– five at a time, "to keep up the family ties." It was the belief of the widow of the former senate president von Quindt that her late husband would want her to maintain the relationship with his family. "My, my, we've never been so closely related before," Old Quindt noted.

The widow Schimanowski from Arnswalde wrote to say that she often thought of the charming, uneducated girl and would dearly love to see for herself how she had turned out.

And all the former governesses and nursemaids recalled Poenichen estate in the far reaches of Pomerania and inquired whether they might pay a visit to refresh their old, cherished memories. Fräulein Eschholtz, to whom Maximiliane was partially indebted for her sexual enlightenment, and whose son Peter, as she wrote, had taken part in the French campaign and was now occupying Norway, was the first to arrive. A short time later they had a visit from the Fräulein whose fiancé had fallen at Arras during the First World War.

Everyone savored the peaceful life on the estate—no air-raid shelters, no blackouts, neither sandbags nor fire buckets outside every door, not even sirens! They warmed themselves at the tile stoves, they ate chicken fricassee, perch, or game stew. Their travel food coupons were not even accepted in exchange. At night they met to listen to the army report, which in Poenichen lost its importance and reality.

First thing every morning Martha Riepe went to the workers' canteen and entered any changes in the front lines on the map of Europe Old Quindt had hung there. Pins with colored glass heads served as the advance outposts, yarn showed the connections between bridgeheads and the cities named in the army reports. Further, she placed the *Völkische Beobachter*, the official newspaper, in the room after the Baron had read it and had underlined what he considered significant—such sentences as "The humiliation of 1918 has been effaced, thanks to the Führer and Commander in Chief of the Armed Forces. His actions continue to compel us to silent and unlimited service." The word *silent* had been underlined twice. When Kalinski asked Quindt his opinion of the situation, the Baron answered, "Yes, Herr Kalinski, what is there to be said? The war!"

As soon as visitors were in the house Quindt suffered from hearing loss, so that some statements had to be repeated three times: "You have no idea, Baron, how things look in Berlin."

The constipated Fräulein also appeared. She and her husband had opened a sauna in Dortmund, but now her husband was at the front, she was alone, and who felt like going to the sauna when there were constant air-raid alarms? Besides, there was a shortage of heating fuel. "You have no idea, Herr von Quindt, how matters stand in the Ruhr region."

"No," he replied. "I can't have so many ideas."

More and more frequently the old Quindts asked to be excused: "They're not feeling up to snuff." The Polish girl brought their dinner to the Ladies' Parlor. Was it any wonder, then, that Quindt's digestive difficulties grew worse, his permanent constipation, now that he had to keep all his opinions to himself?

The large truck had been requisitioned at the beginning of the war, as had most of the horses. They acquired draft oxen that plodded unshod along the sandy paths, pulling plows, harrows, and harvest wagons. They were allowed to keep the little car, but the tires had to be turned in, so it stood on supports in the coach house, where it gradually rusted out. The coaches were repaired, and whenever his rheumatism permitted, Riepe climbed on the block. Most of the time Maximiliane drove the Plaid or the sleigh to the railroad station to fetch the visitors, cracking her whip and tinkling the bells.

Peaceful, satisfying vacation days for guests in Pomerania. "My God, but you live high on the hog! Do you have any idea how good you've got it?" Again Old Quindt corrected the speaker. "No more than halfway up the hog, my dear Fräulein."

There was a lot of repetition; it was repetition that wearied him.

One day a young woman appeared unannounced, holding a little girl by one hand, a suitcase in the other. Unsure of herself, she stood by the round flower bed and examined the eighteen windows along the front of the house. She must have walked to the manor—at least, no one had called for her. Maximiliane was the first to become aware of the visitor. Assuming that it was another one of her Fräuleins, she went up to the two with arms outstretched, greeted the little girl, who made a polite curtsy, then turned to her mother.

"My name is Hilde Preissing."

Maximiliane tried in vain to remember someone of that name. She took a closer look at the child, then at the woman. Recognizing the hairpins, she understood.

"The girl's name is Edda."

Edda, like the daughter of Reich Marshal Goering. A child for the Führer. Ideologically there could be no objection to the girl.

Maximiliane remembered Viktor's words. "Germany needs genetically sound new blood so that a people without space does not turn into space without people."

She took the two to the breakfast room, asked Anya to order warm milk and sandwiches from the kitchen, and tried to start a conversation. "It's a long way from the railroad station to the estate. Did the little girl—"

"Edda," said the little girl.

"Did Edda manage it on her own?"

It turned out that the dairy cart had given them a lift. The conversation faltered as the snack was coming up in the dumbwaiter. Maximiliane had plenty of time to look over Fräulein Preissing and especially the little girl, who resembled Viktor so much—as much as a three-year-old girl can look like a thirty-year-old man: straight dark-blond hair, narrow lips, close-set blue eyes, a flat forehead, rigid shoulders. The child seemed a little bewildered and bristly but appeared to know what she wanted. Her mother was an urban edition of Maximiliane,

268

Nordic and distinctly blue-eyed—at least Viktor had remained true to the physical type—a woman of the world, smart-looking even in the third year of the war. By comparison, Maximiliane, just on her way to the chicken coop, was a simple peasant, wearing the shabby uniform vest she was no longer able to button now that she was in her seventh month.

Fräulein Preissing wiped little Edda's hands and mouth, pushed plates and cups aside, and came to the point. She wanted to get married.

"Does Viktor know?" Maximiliane asked.

"My marriage is my business," Fräulein Preissing declared. "My fiancé doesn't want the little girl. The little girl is in our way."

"Should we be talking about it in front of the child?" Maximiliane asked.

"She's used to it. She knows the score," Fräulein Preissing said before getting down to details. The workday had already been extended again, and most of the saleswomen were employed in defense industries by now. Two months earlier her mother had fallen down the stairs on her way to the air-raid shelter and died. Though her father could take care of himself, he could not look after the child as well. "You've got plenty of space. Here one kid more or less can't make much difference." She spoke as if she had given the matter very careful thought.

"Does Viktor know you came here?"

"No."

Maximiliane reflected and did some quick arithmetic: Joachim would be four in May, and Golo three in September. Then she asked, "When is the little girl's—"

"Edda!" said Edda.

"—when is little Edda's birthday?"

"On March fifth," the child answered.

"She was born on a Sunday—a lucky day, a lucky child." Fräulein Preissing's voice swelled with pride. Then she fetched the little suitcase. "Here's everything she owns. She hasn't got much to wear, only what you can get with coupons."

A doll with eyes that could close and real hair was produced, along with a knitted teddybear. Then an envelope containing her papers: birth certificate, immunization certificate, registration at the local police station, notice of departure from the Pankow police precinct for food ration coupons, as well as the waiver, confirmed by the youth office. In addition, the ration coupons for the current quarter, exchanged into travel marks.

There was a knock at the door. Anya inquired whether to announce the visitors to the Baron.

"No," Maximiliane said. "But tell them in the kitchen to hurry up with the box."

Fräulein Preissing stared at Maximiliane's stomach. "When are you supposed to be due?"

"In six weeks." Maximiliane got to her feet. "Come with me, Edda. I'll take you to Joachim and Golo; you can play with them."

Edda looked at her mother, and when she nodded, the child got up and took Maximiliane's hand. In this way the transfer was completed.

At first Joachim hid his hands behind his back and closed his eyes so as to be able to ignore the hand Edda held out to him. Golo asked, "Who's she supposed to be?"

"This little girl's name is Edda. She comes from Berlin. She'll be staying with us. She's almost your sister."

"But you promised us a tiny baby sister!"

"You'll get the baby sister too. There's no such thing as too many children. Edda was born on a Sunday." With this, she had told them just about everything she knew.

Then the Plaid took Fräulein Preissing to the evening train. On the verandah Maximiliane handed her a box containing lard, bacon, and fresh eggs. The two women

270

parted cordially, but one of them did not say, "Thank you," and the other did not say, "See you again."

While Maximiliane put the children to bed with Anya's help, the old Quindts sat by the fire in the study. "The fox in the chicken coop, Sophie Charlotte. Do you remember? When Quint first set foot in this house, you said, 'Aren't we letting the fox into the chicken coop?' And now he's actually dropped a cuckoo's egg into the coop."

"It's already hatched, Quindt."

"You're right. The cuckoo is here."

Old Quindt never called the child anything but "Cuckoo." Therefore the two boys also called her Cuckoo, and for a time the name Edda was quite forgotten. The little girl said "Grandpa" with a distinct pause after the "Grand," and she introduced the appellation "Gamma" for the old Baroness. Old Quindt tolerated this form of address. His aversion to small children and puppies had mellowed with advancing age, nor was he as sensitive to the smell of milk and urine that came from the dogs' chamber and the nursery.

The very first morning the little girl called Maximiliane Mother and was corrected by Golo. "That's not your mother, that's our mother."

"I know that! I call my own mother Mama.

Since Pomerania was colder than Berlin–"Siberia begins at the railroad station," Grandmother Jadow always declared–and since the child had only a thin little coat that she had already outgrown, the Baroness pulled one of her handwoven wool jackets from the chest, turned up the sleeves, wound a cord into a belt, and thus turned it into a child's overcoat.

The Cuckoo moved into the sideboard that stood in the salon and was as large as a small kitchen–not to hide, but to be able to play undisturbed. Presumably the rooms on Poenichen were too large and too high.

She shoved the tureens and sauceboats to one side, making room for herself and her dolls. Sometimes Quindt walked through the room and called, "Where can the Cuckoo be?" Then the child stuck out her head with its scanty little braids and answered, "Cuckoo."

On the whole she adjusted with commendable speed to her new surroundings. She even let Joachim play with her doll, which he alternately undressed and dressed. The tin soldiers inherited from the possession of Great-grandfather, which reenacted "Lützow's wild and daring pursuit," disappeared once and for all into their box. Horsemen with flashing sabers and helmets, horses and guns. "All go to sleep," he said, wrapping them in cotton wool.

Having come from Berlin, Edda was considerably more advanced than her new brothers. When she felt put in the shade, she sang a mocking doggerel her grandfather Preissing had taught her.

> In Pomerania they're even dumber
> In winter than they are in summer.
> Only when it's spring
> Do they catch on to anything.

Ever cautious, she always ran away as she sang the last line. She could run very fast. They had received the little girl in February, when her skin was city-pale, and by April her face was sprinkled with freckles—speckled like a cuckoo.

Whenever she thought it necessary, Maximiliane introduced the new child, always with the addition "a child born on Sunday—a lucky child." She said it with so much conviction over such a long period of time, and she treated the little girl so much like Sunday's child, that Edda led almost a Sunday existence, to the extent that the times allowed it. She grew up in the awareness that she could not fail at anything. Perhaps, too, she had inherited her mother's sturdy energy along with her father's exalted feeling of self-worth.

Viktor announced his impending arrival in the following words. "This time I shall be able to be by your side in your hour of need. Besides, I have a surprise for you and the children."

Since her labor pains might start at any moment, Maximiliane did not drive to the railroad station to meet him. Old Riepe went, taking Joachim and Golo along. Golo immediately informed his father, "We've got a new sister."

Viktor could therefore not help but assume that he had arrived too late for the birth of his third child, as he had on the previous two occasions. Since he had given up his room in Berlin, his luggage consisted of two valises and a crate. Pech, the stationmaster, had to lend a hand.

On the drive back, the boys' father pulled a wrapped object from his pocket and handed it to his oldest son. "This is what I've brought you, Joachim. It's a splinter from a bomb, one that burst right near my barracks."

But if the quiet, anxious Joachim did not care for shrapnel, Golo was all the more interested. Taking the splinter from his brother, he shouted excitedly, "A pomp! A pomp!" which did not go at all with the long-lashed eyes, the curly brown head, and the cherry-red lips. He threatened his father and old Riepe, jabbing their knees and backs with the piece of shrapnel, just as he did at home with the heavy poker, which he stuck under his arm like a gun as he ran with it through the halls, reducing desire and ability to a common denominator, rushing up and down stairs, tripping over his words and his legs, poking his weapon into trousers and skirts, shouting, "Pang! Pang!" and attacking everyone–Anya, Frau Pech, his grandfather, the bitch Texa–except his brother, whom he respected and protected.

This was the first visit at which Viktor Quint wore his uniform, already that of a sergeant who lacked only a few weeks of frontline service for his next promotion—the surprise he had announced in his letter. It did not, however, have its full effect, since Maximiliane also had a surprise for him. She was waiting on the stairs for the carriage to drive up—which would have been surprise enough, because he believed her to be confined—but then she was also holding a little girl by the hand.

"Whom have we here?" he asked, although he was the only one who could have known the child from his occasional visits to the Preissing family in Pankow. Edda curtsied and, without letting go of the new mother's hand, said, "Hello, Uncle."

When he learned the details, he reproached his wife most earnestly. "I really don't understand you. Why did you leave me in the dark about this state of affairs? You should have prepared me by letter. You're putting me in a most embarrassing position."

Maximiliane persisted in her silence until he understood that he too had put her in an embarrassing position.

"Do you expect the child to stay here?" he asked.

"Where else can she go?" Maximiliane countered.

During supper, which they took without the children, the four adults sat at the long table in the breakfast room. The appearance of harmony between Quint and the Quindts was maintained as usual. All dangerous topics were avoided as far as possible. But even train connections, which were thwarted by air attacks, even the weather, which also affected the aerial warfare, turned out to be risky subjects. The old Baroness, already beginning to feel the first pangs of her colic, was the only one to remark on Viktor's uniform. "Don't you want to make yourself a little more comfortable while you're on furlough?"

Irritated, he explained that he was not a civilian. In a certain sense that she—the daughter of an officer, and the wife of a former cavalry captain—must surely understand, there was no such thing as a furlough from war. A soldier was never off duty.

Because of her condition, Maximiliane sat sideways to the table, a position cumbersome not only for eating but also for conversation, since it meant that she had to turn her back on her husband. The matter of Edda, like most of the topics in the air, was not broached. Instead Viktor gave a detailed lecture on population policies for the East.

"The Baltic Germans are already undergoing large-scale relocation. Even the Germans from the old settlement areas of the Balkans are being brought home. A momentous movement of return to the Reich has begun! Paralyzed Europe is on the move! German nationals and ethnic Germans! Only a few more days before my unit marches into Russia. I shall be in the foremost line, I shall see the whites of the enemy's eyes! Soon I shall catch up with those who are ahead of me. We shall conquer Russia! Russian soil! Pomerania has given me a taste of the East, the coming Greater German living space!"

A couple of times Old Quindt had tried to interrupt, but his wife's glance condemned him to self-restraint. "Quindt! Keep it to yourself," she said when no glance and no soothing hand sufficed. Quindt laid down his knife and fork and leaned back, but a lot was dammed up in him; it had to be vented.

"Since you're on the subject, you have now conceived four Quints," he said. "Surely we can count the little Berlin Cuckoo among them, and the next kid is as good as here." He cast a glance at Maximiliane, who blushed and supported her swollen belly with folded hands.

"Just assuming," he went on, "that this is the end of procreation—a supposition we can take to be groundless—even these four Quints will quadruple in the next generation, and for all anybody knows, they will multiply eightfold. Recently I read some statistics about the population density of Pomerania, which is renowned for the sparseness of its population—eight inhabitants to the square kilometer. We can therefore easily forecast how long it will take before Pomerania is populated entirely with Quints. But why stick to Pomerania when within a short time the Greater German Reich will have at its disposal all of Poland and Russia, the Tatar kingdoms, the realms of Genghis Khan? We shall be able to name one of the new Eastern border provinces Quintland."

At the outset his tone had been jovial, but as he went on it grew increasingly vehement. Maximiliane anxiously observed her husband and saw him grow white with anger.

"I'm certain any comment on my part is superfluous," he said loudly, his two fists clenched on the tabletop, "but the idea that my sons must grow up in a politically poisonous atmosphere—"

"They eat their fill and need never be cold," Old Quindt objected.

"Soon there won't be a single German who has to go hungry or cold. We have conquered the granaries of the Ukraine!"

"But they are not full."

"It does not matter whether one or another individual is hungry or cold. The only thing that matters is the idea! My sons—exposed to your speeches, looked after by a Polish foreign laborer!"

"Anya has been declared an ethnic German! Her home is in the protectorate." Maximiliane's attempts to soothe Viktor failed in the same measure as the old Baroness's efforts on behalf of her husband.

"Stay out of it," Viktor snapped at her.

There it was again, the sentence that had been spoken at the same table fifty years before and never forgotten. Maximiliane curled her fingers into claws.

276

This time the old Baroness suffered her colic attack the very night of Viktor's arrival. Dr. Christ from Dramburg had to be summoned by telephone in the morning, and he was therefore on hand when it came time to deliver Maximiliane of a daughter. Even before breakfast Viktor had had a horse saddled—an old mare, since all the other horses had been requisitioned or were out for the spring sowing—and had ridden off in the direction of Poenichen Heath. He still believed that a horse must be made to feel the rider's hard hand.

After a sleepless night Old Quindt was in the study behind closed shutters, his green desk lamp still lit at noon. He sat and stared into the fire. Anya ran from the bed of the bilious Baroness to the bed of the delivering mother, taking the hot-water bottle and chamomile tea to one, the Quindt cradle with fresh linen to the other, along with cloths and buckets of hot water, and in between a quick dash to throw a few pine logs onto the study fire.

Old Frau Pech was supposed to look after the three children. Golo had turned on the radio, and a special bulletin rang through the house all the way into the sickrooms. The German navy had sunk thirty-eight thousand enemy gross tons. The news was followed by a rendition of "We Are Moving Against England," which Old Quindt called the Gross Tons song.

Martha Riepe turned down the radio and sent Golo to join the other children in the great hall. Frau Pech was in the process of pulling little Edda from the sideboard, where she was once again playing with her dolls. She was fishing for the child's foot with a soup ladle while Golo, in an effort to assist his new sister, poked a large serving fork into the old woman's skirts. Frau Pech managed to get hold of the elusive foot, at the same time grabbing the unruly little boy by the arm. Edda struggled and emitted piercing shrieks. Golo wrenched himself free but stumbled, pulling the old

277

woman and Edda down as he fell. Edda was on her feet again at once; Frau Pech rose slowly. Only Golo remained on the ground, his left foot dangling loosely in its socket. When Joachim caught sight of it, he burst into heart-rending sobs. Golo, taken by surprise, began to bellow ferociously. Edda's shrill screams echoed through the house.

In the meantime Maximiliane, under the usual conditions and with the ease imparted by practice, gave birth to a healthy child—not the expected third but the fourth, and not the desired first daughter but a second daughter, displaced from her position even before birth by the Cuckoo.

Dr. Christ diagnosed a broken ankle for Golo, a simple fracture like the previous injury he had sustained to his right leg in jumping from a branch of the copper beech. The foot had to be set and put in a plaster cast. Suggesting that in future he would keep a sack of gypsum on reserve on Poenichen just for Golo, the doctor packed the boy into his car under the careful scrutiny of Joachim and Edda, old Frau Pech, Anya the Pole, and Martha Riepe. Then he drove off.

In the avenue he met Viktor Quint leading his limping horse by the reins. Dr. Christ stopped, pointed to Golo cowering in the back seat with his broken ankle, explained the situation briefly, and quite forgot to announce the birth of a daughter to the new father. Viktor only learned about it from the beaming Anya's lips when he arrived at the verandah steps. He quickly ran upstairs, hesitated at the door to the Green Rooms, and gave a short knock.

Wearing a clean nightgown, her hair freshly combed, his wife rested against the clean linen of her pillows. The April sun fell through the dotted-swiss curtains onto the cradle. Joachim and Edda, their faces reverent, stood at either side. A genre painting, in which the father briefly takes his place.

278

In spite of the ill feeling of the previous night—he had slept in one of the guest rooms—he addressed a few words of praise to his wife, who, unaccustomed to such treatment and equally intent on giving him pleasure, therefore suggested that the child be named Viktoria after her father, especially as she was born at the moment of a major German victory announcement, the sinking of thirty-eight thousand gross tons!

Viktor expressed pleasure at both the name and the special bulletin. He stayed with Maximiliane for a quarter of an hour, which seemed long to both of them, and Maximiliane revealed one of her secret thoughts—an act that could be explained only by her exhaustion.

"You know, this is the way I think it is. Somewhere somebody dies, and his soul is liberated and finds a new home in our child. Can you imagine that?"

"With the best will in the world, I certainly can't!" he said. "You should get some sleep. The delivery must have taken its toll on you."

She would have liked to explain that a birth was not a delivery but a reception, but before she could begin, he declared that he would now enter the child on the Quindt oak tree. He leaned down to Joachim. "Do you want to come with me?"

The little boy grew frightened, as he always did when his father spoke to him. He nodded and stammered some unintelligible words.

"Enter Edda too, Viktor."

"Maximiliane, I beg of you!"

"Enter her! And when you go to the town hall to register Viktoria, fix up Edda's papers, too. Before you go off to Russia."

"You need your sleep now. But if it makes you feel better."

Edda took her father's hand and said, "Come, Uncle." She continued to call him Uncle, while she used Mother for Maximiliane.

Maximiliane closed her eyes and begged Viktor to send Anya.

"I can't understand, Maximiliane, what you see in that Polish—"

"Send Anya."

For the first time his mind formed the thought that he had not, after all, married a Pomeranian goose.

Anya was holding a casket in both hands. The Baroness had asked her to deliver it. Placing it on the coverlet, she opened the lid to reveal a necklace, a bracelet, and earrings—sapphires pale as water, rimmed with diamonds. Anya insisted that Maximiliane put on the jewelry, and she helped her before fetching the hand mirror. She took the baby from the cradle, laid it beside Maximiliane, and said reverently, "Beautiful mother."

After a while Viktor returned, also bearing a box. He had bought some amber jewelry for his wife to celebrate the birth of the child—also a necklace, a bracelet, and earrings, not the pale amber but the brown-gold kind, East Prussian gold, more suitable to Maximiliane both in color and in shape than her grandmother's sapphires and diamonds, which she was already wearing.

Viktor, too, kept having trouble with these Quindts! Always he was the one who had married in, the one without possessions, a man who made a gift of amber. A Quint without a *d* and without a prefix of nobility, with only a Party badge and a Party card as counterweights. Instead of handing Maximiliane his present, he placed it on top of the bureau, which had been fitted out for changing the baby. It lay there for days, unnoticed, until Maximiliane finally discovered it and was pleased to the point of tears. Though the jewelry was heavy and uncomfortable, she wore it day and night. But by then it was too late to make up to Viktor for his initial disappointment.

Maximiliane, whose feelings could still be summed up in a single word, devotion, once again did not have a chance to get used to her husband. By the time she had begun to have a little confidence in him, he was back at the railroad station.

That first evening after the birth, she heard her grandfather's footsteps in the hall. He was audibly limping. Again tears clung to her lashes, and her vision blurred. Old Quindt had not counted on that; he misinterpreted her tears.

"Last night—that really didn't have to happen. I'm so sorry, my child. When people get old, they ought to gradually unlearn all the words they gradually learned when they were children." Then he pointed his cane at the cradle. "How does she look, anyway?"

"Like the others. Please sit down."

"I'll stand by the stove. I never liked sitting at bedsides." His eyes came to rest on the necklace. "Look at that! Sophie Charlotte! It was my gift to her when her son was born. She never wore the jewelry. She was always a long-sleeved, high-necked person. But it's found lots of room on you, or so it seems." Then he added, "It won't be long now."

"What, Grandfather?"

He shrugged, leaned against the side of the stove, and almost attained his former height. "Everything."

Silence. Only the ceiling light was turned on. Rain beat against the windows. The baby whimpered softly.

Maximiliane tried again. "What I think is that somewhere somebody died. His soul is liberated and seeks a new home. Whose soul might this child have gotten, I wonder?"

"If that's true, many souls must be abroad just now," Quindt said. "All of them the souls of heroes. I never did understand about souls. More about trees."

"Do you know what I've been thinking?" Maximiliane asked after a while.

"You seem to have been doing a lot of thinking."

"When people get old—old enough, I mean, like you and Grandmother will be someday—then they should come to a stop and put down roots. They should live on for a while as trees and not have to go underground at once and be weighted down with a stone. Are you listening to me, Grandfather?"

"Yes. I'm listening very hard. The idea isn't at all bad. But who gave it to you? Our good Reverend Merzin isn't the right man for it. He never understood anything about trees; he's better on pike. And the new minister, Kühn? He uses God's word to slaughter bunny rabbits; I shall have to give him a rifle. Theological reform can't be expected in Pomerania. 'Dust you are, to dust you shall return,' or however it goes. That doesn't have to be permanent. All the same, a piece of Pomeranian earth, that's worth something."

"You'll live on in your grandchildren," Maximiliane said after a long silence.

"To be precise, they are my great-grandchildren, and they ought to call me Great-grandfather, not Grand-father. Imperceptibly one generation has fallen away—your father was a victim of that collapse."

The conversation died away again, and the infant whimpered more loudly. Old Quindt said, "I'll send the Polish girl to you now. Once again—I'm truly sorry."

Apologies from him were rare. He leaned down and kissed his granddaughter's hand. This was the moment her tears had been waiting for—they sprang from her eyes. How many tears fell on this newborn child! April's child, changeable, unbalanced, in spite of her glorious name a child of the shadows.

Two days after the delivery, the marriage bed was fitted out for Viktor again. Several times in the course of the night—three times, to be exact—the door burst open, childish footsteps pattered through the room, little hands groped across the coverlet and faces; one child after another, they all sought shelter with their mother. When the places to her right and left were occupied, the third child groped around the wide bed and lay next to the father. Maximiliane, who was used to this activity, did not even wake up. But Viktor tossed sleeplessly and restlessly in bed until the child in question had enough of it and took off, bumping into chairs and tables on the way. The same pattern was repeated for three nights; then Viktor thought it better for Maximiliane to sleep in the nursery again along with the infant, who had to be fed as early as six in the morning. He needed his rest.

The next day Viktor rose early, as he always did even on Poenichen, left his room, crossed the hall, and softly opened the door to the nursery. What a sight met his eyes! His wife was fast asleep, one arm laid across her face to protect her from the approaching morning light, a child's head on either side of her: Golo's brown curls and Edda's little braids; both children were also fast asleep. The newborn, nursed an hour previously, snoozed in her cradle. And his oldest son sat peacefully in his bed playing with Edda's doll. He greeted his father by placing a finger across his lips and then smiling. Viktor tarried a few moments, felt very close to the fulfillment of all his desires, etched the image deep within his mind, and took it along to the front.

On the last morning of his furlough, when he intended leaving on the ten-o'-clock train—not back to Berlin this time, but to the front—Viktor woke even earlier than usual. On his way to the nursery, already fully dressed in his uniform, he ran into Anya, who was creeping along the hall in her bare feet toward the stairs that led to her attic room. She wore nothing but an old overcoat, which she held closed with one hand while carrying her shoes in the other. Her hair was mussed, her cheeks even rosier than usual, her eyes glistening more brightly.

Viktor confronted her and eventually discovered that she had spent the night with Claude, the gardener, a French prisoner of war. "Excuse, sir," she stammered.

After breakfast Viktor asked the Baron for a short interview. It turned out that he was not telling the old man anything new. Old Quindt merely agreed to advise the two to be more discreet.

Viktor was outraged. "You tolerate this sort of behavior under your roof?"

"Oh, well, a roof—it tends to cover quite a few things, whether I tolerate them or not," Old Quindt replied. "Besides, I presume that those two do their hot and heavy business in the hothouse, where it's warm. But to tell you the truth, I never bothered to concern myself with the details of lovemaking. When it's spring, they all pair off. Claude, the Frenchman; Anya, the Polish girl—they're my best people now. They are attached to me in both senses of the word. I believe that they'll stay if all goes well—I mean, well for us. They'll be better off settling down on Poenichen than in occupied France or occupied Poland. Claude comes from the Medoc region, and I enjoy talking to him. His father owns a vineyard. Claude can't make a vineyard of Poenichen, but the tobacco he's been planting is quite remarkable. On the south side of the hothouse. Poenichen sand leaf, doubly fermented. To the best of my knowledge, he uses honey for the fermentation process."

Viktor interrupted. "It was not my intention to discuss tobacco raising with you."

"Really? It would have been a neutral topic," Quindt said.

"It causes me considerable worry and distress to see this infiltration of our home by the prisoners of war and the forced laborers."

Old Quindt lost control. "By comparison, theirs is a peaceful infiltration. To be conquered by German troops is—"

284

Viktor cut him short. "Not another word. Otherwise I shall be forced–"

"Not another word under my roof!" Quindt spoke curtly and rose, putting an end to the interview.

That evening, when they were alone, Old Quindt asked his wife, "Do you understand it, Sophie Charlotte? I was an idealist when I was young. Then I became a nationalist. To the extent that a Pomeranian can be passionate, I was even a passionate nationalist. And now I come to realize that I am more and more a pacifist. A Prussian pacifist! Right in the middle of the war, during the victorious advance of German troops on every front. But I'll tell you this much: we'll win ourselves to death."

The birth of the child was broadcast by printed announcements: "The parents' joy is shared by the other children–Joachim, Edda, and Golo." The wording served to make Edda's arrival public as well. Congratulations poured in from everywhere. "How happy you must be, Maxi! It seems like yesterday that we clustered in the reeds on our island and you read poetry to us." "Children are the best proof of a happy marriage."

A congratulatory note arrived from Ingo Brandes, a fighter pilot with the rank of lieutenant. "After a brief furlough at home, I am back with my unit," he wrote.

Years ago, if I did not wear a muffler in the winter or wanted to go swimming on a chilly day, my mother always said, "One of these days you'll catch your death, my boy." She's stopped saying it. She lets me go off without warning me to be careful. Surely a bad sign. I have nine hits on my record. I was even cited by name in the army report. I'm highly thought of in Bamberg, which esteem is reflected in the sales of my father's beer. Whose hit list has my name on it, and how far down the list am I?

I'll tell you this much, Maxi: killing is almost as quick as begetting, and just as enjoyable. But the raising of new people, which can quench the lust for killing, still takes too long. I understand too little about begetting and nothing at all about rearing. Your knowledge is all the greater, judging from your announcement. Do you still sleep so deeply? Do you still sleep through everything? Oh, when the owl screeched while the moon rode high over the valley. . . .

How could Maximiliane help bursting into tears over such a letter from the front? A few weeks later another letter came from the front, though it made no mention of the newborn child; it was from Major Christian Blaskorken. They had lost touch with him years before. The letter explained that when universal conscription was reintroduced, he had had himself reactivated as an officer, that he was presently stationed at the Eastern front as a battalion commander, and that the flat Eastern landscape reminded him more than ever of his years on Poenichen. "When the war is over," he concluded, "the first thing I'll do is pay a visit to Poenichen." This letter, too, made Maximiliane cry.

News of the death of old Max von Quindt arrived from Königsberg. Heading the list of mourners was Erwin Max von Quindt, "major general, at present stationed in the East." Klaus von Quindt, the second son, had worked his way up to colonel. Old Quindt studied the announcement and remarked, "A promotion list, pure and simple."

Maximiliane's milk stopped sooner than it had after her first two births, so little Viktoria was not nursed for long; she became a bottle baby. Her christening took place only after her father's departure, among a small circle of friends. Having looked in vain for a baptismal certificate among the papers Fräulein Preissing had turned over to her, Maximiliane concluded that Edda had never been christened. So they would have to arrange for a double ceremony, and it would be best to have old Reverend Merzin officiate.

Since she was older, Edda was christened first. Next the infant was held over the font by Martha Riepe, serving as godmother. During the ceremony Golo, who was feeling neglected, began to bellow at the top of his lungs. In order to silence him, the Reverend Merzin sprinkled some holy water on him as well—a twice-christened boy! Maximiliane was able to stop Joachim from joining in the din only by whispering "Mose" while pulling his head, which sported the clergyman's wig, to her side.

At that moment she was flooded with images: Mose in his basket on the lake, the Führer's piercing eyes, Fraülein Preissing leading the little girl by the hand, Golo in his plaster cast, Viktor in the window of the train compartment. She grew unsteady. At the identical moment she felt her son's slight body tauten under her hand, lending her support. A child who needed responsibility.

27

Why is the writer not given the power to prevent the outbreak of war so everything can continue as before, with sun and rain, thanksgiving for the harvest, hunting parties, and at regular intervals a christening dinner? The writer is constrained by the unalterable course of history. In view of the Second World War and its consequences, one wonders how Maximiliane lived through it all. At least she had a sound constitution as well as the inborn faculty of being able to sleep in just about any situation. In addition, she had been trained to adaptability. These had to carry her through. The fact that she kept giving birth to children, thus increasing the difficulties ahead of her, is further proof of an author's impotence.

Even in Pomerania such statements as "We better enjoy the war while we can, who knows what the peace will be like" were already gaining currency. Matchboxes bore the admonition "Loose lips sink ships," and the black "coal filcher" threw his menacing shadow across brick walls. A nation was conserving. A nation had adjusted to the duration of the war. The East became the Reich's air-raid shelter. Still no alarms in the farther reaches of Pomerania, still no enemy planes over the countryside. On Sunday mornings on Poenichen they listened to Bach cantatas from Leipzig; those who felt like it could also listen to the request program on Sunday afternoons: popular and patriotic melodies. Martha Riepe took charge of the radio and knitted socks, ear warmers, wrist warmers, knee warmers.

"What is it you're constantly knitting?" Frau von Quindt asked.

"Things to keep our frontline soldiers warm."

"Of course," said Frau von Quindt.

They clustered together to save fuel and light and to listen to army reports and special bulletins. The differences of which Quindt used to speak so frequently were disappearing steadily. Anya's facility in German improved. There was no way of avoiding the children's learning a few words of Polish at the same time.

The church bell had already been "drafted," to use Quindt's word. The latest plan was to melt down the war memorial as well as the iron fencing surrounding the church and the cemetery. Herr von Quindt had to grant his formal approval.

Priebe the dairyman came to the manor in his capacity as local Party leader, no longer taking off his boots. He planted himself before his master. "We need cannons, not monuments, Herr Quindt."

He was prepared for resistance. Instead, Old Quindt agreed with him. "Anything left over after the war in the way of cannons can be melted down again for a new war memorial—just a little smaller next time. Iron gets used up; a little piece gets lost here and there. But recycling makes sense to me. Monuments to heroes during peacetime, then cannons again during war for the manufacture of future heroes, and so on; always more heroes for smaller monuments. Though I do see one little problem, Herr Priebe."

Priebe, not understanding, stared at him.

"Melt it down, Priebe. Keep on melting it down. Away with all monuments," Quindt repeated.

But Priebe was not ready to leave. He had another matter on his mind. "Another one of those messages came, Herr Quindt. Klukas's oldest." Would the Baron take the message to Klukas's father?

"Klaus? No, Priebe, I'm afraid you'll have to do it yourself. They're your people, after all. No grave, hmm? And now not even a monument to his name. Where is Klukas supposed to place his wreath? No, you can just go there yourself."

"No way, Baron. Klukas will come after me with his rifle."

"Then my granddaughter will have to do it, Priebe."

Maximiliane put on her black confirmation dress, which Frau Görke had already had to alter twice, and took Joachim with her. Klaus Klukas, her prince, Klaus with whom she had played doctor in the juniper bushes, fallen in Russia near Bryansk. . . .

Like the angel of death, from then on she made the rounds of the village, calling twice at three cottages, four times at one, always holding the little master by the hand. Joachim closed his eyes tight, pressed his lips together, and trembled a little whenever his mother said what had to be said. Then he straightened up and made himself strong so that she could lean on him. Ladybug, ladybug. His father was away at the war. Joachim was still very young, but he had a great deal of time to grow into his burdens.

"Oh, the little master," said old Frau Klukas, Klaus's grandmother. "What a fancy little gentleman." She came from Masuria and was more talkative than the other village women.

Of all the Polish prisoners of war and forced laborers, only Anya remained. Of the French prisoners of war, only Claude was left. To replace the others, Poenichen estate was assigned Russian prisoners of war, thirty men who were brought in a truck every morning, watched by a single guard. There was no danger of their trying to escape; Russia was too far away, and the front was still moving farther to the East.

290

When the truck arrived in the mornings, old Riepe–whom the Russians called Little Father–climbed on. Good-naturedly they helped him up. He supervised the work in the fields and the forest, an old unloaded gun slung over his shoulder.

"Turn back," Old Quindt commanded his fifteen-year-old coachman Bruno, the oldest grandson of the widow Slewenka, whenever he caught sight of the column of prisoners from afar.

He had begun avoiding everything.

Since the time years before when his daughter-in-law had published the photographs in the magazine, he clumsily and awkwardly alighted whenever he wanted to speak to one of the farmworkers; he no longer spoke down to them from his seat in the carriage. On days when his rheumatism was worse than usual, he ordered, "Get in. Sit across from me on the coachman's block." So Vera's presence on Poenichen had not, after all, been entirely without consequence.

Quindt's digestive difficulties had temporarily abated during the early war years, as had his rheumatism, improvements for which the simpler, lower-calorie diet deserved credit. He rarely came to the kitchen, where the Russians' dinner was prepared in the big laundry kettle–boiled storage potatoes, not sorted to eliminate the moldy ones. The dish bubbled and had a fermented smell.

"They're not used to anything better; they're no better than animals," old Frau Pech declared, repeating what she had heard on the radio.

"Then we'll have to entrust the dairyman with the feeding of the prisoners; he takes proper care of the cows."

Such statements from Quindt annoyed the old woman but did not change anything. She hated and despised the Russians, but she did not fear them yet. No more borscht as there had been in Anna Riepe's

291

time, twenty-five years earlier. Nevertheless, as though the October Revolution had never happened, the prisoners sang the same old songs.

Maximiliane opened the windows in the nursery. "Listen," she said. "They're singing again." She tried to copy the melody on her recorder, but no breath of wind blew the sounds across the trees back to the prisoners; the relationship remained one-sided.

Claude supplied the Russians with his homegrown tobacco, Anya providing the rolling paper: one special edition after another, all of them printed on thin paper, disappeared from the library. Shakespeare's history plays went up in cigarette smoke unnoticed, since Quindt, because of his rheumatism, no longer reached down to the bottom shelf of the bookcase.

For decades a bookseller in Stettin had sent regular shipments of new publications to Poenichen, but now Quindt had put an end to even his literary connection with the world. "In future please spare me this blood-and-soil literature." He, who used to like to travel often and far—to Sicily, to the Crimea, to Lisbon—now did not even go to Berlin; only once, when it was absolutely unavoidable, he went as far as Dramburg. For years he left the discomforts of travel to others, to Gobineau, Alexander von Humboldt, Thomas Cook; he walked with Seuma to Syracuse, spent long winter afternoons in the Uffizi, which he held on his lap engraved in steel. When even these travels became too strenuous, he reached for Fontane and read *Travels Though the Mark Brandenburg*, where there were many familiar landmarks and many sights resembling Pomerania. He even shared one or another sentence with his wife.

By now they were spending many joint hours in the study—the Ladies' Parlor was no longer heated. The old Baroness sat idle; her eyes were beginning to fail. Enough hands of solitaire laid out, enough coronets stitched, enough dogs bred. Texa, the last wirehaired

292

bitch, lay always at her feet, even at night. Quindt smoked Claude's tobacco in his short-stemmed pipe. Sometimes the two could be seen walking back and forth along the avenue, three hundred meters one way, three hundred meters back. Sometimes they only took a turn around the flower bed. A marriage takes time.

In the evenings, after the children had been put to bed, Maximiliane joined them in the study. She took books from the shelf, sat down at the desk, and in the glow of the green lamp wrote to Viktor. That is, in her large, round script she copied out poems. Even in those days her handwriting revealed her true nature, which had not had a chance to develop to the fullest its elements of expansiveness and generosity, its need for a lot of room. She still did not have a pronounced profile, which might have been due to Pomerania, where the landscape did little to mark the features, but was more particularly due to Old Quindt. In any family only one original can flourish at a time.

Twice a week Maximiliane sent a poem to Viktor's army postal number; he too wrote regularly, letters that continued to resemble official army reports, maintaining complete secrecy about the military situation and his feelings. Poems in one direction, slogans in the other. Any stranger could safely have read Viktor Quint's letters. Maximiliane pored over them attentively and even read them out loud, searching for some hidden, more intimate meanings. She was so spoiled! She knew the correspondence between Heloise and Abelard, Goethe's letters to Frau von Stein, the letters to Diotima. What could she have written in return? That Joachim was losing his baby teeth? That Viktoria's first tooth had broken through? That Erika Schmaltz had been drafted into the auxiliary, as had Lenchen Priebe—one assigned to antiaircraft, the other employed in a munitions factory? That someone or other had brought lice into the house? That all four children had had lice? After all, some baby or other was always teething, and Viktor had never been interested in the lives of the housemaids; unsuitable news, and so she left it out.

Instead she searched for the right poem, instinctively roaming through the fullness of German poetry. At harvest time she copied out the appropriate lines. A long poem, and under it she wrote the name of the author before signing her own large *M*. Viktor replied, "The efforts of the Russ. pris. hopefully suffice to bring in the harvest, so that the victualing of the troops and the civilian population can be guaranteed. We must demand the utmost in effort and sacrifice from all."

Maximiliane did not begrudge the labor of copying out poems covering two and three pages. She wrote what she had written to the ensign in Potsdam years before–without, however, giving him a single thought. "Love speaks to love: what is not yet mine?" This time the question was put with greater justification.

No soldier can ever have received as many poems as Viktor. But how else could she have let him know what moved her? Her own words? She had little faith in them; hers was not a communicative nature. So, as the moon waxed, she sent him a poem that spoke of the moon shining so brightly over the valley as to wake the sleeper.

Well before the next new moon Viktor's answer was at hand, but the moon over the copper beech on the grounds was not the same moon that made their position along the Dnieper so dangerous. "We are stationed along the D.," Viktor wrote. "Our unit has suffered negligible losses, and the advance continues inexorably. We shall cross Russia's rivers one after the other; nothing can stop us. You should see my unit. Each fellow deeply committed to all the others." A postscript explained that after a successful reconnaissance mission, he had been promoted to lieutenant.

294

Joachim was old enough to have his father's letters read to him. He stood very still, clenching his hands into fists, pressing his lips together, and trembling. Each letter robbed him of the power of speech for several hours, but he carried the latest one around until the next arrived, only then placing it in a shoebox Martha Riepe had fitted out with blue velvet for the purpose. It stood next to the other box on the mantel.

Maximiliane and the children brought rushes from the shores of the Blue Pond and wove them into little baskets as Fräulein Eberle had taught her to do. These they sent to the front, and in summer wreaths of heather. She never sent a poem without adding a pressed flower—rape blossoms, flax, and immortelles. The poems she chose dealt with the seasons, wars of liberation, and love. "The rooks are cawing," she copied, while outside the window hooded crows cawed in the dusk before settling in their communal sleeping place, untold black-headed birds roosting in a single tree. The frost had driven them from Russia to Pomerania. "Woe to the homeless wanderer."

Viktor wrote back, "A huge sphere of action lies before us! It will take time before this underdeveloped agrarian country can be turned into a civilized and cultivated land. Pulley wells in the villages! No electricity, only crude oil lamps! The population sleeps on top of the stoves—whole families of them! Vermin abound. We have preferred sleeping in tents, but the approaching cold forces us to spend the night in these shacks."

Having noticed the word *tents* in his letter, Maximiliane copied out for him Münchhausen's poem "Beyond the Valley Stand Their Tents," which she had sung so often at Hermannswerder. She pasted a yellow maple leaf in the margin. And Viktor replied, "It would be a good idea for you to start learning Russian. I'm sure you can find a textbook; I do not consider contact with the prisoners advisable. This war will be followed by a long period of occupation. I am considering whether my place might not be in the Eastern territories. Until Joachim reaches his majority, Poenichen can be administered by a good estate manager, but here, where they are used to having the master watch over everything, a physical presence will be imperative. You ask about a possible leave. In every fiber of my being I am anything but a leave taker. 'Return as a victor.' You will recall this admonition by the women of Athens to their husbands and sons. It is as true today as it ever was. Our goal is called Moscow. We shall conquer the heart of Russia. I trust that you are raising my sons to be brave and courageous men, according to His slogan 'Tough as leather, hard as Krupp steel, quick as greyhounds.' And the girls as befits their future tasks as mothers."

Maximiliane answered with another poem, calligraphy shaped by a calm hand.

"Rain and mud," Viktor wrote, "can slow down our advance, but they cannot halt it. For the time being the soil has been transformed into soft soap. But the frosts will come and, like last winter, will make an alliance with us; then we shall move on, ever eastward. Tell the children that their father has become the holder of the Iron Cross Second Class. That shall not be the end of it! In your letters I miss news of home."

Thereupon Maximiliane informed him that an emergency order from the Führer had declared Willem Riepe "worthy of bearing arms" for the duration of the war. His family was now living in the distillery, and the foreman's cottage had been fitted out for evacuees. She added another poem.

But what did Viktor care about news of Riepe, the ex-concentration-camp inmate? And what did he care about poems? Both were wasted on him. He threw a hasty glance at the page with the pressed flower and handed it over to his dispatch rider, who had a feeling for that sort of thing—Rudolf Hebe, private first class, a high-school teacher from Gera, a reserved, shy young man who never got any mail from girls. Viktor regularly passed Maximiliane's letters on to him, and Private First Class Hebe read them over and over and saved them. He waited more longingly for the letters than did the lieutenant to whom they were addressed, he fell in love with the woman's handwriting, he forgot that the poetry was not meant for him. He took Maximiliane's large *M* to stand for Maleen. Each word of every poem went straight to his heart. Somewhere there lived a woman who understood him, who loved Stefan George and Rilke.

Falling snow, driving snow, blizzards of snow! And Viktor's Emanuel Quint-like dislike of snowstorms, now transformed into hatred of the enemy. As cold as twenty degrees below freezing. Just in time, before the Russian winter set in, Martha Riepe's secret packages arrived: balaclava helmet, knee warmers, and socks of sheep's wool.

Maximiliane sent homemade stars of straw so that he could decorate the earthen bunker for Christmas, along with a candle and a little dog Joachim had modeled from window putty and painted. She also included the "Kashubian Christmas Song" with its reference to the good beer of Putzig, mentioned once before in the context of the Polish lieutenant and the dunes of Zoppot. What joy and happiness for Private First Class Rudolf Hebe! He gave Lieutenant Quint more than half the Thuringer salami his parents had sent him.

Viktor Quint suffered his first wound during the defensive warfare south of Smolensk. That same night on Poenichen they heard the armed-forces report: "All quiet in the central sector." So they were reassured in the study. "Thank God," Martha Riepe said, though without doing so, and turned off the radio.

One more Second Lieutenant Quint—as he announced in a letter from the field hospital in Minsk—

had received a bullet in the lung, but not of the fatal kind. An infantry gun, missing its target, had hit him. Another got Private First Class Hebe, and his wound was fatal. His effects, among them the poem-covered pages in chronological order, were sent to his family in Gera. His mother and father felt a little comforted in their grief over the loss of their son by the thought that he had found someone who loved him and wrote to him. They saved the pages with the pressed Pomeranian flowers forever. Nothing is as dependable as the effect and permanence of poetry.

They still had no baby carriage on Poenichen, though by now it would have been worthwhile. But which child should have been walked in it, and who would have pushed it? Too many children and no Fräulein, as in times gone by. Instead, Martha Riepe painted the old handcart blue.

In good weather–that is to say, almost every day, since the demands made on the weather were not excessive–Maximiliane filled the cart with pillows, children, apples, and books after dinner. Joachim and Golo flanked the shaft and pulled, Edda was made to push. As soon as they reached the sandy path, they all took off their shoes to take better care of them, thus strengthening their feet. Though they could not go far with their vehicle and never made it to Poenichen Lake, they did get almost to the Blue Pond, the wind-sheltered hollow from the Ice Age. At the edge of the grainfield they stopped; blankets and pillows, dolls and children were unloaded. Each child received an apple. Joachim first played with his a while, then ate it–seeds, stem, and all, like his mother. Golo ate his apple at once but left almost half the juicy pulp clinging to the core, giving his mother the rest. Edda pressed her apple close, making sure no one took it from her.

Once again Maximiliane in her full blue skirt crouched at the edge of a field. The world was never as vast as at noon during the height of summer in Pomerania; at that time the earth breathed and stretched. When she closed her eyes, Maximiliane thought she could feel the world turning, repeatedly passing the sun; she thought she could feel its centrifugal force, and she anxiously laid her hands on her children so that they would not be whirled away. Then she reached for a book, but Golo knocked it out of her hand. He was jealous of the books from which his mother fetched witches, queens, and bears. "Tell!" he commanded, and his mother told the fairy tales she remembered, including the one about the fisherman and his wife, which Amma had told her by the big stove in the kitchen.

Joachim, wearing that sensible expression of his, asked, "What are you supposed to wish for if you already have a castle?"

"Oh, Mose," his mother replied, pulling her oldest child close.

Every day she had to tell the story of the goose girl: "Alas, Falada, hanging there!" Joachim pressed his fist to his lips, frightened. Golo looked around wildly, brandishing a stick. Edda repeated everything in a babble and pulled the hairpins from her mother's hair while Maximiliane sang,

> Blow, blow, thou gentle wind, I say,
> Blow Conrad's little hat away,
> And make him chase it here and there,
> Until I have braided all my hair,
> And bound it up again.

By the time she had told three stories, all were asleep: Viktoria, pale-eyed and sensitive, in the shade of the cart; Edda, in spite of her freckles, in the bright sunlight. The corn was in bloom, and the seeds dusted them. Silence. Until the cry of a buzzard circling overhead roused the children, but not their mother. Maximiliane did not awaken until the buzzard plummeted down on a young hare and the children drove the bird away with their screams.

At night in the nursery mother and children continued to sleep. Five beds were lined up in a row, one of them in reserve; Viktoria still slept in the cradle. Maximiliane still sought a clean, cool bed whenever her own—additionally heated by Joachim or Edda, and doubly so when Golo, who always slept himself into a sweat, lay next to her—grew too warm for her. When after a time any given child missed the maternal closeness, it got up, looked for her, and lay down by her side again. A silent changing of places; in the mornings no one woke up in the same bed in which he had gone to sleep.

The last sheaf was tied and burned. Old Frau Klukas undertook this chore, muttering and leaping in the noonday sun—a ritual about which neither Quindt nor Kalinski, let alone Local Party Leader Priebe, knew anything. Thus the grain demon was banished for 1943. A short while later Viktor returned to Poenichen on convalescent leave. When his wife and the cartful of children set out again for the Blue Pond, he went along. He lifted little Viktoria onto his shoulder, where, blissful and anxious all at the same time, she sat enthroned, wavering and dizzy at that great height, held fast only by her feet.

It was a hot day in August, the hottest day of the year. The air was filled with summer sounds: the threshing machine, the chirping of crickets, dragonflies in the reeds. The children splashed in the water, screeching with pleasure. Edda gave one of her piercing shrieks; Golo, unhampered this summer by a plaster cast, beat his stick on the water; and little Viktoria crawled, still awkward but at least on her own legs, in the warm sand. Their parents were thus undisturbed for a time, something that was never the case at night. When the door to the Green Rooms was not locked, the children

300

stormed the marital bed; when it was locked, they began to holler.

So this was their first peaceful moment during the leave. Because of the heat, both were wearing bathing suits. Maximiliane's skin was evenly tanned, her hair unevenly bleached; she was the most beautiful thing under the sun far and wide. For the first time she saw the red-rimmed scars on her husband's body by daylight: the smaller one on his chest, the larger one on his back. She covered them with her hands, as if wishing after the fact to protect his body or to heal it. What a surprise—Viktor was vulnerable. Once again under her stroking fingers the gooseflesh effect set in; she had power over him. She felt something like magic.

They looked at each other. Maximiliane pointed to the small secluded bay, the hiding place in the reeds that twenty years earlier had served the same purpose for the governesses and Christian Blaskorken: invitingly warm, sandy soil.

But Blaskorken had been less timid and had not just come back from being wounded in some Russian forest. A noise in the reeds, then the cry of a bird overhead, and already the children's screams had shooed away their father along with the buzzard. Thus they prevented their mother's fourth pregnancy.

There would not be another baby, then, one not old enough to walk when Pomerania had to be abandoned.

28

"The war is going downhill," Old Quindt said.

German troops were being forced to retreat on all fronts. American units were landing at Salerno. The Allies' storming of Fortress Europe had begun.

On the map of Europe that hung in the farmworkers' mess Martha Riepe halted the retreat of the German forces. On Poenichen the pins remained stuck into the most advanced strongholds, and the threads of yarn continued to hold fast to the battle lines of November 1942 on the Atlantic Coast and at the Black Sea; Rhodes was occupied, and the Lofoten were in German hands. The old issues of the *Völkischer Beobachter* were no longer replaced with new ones; the edition of November 20, 1942, remained hanging on the wall, as if the news of that day would be valid forever.

Along the Channel coast, where Second Lieutenant Quint and his unit had been stationed for some time, all remained quiet.

His unit was "stationed," but he himself was "posted"–"to an advanced position, in expectation of the enemy." "Not in fear!" as he reported to Poenichen. "Should they be so bold as to attack us, we shall make things very uncomfortable for them. We lay mines along the beach, we ram tree trunks into the ground, we set up steel obstacles. If they expect to find the coast dotted

302

with resort hotels and dancing pavilions, they are mistaken. We keep our eyes fixed ahead, on the enemy!"

At some moment he must have turned his eyes away after all. His next letter mentioned "apple orchards in bloom," "meadows dotted with herds of sheep," "calvados and camembert." By now Viktor had been conquered by a French schoolteacher from the village of Roignet, Marie Blanc by name. She had achieved what Maximiliane had never been able to achieve—for a few weeks Viktor was more man than soldier. A brisk exchange of pampering and tenderness began. Dried pears and smoked boar from Pomerania in French cooking pots, and Second Lieutenant Quint in a French bed, not always easy in his mind. But what was he to do with his fighting spirit during this long, nerve-wracking period of waiting?

Because Hitler was convinced that the Allies would cross the English Channel at its narrowest point, between Dover and Calais, he massed the German troops at Calais. As a result widespread peace of mind prevailed along the Normandy coast. One June night the officers of the regiment to which Viktor Quint was assigned had a party in the mess of the little castle at Roignet, more lighthearted than ever thanks to the 140-proof calvados and the inclement weather. The enemy would certainly not begin an offensive under such unfavorable conditions. In this context one of their frequent strategic discussions unfolded: "Where will the Allies attack?" One of the officers, a lieutenant, declared that all signs pointed to an attack on the steep Normandy coast—in their own sector, and not, as the Gregenalt claimed, near Calais; *Gregenalt* being his acronym for "Greatest General of All Time"—Hitler.

Second Lieutenant Quint reached for his pistol, as quick on the draw as his son Golo, even after five glasses of calvados. The regimental commander managed to calm him down and administered a rebuke to the lieutenant who had been so disrespectful. The party would have run its course like many others before it had there not been one officer who was a pyromaniac, a man with an almost pathological drive to set fires. To bring the festivities to a glorious finish, he had used the powder from shells and grenades to set off fireworks on the castle terrace. To "fan the flames," as he put it, he poured a bottle of high-proof calvados into the fire, and to add the crowning touch, he emptied into it all the bullets in his pistol, creating a grand display into which the wind blew and which brightly lit up the facade of the darkened castle.

Second Lieutenant Quint did his best to stop the spectacle, and in his effort he came too close to the flames: a detonating shell tore into his right arm. The commander's car took him to the field hospital at once. There he was the first casualty of the invasion.

Two hours after the fireworks of Roignet, Operation Overlord, the Allied invasion, began along the Normandy front. In the general confusion there could be no disciplinary action, much less a court martial, for willful discharge of fireworks in the vicinity of the enemy. Instead, Second Lieutenant Quint was given a commendation for his fearless defense of the Führer and Commander in Chief of the Armed Forces. Since the flesh wound was extensive and the bone of the upper arm was splintered, the arm had to be amputated at the shoulder.

Maximiliane's letters and Martha Riepe's packages came back stamped "Hold for new APO number." The next letter from the front to arrive on Poenichen was addressed in a woman's handwriting.

Martha Riepe, who brought in the mail, tore open the envelope in her worry and eagerness and rushed to the study to let the Baron be the first to learn the news of the young master's severe injury. On her way, the Baroness intercepted her. "Martha! Martha! Call my granddaughter–she's sure to be in the garden–and give the letter to her."

Maximiliane read the letter, which had been dictated to a Red Cross nurse, out loud. It was short. Not one word this time about world events, but no word either about the circumstances and nature of the injury. There was, however, the sentence "I shall learn to write with my left hand and to fire with my left hand. There will be a position where I can serve my fatherland even with only one arm."

"Heil Hitler," said Quindt.

At which Martha Riepe also, though in a different tone, said, "Heil Hitler."

"I feel like I'm hearing old von Kalck, who was still young then," Quindt said, turning to his wife. " 'Eighty-five thousand captured Russians–what price one measly arm?' "

"But that's not a proper comparison, Quindt," the Baroness objected.

"No, Sophie Charlotte, that's no comparison, and an arm isn't an arm, and war isn't war."

"We're not alone, Quindt," his wife warned.

Whereupon Martha Riepe excused herself and left the room.

Maximiliane read out the closing sentence. "I am now the proud wearer of the German Cross in Gold."

"I'm sure he'll be able to wear the medal with one arm." Quindt sounded bitter.

When Maximiliane had overcome her initial fear, she said, "Perhaps Viktor is safe now. They can't send him to the front with one arm, can they, Grandfather? Perhaps he'll come home for good."

" 'Dear God in heaven,' old Frau Schmaltz would have said."

"I beg of you, Quindt," his wife admonished.

"It's all right, Sophie Charlotte, I won't say anything more."

Before the Allied ring closed around the German units near Falaise, Second Lieutenant Quint had been transferred to the Luxembourg field hospital. There he heard the news of the July 20 assassination attempt on Hitler, when a bomb intended for the Führer had exploded in his headquarters near Rastenburg in East Prussia. In the aftermath of the attempt, seven hundred officers were arrested. Just about every aristocratic family was involved in the resistance movement through a father, son, or son-in-law.

For the first time Viktor wrote in his own hand—his left one. "I can only hope and pray that no member of the Quindt family is guilty of treason against our people. Since that fateful day a chasm has opened between the Quints and the von Quindts! If there were even a single Quindt among the traitors, my first bullet would be for him, the second for myself."

After listening to the letter, Old Quindt said, "I can only hope, and in this case I'm even prepared to pray, that a Quindt was among them."

"The swan song of the German nobility," he said, hours later, to his wife. And he added, "It's not worth it anymore."

After that day all the mail that reached Poenichen had been opened; the telephone was bugged, Baron von Quindt was interrogated twice, and the house was searched twice. And once again they owed it to their relation to Viktor Quint, a former department head in the Reich Genealogical Office and wearer of the German Cross in Gold, that though they came under suspicion, they were not further molested.

Viktor Quint had been transferred to a hospital within Germany, to Berlin in fact, in accordance with his specific request. If she wanted to visit him, he wrote to his wife, he would be pleased to see her; as for himself, given recent events, he would not again set foot on Poenichen. Painful as it was for him not to see his children's development with his own eyes, he advised that they not be exposed to the constant air raids that had to be expected in the capital. He begged for photographs.

All four children were therefore lined up against the white pillar that appeared in almost all the snapshots taken on Poenichen, and Maximiliane made the trip to Berlin alone, carrying the pictures in her purse.

The first evening Viktor took her to a cellar bar. An old man wearing an old tailcoat sat at an old piano and played old songs. The two shared a bottle of wine and danced. Viktor's one arm held her as tightly as, in previous years, his two arms had done.

The mood was cheerful. Most of the patrons, including Maximiliane and Viktor, sang along when the piano player played the song of the brave little soldier's wife. Maximiliane's eyes glistened; she was wearing her best dress and her amber jewelry, she had pinned up her hair, and she looked surprisingly grown up. She sent a glass of wine over to the piano player and asked him to play her favorite, an old number about the love of home. She stood next to the piano, sang along, and was applauded. The waiter, listening to the aerial-warfare report on the radio, announced that enemy squadrons were approaching Berlin. It was not long before the sirens howled the preliminary alarm, and a few minutes later the alarm proper. But there was no reason to leave the bar since they were already underground. On the other hand, there was every reason to turn out the lights, except for a few soft, red lamps. "Red light, let's dance the tango . . ." Dancing more quickly, laughing more loudly, everything passes, love of home . . .

After the all-clear Viktor took Maximiliane to her hotel; he himself had to return to the hospital.

Maximiliane fell asleep and slept through the second alarm of the night. The sirens did not wake her, nor did the night clerk's knocking. She did not come to until broken glass and a window frame fell on her bed. She lay unharmed under the shards, her face protected by her arm. For a time she did not move. Through the empty window she saw a piece of sky brightened by the flares, heard the crackle of fire, screams and detonations, the cough of the antiaircraft guns. All of them were noises unknown to her until now. Jumping out of bed, she looked for her clothers, dressed hurriedly, left her room, and went down the rubble-covered staircase. On the street two men on fire watch yelled at her and pulled her into a cellar, where she sat among strangers until the all-clear sirens freed the city. She began to walk among burning and collapsed houses, picking her way through the streets in the direction of the railroad station.

That night she arrived on Poenichen without her luggage, dirty, her clothes torn.

In Roignet on the Normandy coast the schoolteacher Marie Blanc, who had remained in hiding, had her hair shorn publicly because she had gone with a German officer during the Occupation. She was denounced and defamed as she was led through the village. For years she was barred from practicing her profession.

The miracle weapons, the flying rockets, would change the fortunes of war and bring final victory, Hitler announced, and Viktor passed the message on to Poenichen. The wounded stump had healed over, and he was posted to the Führer's headquarters in the Taunus mountains, from where for the present Hitler directed military activities in the West.

Maximiliane told the children that their father was now an ordnance officer with the Führer. When Joachim asked what that meant, she explained that an ordnance officer's chief duty was to expedite secret letters.

"Then Papa is a mailman, like old Frau Klukas?" Joachim pursued.

"Something like that," his mother agreed.

"The Western ramparts will withstand the enemy!" one of Viktor's subsequent curt letters declared. But the Western ramparts were breached. The enemy set foot on German soil—"Not with impunity!" as Viktor wrote.

During all these earthshaking events Viktor's mother, who expected and received regular reports on the state of her grandchildren, wrote letters from Breslau concerning "the care and feeding of infants," as Quindt put it. "I cannot understand why Viktoria is still not toilet-trained at more than two years of age! I never needed a single diaper for my children. Prevention! From the first, prevention."

Quindt, to whom this letter too was read, commented, "Prevention as a way of life. Nothing but prevention. What's the woman got against diapers? She doesn't have to wash them."

The manor house had filled with people from the West, some who had been bombed out, others who were evacuees. It became harder and harder for them to keep out of each other's way. Additional cooking and laundry facilities had to be devised. Crates filled with linen and silver and everything that was of greatest value to the Quindts with or without the *d* had to be stored away against robbery in dry attics and empty rooms. The only help left in the house was Anya, and only Claude to work on the grounds. There was no one to pick the fruit, so that chore, too, fell to Maximiliane.

Watching four children at the same time, she picked strawberries, gooseberries, and currants, spent whole afternoons among the raspberry bushes, where the heat accumulated. "She never stops," they said approvingly in the village. By the time she had picked the last row of raspberries clean, the next batch had already ripened in the first row. Joachim, the young master, stood by idly. Golo dipped both arms deep in the filled buckets and smeared the juice all over little Viktoria, who was tied by a long line to one of the cherry trees, always in the shade but nevertheless tormented by sunburn. Only Edda helped with the picking, a five-year-old little housewife with clever hands, always chattering.

In this, the final summer, Maximiliane still loaded up the handcart occasionally and led her children barefoot along the sandy path to the Blue Pond, still told them stories about Conrad's little hat and the fisherman and his wife.

One day Joachim interrupted to ask, "Did you not have a father either, just like us?"

"But you do have a father, Mose," Maximiliane said, lifting Viktoria from her lap and drawing her oldest

310

child to her. "Father is away at war, he only lost his arm."

"But I can't remember," Joachim insisted.

"Uncle is your father, boy," Edda said,

"And you didn't have a mother either?" Joachim continued the interrogation.

"I had the Fräuleins. And besides, I had Grandpa and Gamma."

"We have only you."

"Mose, you do have a father. When the war is over, he'll come back."

"Are you absolutely sure? Do you promise?"

"The only thing I'm absolutely sure of is that tonight the sun will set in the west and rise again tomorrow morning in the east. I promise you that much."

The August apples ripened, and none was allowed to spoil; an entire nation was in need of food. Every morning Bruno loaded the baskets of fruit on the milk wagon and took them to town. In the baking ovens pears were dried. Anya ran even more quickly carrying shovelfuls of glowing coals through the house, heating up even more stoves, bringing hot-water bottles and chamomile tea to the Baroness's bedside. Claude had ceased to be any use; he stood brooding around the hothouse, barely working at all, occupied almost entirely with his reflections. He had asked Anya if she would flee with him—his village in France was already liberated—but she had refused; she did not want to abandon the children.

Alarming reports came in rapid succession. Ingo Brandes was shot down on his sixty-seventh mission; Walter Quint, Viktor's younger brother, met his death on the Eastern front; during an air-raid alarm on Breslau, Grandmother Quint suffered a heart attack; the Youth Affairs Office in Pankow reported that Hilde Jeschek, née Preissing, had been killed in an air raid. From Dramburg Riepe brought the news that Deutsch, the attorney, had been deported; and Pech, the stationmaster, claimed that he had seen with his own eyes whole cattle cars filled with deportees. Aunt Maximiliane wrote that Eyckel Castle was unrecognizable; people who had been bombed out, most of them from Nuremberg, lived in the rooms of the youth hostel, "dishonoring our time-honored ancestral abode."

Autumn came and the fields had to be tilled, as in every other year. Griesemann, Bruno, and the youngest son of the smith plowed with the tractors while the women used the slow oxen for harrowing. They left the killing of the geese until later than usual. Edda picked blackberry leaves, which were dried in the stove for tea and tobacco. Claude had even stopped seeing to the curing of tobacco, and his leaves had grown moldy.

In the evenings, when Maximiliane had to produce her letters to Viktor, her eyes closed with exhaustion. In the summer he had written her from the hospital, "This is not the time for poems, Maximiliane! I'm sorry to have to write you this. I had hoped that you, as my wife, would develop a sense of fitness yourself in the course of the war." Thereupon Maximiliane stopped searching out and copying poems, thus saving herself a great deal of time, but her letters grew shorter and shorter, and she wrote less frequently.

"The fall tillage is in difficulties because of the heavy and steady rain. The draw oxen become stuck, but so do the tractors. The boars are wreaking a great deal of damage, so Kalinski has had the prisoners dig holes and cover them with twigs. The distillery is shut down altogether; this year all the potatoes have to be handed over. They're still waiting in freight cars at the railroad station, and most of them are growing moldy because of the damp."

Maximiliane, fearful that every report she gave might either offend Viktor or be of no interest to him, crossed out most of what she wrote, so that her letters looked as if they had gone through the censor's hands. Old Quindt, who followed her efforts from his armchair, finally said, "If there's nothing left to say, it's time for action. Send him a package. He won't misunderstand smoked breast of goose."

"Martha Riepe sends him that."

"Is that right? Does she indeed?"

"The main thing is that he gets it; then it doesn't matter who sends it."

"Objectively you're right, but subjectively . . ."

The few statements of which Quindt still delivered himself were usually left unfinished. Soon after July 20 he had retired to the study and had his bed made up there; a screen concealed a washbowl and the chair for his necessities. He did not wish to meet the many strangers in the manor. Even on warm days a fire was lit in the fireplace, and he would not allow the shutters to be opened or the blackout shades to be raised. The lamp on his desk burned night and day. Quindt rose only occasionally to put another log on the fire. Sometimes his wife sat with him, silent and idle. Everything had been said; what had not been said by now did not need saying. Prussia, Pomerania, Poenichen–the three great P's. For these he had lived, and in the end not even Poenichen would be left. Soviet troops had already crossed the East Prussian frontier, and there would not be a second Tannenberg.

Quindt no longer tore the leaves off the calendar, no longer wound the clock; he merely waited for the end. He had no further desire to see Kalinski, his estate foreman. He no longer asked Martha Riepe to show him the books, no longer even summoned his friend Riepe. He also refused to see the family of his nephew Erwin von Quindt, who had fled East Prussia and had been living in the Green Rooms for almost a week; his response to the news that the major general was in Russian captivity was a mere "Is that right?"

Maximiliane brought him his dinner, moving the table close to his chair. "Grandfather! Eat something. Sour game stew, just like Amma used to fix it."

"Sleeping and digesting," he said. "In the end, that's all man's well-being depends on." He pushed the plate aside. He was incapable of the one or the other.

The following day when she took him his dinner, Maximiliane brought the children along–a chain, each clinging to the next, the smallest clinging to her mother. "Think of the children, Grandfather."

"Why should I do that?" He looked at them one after another, from Joachim to Viktoria. "All my life I worried about who would inherit Poenichen one day. Four heirs, and nothing to inherit." He laughed. No one had ever heard him laugh out loud before.

Now the children were afraid of the dark room and even more afraid of the greenish light. They did not dare go in by themselves, with the exception of Edda. Sometimes she quietly opened the door, crept to the armchair and climbed on, held her doll on her lap, and stared unswervingly at the old man with her inquisitive eyes.

"Well, Cuckoo?" he finally said.

After a while she slid from the big chair, set her doll in it as her deputy, turned its head so that the glass eyes stared at the old man, and carefully left the room. With the same caution she returned later to rescue the doll.

On New Year's Day old Reverend Merzin appeared on Poenichen. He refused to be deterred. Without knocking, he abruptly entered the dusky room. He wished to say good-bye. He would retreat to Dresden, where his wife had grown up and still had family. "The enemy seems to want to spare Dresden."

The fire on the hearth had died, the room had turned cold.

314

"Pomerania has repeatedly fallen into the hands of its enemies, Quindt," Merzin continued. "Many enemies, much honor! Or, as it says over your mantel, 'The foe rebuff!' Sweden, Poland–and now the Russians. But Pomerania is German. God is just."

"The Lord's justice–Hitler appeals to it as well," Quindt replied. "He says so himself–Providence saved him on July twentieth. Surely his god can't be the same power about which you've preached for a lifetime, Merzin."

"God is greater than Hitler's Providence and greater than the God I proclaimed. He will be merciful to us."

"Is that right? Will he indeed? Just or merciful, Merzin–which?"

"Both. Everything in its own time."

"And what happens in our time? Is God a Pomeranian or a Pole or even a Russian? Perhaps he's an American and we don't know it. 'The victory to the most worthy'–that's what Hitler thinks, too. Poland was divided for almost a hundred and fifty years. But Poland turned out to be indivisible. The inhabitants remained Poles, no matter under what flag they lived."

"It will be the same thing with Pomerania, Quindt."

"My hearing isn't what it was. Say it again."

"It will be the same thing with Pomerania, and with our German fatherland as well. It is indivisible."

"You think so? For weeks I've been sitting here thinking. Prussia, Pomerania, Poenichen. My three *P*'s. During the First World War twenty-two of our men from Poenichen took part, three of them died. This time already four times as many are involved. Each time a Quindt was among them. And now some people flee northward, others westward, some will probably stay, and a few will decamp upward." His thumb jerked toward the ceiling. "Everyone to the place he's least afraid of. You, Merzin, pack up your God and take Him to Dresden.

You'll be paid your pension there, too. Go with God, Merzin."

He did not look up, did not even put out his hand. The Reverend Merzin forgot to take his wig from Joachim, who had waited for him outside the room.

That evening Quindt said to his wife, "The chicken coop, Pia. Now they're taking the chicken coop away from us too. And all we've got left is the fox."

In mid-January 1945 Hitler moved his headquarters to the bunker in the Reich Chancellery. The last of Viktor's letters to reach his wife read, "Should it come to a–temporary–evacuation of Pomerania, don't do anything rash. Our shared life's goal is in the East! You can still count on me! At the crucial moment I shall bring you and our children to safety."

"Do you want to hear what Viktor has to say?" Maximiliane asked. These days you had to get Old Quindt's permission before telling him anything.

"Let's hear."

After Maximiliane had read out the letter, he said, "Is that right? He intends to lead you to safety. Where is that? Once I assured your mother's safety. Her safety lay in the United States. A place in New Jersey, unless she's moved on–it's been a long time since I've heard from her. Remember her address, but don't write it down."

For weeks evacuees from East Prussia, and later from West Prussia, spent the night in the great hall. They lay on straw pallets, and the horses of their caravans were kept in the barns. People and animals had to be looked after, the instructions on the billeting slips had to be followed. The caravans generally moved on after two nights, and then the next ones arrived, bringing more alarming news. People who had been bombed out in the West exchanged stories with evacuees from the East, one set wanting to go where the other had come

316

from, each assuring the other that they couldn't imagine. Hatred of the Soviets, harbored for years, turned to fear.

Pigs, calves, sheep were killed, and the meat was boiled and canned; there was no time for smoking. Frau Pech began to put big pieces of meat into the soup she cooked for the Russian prisoners. But one day the truck with the prisoners did not arrive. The prisoner-of-war camps, it was said, had been broken up, workers from the East and ethnic Germans having been discharged from wartime labor service. The village men secretly repaired their hay wagons and carts, and Priebe, who was more afraid of his district Party supervisor than of the approaching Russians, threatened to shoot anyone trying to take off for the West before obtaining written permission. The district leader had not yet issued orders to evacuate. Priebe chased the women down from wagons that were already loaded with bedding and chests of food—until old Klukas confronted him with the dung fork and disarmed him.

In the study old Frau Görke, unperturbed, worked the sewing machine. She was making floor-length nightshirts for the children from bed sheets. She turned blue-checked sheets that Martha Riepe had gotten from bombed-out travelers in exchange for bacon into shirts for the boys and dresses for the girls, and she made blue-checked dresses for Maximiliane and Martha Riepe as well, both from the same pattern, putting in darts at her own discretion. The last of the jackets the Baroness had woven twenty years earlier were taken from the chests and distributed.

One morning the housekeeper and her mother disappeared. They had left, it was said, for the railroad station, where the stationmaster had found them room in a military transport. A few hours later, Claude and Anya were found to be among the absentees. They were rumored to have joined a group of released French prisoners of war.

Maximiliane wandered from one room to another; things looked bad everywhere. Sideboards and wardrobes stood like bulwarks amid the chaos; they were unsuited to moving and had never budged from their locations. She gave certain instructions, but Martha Riepe ordered the opposite. One commanded, "Take it along"; the other said, "Leave it here." In the dusk Maximiliane had Bruno bury silver and jewelry; at dawn Martha Riepe dug them up again.

During these days of preparation for departure, it became clear that Maximiliane was not one of those splendid estate women from the East who led their caravans to the West with energy and caution. Filled with anticipatory grief, she packed up everything that eyes, ears, and nose could pack up: noises, smells, images. She took her farewell a few days earlier than the others.

Stricken, Joachim sat on the edge of his bed crowned with the abandoned red wig. Golo ran excitedly through stables and barns, climbed on carts, managed to get hold of a gun, and brandished it until old Riepe caught him and delivered him to the manor. Edda stuffed clothing, dolls, and shoes into pillowcases, dragged her bundles down the stairs, and loaded them on the blue handcart. She was the only one who remembered "the casket" that held the photographs and medals with which the children had been allowed to play on special days. Martha Riepe was the only one who remembered the box containing Viktor's letters from the front, which she tucked away among the rest of their baggage even though it was a liability: the letters of an avowed National Socialist. She cut the ancestral portraits from their heavy frames and rolled them in rugs, though she left behind the German rulers—Frederick the Great as well as Queen Louise and the Führer of the Greater German Reich. She packed up the table linen, the bed linen, and the Courland china service, including the christening bowl.

318

At night old Riepe and Bruno buried boxes filled with the valuables of the evacuated relatives behind the barns, where the soil was only slightly frozen. The hunting rifles had to be buried as well, and the ammunition hidden in the hayloft. Rumor had it that the Pichts had set out ten hours ago, the von Kalcks two days earlier. People said that Friederike von Kalck had locked every door, even cellar compartments and larders, taking the heavy key ring with her.

That afternoon the sky turned red in the east. "The sun, Mama! You said the sun always sets in the west."

"Now isn't always, Mose."

Scattered groups of German soldiers looking for their units passed through, as did Polish and French marauders. The locks and seals on the distillery were forced open, the stores of schnapps were emptied, stray chickens were caught and carried off. Viktoria stood in everybody's way until someone sat her in a chair or put her in a corner where she was in no danger of being run down. The Führer's picture and the swastika flag were burned on the round flower bed, but the map of Europe and the old issue of the *Völkischer Beobachter* remained hanging in the workers' mess. Willem Riepe was back, it was said–a deserter. He remained in hiding, waiting for the arrival of the Russians.

Thursday was set as the starting date for the Poenichen caravan. Approval from the district administrator arrived just in time. The old Quindts, wearing their driving furs, sat in the unheated study. For days Quindt had not uttered a word. Outside, the cattle were lowing, people were shouting, cannons boomed in the distance. The study became the eye of the storm–it was silent; walls, windows, and doors were tightly shut.

"And now?" Frau von Quindt asked her husband.

"Do you remember your son's wedding at the Adlon?" Quindt replied. "I said then that I intended being the first Quindt to die in his bed of natural causes. It seems that for us Quindts there is no such thing as natural causes."

"You mean—voluntarily?"

"Yes. But what will become of you?"

"The same thing, Quindt. You'll have to do it. You know I can't shoot."

When this matter was settled, Quindt arose and during his final hours once again became the master of Poenichen. He appeared on the verandah to give instructions to those who wanted to stay and those who were setting out on their flight. Let the cattle off the chains! Feed them and milk them as long as possible! Put the yoked slow oxen at the head of the caravan, let the tractors bring up the rear.

He summoned Riepe. For the last time he said, "How do, Riepe."

"Oh, Baron, sir."

"How about it? Are you going or staying?"

"If the Baron is going, I'll go too. If the Baron stays, I'll stay."

"There's no more Baron, Riepe, and no more differences at long last. You're a worker and you're old; they won't do anything to you. Your mother was half Polish, and your Willem is a Red. 'Who knows what good will come of it,' your Anna always said. So stay. Here's an envelope. Put it away somewhere, and later give it to whoever is going to carry on Poenichen estate. It's the drainage plans. The place won't run without them. The land doesn't care whose feet walk over it. And one more thing, Riepe. See to it that we are put underground."

"I couldn't do that!"

"You're still in my employ!"

"Yessir, Baron." Riepe reached for Quindt's hand, bent over it to kiss it, then kissed the hand of the Baroness.

"Otto! Otto!" As in the old days, when she thought he was driving too fast.

Quindt summoned Kalinski, but the foreman refused to leave the wagon where he had been ensconced for hours. His fear was greater than his obedience. So Martha Riepe would have to lead the caravan. Quindt handed her a number of sealed envelopes.

As a final gesture he turned to Maximiliane and the children. "The two of us will not be leaving Poenichen," he said.

"In that case we'll stay too," Maximiliane declared.

"You always were a runaway. Think of the horses, how they preserved their kind by running away. You'll always be a Quindt, even without Poenichen."

"That's not possible, Grandfather!"

"Gamma! Gamma!" Edda shouted, stretching out her arms.

"Oh, the hell with it," Quindt said, and returned to the house.

Maximiliane dressed the children in double sets of clothing–shirts, pants, jackets, stockings. Mummified, Joachim, Edda, and Viktoria stood ready to be loaded when it turned out that Golo was missing. It was high time that they get started. They had to reach their first stopping place before nightfall, and the dull barking of tank columns and the thunder of guns were coming closer. The horses snorted. The shouts and sobs of those remaining behind mingled with the cries of those who were fleeing.

Maximiliane made the three children link arms and ran off to find Golo. There was no answer to her shouts. Finally she came to his favorite spot, which had also been her favorite spot–high up in the copper beech, where he was clinging like a cat. He did not want to leave, and he began to bellow. If he were to jump down now out of defiance, he would be sure to break his leg! She put her arms around the trunk of the copper beech, pressed her face against the bark, and stopped hearing the shouts and the booming of artillery. When Golo realized that no one was calling him any longer, he was seized with fear. Carefully he climbed from branch to branch, dangled from the bottommost one, and jumped to the ground. Then he took his mother's hand. "Mama, come."

The caravan began to move. Two teams of oxen, four teams of horses, two tractors, a hundred and forty-three people in eight wagons. Four men on horseback, among them Griesemann the teamster. Six dogs ran alongside the wagons, four cats hid among the bundles; a little more than a mile outside the village they jumped off and ran back. Stable lanterns served as taillights. A gentle snow began to fall. From the last wagon hung a slate: "Quindt–Poenichen."

The old Quindts stood on the verandah beneath the frozen potted palms that had been forgotten the previous autumn and had never been taken indoors. They waited until the last wagon had turned from the avenue into the road. Then three shots rang out. The first one was for Texa, the wirehaired bitch.

30

Flight, expropriation, declassing, displacement, expulsion, pauperization—of all these horrors offered by the end of the war, Maximiliane had presumably chosen the least horrible at the moment the Quindt caravan turned into the road: flight. She became one of many millions of Germans flowing over Germany from the East in a wide stream, growing thin, eventually trickling away.

It is not certain that Maximiliane heard the three shots. In any case, she did not turn around: no backward look. The only one who did was Joachim, the young master, a child who would always turn back, always leave something behind. This time it was the wig. He wept softly to himself while his mother pressed him close.

"Mose, my Mose. Soon we'll go back, and then you'll have your wig again."

"Do you promise?" He needed promises, needed someone to help him stand up for his rights.

It was otherwise for his brother Golo: the best years of his life were beginning, and no one had to help him claim his rights; more precisely, he had to be restrained from committing wrongs. To him flight was an unmitigated adventure. Nor was there cause to worry about Edda: a child born on a Sunday. Only Viktoria would always and everywhere come off badly, even though people liked to slip her a little something, saying to her mother, "Look after your little girl, why don't you." More than ever she ran the risk of getting lost, being crushed or trampled to death.

Advances are easier to organize than retreats. Populating an area also goes more smoothly according to plan than its evacuation, in spite of printed procedural instructions forbidding random quartering and allowing days of rest only when the draft animals were exhausted, in spite of marching orders that led the caravans from one supervising office to the next, where provisions for travelers and animals were apportioned to the extent that they were available. As soon as units of the German armed forces required the roads, the caravans drove to the side and stopped.

Late that first night the Poenichen caravan arrived at its first stopping place. "The Quindts on Poenichen are here." The shout went up, followed by the question, "And where is Baron von Quindt?" No time to wait for an answer; that caravan was already being assembled to leave. "Four children? Will two beds be enough?" Still the differences—straw pallets for the manor's workers, beds for the manor's owners. Martha Riepe was considered a worker.

As on the first day, on the second their caravan advanced only seven miles—the slow draft oxen could manage no more. In the village of Bannin they spent the night in the schoolhouse. While looking for clean diapers for Viktoria, Maximiliane discovered the Reverend Merzin's red wig in one of the overstuffed bundles. Joachim's expression brightened. He wore the wig like a magic hat and refused to take it off day or night—a gnome who wished to make himself unrecognizable. The bundles packed up by Edda proved to be magic cornucopias, spilling forth crayons and the slate and the recorder.

Before they went to sleep, Maximiliane pulled her four children close. In times gone by, she had said to each one, "God preserve you"; now she said, "God preserve us."

"Do you promise?" Joachim asked.

"I promise."

Without guidance from psychological or pedagogical texts, Maximiliane gave her children what she had most missed when she was a child: closeness, affection, a sense of belonging.

When the caravan was stopped for hours by the side of the road with the freezing east wind blowing across the open fields and their only meager protection the big rug from the great hall spread as a sort of awning over the wagon, Maximiliane told them stories or drew pictures on the slate, drew "our house with many windows," and once again she did not sketch in window frames or door frames—an image that by now corresponded to reality. She drew paths leading to the house or away from it. "Where do they go?" Golo asked, and she replied, "This one leads to Kolberg and that one to Berlin."

And Joachim asked, "Where does that road go?" and she said, "All roads lead to Poenichen." As she had done as a child, she still began each picture by drawing the sun, and at the finish she drew a child into every window of the house, little suspecting that she was anticipating the future.

Everything Maximiliane had learned in her life until now, at home or in school—English, a few phrases of Polish, a few words of Russian, poems by Rilke, raising chickens, horseback riding, rowing, and how to make a Cumberland sauce—all of it was suddenly useless. An era had opened in which Cumberland sauce had lost its importance. Even the recipe for the famous Poenichen game pâté, praised by Bismarck in a letter, had been lost, perishing along with the housekeeper; but the letter

325

from Bismarck was preserved as proof of the legendary concoction. It was a time for one-dish meals and foot marches and hymns. New stories had to be invented—stories without princesses and castles.

When the caravan stopped in a small pine forest to hide from enemy strafing, Maximiliane invented a little boy named Mirko, who had lost his father and mother in the war and now had only his little dog.

"What should the dog be called?" she asked.

"Texa!" the children replied with one voice.

"The dog was so little that Mirko could carry him everywhere, and Texa always barked twice when Mirko was in danger. Guns were going off in every direction, and Mirko did not know where the enemy was—ahead of him or behind him. He could speak Polish and German, he lied and stole and lived from hand to mouth, and he could always find someone to give him a warm corner to sleep in and something to eat. And always he shared whatever he had with his little dog."

Joachim alternated between fear of the planes in the sky and fear of the planes in the stories about Mirko. Viktoria chewed her fingernails and daydreamed. Only Golo and Edda learned lessons from Mirko.

"Why doesn't he make a fire?"

"The fire would give him away."

"Why doesn't he break the goose's neck?"

"He doesn't have a pot to cook the goose in."

"Why doesn't he shoot? Why doesn't he build a raft if he wants to cross the river?"

Their ultimate destination was Mecklenburg, and their direction westward, but they could not proceed in a straight line; they had to make many detours toward the West. Each day their progress grew slower. Under the heavy rugs covered with snow, the wagon hoops splintered. The oxen's hooves began to bleed; they were not shod with iron, and they were used to walking on sandy summer paths, not on icy paved roads. Additional

326

caravans coming from side roads daily joined the stream of refugees. Since the camps and field hospitals were being abandoned, prisoners and wounded soldiers joined them as well, taking unilateral action to return home on crutches, with bandaged heads. Day and night the rumbling fire and dull detonations of the German heavy artillery could be heard–and the bark of the Russian tank cannons. The oxen could not be shod, so the animals had to be left behind and the baggage reloaded. Only the old and the ill were still allowed to ride in the wagons; everyone else had to walk.

Martha Riepe kept the Poenichen caravan together as best she could, running in her heavy boots from the last to the first wagon and back again, shouting instructions. Her special concern was to see that at night nothing was unloaded that was not essential. It came to a confrontation between Martha and Maximiliane concerning the handcart, which was chained to one of the horse-drawn vehicles. Maximiliane wished to unhitch it, but Martha Riepe refused to make any exceptions.

"Public need before private greed," she said.

"You are riding a caravan that belongs to the Quindts, Martha," Maximiliane replied in tones reminiscent of Old Quindt.

A community forged by propaganda and terror was falling apart.

The following night their caravan was quartered on a small countryseat near Kolkwitz that had already been abandoned by its owners. Maximiliane and her children retired for the night to a small, secluded living room, and in the morning she slept through the general departure. Martha Riepe led the Poenichen caravan on without them–who knew whether by design or accidentally? Perhaps she acted out of spite and rebellion–she was, after all, Willem Riepe's sister–or perhaps she was expressing unconscious jealousy of Maximiliane's husband and children. In any case, by the time the contingent realized that the mistress and her children were missing, it was too late to turn back.

All that was left outside the abandoned manor was the overloaded handcart. Viktoria, not yet three years old and a poor walker, was stuffed into a fur jacket and tied to the top of the laden cart. Joachim and Golo took the shaft, with Edda and Maximiliane pushing, as in the days when they had set off for the Blue Pond.

Sometimes they fell in with a stream of refugees and were allowed to hitch their cart to one of the horse-drawn wagons. But they soon had to release it again because they could not keep up. Once an army truck gave them a lift, along with their cart. Then they took their place in yet another column of wagons.

"Where do you come from?" they were asked. When Maximiliane replied that she was a Quindt on Poenichen, she looked into uncomprehending faces; she had long since left the world where her name meant anything.

"Don't the people know who we are?" Joachim asked. Astonishment and fear took up permanent residence on his face, which daily grew more gaunt.

Since all their identification papers, billeting slips, and ration cards were with Martha Riepe, leader of the caravan, Maximiliane possessed no documents entitling her to lodging or food. At night they sought quarters in abandoned farmhouses, taking what they needed. When one of the children brought something they did not need, Maximiliane ordered it returned. The milking rooms still contained cans of milk, the kitchens held jars of jam and syrup. They slipped into beds that were still warm, and often they needed to do no more than place a piece of wood in the burning kitchen stove. The children knew that where there were chickens, there would be eggs, and they knew where chickens were likely to nest. Edda searched the cellars for apples for her mother, wrinkled ones, which always tasted of Poenichen.

Before she fell asleep, Maximiliane tied the children to her so that they would not be lost; once more she made use of the umbilical cord. When they had to sleep in the hay, they made a nest. Maximiliane drew Viktoria, who was always chilly, into the curve of her abdomen while one of the other children snuggled spoon-fashion into her back, the rest taking up the same position in a row. Whoever was at the end began to complain of a cold back and climbed over the others to the front, closer to their mother; then the new occupant of the end position began to complain and went through the same maneuver, until all of them had rolled over and around each other, grown warm, and fallen asleep.

Along with the flood of refugees, they crossed brooks and small streams; they still had not reached the Oder, and the morning sky and the night sky at their backs was still red; the thunder of cannons could still be heard, now closer, now farther away. The stream of refugees grew longer and wider, with ever more wounded soldiers among them. Whenever one of them had a sleeve dangling loosely from his shoulder, Joachim shouted, "Papa!" Sometimes they met a caravan that had turned around and was going back to the East. Someone said, "They're half-Poles themselves." Joachim's head, heavy with thought and weariness, swayed under the red wig. "Lost his arm," "half-Poles"—such phrases confused him. He stared at his mother.

"Which half of those people is Polish? How can you tell?" he asked, and "Where did Papa lose his arm?"

"In Normandy," Maximiliane replied. "It's in France, the west of France. Near a castle called Roignet."

"Can we go look for the arm after the war is over?"

"No. They buried it."

This, in turn, gave him more food for thought—a lone arm buried in Normandy. "But which half of those people was Polish?" he asked once more.

"What do you mean, Mose?"

"The people said, 'They're half-Polish.' "

"Some people have the hearts of Poles, and some have the heads of Poles—" She broke off. "Mose, you have to go to school. I can't explain everything."

"Do you promise that I'll go to school?"

"Yes, in Berlin."

Once more they faced an obstacle—one more river to cross. "Why do all the rivers flow north?" Joachim asked. "Why do we always have to get to the other side?"

"The Baltic is to the north, Mose, you know that. It's at Kolberg. And all rivers flow into the Baltic."

"All of them?"

"All the ones that come from Pomerania."

"Why don't we walk along the river? That way we wouldn't ever get lost."

"Because we have to go to Berlin."

Maximiliane's answer to every question was "Berlin."

The children learned to be cautious but also, when the occasion demanded, to be trusting. Maximiliane decided what was best in particular situations—to send one of the children ahead or to send all four of them or to send out a timid little bird like Viktoria. Golo had long since understood when it was appropriate to say "Heil Hitler" and when to say "Good evening"; sometimes he spoke in the Pomeranian dialect, or when Polish marauders discovered their hiding place, he fumbled around in broken Polish. To his mother's skill in filling her round eyes with tears at a timely moment he added his ability to press dimples into his cheeks; in really risky situations he managed to apply both techniques brilliantly.

Martha Riepe had also kept possession of the map, so Maximiliane had to take her bearings from the sun and the stars; she had learned to do both from her grandfather. Columns of refugees crossed their path, heading north to get to the coast and seek safety on ships.

Undeterred, Maximiliane continued to lead her children westward. Berlin. She had always gone to Berlin; all roads from Pomerania led to Berlin. "You can count on me in your hour of need." "I shall be by your side." "I shall suppoort you." For the first time she seemed ready to take Viktor at his word.

No radio bulletins reached them, no newspapers, barely any rumors. The snow melted, at dawn the puddles were no longer covered by a layer of ice, the sun began to warm them, buds began to sprout—earlier than in other years; they must be deep into March. The first freckles blossomed on Edda's forehead and nose. "Cuckoo," her mother said, and each night she counted the freckles, tapping each brown dot and singing, "Who can count the stars in the sky?" She had not lost her love of singing.

They moved on, always accompanied by Mirko and his dog Texa. "One night the two of them came to a river too broad for them to swim to the other side. The moon stood high and white in the sky, turning the river and the bushes along the shore and Mirko and his dog Texa into silver. Mirko looked for a boat under the willow bushes, and the moon helped him. Mirko knew: there are boats wherever there is a shore, and people always hide the oars so that no stranger can make off with the boat. But Mirko also knew the places where oars were hidden. He found a wonderful boat, and he found strong oars as well. He put his dog in the boat, ordering him not to bark, and he began to row across the river.

"But the night was much too bright. They would see the black boat on the silver water, and they would shoot at it because they could not tell that only a little boy and his little dog were in it.

"So what did Mirko do? He stretched out his arm as far as he could and even farther, all the way to the moon, and he plucked the moon from the sky. Then he slowly drew back his arm and tucked the moon under his jacket. The sky grew dark, and the earth grew dark. The only light came from three thin rays shining on the water through a tear in Mirko's jacket and through the buttonholes. They gave off just enough light for Mirko to see the opposite shore.

"After he had landed, he tied the boat to a willow and hid the oars for the next person who had to get to the other side. In the meantime Texa snuffled in the sand until he found a warm hollow, and then he barked softly two times. Before Mirko lay down in the sand with his little dog, he unbuttoned his coat and let the moon float back up to the sky. And then he hugged his dog and went to sleep."

Golo found a cooking pot, tied it to his stomach, and drummed on it with a wooden spoon. Let the drummer boy lead the way! Maximiliane tied the soles of her shoes on with twine after they had come loose. When she had walked through the twine, she lost the soles and went on walking in stockinged feet. Two hours later Golo brought her a pair of army boots, a little too big, but she managed by wrapping two of the batiste diapers around her feet. She did not ask where he had found the boots; he would surely not have taken them off a live soldier.

No more advantages, to say nothing of rights, and she had to share compassion with hundreds of thousands. There was not much left for one individual.

When a peasant woman agreed to give her some milk for the children only in exchange for the fur in which Viktoria was wrapped, Maximiliane said, "May God reward you," and moved on.

"Why did you say that?" Joachim wanted to know. "Usually that's what you say when somebody gives us something for nothing."

"God doesn't reward only good deeds, Mose, he also repays evil."

"Do you promise?"

"Yes," said his mother.

Viktoria cried softly to herself, grew more transparent by the day, and was lighter to carry each time her mother lifted her from the cart. Several attacks of diarrhea had reduced her weight even further. Maximiliane chewed oats she found in a granary, separated out the bran, and fed the child mouth to mouth, in the manner of birds.

Edda complained that her fingernails had grown so long that she made herself bleed whenever she itched—and when did they not itch now that they slept in haylofts and had no chance to wash? Maximiliane suggested that she bite her nails like the others did. But then Golo, in one of his house searches, found a sewing basket with a pair of scissors, so that nails could be clipped. Except for the scissors, Golo had to take the basket and all its contents back. "We'll take the scissors, we don't need the rest," Maximiliane said, setting guidelines for his future dealings. But Golo also appropriated her principle "It is better to steal than to beg." He stole like a highwayman but distributed his loot like a prince. He somehow managed to get hold of hand grenades and pistols thrown aside by German soldiers—even an antitank grenade launcher. His mother had to disarm him several times a day.

They strayed between the fronts, turned away onto side roads, and suddenly found themselves back in no-man's-land, where they met not a living soul. Anyone left behind stayed in hiding. The spearheads of the quickly advancing Russian tank units had taken the main roads to the right and left of them.

For half a day a German soldier on crutches limped along beside them, his head scantily bandaged, his only piece of luggage a gas-mask case. When the Quindts stopped to rest, he stopped as well. Maximiliane made him a fresh bandage from one of Viktoria's diapers. Private First Class Horstmar Seitz from Kaiserslautern in the Palatinate would save the diaper with its embroidered crest and remember the woman and her children. "A baroness from the East made me a bandage with her own hands at the edge of the road." He took chocolate and cigarettes from his case and distributed them. Maximiliane smoked, as did Golo. Why shouldn't a five-year-old who stole cooking pots and took the boots off dead men smoke? Then, as they moved on, they lost sight of the soldier.

Edda searched out the first nettles at the side of the road–a city child who knew that they could be cooked like spinach. And Joachim, the dreamer, picked the first daisies for his mother. Viktoria no longer wet her diapers– no more could be expected of her. What a relief for a mother who never in her life had washed anything with her own hands. "With her own hands"–a phrase Maximiliane was coming to recognize and which would later be used as the highest form of praise.

A noncommissioned officer of the military police, scouring the area for German soldiers, asked to see their billeting slip and personal identity cards.

"My dear lady," he said. "How do you expect to make your way without papers? Where are you headed, anyway?"

"To join up with my husband."

"Do you know where he is?"

"In the Führer's headquarters."

"Oh, my God." And he let her go.

334

Later Joachim asked, "Why did the soldier say, 'Oh, my God'?"

"That's what people say when something is difficult, Mose."

By the end of March, Soviet troops and the five Quints stood at the banks of the Oder.

31

"Watch. Watch."

The primitive sound of Russian soldiers thirsting for retribution and booty. Maximiliane held out her bare wrists; for days Joachim had been wearing the gold watch on his skinny upper arm. The children thought "Watch, watch" was a form of greeting and shouted back, "Watch, watch." Most of the Russian soldiers laughed, but one of them felt he was being made fun of and pointed the muzzle of his gun at Maximiliane. "Pang! Pang!" Golo shouted loudly, brandishing the empty stem of a hand grenade. The soldier whirled around and looked into the boy's laughing face. Joachim, ever fearful, had already taken off his coat and said, "Watch." Whereupon Maximiliane undid the strap and handed the soldier the watch.

No more telling time–but only for two days, until Golo brought a substitute, not a gold watch but one that ticked clearly, a pocket watch with a lid that opened on a spring mechanism. "Watch!" Beaming, he held it out to his mother, and this time too she forbore asking him where he had got it.

A few times Russian soldiers threw bread or cans of meat to the children. They took and they gave, they shot or they helped. They, too, were near their goal–Berlin, the end of the war. Tanks and armored cars rolled by, and over and over long lines of German prisoners between them, disarmed, stripped of their insignia. Still Joachim shouted, "Papa!" whenever he saw a one-armed man among them.

The Oder barred the refugees' way. By the thousands they were dammed up in the villages on the east side of the river.

The children stood in a battle line to guard their young mother, no weapons to defend her except their earsplitting screams. Maximiliane did not blacken her face like the other women; no Russian would believe that an old woman would be on the road with four young children. Nor did she run away like the others. When danger threatened, she did not move from the spot; she commanded, "Scream! Scream as loud as you can!" And these children could scream very loudly and continuously, could erect a wall of screams around her. But when a Russian soldier searched the air-raid shelter where they had been staying for two days, the children did not scream because their mother was asleep.

"Come, woman," the soldier said to Maximiliane, but she was sleeping the heavy sleep of the exhausted; she lay still, her throat exposed and her face covered with a cloth because of those eyelids that allowed the light to penetrate. Joachim, his bravery all the greater than that of the fearless Golo because he was so fearful, stood in front of his mother and placed his finger against his lips. "Mama asleep."

The Russian did not understand what the child was saying, and he poked the woman's knee with the butt of his gun. Accustomed to shoves, she did not wake even then.

He took her for dead and left.

When it happened after all, Maximiliane did not make much of a fuss, nor did she inflict any lasting psychic damage on the children. "Go outside for a while and watch the cart," she commanded. Her back to the cellar wall, she stared at the Russian soldier, an Asiatic with slanted eyes and prominent cheekbones. His hand pushed her kerchief back as he said, "Come, little woman." A mere additional adjective, but it made the whole business a little easier.

When Maximiliane saw that there was no way out, she grew calm. She was overcome by great compassion—for the strange soldier, for herself, and for the children—a compassion that encompassed the whole desolated world. Her eyes filled with tears, causing the soldier to say "No cry, little woman," half in Russian, half in German. What happened was not exactly rape. As Maximiliane put it in later years, she had been feeling "so universal" for days. She was someone who embraced trees. The difference between this encounter and Viktor's advances was minimal.

The Russian soldier came to the shelter three more times, bringing bread, vodka, and cigarettes for her and her children; once he even gave them a coarse blanket. The last time he sat on the edge of the iron cot, smoking and talking. She listened and memorized a few words. "Kirghiz," "Ala Tau," "Lake Balkhash." As he spoke she looked at him, at the flat planes of his face, at his skin of earthen gray, at his shaven head. When he finished smoking and talking, she said, "*Nyet plakatye.*"

Once again she sensed that she had conceived, but she had no question that this child would be hers, just like the others. She too had never had a father, and her own children had seen little of theirs. Besides, she considered the man's share in conception insignificant.

One night when the moon was full a local woman took Maximiliane and her children and her cart across the Oder in a barge in exchange for a gold brooch.

The following night they asked for shelter at a rectory, but it was already full to the rafters with refugees and people who had been bombed out. With the best will in the world, there was no room for a woman with four little children. Might she at least look up something in

338

the encyclopedia? she pleaded with the parson, who granted her wish.

Maximiliane sat the children down on the outside stairs. "Watch the cart. Scream," she commanded. For almost half an hour she squatted before the parson's bookshelves and, using a 1912 encyclopedia, informed herself about the Kirghiz. She learned that they traced their descent to Genghis Khan, that their language was a pure Turkish dialect, and that they had a rich lyric and epic folk literature. The nobility was set apart from the commoners. They primarily raised cattle, agriculture being restricted to a few areas with heavy precipitation. They lived in dome-shaped tents covered on the outside with felt blankets and furnished on the inside with grass mats and rugs. Their clothing consisted of shirts, trousers, and wool coats, their shanks being wrapped in felt strips. The men wore colorful caps over shorn pates, covering both with pointed felt hats. The women wrapped two white cloths around their heads, one formed into a high, pointed cap while the other was passed under the chin and allowed to fall across their shoulders and backs.

Kerchiefs had become a familiar headgear to Maximiliane, too—they were the only kind she ever saw now. Women from the East tied them under their chins, those from the West knotted them on top of their heads.

Kirghiz wives were bought, she read, and remained the property of the husband's family. Only the well-to-do occasionally had two wives. The Kirghizian steppe was a large, sandy plain, sometimes wavy, dotted with lakes into which no rivers flowed; Lake Balkhash was an example. There it was, the lake he had mentioned. And there was the other word—Ala Tau, a mountain range. Mountains as high as 7,000 meters. Nomads leading their herds from well to well, living off the proceeds of sheep, goats, horses, camels.The principal foodstuff was yoghurt, made from sheep's milk. One felt blanket served sleepers as a mattress, another as a cover, their saddle as a pillow.

She took the globe down from the top of the bookcase, spun it, stopped its motion, and placed her hand on Asia. Then she looked for the Oder. A hairline on the globe—that represented the stretch she had covered in two months on horse-drawn wagons, in trucks, on foot. She put the globe back and read on, as if devouring a tale from the *Arabian Nights*. Her Kirghiz with his two blankets under his arm! Already she was endowing him with a possessive pronoun. He smelled of sweat and sheep. Primal odors came back to her: her grandmother's weaving room, where as a baby she had lain in the wool. The sheepfold at Poenichen Lake rose before her eyes, Blaskorken with silvery fish scales on his bare arms; the reeds and Mose in his wicker basket; her horseman, the black cap with the skull. For a moment she staggered under the weight of reminiscence.

"Are you unwell?" the parson asked with concern when he saw her damp eyes. Receiving no answer, he added encouragingly, "You'll make it."

Maximiliane returned the encyclopedia volume to the shelf and thanked him.

Outside, she sat down among the children on the steps. "We're going to have a baby," she announced.

"How do you know?" Joachim asked.

"I read it in the encyclopedia. It will be a while yet, but we can start getting used to the baby."

"A dog would be better," Golo objected, "like Mirko's little dog Texa. It could at least walk right away. We've only just gotten Tora to that point, and now it'll start all over again."

"Tora can walk pretty well," said Maximiliane as she opened her lap to her problem child, who had given herself the name Tora. "Besides, soon we won't have to move on every day."

"Do you promise?" Joachim asked.

340

"Yes, Mose, I promise."

Still on the steps of the rectory, they agreed that the child would be named Mirko. Effortlessly the Polish boy stepped out of the fairy tale into reality.

"Take your places," Maximiliane ordered. "It's time to move on."

As they got ready to leave, the parson appeared with a box almost as big as the boxes given to travelers on Poenichen. "If you'd be so kind as to accept this from us?" Compassion, of which there was enough for only a few, had chosen the five Quints this time.

Joachim bowed. "May God reward you."

"Thank you, my son," the minister replied.

Some time later Joachim asked, "Why did the pastor say 'my son' when he isn't my father at all?"

"He stands in for God, and because you are a child of God he calls you 'my son.' "

"Are all of us children of God?"

"Yes." On the road Maximiliane gave lessons in geography, history, theology.

Joachim learned to read; crumbling house walls and boards nailed up over doors were his primer. "Everyone alive," scribbled in chalk. "Fritz dead, Anna with Grandpa," he spelled out.

At the same time Golo learned mathematics through the currency of cigarettes. One cigarette cost three marks, and for three cigarettes you could get a loaf of bread. He still used his fingers to count but was already managing by judicious use of his dimples and long eyelashes to lower prices.

Hard times for children of tender years, but they had a mother who could keep the sun from setting–a conviction that could not be shaken by anything that happened later.

They had stopped at the foot of a hill; the sun was going down, dusk was approaching, and they had not yet found a lodging for the night. Viktoria with diarrhea,

Edda with blisters on her feet, Joachim tottering from exhaustion under his red wig, and Golo cursing.

Maximiliane stretched out her arm and pointed to the sun. "I'll show you that the sun isn't ready to set yet. Watch. But we'll have to hurry." As quickly as they could, they pulled their rickety cart up the hill—and it was true: the sun was still high in the sky. But behind the next hill it was already beginning to sink again.

"It still isn't setting," their mother promised. "You'll see. We'll have to hurry some more."

They ran up the next hill, and again the sun was well above the horizon.

Exhausted and relieved, Maximiliane said, "Now we'll let it set. There's a barn over there."

"One more time," Joachim begged.

"It's enough, Mose. I can stop the sunset three times, but no more."

"You just did that so that we'd move faster," Edda noted.

Sometimes you could tell that Edda had a different mother.

get as far as Pankow before she reached the end of her rope. She did not know where to turn next. Should she go looking for Viktor? But where? The Führer's headquarters had long since ceased to exist. In his boardinghouse? He had moved away from there three years before. Should she turn to Grandmother Jadow in Charlottenburg? But how was one to find out whether she was still there, whether she was even alive? She could hear her grandmother say, "What im-pu-dence." In her mind's eye she saw doilies and eliminated Charlottenburg as a possible destination.

Should she go to Hermannswerder? But the island, they said, was occupied by the Russians and out of bounds to civilians. And then she remembered another name: Hilde Preissing, Edda's mother, who used to live with her parents in Pankow before her marriage. Pankow! She plunked Edda down on the wagon, facing her, and took her by the shoulders. "Think, Cuckoo. Where did you live? What was the name of the street?"

Edda thought hard. Her face turned red with the effort, and she clenched her fists like her father. But she could not remember.

Maximiliane shook the little girl. "Think! What did the street look like? Were there trees on the sidewalk?"

Edda shook her head.

"Was there a church nearby? Did you hear bells?"

Again Edda shook her head. Suddenly she said, "Paul the Coal Man! The corner store, that was Paul the Coal Man. That's where Grandpa always got briquettes."

"That'll do," Maximiliane decided. "We'll find him."

As she moved on with the children, she kept on asking passersby, "Do you know Paul the Coal Man?"

Suddenly a line of people barred their way—men, children, and old women holding buckets. The throng snaked all the way to a rear yard where a butcher was selling sausage soup. At that, Edda left the cart, ran as fast as she could to the line, pulled a man's sleeve, and clung to his arm. A Sunday child! In the midst of the crowd she discovered her grandfather.

Edda waved to her mother without letting go of the man, as if afraid of losing him again.

"Watch the cart," Maximiliane ordered as she went up to the man. "Herr Preissing," she said. "Dear God in heaven, Herr Preissing." She put her arms around his neck, laid her head on his shoulder, and broke into tears.

"All right, all right," he said. "I'm not really God, you know." He pointed to the cart. "So that's the manorial estate in Pomerania?"

Maximiliane nodded. She never doubted for a moment that the stranger would take in her children and herself, and he did so with the same matter-of-factness.

"Let's go, then," he said. "My place is still standing."

Their lodging consisted of a large kitchen, bedroom, hall, and lavatory on the landing serving four apartments.

"A pigsty," Golo declared when he had explored it all. Boarded-up windows, but one of the kitchen windows had already had new glass put in. No water, no electricity, no gas, but a stove with its pipe sticking through the wall, two beds, and a sofa. Joachim took off his wig and laid it on the kitchen table. His face was tanned, but his forehead and scalp had remained white—a thinker.

That night, when all the children had been washed and were lying in the beds, Joachim asked, "And where will Mirko sleep?"

"You don't mean one of them's still missing?" Herr Preissing asked.

"I'm expecting a baby. I'm broody, as my grandfather used to say."

Herr Preissing banged his palm against his head twice. "I'm dreaming! I used to feel that one was too many, and now they're bringing me back five!"

346

He offered Maximiliane the sofa in the kitchen; he himself would fix something up on the floor. But Maximiliane explained that the children had been used to having her in the same bed from infancy.

"In that case I'd like to know how you got them all in the first place," Herr Preissing said.

The two of them sat in the kitchen a while longer. Maximiliane described their flight, and Herr Preissing related how he had lost first his wife and then his daughter in air raids, explaining that the daughter's apartment at the center of town had been destroyed. He had recently had news of his son-in-law Jeschek, so that he might well be alive, only taken prisoner. He himself had been drafted into the home guard shortly before Christmas, but he had gotten away tolerably well; all that had happened was that the blast from an exploding blockbuster had split his left eardrum, so that he was hard of hearing on that side, the more so because he had to stop the ear up with cotton.

"Do you have any money? Do you have papers?" he asked.

"Money, yes. Papers, no," Maximiliane replied.

"Better than the other way around," Herr Preissing decided. One of his card-playing buddies, he said, was working at the registration office and could probably be helpful in procuring papers if Preissing told him that she was related to him. "If there's such a thing as stepfathers, there must be stepgrandfathers as well. The main thing is that the war is over."

The following morning he used his own judgment to translate Maximiliane's statements about the family's status at the registration office. Between sentences he repeated, "Man, Lehmann, just look at them! Four itty bitty things like that, and another on the way." He reported that she had lost all her papers on her flight from Pomerania, from where she had been evacuated, that her husband was a Berliner and a civil servant, that he had been drafted and had ultimately achieved the rank of second lieutenant, that he had been severely injured, had had an arm amputated, and had been missing for months. He said not a word about Viktor's employment at the Reich Genealogical Office, and he made no mention of the Führer's headquarters.

Her biography revised, Maximiliane was given a registration card and ration cards for four children, along with coupons for an expectant mother. When the appointment was over, she posted a notice in the schoolhouse corridor. "Looking for Second Lieutenant Viktor Quint, last heard from in January 1945, Berlin." One announcement among many.

During the following weeks something like ordinary life was created in the Preissing apartment. Herr Preissing, a trained metalworker, donned his wornout coveralls and went out assembling again—or, as he put it when he came back at night, dissembling.

Golo, who took only a few days to master the Berlin dialect, set out for the black market. To arouse sympathy, he had his mother bandage his knee every morning, and thus attired he limped off on his errands. One evening he brought home twenty pairs of gray knitted knee warmers that had come too late to be sent to the front.

Edda went out with an empty potato sack and climbed around in the ruins looking for charred pieces of wood, picking nettles and dandelions.

Joachim, the most patient of them all, stood in line outside stores for bread or skim milk or gooseberries.

And Maximiliane, still wearing the boots of the unknown soldier, learned to sweep a room with her own hands, to saw wood in the courtyard with her own hands, to fire up the stove, to make a meal out of whatever the children brought, and to clean the hallway, the stairs, and the lavatory.

"No gem will fall from your crown," Herr Preissing said, and Maximiliane nodded.

"They're stuck tight," she agreed. "They won't fall out even if I bend down."

When he asked, "Can you do that?" she answered, "Well, I could try."

At night they all sat in the kitchen. Edda unraveled the knee warmers, Golo wound the yarn into balls, and Maximiliane tried to knit it into a pullover with her own hands. Joachim sat at the table drawing letters in rows, adding a line of tilted, crooked swastikas.

Maximiliane noticed. "Mose, unlearn that," she suggested. And Herr Preissing advised, "Now you'll have to learn to draw hammers and sickles. I'll show you." He drew the crescent-shaped, pointed blade of the sickle.

"What does that mean?" Joachim wanted to know.

"It's a symbol, Mose," Maximiliane said.

"He can't understand that!" said Herr Preissing, sketching a handle onto the blade. "Farmers use a sickle and workers a hammer, and from now on there are only farmers and workers."

"But farmers have scythes, and they have machinery."

"You're right, my boy, and the workers used to have machines too, not just hammers. So it probably is a symbol after all," he said. He turned to Maximiliane. "The boy thinks too much." Then he held up the piece of paper. "I should have been a painter," he said, laughing like someone who had forgotten how to laugh.

"Won't they ever shoot anymore?" Joachim asked.

"No, Mose, there won't be any more shooting," Maximiliane assured him.

"Do you promise?"

"I promise."

In the meantime the victorious powers divided Germany into four unequal parts and Berlin into four sectors—historical decisions about which those most immediately

349

affected learned the least. No newspapers, no mail, no telephone; the population made arrangements to survive the postwar period as well. Maximiliane did not take part in the great balancing act of destiny. Nor did she believe in the possibility of an equalization of burdens. "Each of us shoulders the other's burden," the Reverend Merzin had preached. "Why shouldn't each shoulder his own burden? Why should he load it onto the next person?" An attitude that eased her life considerably.

She continued to stick queries about Viktor's whereabouts onto hoardings and bulletin boards, and she tried to get news about Pomerania and about what had happened to her caravan.

One summer Sunday they visited Grandmother Jadow in Charlottenburg. A visit to the American sector of the city meant a day's journey from one sovereign territory to another, from one ideology to another. A transit slip as legitimation, for each child a slice of bread and molasses and one boiled potato, as well as two beer bottles full of skim milk. Freshly washed and combed, their shoes polished, they set out.

The house was still standing. Not even the attics were burned out, and there was glass in every window. No stovepipes stuck out through the walls, no rubble covered the stairs, and the brass shield for the fourth floor was brightly polished: "v. Jadow." Admittedly, three handwritten slips of paper were tacked next to it, each bearing a name and instructions about how many times to ring. One ring for Jadow.

They heard Grandmother's voice. "Who's there?"

"Maximiliane."

The door opened cautiously. Grandmother Jadow appeared, white trim on her collar, her white hair waved, unchanged though a little shrunken.

"Wipe your feet, children," she said in welcome. And she added, "The children must learn that they have to wipe their feet."

350

mother. He pointed to a bare, splintered tree. "Is that what Grandfather's forest looks like now?"

"No! It's much too big, it's impossible to destroy that many trees."

"I wish I were a tree right in the middle of the forest," he said, and then he spelled out announcements on a nearby bulletin board—the next lesson in his primer.

A passing jeep stopped for a second. "Hello, Fräulein!" Then it drove on. A couple of tattered soldiers released from internment walked past.

Maximiliane got them going again, for they still had a long way ahead of them. The trenches in the park had already been filled in, and the soil broken up into vegetable patches; most of the trees had already served for firewood. The Brandenburg Gate with the Quatrika came into view. The roof beams of the southern gatehouse were exposed, and the Prussian-blue sky shone through. The Greek model stood out all the more, reminiscent of the manor on Poenichen.

Maximiliane picked up Viktoria. "Tora, do you see the woman up there on the wagon? Her name is the same as yours—Viktoria."

In the shattered arm of the statue of victory someone had stuck a flagstaff. The east wind billowed the red flag with its hammer and sickle.

Maximiliane remembered the night in Berlin when the Führer's piercing gaze had struck her and Viktoria was conceived. She looked at the little girl as if she were afraid of seeing the Führer's eyes, looked at the light-blue eyes, pale like the girl's skin and hair, like all of her. Frightened, Viktoria began to cry and wanted to be carried.

Maximiliane continued walking with the children toward another street. "This is where your father lived at one time."

"Where?" Joachim asked. But his mother could not place the boardinghouse.

"Where is Papa now?"

"In a prisoner-of-war camp."

"Does he have to work in the woods? Like our Russians?"

"I don't think so. He has just the one arm, so he's not much use to them."

When, tired and dusty, they returned to the Preissing apartment, Golo pulled a pack of Chesterfield cigarettes from one of his pockets and white sewing thread and a packet of needles from the other. The latter had come from his grandmother's sewing table.

"We can use all that," his mother declared. She pulled out a pot of stewed barley from under the bed, which she used as a larder.

"Everyday is one-dish Sunday now. If the Führer knew!" said Herr Preissing. "I've got to hand it to you, you do know how to cook."

Golo asked for a second bowl of soup. "Give mine some more!"

Maximiliane corrected him, teaching him the difference between "me" and "mine." Later on she would have to instruct him in the difference between "mine" and "yours," which would take longer.

"Look at you handling it all," said Herr Preissing. "You're a born widow."

There was a knock on the door. Outside stood a man, a repatriated soldier in a German army uniform with a large PW on his back—a released prisoner of war. It was Jeschek, Herr Preissing's son-in-law, whose own apartment was totally destroyed.

Maximiliane and the children retired to the bedroom. They could hear the voice of the new arrival coming from the kitchen. "Strangers . . . brats . . . Nazi pig . . . Hilde palmed the kid off . . . estate owners, capitalists, militarists. . . ."

The following night Maximiliane told Herr Preissing that she had decided to take her children and move on.

"But where will you go?" Herr Preissing asked.

Maximiliane's arm sketched a vague but grand gesture. "When you've got no home, you can go anywhere."

Joachim sat on the edge of the bed wearing his worried expression. "Can't we go back to Poenichen to Grandpa and Gamma?"

"No, Mose, not right now. But we can go everywhere else. We'll look for Martha Riepe and Kalinski and the Griesemanns and all our people, the whole caravan from Poenichen. And Falada! And then we'll move in with Aunt Maximiliane, who lives in a real castle. And then we have uncles and aunts and cousins in Sweden, and you have a grandmother in America. But first of all we have to find a place for hatching, for Mirko."

"You can stay with your grandpa if you don't want to come with us, Cuckoo," she said to Edda, who was chewing on her braids. The little girl began to cry, and she cried so keenly that the others began to weep along. Herr Preissing appeared. He made a few excuses, blamed everything on his son-in-law, and said in conclusion, "Of course Edda will stay here."

"No!" the little girl shouted, banging the wooden bed frame with both hands and stamping her feet just as her father used to.

"My husband and I adopted the child, Herr Preissing," Maximiliane said.

"You don't have any papers to prove it."

"Neither do you, Herr Preissing."

The following day she learned at the district registration office that someone had responded to her notice, a man who had been employed at the telephone switchboard at the former Reich Chancellery. He had reported that Second Lieutenant Viktor Quint, lastly ordnance officer in the Führer's headquarters, was officially missing.

33

"Good luck!" Herr Preissing had said; it sounded like "Take care," and it was final. He entered family history as "Grandpa Preissing with the cotton in his ear."

It was difficult to part with the handcart; still another piece of Poenichen had to be left behind. Each of them had two pieces of luggage to carry, even Viktoria; bundles and blankets and sacks on which they could sit or sleep.

First they sat, on a September day in the midst of a crowd of refugees on a siding, waiting for the train that was to take them westward, at least as far as the zone boundary. Wearing the blue-and-white clothing Frau Görke had run up to allow for growing, they squatted side by side, looking from a distance like a heap of jumbled bed linen. Beside them on her own bundle sat a woman from the Warthegau who had lost both her children on the flight. One had frozen to death, the other had succumbed to dysentery. She was too old, she said, to have any more children, and she didn't even know where her husband was; maybe he was already in Siberia. She placed her hand on Maximiliane's stomach and said, "It's going to be a girl. If your stomach is round it's a girl, and when it's oblong it's a boy."

Another prophecy. Some had already come true. "She won't amount to anything, she was born with open hands," Schmaltz the midwife had said to Anna Riepe in the kitchen after Maximiliane's birth. At her
356

cradle the record player had ceaselessly sung of Berlin's linden trees, and now no more lindens stood along Unter den Linden. "Yes, we have no bananas" had also come true. And the eyes of the Polish lieutenant, which Herr von Kalck had called "a fortune for a girl," had already worked their magic several times.

Something large and spacious attached to the name Maximiliane, Old Quindt had said in his christening speech. Maximiliane would now grow into her name: Maximiliane Quint, no longer on Poenichen but from Poenichen. The surprises prophesied for her by the Fräuleins and Herr Kressmann still lay ahead of her. She had learned to stay out of it, as both Old Quindt and Viktor Quint expected of a woman. The runaway had turned into a refugee. The principle "She'll grow out of it" would continue to hold, but Maximiliane would also continue to chew her nails and to sing sentimental songs; she would never outgrow songs about love and home. She would never not feel like singing and laughing, although there would be nothing in her life to laugh about, and she would continue to embrace tree trunks even though for the time being her arms were full of children. Her roots were deep in Pomerania. Would she ever put down new roots?

To pass the waiting time, Edda and Golo played "Come, woman." Edda screamed and ran around the piles of baggage and travelers. Golo chased her, grabbed some man's cane, put it under his arm, and shouted, "Pang! Pang!" until Edda surrendered and dropped on one of the bundles beside her mother.

The man grabbed the boy's arm and rescued his cane. "Aren't you children the least bit afraid of your mother?" he asked.

"No!" Golo shouted.

Nothing that had yet been said of Maximiliane Quint was higher praise.

7-22